KT-417-417

# PROPHET

Before turning his hand to writing, James Hazel was a lawyer in private practice specialising in corporate and commercial litigation and employment law. He was an equity partner in a regional law firm and held a number of different department headships until he quit legal practice to pursue his dream of becoming an author.

He has a keen interest in criminology and a passion for crime thrillers, indie music and all things retro.

James lives on the edge of the Lincolnshire Wolds with his wife and three children.

*Also by James Hazel*

The Mayfly
The Ash Doll

# FALSE PROPHET

## JAMES HAZEL

ZAFFRE

First published in Great Britain in 2019 by
ZAFFRE
80–81 Wimpole St, London W1G 9RE

Copyright © James Hazel, 2019

A CIP catalogue record for this book is
available from the British Library.

ISBN: 978–1–78576–801–9

*Also available as an ebook*

1 3 5 7 9 10 8 6 4 2

Typeset by IDSUK (Data Connection) Ltd
Printed and bound in Great Britain by Clays Ltd, Elcograf S.p.A.

Zaffre is an imprint of Bonnier Books UK
www.bonnierbooks.co.uk

To Oliver
*Chase your dreams; to the end of the Earth*
*if that's what it takes*

'There is no sin, no matter how great, that God cannot pardon.'

Last words of Gilles de Rais before his execution
in 1440 for serial murder

# Preface

## *The Snake and the Boy*

There was once an angel named Samyaza. He was the leader of a band of angels known as the Watchers; the holy ones who descended from heaven to be with man.

It was propagated that, in the beginning, Samyaza changed his form into that of a snake: a copperhead serpent said to be the most cunning of all of God's creatures. It is in this form that Samyaza took up his position in the Garden of Eden and enticed Eve into eating the forbidden fruit, telling her that the fruit's consumption would give her the powers of God.

Like Prometheus stealing fire to give to man, which angered Zeus because he knew that, with fire, man would eventually find little need for gods, so the Christian God was enraged by Samyaza's trickery. Adam and Eve were expelled from the Garden of Eden, but man's ultimate punishment was to live forever under the crushing weight of his own morality.

From high above, Samyaza watched as God punished man, no longer welcome in the celestial outworld of Heaven. Resentment, anger and lust boiled within him. And something else too. Hatred of God, and the burning desire for revenge.

Then one day, Samyaza felt a cold hand on his shoulder. In his rage, he made to throw off the hand, break it, smash it, tear it apart. But when he turned, his eyes flooded with bloodlust, and he met the cool, unrelenting gaze of the only creature who still had any dominion over him. Satan. And into Samyaza's receptive ears, Satan poured a devilish plan.

Later that day, in accordance with Satan's plan, Samyaza proposed to his followers, one hundred and ninety-nine other Watchers, that they descend to Earth, permanently, and make wives for themselves of the humans below waiting for them. It was a dangerous enterprise, one that would draw the ultimate wrath of God himself; Samyaza would take personal responsibility if they were uncovered. But the one hundred and ninety-nine drew a pact together – they would not let their leader sacrifice himself alone.

And so a covenant was reached – each Watcher was bound to himself, his kin and to Samyaza. Together, they descended to Earth, and in so doing became the Fallen Ones. Others called them Demons. Each took a human woman as his wife. And they procreated. Their offspring, a hybrid race of demon and human, were known as Giants.

But the Giants were a blasphemy. Nothing has ever existed that was more malevolent. They were a union that was supposed to be forbidden in every sense. Soon, God's greatest creation had become corrupted, ravaged and ruined. When the Giants began to outnumber the purebloods, they turned upon their cousins – devouring them like the monsters they really were.

From his demonic castle in the clouds, Satan observed the chaos below with gleeful eyes, knowing that his tenure became safer with the death of every pureblood. He knew about the prophecy; the Bible told of it. The one to overthrow him will be a man. Well that can't happen if there are no men left, can it . . .

In retaliation, God sent a flood to cover the Earth, and destroy all living things, including the blasphemous demon hybrids. But in order to preserve the purebloods, God saved Noah and his family. Noah, who was perfect in his generations. The purest of pure, whose lineage was untouched by the demons. The Earth's last hope.

But Satan was not done yet.

Janus was the son of a farmer; honest and hardworking. The kind of man who would have lived and died in total obscurity, ploughing the oil seed fields or tending to cattle in the arid wilderness of southern Mesopotamia, now modern-day Iraq. That is, were it not for one fateful day.

On that day, Janus was sent by his father to recover a lost sheep, a journey which took him across the unforgiving wastelands for two days. Starving and dying of thirst, Janus was about to give up on his pursuit when he tripped and fell, a sharp pain rippling up his leg. When he looked up, he saw he had been bitten by a snake; a creature with deep crimson scales, the colour of the Arabian sunset. The same copperhead serpent that curled artfully around the Tree of Life, and who lured Eve into sin. This was God's partisan, the wicked Samyaza.

Afraid, Janus was about to strike out with his crook, when, just as the serpent of the Garden of Eden had, the snake spoke to him, warning Janus of the forthcoming deluge. The snake advised Janus that there was no hope for his father and mother but that he, Janus, might survive if he were to stowaway on the Ark built by Noah, which was then nothing more than a wooden carcass, a giant timber skeleton jutting out of the desert.

Then the snake writhed away, and where it slithered, crops grew and water flowed. Not one to look a gift horse in the mouth,

Janus set off to find the Ark. When he did, he disguised himself as one of the labourers, but whereas those men hired by Noah to unwittingly build his vessel of survival went about blindly following Noah's directions, Janus constructed a small, secret room below deck where he stayed until the Ark was complete.

There he remained, as the rain lashed and the wind hurled the Ark around for forty days and forty nights until the highest mountains were covered with black water and all life on Earth was extinguished, save for Noah, his family, the animals aboard the Ark and their stowaway.

When the clouds parted, and the rain relented, Janus picked his moment and crawled away, the demon bloodline pulsing through his veins.

Above him, Satan smiled. His plan had worked. It would not be long before Janus spread his demonic seed. Soon, the age of the demon would be born again.

# Chapter 1

*Monday*

Emma woke in the early hours of the morning with a pounding head and a pain in her left side she didn't recall falling asleep with. She must have gone to bed and left the skylight shutter open because the room was bathed in moonlight. She lay still for a moment with her eyes open. It was oppressively hot; she couldn't hear the air-conditioning unit, although she was sure she had set it to automatic yesterday. Perhaps it was the heat that had roused her.

Her dressing gown was slung over a chair in the corner. It was a dull blue colour with an ugly design of roses weaving their way around each other up both sides, their heads finishing gracelessly below the breast. A present from Harry last year. She hated it. She had been with Harry for two years now – a new record – but, at thirty-three, she regarded herself as too old to call Harry her boyfriend and too uninterested to call him her partner. She was terrified that he was going to propose soon, although thankfully his work meant he was abroad a lot.

Emma closed her eyes. The pain in her side subsided – she must have just slept awkwardly. She should turn on the air-conditioning but she knew as soon as she got out of bed she wouldn't go back to sleep. She turned over. The full moon shimmered through the skylight. In the morning, she would ditch Harry by text and burn that fucking dressing gown.

There was a noise. Her eyes shot open. A definite thud, from downstairs. She held her breath for a moment. Had she imagined it?

There it was again. Like a heavy object falling off the shelf and hitting the floor.

Emma was used to living alone; she had been doing it since she was sixteen. Harry rarely stayed for more than a few nights at a time before gallivanting off to the next conference. Everyone else was kept at a distance. Did she mind? Not really. She liked living alone; never having to compromise or accommodate other people's little habits and rituals. But she didn't like noises in the night.

*Thud.* This time louder.

Emma felt her heart rate quicken. The sheets were clammy, the heat suddenly unbearable. *What the hell was that noise?* Her apartment had two bedrooms on a mezzanine floor overlooking the living room. Her room had its own balcony. Downstairs, there was a separate kitchen, along with a bathroom and study. The noise could only be coming from inside her apartment.

She cursed under her breath. She was wide awake now. *Was someone. . .?* No, she couldn't bring herself to complete the thought. It was ridiculous. She was alone, as always. Nobody could get into the apartment block without a key, let alone her flat. She closed her eyes. If she heard the noise again she would get up and investigate; if not, then she could put it down to the boiler playing up.

Moments passed. A longer interval than before. Her head began to spin.

Then, *thud*.

Emma threw back the covers and stood up, swaying naked in the room for a minute. She felt dizzy and nauseous. Her chest fluttered with unease. She pulled the dressing gown around her and stopped to try and clear her head. What if someone *was* in the apartment? What if there was a gang of men carrying her electrical goods away right now? Wouldn't it be better to stay up here?

She threw the thought from her mind and stared over the glass railing. The living room had taken on the same ghostly feel as the moonlit bedroom. She couldn't see anything out of place, but there it was again. *Thud*.

The staircase arched around one side of the cavernous space below. Emma descended slowly. The wall leading down was plastered with Emma's award-winning work. The photographs were varied, a mixture of black and white, sepia and colour: a regiment of elephants wading knee-high in water in front of the Savannah's setting sun; children no older than ten crowded around a UN convoy, braying excitedly at the arrival of a tank; a woman wailing at the foot of a crumbled ruin, pawing at her blood-stained clothes. Emma had an eye for capturing the soul of human suffering through a lens. The thought steeled her resolve. She had lived in warzones; she wasn't going to be scared in her own damn house.

Nonetheless, when it came again, the thud still made her jump and she hurried down the stairs.

Everything was still in the living room so she opened the double doors into the kitchen underneath the bedrooms. She fiddled with a cluster of switches near the door; everything was instantly illuminated with splashes of mellow blue light from the LEDs peppering the ceiling. She was met with an array of sleek appliances built into a black range that dominated the far wall behind an island of gleaming white units. There was no noise, except the gentle hum of the giant American-style fridge. Green digits glowed like cat's eyes from all sides. Everything was spotless.

She left the light on and checked the bathroom, which was as she had left it. Same with the study. She took one last look at the living room. The walls were high on one side, spanning both floors: white-washed brick adorned with abstract artwork. It was sparsely furnished with odd shaped chairs. A hammock was slung between two iron pegs in the corner. The main feature was three enormous black-framed arched windows to Emma's left. At twenty-five storeys up, it seemed as though most of London was laid out like a blanket below her.

There was nothing wrong, nothing out of place and nobody here but her. Emma felt her body relax, her breathing slow. Her disquiet was replaced with annoyance; precious sleep had been lost.

She turned all the lights off and went back upstairs. Removed the dressing gown and threw it in the corner of the room. It didn't even deserve a place on the chair. She slumped back into bed, half pulling the cover over her naked body.

Emma closed her eyes.

She started to write the text message to Harry in her mind. But she didn't get very far.

She realised, far too late, that the thud had been intended to lure her downstairs, giving whoever it was in the room with her now the chance to sneak in and hide.

Emma tried to scream, but a pair of strong hands were already wrapping around her mouth. She felt the weight of a man straddling her, crushing down on her chest. His knees pinned the tops of her arms. She tried to kick, thrash around, but he was too strong.

The last thing she remembered seeing was the moon through the skylight, igniting the cloudless sky with pale light. Then a strange sensation of floating as her assailant took a hammer and, with one life ending strike, drove an eight-inch galvanised nail into her skull.

# Chapter 2

*Tuesday*

The corner property of Walnut Avenue was a rundown grey-bricked Georgian townhouse with peeling sash windows and black railings. There were five floors: one below pavement level and the top floor signified by three smaller windows peering over the visible roofline.

Two cars were parked on the opposite side of the road a little further down. In the front seats of the first – a blue Mercedes – two people were watching the house. The driver was Sasha Merriweather, a partner in the law firm Merriweather, Stevens and Shuttler. Her passenger was Henrik Vose, Sasha's client's representative, who sat fidgeting with his tie and anxiously checking an expensive-looking watch.

'He's late,' Henrik remarked.

'Don't get upset. He'll be here.'

Henrik pulled the rear-view mirror towards him and glanced at the people carrier parked behind them. Three men and one woman occupied it. Henrik knew their names but little else about them. They were hired help from Sasha's office brought in at goodness knows what expense by Henrik's employer. It was a good job that the people carrier's rear windows were tinted; they stuck out like a sore thumb as it was.

'We were supposed to execute the order at nine thirty precisely.' Henrik shuffled in his seat. 'It's five minutes past that time already.'

'He'll be here,' Sasha repeated.

He was struggling to hide his frustration. Whilst he had become accustomed to Sasha's abruptness, the supervising solicitor's timekeeping was agitating him to the point of intolerance. Henrik sighed heavily. He wished he was back at home; nobody was ever this fucking late in Germany.

'You are sure this person has no connection with Professor Owen?' Henrik asked.

'He has no connection with anybody involved in this case, Henrik. Stop fussing, for God's sake. You're making me hot.'

'The sun is making you hot, not me.'

It was true. Since Sasha had killed the engine, the temperature had been slowly rising. Even though it was still early, the sun was already starting to bake the city. The newsreader had reported this morning that there hadn't been a heatwave like it since 2003. Henrik had removed his jacket and loosened his tie but he was carrying extra fat around his belly these days and sweat patches were already forming under his arms.

'We've got to have some air in here,' he muttered.

Sasha turned on the electrics and Henrik opened the window. Mercifully, there was at least some breeze, although even that was abnormally warm.

'I'll ring him,' Sasha said, picking out her phone from one of the Mercedes' central compartments. 'I have his number here.'

Henrik looked at her. 'He'll be subtle, won't he?'

She stopped scrolling through the phone and returned his look. 'He's overseen search orders before. He knows the drill.'

'What car does he drive? You can tell a lot about a man from the car he drives.'

'A clapped-out old Volvo.'

Henrik whistled. 'Great. Probably broken down somewhere, then.'

He shuffled back into his seat and wiped his brow. His trousers were saturated. He wondered whether, with her new investor onboard, it was time to ask his employer for a pay rise. Fat chance. Henrik had worked for the reclusive Elisha Capindale for six years now having answered her advert for a bookkeeper and personal assistant he saw in the local paper. He had worked for Deutsche Bank for the best part of a decade before being transferred to their London branch where he somehow managed to survive the financial crisis of 2007 only to be made redundant in a wave of cuts when the bank started to move its euro clearing business back to Germany several years later. Disillusioned, he had decided to stay in England and moved to Ely where he took up residence in an annex attached to Elisha's manor house – the main pull of the job being that it came with a home.

Henrik chuckled to himself. *Manor House.* The damn thing was a near-ruin. He would have preferred for Elisha to have spent some of her new investment money on his dilapidated accommodation (the boiler hadn't fired properly since last year) rather than expensive lawyers.

But the Book came first. He understood that, although he didn't have to like it.

'Where is he?' he grunted, exasperated. 'If Owen gets wind of what we're doing before your man gets a chance to serve the order, then he'll destroy the Book.'

'Henrik, relax, for God's sake. The point of having to appoint an independent supervising solicitor in cases like this is that he is experienced. He's not going to roll up and . . .'

Sasha was interrupted by the roar of a powerful engine and a car pulling up on the other side of the road, right outside Owen's front door. Henrik strained to see. The driver was male, maybe in his early forties, dark hair; that was all he could make out.

'That's him,' said Sasha, getting out of the car.

'What?' Henrik paused, looking on in dismay. 'You call that subtle?' He scrambled to get out of the car and joined Sasha on the pavement.

The Aston Martin Rapide S shimmered like a mirage in the bright sunlight. The deep red paintwork was flawless, as if it had been driven straight out of the showroom, and the engine purred dangerously as the driver powered it down.

Henrik was breathing heavily, checking the upper windows of Owen's house. The curtains were still drawn but surely anyone would check outside if they heard that beastly noise pull up at their front door. He resisted the temptation to run over and punch the guy driving it. *Owen must not be given a chance to destroy the Book.*

A tall, broad-shouldered man got out of the driver's side and slammed the door shut. He was clutching a file of papers and wearing a white shirt and waistcoat but no jacket or tie. He spotted Henrik and Sasha and started to make his way towards them, checking his watch as he crossed the road. As he came closer, Henrik felt his tension levels rise to breaking point. He didn't look like a lawyer. He looked like an art collector.

'That's not a fucking Volvo,' Henrik growled under his breath as the man drew closer. When he reached them, Sasha smiled and extended her hand.

'You must be Charlie Priest.'

'That's right,' Priest nodded. 'You're Sasha Merriweather, no doubt, and . . .' Priest turned to Henrik who glared back, then reluctantly took Priest's hand. The grip made him wince.

'Henrik Vose. I'm one of Elisha Capindale's senior advisors. I must say this is a bad start, Mr Priest. This case is of vital importance to Ms Capindale so—'

'Of course,' Priest cut him off, looking past him. 'So, Ms Capindale is where exactly?'

Henrik pursed his lips. Priest must have seen the four people in the car, but they wouldn't move. They had been instructed to sit tight until they had the go-ahead to conduct the search. He looked at Priest. He had a strong jawline but his shirt was crumpled and he hadn't shaved. Not his idea of professional.

'Ms Capindale is on business elsewhere,' Henrik said coldly. 'I am her representative.'

The lie rolled off his tongue easily; it was a well practised deception. Elisha Capindale didn't leave her house. Her condition didn't allow her to. She didn't need care as such, but Henrik acted as her ambassador in all matters that needed a personal attendance. He could have told Priest this, but he chose not to. Elisha was sensitive when it came to people knowing about her condition.

'I see,' said Priest. 'This case isn't important enough for her to attend in person, then?'

Henrik opened his mouth but Sasha interrupted, turning to Priest. 'Do you have the papers?'

He tapped the file under his arm and grinned. 'All here. It's been a while since I've overseen an Anton Pillar order. Congratulations on getting it, by the way. Very tough to persuade the courts to grant these types of things – they're so damn messy to execute.'

'They're called search orders, now,' Sasha retorted. 'And have been since 1998.'

'Oh, you'll be telling me they've changed the name of Marathon bars next, Sasha. Now, Mr Vose.' Priest turned to Henrik, who wrinkled his nose with contempt. *Who the hell did this clown think he was?* 'The court has appointed me as an independent solicitor to oversee the execution of your search order. I'm not here to pass judgement and I'm not taking anybody's side in this. I'm here to see fair play. That all understood?'

'Fine,' said Henrik irritably. 'There are four employees of Ms Capindale in that car behind us. They will conduct the search and take away any evidence and keep it . . .'

'I don't think so,' said Priest. 'This order allows the Claimant's solicitor entry along with the Claimant *or her representative.*'

'Yes, as I said, these people are—'

'Are plural, Mr Vose. These people are plural, whereas the order grants permission only in the singular. One solicitor and one representative.'

To Henrik's total dismay, Priest had the audacity to produce a copy of the sealed order and show him the wording. Henrik stammered and looked at Sasha for support, but she shook her head at him.

'That's ridiculous!' Henrik declared. 'The house is massive; it will take me hours to search it on my own!'

Priest shrugged and moved on. 'Professor Owen has the right to take independent legal advice before the order is formally executed, so nobody goes in without my say so. And of course, nobody removes anything without going through me. No doubt Ms Merriweather has explained all this to you, Mr Vose?'

Henrik nodded. He could feel the veins in the side of his head expanding. 'Yes, yes. Just get on with it.'

'Very well,' said Priest, straightening up. 'You can sit tight for the next four hours.'

Henrik shook his head, incensed. *Did he hear that correctly?* 'Four hours?'

'Professor Owen is entitled to a reasonable amount of time to take advice. Four hours might be pushing it but we'll review that as we go.'

'It can't take that long to find a lawyer in the middle of London on a weekday!'

Priest raised an eyebrow, then leant in towards Henrik. 'I dare say you'd find one in that time. It's negotiating the fee that's so time consuming.'

Priest winked and meandered off across the road towards Owen's house, the papers tucked under his arm. He left Sasha and Henrik watching after him, speechless.

# Chapter 3

DCI Tiff Rowlinson stopped just below the twenty-fifth-floor landing to catch his breath, pausing on the final flight of stairs so that the uniformed officers in the corridor didn't see him intake deeply from the asthma inhaler. They'd temporarily decommissioned the lifts to help control who went in or out while the crime scene was still being investigated. Moving everyone out of the building had been hard work. There were a lot of late sleepers and an old woman on the fifth floor had refused point blank at first. Why did a murder in the penthouse mean she had to miss Jeremy Kyle?

Rowlinson pocketed the inhaler and climbed the last few steps. He was met on the landing by a stocky man with a pockmarked face who introduced himself as the crime scene manager. Rowlinson didn't catch his name and it wasn't important. He was anxious to get on with it. While he put on a white coverall, the CSM gave a few details about what to expect. Rowlinson listened but took it with a pinch of salt. He approached all crime scenes with the same basic rule. ABC: assume nothing, believe no one, challenge everything.

He donned a pair of overshoes, nitrile rubber gloves and a facemask before the CSM showed him through to the apartment.

It was stifling inside the hallway. The place was big but airless and the heat must have been locked in from the previous day. The coverall was already starting to cling to him. Various pot plants lined the entranceway. Some were in need of a bit of TLC, except the dragon tree at the end which caught Rowlinson's eye. The SOCO team had already placed foot-markers to step across leading through the hallway and up the stairs, past a wall covered with photographs.

In a sizable bedroom, Rowlinson picked his way across the floor. There were three crime scene officers bent down in different corners scanning for evidence. The sunlight raged through the three large windows on the east side of the penthouse, bouncing off the gleaming white walls. So much so that Rowlinson had to shield his eyes. It was minimalist; only a few pieces of abstract furniture surrounding the bed. The room looked more like a museum of modern art than a habitable space. All very *avant-garde*, although he couldn't see any elephant-shit-on-a-plate. Nonetheless, it made the pool of dried blood which covered most of the grey wood floor seem almost like part of the design.

The bed was a large black and white king low to the floor and made from Italian leather. The victim was spread across it, face up, one arm draped in the epicentre of the bloodstain. She had a nail stuck in her head. The room was swarming with fat, jet black flies, but that wasn't the only thing that caught his attention.

'What's this on the floor?'

Rowlinson's question wasn't aimed at anyone in particular but one of the male crime scene officers turned and answered him.

'It's salt, sir.'

Rowlinson looked closer. There were little crystals dotted around, stuck in the dried blood. *Salt.*

Rowlinson rubbed his forehead, pushed a stray cluster of blond hairs out of his eyes. His fear had crystallised. Four days ago, he'd been called to a house a mile and a half away to a similar scene. A young woman – Jane Vardy – strewn across a hotel bed, her throat slashed. Blood everywhere. No prints, no biological evidence. No apparent motive. As yet, no leads. Just one significant clue. The same clue as here. A symbol, drawn on the wall in the victim's blood.

Rowlinson shuddered. The symbol stared at him mockingly from the back of the bedroom, the deep red blood stood out in perfect contrast to the crisp white walls. This time the killer had been more extravagant: the symbol was almost five foot tall, much bolder and more deliberate. A cross entwined with a sinuous line, like the tilde on a keyboard. It meant nothing, and yet, here and now to Rowlinson, it meant everything.

'Looks like the same as last time,' said a voice to Rowlinson's right.

He hadn't heard her come in. DS Fay Westbrook had been assigned to him following her promotion in June. She was garbed in the same plastic coveralls but underneath he knew her as a slim, attractive biracial woman in her early thirties. She was ambitious and pushy with it but Rowlinson was too long in the tooth to let her enthusiasm wind him up. So far, she'd managed to stay on the right side of him, although she knew how to sail close to it occasionally.

'Seems that way,' he said, almost under his breath.

'We're looking for a serial killer now, boss,' she remarked, although Rowlinson couldn't tell if it was a question or a statement.

'Depends on which definition of serial killer you want to use. We're looking at two murders that are clearly connected. That's all that matters for now.'

'How long before the press gets hold of this?'

'Probably days, hours maybe. Not my problem, or yours. That's what the press officers are for. Now what do we know about this one?' Rowlinson nodded at the victim and Westbrook produced a notepad from inside her coveralls.

'OK. This is Emma Mendez. She's thirty-three. A professional freelance photographer. Shot to minor fame last year when her picture of refugees boarding a train in Syria won her a Pulitzer. Worked for various newspapers and online publications. Never married but does have a boyfriend – we're tracking him down now. She's a British citizen but parents were from Mexico. Father is dead, Mother is in Mexico City and doesn't have much to do with her daughter by all accounts.'

'Who found her like this?'

'The cleaner, Gita Johar. She's back at the nick making a very emotional statement.'

'I don't doubt it.' He glanced at her sideways. 'It would have been a shock to find . . . this.'

Westbrook at least had the decency to look away and change the subject. 'Same as last time, no sign of forced entry. Maybe she let him in. If she did, maybe she knew him, like Jane Vardy.'

Since Jane Vardy's murder, they had assigned a masculinity to the killer, although this was based more on statistics than any empirical evidence. A woman hadn't been ruled out but it was very unlikely.

'He's getting more confident,' Rowlinson said, looking up at the symbol. 'Last time this was slashed across the wall in haste. He took his time with this one; much neater.'

'We need a profiler, boss.'

Rowlinson grunted. 'Profilers don't catch killers, Westbrook. Hard work and luck does.'

'The AC's not going to like that attitude, boss. And she's quite frosty towards you anyway, if it's not out of order for me to make that observation.'

'It's completely out of order, Westbrook.' Rowlinson swatted a fly away from his face. *Funny how those little bastards always find their way into a sealed room.* 'But it doesn't help that I'm pals with her ex-husband.'

'Thought there was . . . you know. History.'

'One thing about this job, Westbrook. There's *always* history.'

They were silent for a while. Rowlinson felt the urge to turn away. The smell of the early stages of putrefaction was starting to get under his skin. He fumbled for the inhaler in his pocket but resisted the temptation to use it.

'What do you make of the salt on the floor, boss?' she asked.

He looked around the room again. The salt covered a large area, almost as large as the pool of blood.

'Did we find salt at Jane Vardy's murder scene?'

Westbrook shrugged. 'I don't remember it but I'll check with SOCO.'

'And you say no sign of forced entry again?'

'No. Same as last time. Just ghosted in, buried a nail in her head, ghosted out again.'

Rowlinson nodded grimly. *There'll be no trace of anything biological on the nail. Like last time.* The Met's resources had taken a beating in the last six months – three senior officers had left and the major crime unit was understaffed as it was. Rowlinson had originally been assigned temporarily from South Wales but they had then offered him a permanent post at Holborn. He'd taken it, but he was already beginning to regret his decision.

He turned away, shielding his eyes from the sun burning through the windows. 'Call a meeting of the senior team this afternoon,' he instructed. Westbrook nodded and pulled out her phone. Rowlinson carefully made his way back out into the hallway. It was going to be another scorching day.

# Chapter 4

Charlie Priest made his way across to the end-terrace on the corner of Walnut Avenue and rang the bell. He'd scoped out the house and its occupant yesterday and concluded there wasn't much opportunity for trouble. Professor Norman Owen was a sixty-year-old man who lived alone. He had divorced years ago and had one daughter in her twenties.

Priest didn't have much to go by. Sasha Merriweather had issued an application for a search order in the High Court without notice, meaning that Professor Owen hadn't been made aware of the court hearing until yesterday. The order had been granted. The judge must have been satisfied that the claimant had a decent case and that, unless restrained, there was a real prospect that Owen would destroy or dispose of the evidence.

Merriweather had contacted him shortly after the hearing. Apparently one of her partners had put his name forward as a possible supervising solicitor. There weren't many lawyers who had the necessary experience, even in London, and although Priest didn't really know how he had ended up being offered the brief, he was a man whose reputation preceded him. Intrepid and resourceful, Charlie Priest was one of London's most sought after lawyers. His firm, Priest & Co., was a boutique law practice based in Holborn that turned away more work than it took on and so far hadn't lost a case since its inception over a decade ago. He had resisted the temptation to expand, or sell out to one of the Magic Circle firms, the five law firms which supposedly outperformed everybody else in London in terms of profitability, revenue and prestige. Apart from its principal, Priest & Co. comprised just three associates: in-house counsel, former prosecutor for the International Criminal Court, Vincent Okoro; Georgie Someday, a young, insatiable solicitor with a brilliant legal mind; and Simon 'Solly' Solomon, a legally trained accountant whose genius was matched only by his social incompetence.

Priest had very nearly blown Merriweather out, but she had made the case sound just about intriguing enough not to turn down.

'What does Professor Owen have in his possession that you're looking for?' he had asked her.

'A book, that's all. Well, a scripture.'

'As in Biblical?'

There had been a brief pause. 'As in like a Dead Sea Scroll.'

After a few minutes, the door opened and a weathered face peered out suspiciously. He had wispy, silver hair that tumbled over his shoulders, milky grey eyes and skin that looked like wax. He kept most of his body behind the door but Priest could make out that he was wearing a string vest. His arms and shoulders were covered with thin hair.

'Professor Owen?' Priest asked.

'Who's asking?'

'My name is Charlie Priest. I'm a solicitor of the Supreme Court here to oversee the execution of a civil search order issued yesterday in the Royal Courts of Justice. It enables one

Elisha Capindale or her representative to search for and remove evidence that may be needed in court in proceedings brought against you for preservation purposes. May I come in?'

Owen slammed the door shut. Priest closed his eyes. Maybe his assessment of how straightforward this was going to be was wrong. He turned back to see Henrik Vose and Sasha Merriweather standing by the Mercedes. Vose had his arms folded. On seeing Priest turn around, he waved his arm irritably, indicating that he ought to try again.

Priest shrugged and knocked on the door, louder this time. It was twelve years since Priest had been a detective inspector in the Met but old habits die hard; doorstop persistence was a particular speciality of his.

'Professor Owen!' he called through the letter box. 'Can I come in? I'm not going away. I'm going to post you a copy of the court order. Please read it and let me in.'

He posted a copy through the letter box and waited. He could hear movement on the other side. It sounded like Owen had snatched the order up and was unfolding it. *Good. It's too bloody hot out here to be messing around.*

According to Merriweather, the claimant was an interesting character. Elisha Capindale had grown up in Ireland and moved to England in the seventies where she had travelled around for a few years before settling in Ely. She was an antiques dealer, with a particular interest in Christian antiquities. Sasha had never met her; all her dealings had been through Capindale's PA, Henrik Vose. By all accounts, she was a recluse, rarely stepping foot outside her residence but nonetheless she seemed to have once been held in high regard, not necessarily as a human being (Sasha had described her as 'carping' on the phone), but as someone able to source and trade unusual relics through an impressive network of archaeologists and treasure hunters. The network had apparently included Professor Owen, up until their recent falling-out at least.

'Professor Owen?' Priest called again through the letter box. Owen had had long enough to digest the order. 'I'm happy to stand here all day but, if you don't let me in at some point, you'll be in contempt of court and liable to criminal prosecution.'

Priest waited a beat. He sensed Owen was standing just on the other side of the door.

'I'll not let any representative of Capindale in here,' Owen barked back.

Priest sighed in relief. Owen would have to, at some point. But at least he was now talking.

'I'm not with Elisha Capindale, professor. I'm an independent solicitor, appointed by the court to oversee the search order's execution. I'm like a referee, that's all.'

'I don't . . .' Owen faltered, and Priest detected the break in his voice. 'I don't know what to do.'

'Look, professor, let me in and I'll explain.' Priest softened his tone.

Merriweather had said that Owen was an archaeologist, as well as a biblical scholar and philologist, an expert who studies languages written in historical sources. He was an academic. A noteworthy individual but one who probably inhabited the often isolated, detached world of academia. Naturally, he was out of his comfort zone.

'It'll be all right, professor. The first thing to do is sit down, make a cup of tea, and I'll go through this with you. We'll arrange for someone to come over and represent you, someone on your side. If that takes all morning then Capindale can wait, OK?'

Priest held his breath. For a moment, he thought Owen might have retreated, but then he heard the latch click and Owen ushered him in. Closed the door behind him and locked it with both key and deadbolt.

'The kitchen's through there,' Owen grunted, pointing down the hall. 'I'll just put a shirt on. I take two sugars.'

# Chapter 5

Priest eventually found a kettle buried behind a pile of dirty plates. There was a cupboard with two mugs of different sizes that looked semi-clean. The rest of the crockery appeared to have been abandoned throughout the kitchen in various states of sanitation, from mildly stained to full-on mould-ridden. Evidently, Professor Owen didn't have much time for cleaning.

It seemed like the house hadn't been touched since the 1930s. The white cooker with black-ringed hob stood on terracotta tiles and reminded Priest of his grandmother's kitchenette. He remembered the smell of burnt scones and the texture of new potatoes from a tin; his older brother, William, trying to play the piano in the hall and squealing with delight when he was told off. His younger sister, Sarah, no older than six or seven, scolding him later for making fun of grandma.

'You found the milk?'

Priest turned and found Owen standing in the doorway, this time wearing an oversized checked shirt and a pair of faded blue trousers, both fraying at the seams.

'Think I've got it,' Priest said. He found the fridge close by and retrieved the milk. By the smell, something was off but he ignored it. Hopefully, it wasn't the milk.

He placed two cups of tea on what turned out to be a picnic table covered with old magazines and newspapers and they sat opposite each other. Priest put his papers beside him on the bench. Owen was still clutching the court order.

'How long have I got?' Owen asked, looking at the order with regret.

'As long as you need.'

'Don't play with me,' Owen snapped. 'I know that's not how these things work. How long have I got?'

'Four hours. Five max, before they'll start to suggest you're stalling.'

Owen cursed under his breath and took a long swig of the tea, although it must have scalded him. Above them, a ceiling fan laboured round, clicking with each rotation but creating enough breeze to take the edge off the situation.

'Do you have a lawyer you can call?' asked Priest. 'Someone you regularly use.'

Owen snorted. 'I don't even have a will. Don't take this the wrong way but—'

Priest held up his hand. 'It's OK, you hate lawyers. I get that all the time. For the record, so do I.'

'You can't advise me?'

'Afraid not. I can interpret the order for you and give you a few names of people I know who are good but, other than that, I'm basically just here to make sure that the order is carried out. That means you do your bit by giving Capindale's representative and her lawyer access and they do their bit by treating you and your property with respect and only taking what they're entitled to.'

'Which is what?'

Priest put his own copy of the order in front of Owen and pointed to the wording. '*Any document, material, artefact, text, or scripture in your possession or under your control connected with the North Qumran Caves Dig.*'

'She wants the Book,' muttered Owen. 'Why doesn't she just bloody well say so.'

'Maybe if you could start at the beginning for me, Professor Owen. I need to understand the basics. What book?'

Owen sighed. Drained the rest of the tea with one gulp. He didn't respond at first. He was deep in thought; his brow was furrowed and sweat had collected around his temples. He had a large frame but was healthy-looking, with clear muscle definition, suggestive of a body that was used to working outdoors in the heat.

'You're an archaeologist,' Priest prompted.

Owen nodded. 'I was hired by Capindale, or someone working for her. Nobody gets to see Elisha Capindale personally, especially not an errand man like me. She's an enigma, that's for sure. I was commissioned to broker a deal for her with a Swiss collector to buy a scripture found north of the Qumran caves, east of Jerusalem.'

'What was the scripture?'

'A Book, one of the Dead Sea Scrolls. But not one you'll have heard of. She got me to sign a contract, that's what this is all about.'

'Can I see the contract?'

Owen paused, perhaps deciding what was best before getting up and leaving the room. He returned a few minutes later and put a hefty document in front of Priest, who picked it up and fanned through the pages. It was an agency contract, from what he could ascertain, giving Owen certain authority to negotiate a deal on Capindale's behalf. Judging by the language, it had been written by an American lawyer trying to imagine what an English lawyer might put into an English contract. Lots of pointless Latin phrases and elliptical sentences.

'So you bought it, the Book, I mean. You used her money. You'll need to hand it over. Have I over-simplified it?'

'You have,' Owen replied. 'The contract doesn't say what it was I was buying. I only found that out when I got there.'

Priest scratched his head. 'They say that makes you in breach of contract.'

'The Book of Janus belongs to me. That's the end of it.'

'The Book of Janus?'

'That's what we're calling it for now, but it'll take months to analyse properly.'

Priest put the contract down. The kitchen looked out over a small enclosed garden at the rear of Owen's house. In contrast with the kitchen, it was neatly kept. Priest could see an arbour seat was nestled in between rose bushes behind a stone sundial that looked new.

'I'm not here to cast judgement, professor. But Capindale's lawyers managed to persuade a High Court Judge that they had a damn good case. Not just reasonable prospects of success but a sure-fire winner. They also managed to persuade the judge that you intend to destroy evidence.'

Priest had expected Owen to react toxically to this suggestion but instead he nodded in agreement. 'I can understand why. When I started to receive threatening letters from Capindale's lawyers I may have said, to my shame, that I intended to burn that damn thing.' Owen shook his head and looked away. 'A stupid thing to say but I was trying to buy some time. I thought if I threatened to destroy the Book they might back off a little. Instead, it seems to have just increased the pressure.'

Priest exhaled, empathising with Owen's miscalculation. He opened the contract again and quickly navigated to the relevant provisions.

'Whatever you acquired belonged to her, if it amounted to a *text, material, document or scripture forming part of the Hebrew Bible canon or being Masoretic in nature or otherwise written in the celebration or account of God.* What is this Book of Janus?'

'It's a Hebrew text, of sorts,' Owen answered. 'I propose to arrange for it to be formally radiocarbon dated in due course, once we have resolved this dispute, but I am confident that the tests will show that the Book of Janus was written in the first century BC.'

'My scripture knowledge is a little rudimentary, professor, but I've never heard of the Book of Janus.'

'Do you know the story of the Dead Sea Scrolls?'

'A little. They were found by chance in the forties, but there was so much academic squabbling over them that they weren't properly analysed until much later.'

'That's right.' Owen wiped his nose on his sleeve. 'Somewhere between 1946 and 1947 three Palestinian Arabs of the nomadic Taamire tribe were searching for a stray goat on the rocky cliffs not far from the Dead Sea. One of the Arabs was throwing stones into holes in the rocks. He was surprised when, on one successful shot, he heard the sound of breaking pottery. At first, the local Bedouins, other nomadic Arabs, tried selling the first few Scrolls that were found. They changed hands several times before eventually finding their way back to Jerusalem, but by then the story of the Scrolls had spread like wildfire and every archaeologist worth his salt was looking into the great find. It wasn't until various individuals and organisations, including the Israeli Government, intervened that the Scrolls were eventually published in 1991.'

'Why wasn't the Book of Janus published at the same time?'

Priest saw something flash across Owen's eyes. The professor paused, as if assessing whether he could trust him. 'The Book of Janus went missing at the very early stages of the Scrolls' discovery. Most likely it was stolen and sold by the Bedouins, who were constantly interfering with the early digs and finding fragments of their own. They would spend months piecing these together as best they could, often using the adhesive from postage stamps. When they thought they had something resembling a complete document, they would sell it. No wonder the Book of Janus has been lost for so long. Who knows how many other scriptures remain missing?'

'That said, you don't consider that the text falls within the definition of documents that belong to Elisha Capindale under this contract?'

Owen folded his arms and said firmly, 'I do not.'

Priest waited for Owen to expand, but he didn't. The ceiling fan was still clicking above them. Priest wasn't religious. The last time he was in a church he was there to marry Dee. Three years later, they had divorced. Priest no more believed in God than he believed that divorce lawyers' fees were fair.

'It's not a Christian or Jewish document, then?' he asked.

Owen straightened up. 'The Book of Janus is an account of a stowaway on the Ark at the time of the Great Flood detailed in Genesis.'

'And that isn't a text written in celebration or account of God because . . . ?'

'Well, that's simple, Mr Priest,' said Owen confidently. 'It's because the Book of Janus was written by the Devil.'

# Chapter 6

*One year ago*

St Swithin's church in Hackney is one of the loneliest places you'll ever see. A small Norman building with a single spire sat on a moss-covered knoll surrounded by former council houses and dead trees. No one has been buried in the graveyard for fifty years and the gaps between the floorboards are wide enough to lose your phone down.

To my knowledge, there is no resident pastor, just a caretaker who comes every two weeks to see if the place is still standing. They open it up at Christmas and some vicar nearby might pop in to mumble a few words in front of an uninterested crowd, but other than that the church is redundant.

And this makes it perfect for me, because it is an outpost, one of the last. It is not Godless – the jackdaws still nest in the rafters to keep the Devil at bay – but it is close to soulless. What better place to build an empire from?

A modest empire, I mean. One whose people flounder at the very bottom of society, in the gutter. The people who feel that they are drifting in an endless sea of grief and despair. Those caught in an unbreakable cycle – drink, self-destruct, fall apart, drink, self-destruct, fall apart, repeat. I don't know which of the phases they started on. They're all different.

*Today there are ten of us. An impressive number, and one that includes two new members. I don't know their names but I will find out eventually – we do not leap on people and extract their personal details immediately. This isn't a training course, or a school. They tell us what they want in their own time and in their own way.*

*Admittedly, I'm a little concerned about Sue today. She looks tired, but it's more than that. So I reach out to her and try and encourage her to talk to us. I don't put pressure on anyone to talk – many will come to these meetings and say nothing at all but take away with them a tiny glimpse of hope and if that's all they achieve then I have succeeded. I know, because I once sat in their chair. After the fire, I lost everything.*

*'Sue, it's lovely to see you again,' I say tentatively. 'Would you speak to us all later? We'd love to hear from you.'*

*There is some unenthusiastic nodding. Note how I didn't say, 'Would you like to speak now?' I said, 'Would you like to speak later?' Just a little way to relieve some of the pressure.*

*Sue looks at me with a mixture of curiosity and alarm. She's been coming here for a while now, maybe a few weeks, but she is yet to progress to step three.*

*'I'll try,' she settles on, which is good enough for me.*

*The AA twelve-step programme is as famous as it is misunderstood. For a start, it isn't necessarily religious. The idea is to submit to a higher intelligence. If that is God, then great. I certainly encourage that. But if it's something else, then fine. I shy away a little bit from other gods – this is after all a Christian church – but if it's a space alien, or, as we had one year, a stuffed animal, and it works, then I'm happy. The important thing is that you determine your own healing process, and whatever you believe in (it's God ultimately, even if you don't see that straight away) will give you the grace to get better.*

*I'm not sure what Sue's higher intelligence is, which is part of the problem. She's stuck on 'believing that a Power (the higher intelligence) greater than ourselves can restore us to sanity'. Step two. She spoke to me last week, expressing her desperation to move on. I gave her some advice, but said that if she isn't getting anywhere by this time next week I would speak to her in private at the end of the meeting. It looks to me like that's where we are headed.*

*For me, the higher intelligence is God, but I have learnt patience. It took me a long time to understand what my purpose was, where I fitted in the world, and, more importantly, what His plan for me was. Unsurprisingly, it is not to see out my days in this backwater church watching the dregs of society pathetically hauling themselves up an impossibly long ladder, only to fall right back to the bottom again with one shot of vodka. No. It's something else. But we all have to start somewhere.*

*At the end of the meeting, I invite Sue to join me. As the others mill out into the glorious sunshine, shielding their eyes and muttering to each other about enlightenment, and God and horse racing, Sue just looks at me, unsure. She's one of those people who could be attractive if she tried, but the alcohol has washed away a lot of her humanity and respect, leaving behind a brittle creature with etiolated skin and thin arms. But there's life in her eyes and she's young. She has potential.*

*I invite Sue back to the vestry. It's a little bit more private and, although there is no chance of us being disturbed, I think the intimacy of a smaller room will seem less daunting to her.*

*She sits like a prim schoolgirl, perched on the edge of an ancient chair with her legs crossed, looking earnestly at me and I feel like putting my arm around her, she looks so wretched, so desperate for me to wave a magic wand and make her better. If only I could. But I can try.*

*'Sue, how do you feel you're doing?' I begin.*

*She looks down at the floor, as if the answer is written in the flagstone. 'Not very well. I'm still on step two. I need to move forward. But it's hard.'*

*I sigh. 'Well, I've done a lot for you, Sue. There's only so much I can do. You have to take the next step.'*

*She looks at me, alarmed. Am I abandoning her? 'No, please. You've been so helpful. If I can just get to step three, get some momentum.'*

*I shake my head. 'The guide is clear, Sue. There isn't much I can do now.'*

*'There's nothing?'*

*I sigh again. It's a well-rehearsed routine. 'You really want to make it to step three?' She nods. Knows what that really means: will I clear her? I'm the one that determines her steps. She needs me to sign it off.*

*'OK,' I say, reluctantly. 'This is unorthodox but there is a way. I warn you, it's not for everyone. But I think you have the right constitution.'*

*'I'm willing to try anything.'*

*'Very well.'*

*I've been here before, and this is the part that blows people away. It's the raw shock on their faces, the little gasp, the searching, confused look. The horror. Sue was no different. When I place the bottle of gin on the table to the side of us, her eyes widen in alarm.*

*'You have to fail, Sue,' I say sadly.*

*She looks at me, complete incomprehension. 'What?'*

'You have to fail. If you don't fail, you can't learn to get back up again. Everybody fails at some point. If you fail at step eleven, forget it. Game over. You'll never get back up there. I've seen it. Fail now, get it over and done with, and you'll be free. I promise.'

She twists in her seat and I can see her searching her inner soul. Is this right? She probably, like the others, concludes that it isn't. But what keeps her rooted to the chair isn't me. It's the bottle.

I take out two small glasses and pour a shot, neat, making sure that the glass clinks a little – I'm delighted to see her react to the sound, that familiar, comforting sound. She'll be imagining already what the liquid will feel like trickling down her throat, mixing in her blood. Sending her back to the only place that seems sane to her.

'I don't understand,' she says, without taking her greedy eyes off the bottle.

I hand her the glass, and take the other one in my hand. Then I down it in one. She gasps. Looks down, back up. I nod encouragingly.

'If you don't fail,' I repeat, 'you'll never move on. It will be our secret.'

Now here there's usually some negotiation. Some of them have wanted assurances: don't tell anyone, will the Fellowship know? But not Sue. She just drinks. I confess I'm a little surprised. Some of it ends up on her chin. She licks it off, looks at me.

So I pour again.

# Chapter 7

Priest took a sip of tea and waited for Owen to collect his thoughts. The professor had declared himself famished and was making toast. A loaf of wholemeal bread had been produced and the kitchen was now filled with a burning smell. Priest had declined a slice. He had thought Owen might expand on his melodramatic statement but he seemed too preoccupied with trying to find a clean plate to put his toast on.

*The Book of Janus was written by the Devil.*

Priest felt he had to tread carefully. He was cynical but conscious not to offend. He was beginning to like the professor; his aloofness reminded Priest of himself.

'When you say the Book of Janus was written by the Devil,' Priest began, 'do you mean it is a Satanic text or do you mean it was actually conceived by the Antichrist?'

Owen avoided the question. 'Do you believe in God, Mr Priest?'

Priest clicked his tongue. Owen was staring at him intently, sizing him up. None of this was strictly relevant to the search order but Owen was taking Priest down a particular path and the lure of seeing what was at the end was overwhelming.

'No. I'm an atheist.'

'Very well,' Owen said. 'Do you believe in the existence of evil?'

Priest's mind wandered uncontrollably to his brother: Dr William Priest, languishing in Fen Marsh High Security Psychiatric Hospital; a place where he would most likely die. A man the press had dubbed 'the Dark Redeemer', so called because all of his victims were, to differing extents, supposedly either morally corrupt, or criminals. Like all serial killer cases there had been the usual plethora of questions: *was William born this way, or did something happen to make him how he was? Are the parents to blame, or has society failed again? Is there such a thing as an evil gene?*

Priest chose his words carefully. 'I believe there is potentially no end to the human capacity to cause and permit suffering. Will that do?'

'Very precise. And yet there are limits to almost everything else in the physical world in one way or another. Have you *ever* had faith?'

'I like to rely on what I can touch and feel, professor. I'm a simple man.'

'Really? It's all an illusion, is it?' Owen took a bite out of the toast. Priest shuffled uncomfortably on the bench. His waistcoat was either a size too small or he had been overeating in the hot weather. He wondered about Sasha Merriweather and Henrik Vose, sat outside in the Mercedes, irritably checking their watches. At least they had air-conditioning.

'I think it was the French philosopher Voltaire who said, "There is no God, but don't tell my servant that, lest he murder me at night." Doesn't that sum it up?'

'Precisely.' Owen suddenly became very serious. 'It doesn't matter who wrote it. It matters what people believe.'

'What do you believe?'

Owen smiled, took another bite of toast. Chewed and swallowed. 'The document is written in Hebrew. It is over two thousand years old and almost flawless. There is reason to study it – *carefully* – but the ideas that are contained within it must not be allowed to enter into the mainstream, which is exactly what Elisha Capindale wants.'

'You said it was about a stowaway on Noah's Ark. Why must that be kept a secret?'

'That aspect of the scripture is merely the context. There is a darker, more dangerous secret in those pages. Possibly the most precious secret of all time.'

Priest was suddenly aware that the ceiling fan had stopped clicking. He looked up, the blades had slowed and come to rest with a final clunk. His waistcoat was suffocating. Priest inhaled deeply and undid the top button. A sensation washed through him, passed through his chest. For a moment, he thought he might pass out, but the feeling vanished as quickly as it had come.

'Mr Priest? Are you OK?'

Owen leant across the table, looking concerned.

'Mm. Fine, sorry,' Priest stammered. 'It's this heat.'

'I'll fetch you a glass of water.'

Owen stood up, crammed the last of the toast into his mouth and loped across to the kitchen sink where he started crashing around, trying to find a clean glass. He eventually found one, filled it with tap water and placed it in front of Priest.

'What secret does the Book of Janus contain?' Priest asked, downing the water.

'The point of a secret, Mr Priest, is that it is something that must not be divulged.'

'But you've read the text, and deciphered it?'

'Of course. I am an expert on ancient languages, particularly Hebrew.'

'No doubt that's worth a lot in monetary terms? The biggest secret of all time.'

Owen frowned, clearly offended. 'Oh, come on, Mr Priest. I was just beginning to like you. If this was about money I'd have sold that damn thing to the highest bidder the second I had it in my hands.'

'So you're the Book's custodian, and the biggest secret of all time is safe?' Owen nodded, chewing on more toast. 'How do you know that Capindale doesn't have the same noble intention?'

Owen pulled a face, as if he found the question jarring. 'Elisha Capindale is a rogue trader. She buys and sells relics, and maybe there was a time when she was younger when she commanded respect amongst her peers, but she seems more interested in finding the next Holy Grail than maintaining a name as a reputable antiques dealer.'

'Have you spoken to her since you acquired the Book?'

'We have had one conversation. By phone, of course. No one gets to meet her. In fact, I'm not even sure she is real.'

'What happened?'

'She raved, like a lunatic. *"I want that Book! I want that Book!"*' Owen threw up his hands in mock indignation. 'Threatened me with everything from the police to the Mafia. The woman is deranged. The Book of Janus *must* remain with me.'

'And that's for what? The good of mankind?'

'If you want to put it like that, then yes.'

'Well, how would *you* put it?'

Owen looked sternly into Priest's eyes. 'Like this: if the secret contained in the Book of Janus is revealed, it may precipitate a

Holy war. It will make Jihad look like a playground spat. People will pay with blood. Believe me. I will not let that happen.'

'They'll prosecute you, professor, if you don't comply with this search order. Through the criminal courts. You could go to prison.'

Owen leant across the table. His eyes were watery, but fired with resolve.

'Mr Priest, if I have to, I'll die to keep the Book secret.'

# Chapter 8

Rowlinson looked around the briefing room. There were six desks, three of which were occupied, one by Westbrook. She was staring at a computer, a pen poised on her lips. Her hair was braided today; he hadn't noticed earlier. She wasn't his type, on account of her being female, but he appreciated that she was beautiful. The light above her desk had blown. It had been on somebody's job list for a week now but she didn't seem to mind the dullness, and the light from her computer screen glowed around her dark, flawless skin. The pasty male DC at the desk next to hers kept looking up, stealing a glance whenever he thought he could get away with it.

Rowlinson's desk was tucked into a corner, cordoned off by plastic partitions. His position had been made permanent in the Spring, after he had been covering for nine months, but he was still the new DCI around here. Only Westbrook had arrived after him. He scanned the office for the fourth time but couldn't see what he was looking for. Agitated, he strode past Westbrook's desk to the back of the room where there were filing cabinets and a stationery cupboard. They'd finished at Emma Mendez's place an hour ago but Rowlinson had made time to go home first, shower and change before getting back to the station. His clothes had stunk of death.

'What'cha looking for, boss?' asked Westbrook, without glancing up.

'A board,' he grunted as he poked around the back, checking under the desk. 'I want to make a crazy wall.'

Westbrook took the pen out of her mouth and looked over, frowning. 'We use software for that, now, boss.'

'I like to do things the old-fashioned way. Ah-ha!'

Rowlinson found the transparent board tucked behind the stationery cupboard. He pushed the cupboard aside, the noise of grating across the floor made the others stop and watch as Rowlinson heaved the board out and set it up next to Westbrook's desk. He found a cloth and wiped it down.

'You ought to try *i2 Analyze*,' said Westbrook. 'I can show you—'

'Thank you, Westbrook,' Rowlinson called over his shoulder. He placed pictures of both Jane Vardy and Emma Mendez on the board next to each other. Wrote 'Victim' at the top of each in capitals. 'If your software is so bloody good how come it hasn't solved this case yet? Right—' He turned to her, pen in his hand. 'We're looking for connections between these two victims.'

Westbrook sat back, picked up a cup of coffee and cradled it while studying the board. 'Both female. Similar ages, Emma was four years older.'

'Good.' Rowlinson made notes on the board.

'That's about it, though. There's not a lot more to distinguish them. Jane was married with three children. Emma was unmarried, childless, although there's the boyfriend we're still trying to reach. Jane was a teacher at a primary school, Emma was a freelance photographer. Jane was white, British. Emma has a bit of Latino in her but everyone we've spoken to says you wouldn't notice it. Her father's British.'

Rowlinson finished writing everything down on the board. The photographs were of both women face-on before their murders, innocent faces smiling into the camera. Underneath the notes, Rowlinson pinned a picture of each victim after the murder.

Westbrook inhaled sharply. 'Do you have to, boss? We know what happened.'

'So we don't forget what we're up against.'

Next, he pinned two pictures of the symbol they'd found at both crime scenes.

'We need to focus on this,' he announced. 'This killer wants us to know something. We have to work out what, quickly. Track down an expert we can bring in, somebody who understands symbology.'

'It's like a gang tag,' said Westbrook. 'The killer's leaving his mark so we know it's him.'

'That's guesswork. Serial killers don't leave tags. That only happens in Hollywood films.'

'Heard of the Zodiac Killer, boss?'

'Zodiac used a small symbol in letters to the police. He didn't leave them at the crime scene and nobody really knows whether that was the killer or some sick imitator.'

Westbrook opened her mouth to reply but she was interrupted by the DC at the desk near hers – the one that kept eyeing her up.

'Guv?' he said, covering the end of the phone he was on with one hand. 'Super wants to see you both.'

'Tell him we'll be five minutes,' Rowlinson sighed.

The DC put the phone back to his ear and listened. 'He says you've got one minute.'

DSI John Eaton's office was on the floor above Rowlinson's, a sizable room with files and papers scattered everywhere and a pin-board plastered with pictures of his grandchildren. Eaton sat at his desk, leaning back with his legs crossed, rolling a cigarette. The DSI had announced his retirement three years earlier but had never got around to executing the plan and probably never would. He would probably die in that chair, Rowlinson had concluded. He had a mass of grey ungovernable hair falling over a cobwebbed face and a pair of sunken eyes that had lost none of their probative quality over the years. He came across as a cold martinet, blunt and to the point, but Rowlinson had found layers to his personality and Eaton had been single-handedly responsible for persuading Assistant Commissioner Auckland to offer Rowlinson a permanent post and for persuading Rowlinson to take it.

Standing near him was a slender man with curly hair and acne scars. He seemed self-conscious, fiddling with his tie. He gave Rowlinson a nervous smile and Westbrook an unsubtle once over; eyes lingering on her legs.

'DCI Rowlinson, DS Westbrook,' said Eaton in his thick Yorkshire accent. 'I'm delighted you both found the time in your busy schedules to come and brief me.'

'We were just liaising to make sure our brief was concise, sir,' Rowlinson replied.

'Bollocks you were. Anyway, this is Ethan Grey, brought in at no expense spared to help you with the murders of Jane Vardy and Emma Mendez. He's a profiler.' When nobody moved,

Eaton waved his arm at them all. 'Well, go on then, this isn't bloody Sunday school, say *hello* or something.'

Rowlinson walked across and offered his hand. 'DCI Rowlinson. This is DS Westbrook.' Grey's handshake was weak.

'Delighted,' Grey mumbled.

'Don't take what I say next the wrong way, Ethan,' said Rowlinson, turning to Eaton. 'Do we really need a profiler, sir? I prefer—'

'I know what you prefer, Rowlinson, but Mr Grey here has been assigned to us specifically by Assistant Commissioner Auckland and comes highly recommended.'

Rowlinson stole a quick glance at Grey, who shifted his weight uncomfortably. The man looked as though he was newly qualified; the kind of person that still got ID'd buying glue at the supermarket.

'Profilers don't catch killers, sir. Hard work and—'

'Spare me the philosophical bullshit, detective. We all know what's happening here, this is only going to get worse. Two victims seemingly unconnected in four days.'

'It's a little early to call, sir. We don't know there's no connection; we just haven't found one yet.'

'Well, you know what: I'm happy to sit here and knock this idea around with you for the rest of the day but it makes no difference. The AC says you need a profiler and here's a profiler.'

'Whose budget is this coming out of?' Rowlinson said wryly but he knew he was pushing it. Perhaps it was only because Grey was standing there that Eaton didn't rise to it.

From the corner, Grey gave a nervous laugh and asked, 'Do you have any experience of catching a serial killer, DCI Rowlinson?'

'Do you?' Rowlinson retorted.

Grey's smile disappeared. 'I've read your investigation notes, detective. You've lost four days already. You need my help. This killer is devious and knows what he's doing. It'll take more than hard work and faith to catch him.'

'Look, no offence, but—'

'Have you started a profile on *Analyzer* yet?' cut in Eaton.

'We're using a mood board,' Westbrook offered. Rowlinson turned and looked at her dryly. *Thanks, Westbrook.*

'A board?' Grey laughed. His voice had a public-school boy resonance. Like he was talking with a mouth full of cotton wool. 'Really?' He turned to Eaton, raised his eyes melodramatically. Rowlinson bit his tongue.

Eaton didn't seem to notice. He'd finished rolling a cigarette and had stood up. 'We're going to meet tomorrow for a full briefing. In the meantime, I want you two to let Grey have access to everything so he can start building a profile, which will be used as the focus of this investigation. We have a small window: the media know about the murders and they're giving them mild attention but they haven't made any connection. They don't know about this symbol the killer drew at both scenes, *yet*. Now bugger off, all of you, and make friends.'

Rowlinson left with Westbrook and walked off swiftly to the coffee machine near Eaton's office. He noticed that Ethan Grey didn't follow. When they were out of earshot he turned to his DS.

'You had to mention the board.'

'Sorry, boss. No excuse for Grey being a prick, though.'

'True.'

Rowlinson fumbled around for some change and bought a decaffeinated latte for himself and a black Americano for Westbrook.

She took the plastic cup gratefully and they headed for the stairs. 'Boss, have you ever caught a serial killer? I mean, you know, a *real* serial killer.'

Rowlinson paused. 'No. I only know one person who has ever successfully caught a serial killer.'

'Who's that?'

Rowlinson didn't answer, but took the stairs two at a time.

# Chapter 9

Priest checked his watch. An hour had passed. He got up to stretch his legs; peered through the curtains to look at the Mercedes across the street. He couldn't see whether Merriweather and Vose were still in the car because the sun was reflecting off the windscreen. With any luck, they'd passed out in the heat.

Owen was in another room on the phone. His voice resonated through the walls although Priest could only make out a few words. 'Outrageous', 'terrible state of affairs' and 'they have no idea!' He was talking to a colleague – he didn't specify who. Priest had tried to persuade the professor to take legal advice but he seemed intent on putting his faith in his fellow academics rather than an unknown lawyer, and who could blame him?

Priest sighed. Owen's resolve – his unshakable belief in what he was saying – was troubling him. The man was genuinely afraid. But what secret was he really hiding? What was so explosive that it had to remain hidden from the world at all costs?

*Do I even want to know?*

Jessica was due to arrive at Priest's apartment at seven. He had promised her a gourmet meal, the likes of which she had never previously experienced; she had looked at him sceptically before accepting, a smile playing at her lips. She had incredible lips – the thought of them tortured him at night when he lay awake, alone, in the early hours wishing their time together wasn't so brief. Snatched moments of passion was the sum of their relationship. Jessica's business commitments saw to that. It wasn't a relationship, she had told him. Jessica Ellinder was running one of the largest pharmaceutical companies in the UK, and rescuing it from the brink. She didn't have time for relationships. Snatched moments would have to do. Take it or leave it.

Priest bit his lip. Would she prefer Chinese or Indian takeaway? If his time with her was so limited, he sure as hell wasn't going to waste it by trying to cook something, promise or no promise.

Owen returned, slamming through the door and slumping down in a wooden chair near the pantry. His face was red, anxiety seemed to be seeping from his pores.

'No help at all,' he fumed.

Priest walked over to the sink and filled the kettle. 'Where is the Book?'

'It's upstairs. I'll fetch it.'

Owen disappeared again and returned a minute later carrying a large box, which he placed delicately on the kitchen table. There was a power cable connected to the back, which he plugged into the mains and flicked on.

Priest looked the box over. It was black, sealed and had looked heavy when Owen had been handling it. There was a control panel on the side with a digital display and the whirr of a fan built into the unit.

'This is a portable microclimate storage container,' Owen explained. 'The scripture is contained in the box, which is locked using a combination. The box self-stabilises the temperature to seventy degrees Fahrenheit and fifty per cent relative humidity. There's a battery back-up in case you need to transport it, which lasts a couple of hours.'

'I see. Can I . . . ?'

'No. Any exposure to light, especially in this heat, could be prejudicial to the scripture. It's barely legible as it is.'

'Then how do you know it's in there?' asked Priest.

'There is a trick.'

Owen directed Priest to a small round metal ringlet on the side of the container which turned out to be a spyhole. Priest closed one eye and stared in. There was something there; he could make out a pile of tattered yellowing pages adorned with faint black symbols.

'You've translated it all?' Priest asked.

'As much as I can, although in some places I have had to make certain assumptions where the writing is damaged.'

'Presumably you have the translations safe?'

Owen smiled. 'They're safe, yes.'

'Where are they? Capindale will say they fall within her search order and she has a right to them.'

'She'll never find them.'

'Her people will turn your house upside down looking for them.'

'Mr Priest, if I'm prepared to die to keep the secrets of the Book of Janus locked up, then I'm sure I don't mind the inconvenience of having to tidy up once in a while.' Owen looked around and indicated the mess in the kitchen. 'I hardly live in an immaculate environment anyway.'

Priest sat down. The kettle had boiled but he'd lost his appetite for tea. If Owen wanted to let Henrik Vose rifle through his underwear drawer for the rest of the day then who was he to stand in the way? Priest was here to ensure that the order was executed peaceably, not make sure that Capindale got what she wanted.

He rested his cheek on his hand. 'Shall we get on with this, professor? If you're not going to take advice then I'm not sure that sitting here for the next three hours is going to improve their mood out there.'

Owen's voice almost cracked. 'There's nothing you can do, Mr Priest? Nothing?'

Priest shook his head. 'Professor—'

'Wait.' Owen hesitated, waved his arm at Priest. 'Please. They won't find the translations but it doesn't matter, they'll find someone to translate the text eventually. The content of this book is enough to . . . it will tear a hole in the world. One that we are not likely to be able to repair.'

Priest hesitated, scrutinised Owen. He was desperate. Desperate and credible.

*It's not my job to help him out.*

Perhaps sensing Priest's uncertainty, Owen continued, 'I know how ridiculous it sounds, Mr Priest. And I know I'm asking you to put your belief in something that you can't understand but there are bigger forces at play here, bigger than you, me and Elisha Capindale.'

'I thought we agreed I don't believe in God.'

'Fine.' Owen was disappointed. 'But you believe in the destruction that flows from those who *do* believe in God.'

'I'm not here to judge, Professor Owen.' Priest took out his phone and typed out a text to Sasha Merriweather:

'*When you're ready. Just you and Vose.*'

'I can buy you some time, that's all.'

Owen groaned, put his head in his hands. 'Time isn't enough, Mr Priest. Not even if you could buy me a thousand years.'

Priest took one last glance at Owen. He looked tired, but not defeated. Priest looked at the text. Thought about it.

'*What harm can an old book do?*' Clicked 'send'.

Moments later, Priest saw the driver's and passenger's door of the Mercedes open.

# Chapter 10

Henrik Vose loosened his tie and undid his top button. The heat struck him like a wrecking ball as he climbed out of the car and made his way across the street with Sasha Merriweather. She was fiddling with a video camera.

'You're going to film it?' Henrik asked.

'I don't want a dispute about what happens in there. This is for everyone's protection.'

Vose was pissed off. He hadn't expected to carry out the search himself – what else was the point of the team Capindale had sent with him? Christ, he didn't even know what he was looking for. Owen could hand him any old tea-stained document and tell him it was the Book of Janus. How would he know the difference?

Henrik climbed the steps and pressed the doorbell to Owen's house, turned to Merriweather. 'Will he just hand it over, do you think?'

'Priest knows the score. We could have been waiting twice as long; he's obviously got Owen under control. Stop worrying, Henrik.'

She managed to get the camera working and held the lens up just as the door opened.

Charlie Priest's significant frame filled the doorway.

'You can turn that damn thing off for a start,' he grunted.

Priest stood back and let Merriweather and Vose shuffle into the kitchen. He watched Vose's eyes dart about the place; register the mess, the smell of mould, Owen's desolate form in the corner, then rest on the microclimate container on the picnic table.

Priest cleared his throat. 'Professor Owen, this is Henrik Vose, who is Elisha Capindale's representative and their solicitor, Sasha Merriweather.'

'Pleased to meet you, professor.' To be fair to Merriweather, she extended her hand, although Owen declined to take it. 'I'm grateful for your patience. We don't want to be here any longer than is necessary.'

Vose nodded at the box. 'What's that?'

'That is a microclimate container,' Priest answered. 'It contains the Book of Janus.'

Priest saw Vose swallow, and his eyes narrow. Something troubled him. It was the way Vose was looking at the box. Not with satisfaction or relief. But greed. Cold, raw greed.

'Can we just . . . ?'

'The box has a battery back-up that lasts a few hours,' Priest explained. 'You'll need to get it plugged in quickly if you don't want the contents to turn to dust.'

'We'll take it straight to my office,' said Merriweather, unplugging the box. 'Help me with it, Henrik.'

'Wait,' said Vose, glaring at Owen. 'What about the translations?'

Owen shook his head. 'You can't take them.'

'We have a court order. We can take what we want. Isn't that right, Mr Priest?'

'No,' said Priest calmly. 'You can take certain materials permitted by the order, assuming you can find them.'

'Are they here?' Vose was red round the face and neck. He had a sharp edge to his voice. He looked like a man teetering on the edge.

Owen spoke directly to Vose: 'There's something you should know about what you intend to take away from my property, Mr Vose.'

'Spare me the spiritual bullshit, professor. I already know your position on this. The Book's coming with us. Now where are the translations?'

Owen faltered, his voice trembled. 'Set . . . set out in that book is a roadmap which will lead you to an evil greater than you can possibly imagine.'

Priest saw Merriweather glance sharply at Vose. *She doesn't know what this is. That's interesting.* Vose had taken hold of the container and was testing its weight.

'We'll put this in the car,' he instructed Merriweather. 'Then we will return and, by then, I hope Mr Priest will have explained to Professor Owen that the translations must be handed over to us immediately.'

'Just to be clear,' said Priest. 'I shan't be doing that.'

Vose stopped, balled up his fists. 'You'll do as I say. Remember who is paying you. Or do I need to go back and tell the judge to discharge the supervising solicitor for incompetence?'

Merriweather looked uneasy. 'Henrik—'

'Shut up!' Vose seethed. 'Let's go.'

'Blood will flow,' Owen stammered, getting up. He was starting to sound like a Doomsday fanatic. 'If you do this, Mr Vose. Remember: the world is in debt to Christ and one day He will call in that debt and we will pay. In blood. This book contains the key to a redemption that has been thousands of years in the making and which will be as savage and cruel as it will be glorious.'

Vose looked at the professor with a mixture of pity and disgust. 'You really are a loon if you believe that. This book is a relic. Like you.'

Owen looked over at Priest, aghast. *The world is in debt and will pay in blood.* Priest clicked his tongue. *What had been his assessment of Owen? Desperate and credible.*

Vose directed Merriweather and they picked up the box together, lifted it over the table.

*Desperate and credible.* Priest was rarely wrong about first impressions.

Owen groaned as Vose kicked the door open and they started to manoeuvre out of the room.

'Wait!' commanded Priest.

Vose stopped and looked across at him, annoyed. 'What now?'

'You can't take that.'

'What?' Vose was incensed. 'We've just been through this, Priest.' He turned to Merriweather. 'I thought you said he knew what he was doing?'

'I'm afraid you can't take that, Mr Vose,' Priest repeated, brandishing a copy of the order.

Vose hesitated, then with a huff, lifted the box back on the table. A little out of breath, he fumbled around for his own copy of the court order. Read aloud: '*Any document, material, artefact, text, or scripture in your possession or under your control connected with the North Qumran Caves Dig.*'

He looked up at Priest and lifted his arms in feigned puzzlement. 'There. Satisfied?'

'Completely,' said Priest, nodding.

Vose grumbled some profanity Priest didn't catch under his breath before turning back to the box.

'Of course,' Priest interrupted. 'That means you are, so you say, perfectly entitled to take the Book of Janus. I don't think that anyone could dispute that the Book falls within the terms of the order. But the box within which it is contained does not.'

Vose paused. For a moment, Priest thought he might take a swing at him. Wouldn't be an issue if he did. Priest had forgotten none of his martial arts training from the police force and had a six-foot-three frame pumped with muscle. Vose was overweight and looked clumsy.

'You're being stupid,' Vose accused. 'We can't take the fucking book without the box. You know that.'

'In which case, this order should have been drawn more carefully,' Priest replied.

Owen had removed his head from his hands and was watching with wide eyes.

Vose shot a look at Merriweather, who shrank back in his gaze. 'Sasha – tell me this is a joke.'

'It's . . . well . . .' she stammered.

'Well, say something, woman!' Vose roared.

Merriweather seemed to recover a little and turned to Priest. 'Charlie, the spirit of the order suggests—'

Priest held up his hand. 'I'm not the judge, Sasha. I don't care about the spirit of anything. Only the words, which are clear and unambiguous. You can take the Book, but not the box. You'll need to apply to amend the order.'

Vose exploded. 'He'll destroy the bloody thing! You *ridiculous* man, can't you see that!'

Priest held his hands up in what was intended to be a conciliatory gesture, although he was far from intimidated. 'We have a problem here, Mr Vose. I can see that. You are entitled to the Book, but not the box. But you can't have one without the other.' He turned to Merriweather. She looked alarmed and he suspected the thought of having to report back to her client was filling her with dread. 'My suggestion, Sasha, is that I preserve the Book and its container as an interim measure, until you can amend the order.'

For a moment, nobody spoke. Only Vose was animated, twisting from one person to the next, finally settling on Merriweather.

'Well?' he demanded. 'What do you want to do?'

Merriweather took a moment to collect her thoughts. 'I think he might be right, Henrik.'

Vose buried his head in his hands. 'This is farcical!'

Priest turned to the professor, who looked shaken but relieved. 'You'll need a lawyer, professor.' Owen nodded appreciatively.

Vose stormed out, taking Merriweather roughly by the arm. She cast Priest a reproachful look before submitting to Vose's withdrawal.

'The application should be on notice,' Priest said before she disappeared out of the door. 'There's no emergency – the Book is safe with me, for now.'

The ceiling fan shuddered into life again, kick-started by the vibration that rippled through the house as Vose slammed the front door behind them.

# Chapter 11

Georgie Someday closed her eyes. She could hear blood thumping past her ears, her heart pounding in her chest. She felt a rush of adrenaline. Nothing existed outside of her focus. Everything was perfectly aligned, perfectly balanced. Georgie was a bird, about to take flight.

She heard movement. Bare feet ghosting across the mats. Georgie opened her eyes; her body was coiled. She crouched low, saw the form in front of her feign left but she anticipated the move. She sidestepped, left her trailing leg out and felt the body collide with her knee. It was easy to use the weight and momentum to her advantage, flipping her aggressor right over and watching her land face up on the mat a few feet behind her.

'Aw, Christ on a bike!' groaned Li.

Georgie snapped out of her trance and hurried over. 'Oh my God, are you all right? I'm dreadfully sorry. Are you hurt?'

Li sat up with Georgie's help. 'Yes, I'm fine. And Georgie – that was awesome!'

'I didn't mean to let you fall so hard. I was just trying—'

'Georgie, the point of judo is to try and get the other person to fall on their fanny. Stop apologising.'

Li climbed up, her white judogi fitted her beautifully. But then that girl could look attractive in a bin liner, so perhaps it wasn't a surprise that half the men in the room were mesmerised by her movement, even if she was flying through the air.

Georgie's judogi was from eBay and two sizes too large.

'I think I'm getting the hang of this,' Georgie chimed.

'I think you are,' agreed a man's voice. Georgie felt a hand on her shoulder. She turned and was met with a smile. Their instructor, Andy, was tall, with mousy brown hair cut stylishly like he'd just come from Toni and Guy, a strong jawline and bright green eyes, like hers.

Georgie smiled but the ability to offer some form of appropriate reply eluded her.

Li manoeuvred herself out of Andy's eyeline and motioned with her hands for Georgie to speak. '*Say something*,' she mouthed.

Georgie didn't say anything.

Andy removed his hand and, not sure what to do next, patted her arm.

'Anyway, great work, Georgie,' he said awkwardly. He smiled again and wandered off to where another two students were grappling in the middle of the room.

'Well, as chatting up goes, that was fucking awful,' Li remarked.

'What do you mean?' Georgie asked, fixing Li with a puzzled expression.

'OK. I'll break it down for you. That man, who by the way is very hot, obviously really likes you but every time he comes over to start a conversation you clam up like . . . er, a clam.'

'Oh, don't be silly! He doesn't . . . . I'm sure—'

'Georgie, we've been coming here for eight weeks now. I'm a prostitute. I can tell when someone has genuine feelings for someone else. In fact, even an asexual alien with no understanding of human psychology or desire would get that Andy really fancies you. Seriously, you're in a minority on this.'

'Really?' Georgie looked over but, without her glasses, everything in the middle distance was a bit of a blur. Andy was there somewhere though, probably looking very attractive, like Li said. *One of those fuzzy white bodies somewhere . . .*

'How can you be so intelligent and not see what's right in front of you?' Li chided, sighing.

Georgie turned back to Li. 'We'll talk about it later. We need to practise our small inner reap reversals. OK, I'll come at you this time.'

Li groaned as Georgie adopted an offensive position.

'Fine but go easy this time. I prefer my back unbroken.'

# Chapter 12

Jessica Ellinder leant against the kitchen table, one hand down, the other cradling a glass of pale Rosé. She was wearing a simple white top with a high neckline and half sleeves over a pleated skirt the same colour as the wine. There was nothing particularly fancy about the way she dressed, or the unfussy way she had her auburn hair cut short and straight, or the minimalist way she applied make-up. But the whole effect was as exquisite as it was austere.

'So tell me what happened after that,' she said, eyeing Priest from behind the glass.

Priest paused to unclip the cap off a bottle of beer. Ran a hand across his face. Cringed inwardly. She looked like she was ready for a photo shoot with *Vogue* and he hadn't shaved in three days.

'Well, Sasha Merriweather was very upset for a short time,' he said, continuing to lay the table for two, hoping she hadn't noticed how unkempt he looked. 'And of course I was very patient, as always. So when she calmed down and the chap with her – Vose – had ranted for a while, she gave me the box containing the manuscript.'

'Where is it now?'

'In the study, through there.'

'Can I see it?'

'Sure. It's not very interesting, though. You can just make out the parchment through a little spyhole and some symbols but not much else. I'll show you after we eat.'

Jessica took a sip of wine, brushed her hand through her hair thoughtfully. 'He didn't tell you what the manuscript says? Just that it contains a secret worth dying for.'

Priest poured out two glasses of water. 'That's about the size of it. Maybe the end of the world or something, I don't know.'

'Doesn't it intrigue you?'

Priest hadn't had much opportunity to think about it. By the time he had finished packing the box into the car and talked with Merriweather, Vose and Owen, it was gone five. He'd got stuck in traffic before he had to pull over and stop. Something had caught his eye, in the crowd. A man with a dog's head.

He shook the image from his mind but the minute he remembered, his heart lurched for a few beats before settling.

Priest's depersonalisation disorder had entered a new phase recently. The mental condition that distorted his perception of reality had started as a long, continuous epoch of constant rumination and self-absorption in an emotional wasteland where he felt nothing and everything at the same time. Over the years, the symptoms had faded. By the time he had met Jessica – when she and her late father had engaged his services to help investigate the death of Jessica's brother, Miles – he was functioning normally most of the time. Occasionally, he experienced bouts of depersonalisation – where he was no longer certain that he was real – or derealisation – where he was no longer certain that the world was real. In extreme cases, he experienced both.

More recently, he had also started to see bizarre hallucinations which merged into the real world, like the man in the crowd with the dog's head. Everything else was normal, except for an obvious anomaly. Like a ghost in a haunted house only he could see. Fortunately, they were infrequent, but nonetheless unpleasant (and, at night, terrifying) reminders that he wasn't well, and never really had been.

'What's wrong?' she asked, sensing his hesitation.

'Nothing,' he said. An automated response.

'How's your . . .'

She gestured with her hands. For a moment he looked puzzled, then remembered that Jessica was one of the few people who knew he had depersonalisation disorder, or DPD for short.

'Not too bad.' He tried to keep it casual but the little nod of her head told him that he'd failed. But she didn't dig – Jessica wasn't like that. It had become an unwritten rule that they didn't talk emotionally to each other, even during, or after, sex. The problem was that Priest had lost track of for whose benefit that rule had been established: his, or hers?

*Probably both of us.*

'What were you saying?' he said.

'The Book of Janus. Aren't you intrigued?'

He nodded. 'Yeah, I'm intrigued. Who wouldn't be? But you hear a lot of crackpot theories from time to time and Owen said himself that the manuscript hasn't been completely authenticated yet.'

'What do you think it could be?'

He turned to her, winked. 'Maybe it's a lasagne recipe.'

She laughed, then indicated to where wafts of smoke were seeping through the cracks around the oven door. 'In which case, it's wrong.'

Priest looked over, just as the fire alarm began to blare. 'Shit!' He turned the oven off and opened the door. A plume of thick smoke blossomed in front of him, the heat stinging his eyes. He pressed a button to end the alarm, waved a tea towel around until the smoke cleared. Then peered inside the oven to find the blackened remains of a lasagne's carcass wilting in a baking tray.

'How did you manage that?' Jessica asked, taking another sip of Rosé.

Priest inspected the oven. 'I don't know. Do you like take-aways?'

A takeaway had been the plan all along but a rush of blood to the head on the way back to the apartment, probably stimulated by the dog-head-man, had compelled him to try not to look like the useless human being he actually was.

Jessica sighed. 'It's a good job I don't come here to be impressed by you.'

Priest felt a prickly heat in the back of his head, his good humour felt suddenly drained. She was staring behind him, holding the wine glass close to her face, the colour dancing off her cheek. Fate had fused them together, but the bond wasn't sealed. It was like a sticky tar that peeled apart every time they met but never stretched far enough to break. Being with Jessica was like being deconstructed over and over again and with every new incarnation his judgement was a little more skewed, his perception a little more blurred. When she looked past him like this – cold and detached – he thought that the moment would come when he would realise that he didn't need her. That he was *good* without her. Whole. Or least, close to whole. But it never came. She was too deeply woven into his world; their paths were perpetually entwined by the Mayfly affair. She *infested* him, and he knew he infested her. That was the problem; the reason why they could never be *normal*: settle down and have kids, enjoy mutual friends and swap stories of adolescent love. The reason why they could never just walk hand-in-hand through a park, catch a film, make love and not just have sex. It was also the reason why they could never willingly go their separate ways. The Mayfly was an unimaginable evil – a deadly echo from the Holocaust – but it had never ended; the evil was still there, insidiously hovering wraith-like between them. It bound them together and, in this way, Priest knew absolutely that he could never be the one she needed. He could never offer her proper untainted love, or hold her close at night, be the shoulder she cried on, or the hand to pick her up when she fell. He reminded her too much of what had happened, the evil that almost destroyed her. He could see it in her eyes now, the barrier that could never be overcome, and the lust that tempted them again and again.

He looked away. 'Then what do you come here for?'

She played with the edge of the wine glass but didn't reply – the question hung in the air between them. Priest waited. He felt himself react to her coolness; her languid gaze. The way she sucked her lip, almost imperceptibly, but enough to let him know what she was thinking. What they were both thinking.

She opened her mouth to reply, her high cheekbones rising in perfect symmetry. Priest felt pressure in his groin. He hadn't seen her in two weeks. He was desperate to touch her, but—

The doorbell rang.

She exhaled, lolled her head to one side. The tension subsided. 'Expecting visitors?'

Priest wavered. You couldn't get in or out of the building without a fob – unless someone else let you in. Priest didn't know many of his neighbours and they didn't ever access his floor – there was only one penthouse.

The doorbell sounded again, then a knock. Loud and impatient.

'Better answer it,' Jessica teased. 'Could be important.'

Annoyed, Priest crossed the room, opened the door without bothering to check the security camera. He was about to say come back later when in walked his sister and niece.

'About time. Sorry, assume you didn't get my text. Good job I know the security guard.'

Sarah Boatman bustled in, as if she was expected, followed by six-year-old Tilly, with shining cheeks underneath a mass of tangled brown hair, a toy giraffe tucked under her arm.

'Hi, Uncle Charlie,' she said, skipping past and over to the kitchen table on which she placed a little plastic box and a fluffy rabbit.

'Sarah . . . what?' Priest stammered.

She turned to him, having obviously not seen Jessica. Something was wrong. She was sour, her eyes a little bloodshot, her hair – strawberry blonde, ruffled and always looking salon-finished – appeared unwashed. She was carrying a large bag and wearing joggers. *Sarah never goes out in joggers.*

'Charlie, we need to talk.'

'I can see that, but—'

'Do you have any wine?'

'Er, Sarah—'

Tilly interrupted. She had opened the little plastic box and produced a set of colouring pens and paper. She was busy scrawling away, not looking up: 'Who is that lady?'

Priest looked over to where Jessica stood by the oven. The intrusion hadn't seemed to faze her.

'Oh God, Charlie, I'm sor—' Sarah began but Priest cut her off.

'Jessica, this is Sarah, my sister, and Tilly, my niece. Sarah, this is Jessica.'

'Delighted to meet you both,' said Jessica, pleasantly.

'Hello,' said Tilly.

Sarah looked back at Priest, her eyes welled up. He sighed. Whatever it was, it was serious and any hope he had of wooing Jessica into the bedroom was now as charred as the lasagne.

'Maybe you should sit down,' Priest suggested. 'We were just about to order a takeaway.'

# Chapter 13

*One year ago*

*After the third neat gin, Sue is more relaxed. She's talking to me, about her life. And asking me about mine. Where did I grow up? Marypoint, Cumbria. What did my parents do? My mother worked in an office, insurance, I think, and my father was a vicar. Is that why I do this? Because of my father?*

'I think so,' I admit, pouring another glass and handing it to her. 'I'm afraid, like you, I wasn't blessed with a good childhood.'

*She looks concerned. 'What do you mean?'*

I look away wistfully. 'My parents died in a house fire when I was ten. There was a gas leak, and a spark from somewhere, although no one knows where from, and the whole place ignited. I remember it like it was yesterday. A fire as hot as hell itself, and the smell of burnt flesh. Like a barbecue. Imagine that? Your parents cooking like a barbecue, Sue?'

'That's horrible,' she mumbles. Drinks the gin and offers her shaking hand forward for more. 'Where were you at the time?'

'Well, therein lies a story.' I smile knowingly. 'But it's not one that I often tell people.'

'You can tell me.'

'Can I trust you, Sue?'

She produces a slightly drunken scout's honour salute, which I take to mean an affirmative. 'Well, I should have died in that fire. Without a doubt. But something woke me in the early hours of the morning. I don't know what, the tree branch tapping the window, or a barn owl nearby. I don't know. But I woke up, and I had this irresistible urge to get out of bed. I can't explain it to you. I didn't sleepwalk, or have night terrors. I usually slept like a log. But something was telling me to get out of bed and, can you believe, go outside.'

I take a sip of my drink and I don't mind telling you at this point the alcohol is starting to affect me slightly. Nothing like Sue – I make sure I eat like a horse before I conduct a private session – but enough to make me feel a little woozy.

'What happened?' she asks earnestly. She's so sweet, and I have her in the palm of my hand.

'Well, I gave in to temptation. Got out of bed, and walked outside. Luckily, it was a warm night and I was perfectly happy sitting on a bench in the garden with my dressing gown on, looking up at the house, with its gritty façade and grey slate roof. We had neighbours, but you couldn't see them. The next house was half a mile away. We were surrounded by fields and trees, and an army of rabbits.'

I poured another two glasses.

'And then?'

I frown, like I'm trying to remember, although I have no need to. It's permanently ingrained in me, like a tattoo that never fades. 'There was an explosion, from the kitchen, I think. I jumped up, terrified. It was like a bomb had gone off.'

I clutch at my face, as if the thought is painful. She leans forward. We're a metre apart, maybe less. The room smells of alcohol and she is swaying slightly.

'The fire ripped through the building. You've never seen anything like it. I always thought that fire ate through buildings slowly, gradually. But within seconds, the flames were leaping out of the first-storey windows. The window of my parents' bedroom, and I knew straight away that there was no way they would have made it. Not unless they had also experienced a strange compulsion to get out. But if they had, they would have been standing next to me.'

Sue had her hand to her mouth. 'Oh my God.'

'Sue,' I scold.

'Sorry. Sorry. Gosh.'

'Don't worry about it.' I smile, reassuringly. 'Anyway, I ran to the nearest house: half a mile away. In bare feet. By the time I got there, my feet were ripped to shreds. I could hardly walk. I pounded on the door and eventually my neighbour, Mr Barnes, opened up, stern-faced and exhausted. Hurriedly, I explained what had happened, and of course he called the emergency services. But by the time they got to the house, there was nothing left but charred remains and ash.'

This bit was an exaggeration. The fire was in fact still burning when the brigade arrived. It burned for a day, maybe more, but for the purposes of conveying the horror of the story, a small hyperbole here and there is excusable in my eyes.

'It's just terrible,' she whispered. 'Terrible.'

'Yes.' I look down sadly.

'Who brought you up then? If your parents died, I mean.'

'Well.' I shuffle, as if I'm uncomfortable. I am. The vestry seats are like a hundred years old or something. 'I can't tell you, for the simple fact that I had so many foster parents that I can't remember them all. Except one.'

'Oh yes?'

*I hesitate, pour more gin. The bottle is gone, so I produce another without Sue even realising that the cabinet is full of them. 'I'm afraid, Sue, that, let me put it this way, not everyone in the care system is in it for the benefit of the children.'*

*I look at her with what I hope is a meaningful expression. It obviously is because she catches on straight away. I knew she would, because I know a little of her own history. I know her abuser was her uncle.*

*'I'm so sorry.' She looks down and for one awful minute I think she's about to cry, but she manages to compose herself. I think, flatteringly, for my sake.*

*'Like I said, we all have our crosses to bear.' I smile again.*

*'It must have been God,' she realises. 'I mean, the reason why you woke up that night and went downstairs. That was God delivering you for a purpose. A higher purpose. So you can do this work.'*

*She is so delightedly keen to be right, but her assessment falls short. She is right in that God chose me for a particular purpose, but it was not so that I could waste my time running AA meetings.*

*Nonetheless, so as not to discourage her, she is after all doing so well, I say, 'I think so, Sue, yes. But as it happens, I can be more certain than that, because there was not one miracle that fateful night, but two.'*

*Her mouth is wide open, jaw to the floor. She is rocking back and forth, completely unaware of how comical she looks right now. Her loose top has slipped from her shoulder, too, and I can see the rise of her collar bone, the rash around her neck.*

*'The night my parents died I was visited by God in the form of a jackdaw,' I say, matter-of-factly. She doesn't contradict me. 'The jackdaw told me that there was a plan for me, and for the world at large. Like John of Patmos, tucked away deep in the heart of the*

Cave of the Apocalypse, listening to the word of God that eventually became Revelations, I listened to the jackdaw.'

There was a sudden silence, and I became very aware of Sue's eyes on me, unblinking. She had stopped drinking, despite there being a drop of gin left in her glass; such was the intensity of her concentration, I had temporarily cured her of her disease.

'And?' she breathed. 'What did He say?'

I took a deep breath. 'He said that I am destined to sit at His table, to drink from His cup and to eat from His plate. That I am not His son, but I am to be regarded as His representative on Earth, specifically in the fight against evil. Are you familiar with the Book of Revelation, Sue?'

She nodded. 'A little.'

'Well, I would forgive anyone who is not intimately familiar with the manner of our impending doom. It is a controversial subject, not for the faint-hearted.'

'But how does it all tie together?' She is desperate to understand, I can see it in her bloodshot eyes. 'Are you saying that there is another Book of Revelation?'

Carefully, I put the glass down. For a moment, we sit opposite each other. Nothing is said, but the air between us is thin, the space is hollow. She trembles, like a frightened bird, but wishes to remain strong, upright. But I can see that the drink has taken over: she is in her safe place. In a world of confusion.

This can only mean one thing: it is time.

# Chapter 14

Priest helped sort out Tilly and get her ready to sleep in one of the spare rooms. The penthouse had four bedrooms, all en-suite. Priest had hastily found bedding to make up the smallest room, which Tilly had demanded be designated as hers because the window overlooked Covent Garden and she could watch a small brass band busking on the street below. The penthouse was air-conditioned and Sarah spent a long time patiently explaining why she couldn't have the window open to hear them. At the moment, it wasn't dropping below twenty degrees at night.

When Tilly had finally agreed to go to bed, Priest and Sarah trudged back through to the kitchen and joined Jessica at the table.

'I ordered pizza while you were sorting Tilly,' said Jessica, pointing at a stack of steaming boxes. 'It just arrived. I hope you like pepperoni.'

'I'm so sorry,' Sarah began, aiming the plea at Jessica. 'I didn't want to spoil your evening. I don't usually turn up here unannounced looking like shit.'

'Please, Sarah, it's not a problem,' Jessica reassured her. 'Charlie thinks the world of you and it's really a privilege to meet you.'

She cast a glance at Priest, who shuffled nervously in his chair. He never talked about Sarah, or Tilly. Not because they weren't important to him – they were – but because they didn't talk about their families.

'Oh, that's sweet, thank you,' said Sarah. 'Charlie's mentioned you too, of course.'

Sarah smiled at Priest. He smiled back. As did Jessica. All three of them knew it wasn't true. Priest wondered if there was any chance of the ground opening up and swallowing him whole.

Sarah shared out the pizza and poured wine, then sat down heavily.

'It's Ryan,' she said, taking a bite.

Priest had figured as much – it had only been a matter of time. Sarah had married Ryan a year before Tilly was born. They hadn't been seeing each other for long. Priest hadn't really paid much attention at first: there had been men in Sarah's life before and Priest tended to be over-protective of his little sister, in response to which Sarah tended to avoid introducing him to anyone new unless she absolutely had to. Ryan wasn't stupid. He had trained as an accountant. But he was lazy, and the minute Sarah had started to earn enough he had quit his job on the pretext of developing some great money-making scheme (which had, unsurprisingly, never come to fruition) and relaxed into the life of a part-time husband, part-time father, and part-time human being. And Sarah had been making excuses for him ever since.

'What happened?' Priest asked. He glanced at Jessica. He had expected her to be feeling awkward but, on the contrary, she sat next to Sarah and placed a hand on her arm in support. She was leaning forward, concerned and engaged. He felt a twinge of annoyance. Jessica was perfectly capable of empathy and warmth, but just not for him. Outside of the bedroom at least.

'Whatever happens, please don't say you told me so,' Sarah said, a tear forming at the corner of her eye.

'Admittedly, that does sound like the kind of thing I would say but I'll let you off for now.'

Jessica interjected, softly: 'I take it Ryan is . . . ?'

'My husband. At the moment,' Sarah breathed.

'Did he hurt you?' Priest asked, anger swelling in his throat.

Sarah looked down, ashamed. 'There's someone else.'

For a moment, Priest wasn't sure what she meant. *Who had someone else?* But some invisible feminine message had been transmitted and received loud and clear between Sarah and Jessica. Apparently it had bypassed Priest altogether.

'Who is she?' Jessica asked.

'A girl he met online.'

'Has he done this before?'

Sarah pursed her lips and Priest could see it now: the mixture of ire and betrayal, embarrassment and regret all fighting for supremacy in her head. 'She rang me.'

Priest sat back, arms folded. He knew that he should be the one in control; the supportive, rational, objective friend, not the angry big brother. But his fists were locked shut under his arms. Jessica put her hand on Sarah's back. She was slumped at the table, chin resting on her arms, staring straight ahead.

'What did she say?' Priest growled.

'*I just thought you needed to know,*' said Sarah, mimicking a high-pitched, girly voice, '*that your husband picks out girls on the internet and sleeps with them.*'

There was a silence for a while, just the whirr of the fridge and the occasional drip of water from the tap.

Then Jessica said, 'She was one of them?'

Sarah nodded.

'You get a name?' asked Priest.

'Does it matter?'

'Guess not. How long has this been going on?'

Sarah exhaled, shuddered at the thought. Her voice was barely a whisper. 'Long time.'

'Where is he now?'

Sarah looked up at him, sensing his intonation. 'Don't make this worse. Remember Tilly.'

'I'm just asking.'

She took a gulp of wine. 'Back home. The phone call was this afternoon. So I waited for him to get back, then told him what had happened. He tried to lie at first. Make out it was some loony old girlfriend that had tracked him down but . . . I've known for a while, I suppose. Maybe not the details, but I've known. Just buried it, for Tilly's sake.'

'Did he admit it in the end?' asked Jessica.

'More or less. Said, *what did I expect*? – work always came before him. Fuck.' Sarah shook her head. 'I've been so fucking stupid.'

Priest bit his tongue.

'You haven't,' Jessica assured as Sarah started to cry. 'No one is judging you, Sarah.'

'I'm sorry,' Sarah said through deep, moist breaths to Jessica. 'You seem so nice, and I've ruined your evening.'

Priest got up and walked round, managed to swallow his anger for a moment. Put his arm around her. 'I'm sorry, kid.' He held her for a moment and she responded, putting her head on his shoulder. 'What does Tilly know?'

Sarah wiped her eyes, blew her nose on a tissue Jessica handed her. 'That we're staying here for a while and that Daddy's working away. That's OK, right?'

'You can stay as long as you want.'

'I'll cook for you,' she whispered. 'I know you're shit at that. I'm sorry if you didn't know that, Jessica.'

Priest caught Jessica's eye.

'No,' she said. 'I'd got that one figured.'

# Chapter 15

*Wednesday*

DS Fay Westbrook placed a plastic coffee cup on the table in front of Rowlinson, who lifted the lid and peered inside while she sat down at the briefing table next to him.

'This is decaf, right?' he said.

She huffed. 'You only drink decaf. I can remember simple personality traits after six months of working closely with someone.'

Rowlinson nodded, pleased.

Ethan Grey was stuffed inside a blue pin-striped suit and poring over a file of papers. He looked like he'd just stepped out of the shower, his gelled hair glistened like a marine oil spill in the office's artificial light.

'The killer took more time with the second murder,' Grey muttered, turning over a crime scene photograph.

'The symbol is more elaborate and there's salt spread all over the—' Rowlinson began to explain but Grey held up his hand to stop him. When he was sure he had their attention, he crossed his legs and leant back in the chair, pensive.

'What we're dealing with here, Chief Inspector, is a very dangerous individual; probably a man. I'd say in his early twenties.

He would have had a troubled childhood. Possibly the victim of abuse, from his mother most likely. Hence why the victims are both female. No doubt this is someone cut off from society, with a nihilistic disposition.'

'Look, Ethan, we've got two murders here and a symbol that connects them,' Rowlinson began. 'Let's not be hasty about this.'

'This is a serial killer.' Grey narrowed his eyes. 'There is every cause for haste.'

'You need three murders with a cooling-off period for a serial killer,' said Westbrook.

Grey snorted. 'Only according to the FBI definition, but last time I checked we were in England.' When no one showed an interest in contradicting him, he continued. 'There is every reason to believe that we are dealing with a serial killer and every reason to believe that he will strike again. Very soon, I'd say. Here.' Grey tossed a bundle of papers across the table. 'This is my preliminary profile. I will no doubt tweak and improve it as we progress. It is early days. But you will find this a valuable asset in your hunt, Chief Inspector.'

Rowlinson picked up the papers warily. Pretended to flip through the first few pages. 'What about the symbol?' Rowlinson rested his hand on the picture. Emma Mendez sprawled over the bed. Behind her, the streaks of deep red were clear enough: the cross and the sinuous line.

Grey frowned. 'The symbol? I haven't surmised its meaning yet. But I will. It means something to the killer. He wants to be known, he wants publicity. This is his calling card.'

'It looks like a snake,' Westbrook said, almost under her breath. Rowlinson re-examined the picture. *Yeah – looks like a snake.*

'The Serpent Killer?' announced Grey.

'Excuse me?'

'His name, of course. The Serpent Killer.'

'We're going with Unsub,' Rowlinson mumbled, gathering the papers and standing up. 'Let's not glorify this fucker with a gimmicky name. We're not the FBI.'

'The Serpent Killer has a good ring to it,' said Westbrook, straight-faced. Rowlinson could see she was being facetious but Grey hadn't picked up on it.

'She's right.'

'The killer is Unsub, until I say otherwise,' said Rowlinson. He motioned for Westbrook to follow him out of the room, leaving Grey to clear up the rest of the papers and photographs.

# Chapter 16

Georgie hopped up the steps to Priest & Co.'s office two at a time and half stumbled through the door into the reception. Maureen was on the phone, but gave her a wide grin and a gestured greeting, which Georgie returned.

She waited while the Priest & Co. receptionist finished explaining to someone on the other end of the line that Charlie wasn't available. Her dry responses cut across whatever protestation the other person had like nails on a blackboard.

'Like I said, Mr Ferdinand, I don't think Mr Priest will take on a prosecution under the Salmon Act . . . No, I had no idea that handling salmon in suspicious circumstances was an offence.'

Maureen pushed a pile of mail across the reception desk towards Georgie, who scooped it up to sort through. Some of them were for her, relating to cases that she had taken on herself – the rest were split between Charlie and Vincent Okoro, Priest & Co.'s prolific in-house counsel. A former prosecutor for the International Criminal Court, Okoro's reputation as a skilful advocate was as large as his physical presence.

The final member of the Priest & Co. team, Simon 'Solly' Solomon, rarely got post. Solly inhabited the top floor of the building, from where he seldom strayed. His acute obsessive-compulsive disorder meant he wasn't a people person, but, as a forensic accountant, he was second to none.

Maureen was still on the phone. 'I fully appreciate, Mr Ferdinand, that you can afford to pay Mr Priest but we don't do that kind of work . . . OK . . . That's great . . . Sorry we can't help.'

Maureen hung up and sighed heavily. After four decades of thirty cigarettes a day, it was more of a gurgle than a sigh, but Georgie got the gist.

'Salmon?'

'Don't ask.'

'You're probably right. Where is everyone?'

'Boardroom. Case sifting.'

'Thanks, Maureen.'

Georgie turned to leave but Maureen called her back, lowered her voice 'Honey, Sarah left her husband last night. She's staying at Charlie's house. Just to let you know. He's a bit distracted. More so than usual.'

Georgie raised her eyebrows. She didn't know much about Sarah and Ryan, only that Sarah seemed very nice and Charlie didn't get on with his brother-in-law.

'OK. Thanks for letting me know. I'll be discreet.'

The Priest & Co. boardroom was next to Okoro's office. It was a sizeable area centred around a modern table large enough to seat twelve, with a dark glossed oak top and sleek grey legs set at an angle. The chairs were black leather, high backed with spindly legs that made them look like Steampunk spiders. In the centre of the room hung a bulky, spherical chandelier: a blue web of thin metal strips, through which a bulb the size of a cricket ball was just visible. It reminded Georgie of Neptune, a giant ball of gas and ice, swirling watchfully above them.

Charlie sat at the head of the table, his knee resting on the edge, leaning back. He was wearing dark jeans and a brown wool suit jacket, his trademark cup of Earl Grey tea steaming next to him. His hair was dark, almost black; untouched, yet somehow perfectly ruffled. He had let his stubble take over his face so it was more like a thinly cut beard. It suited his strong jaw line; finished off the stolid, handsome look. Only the bags under his eyes betrayed him.

Okoro was next to him. He gave Georgie a genuine smile as she sidled in and took the seat opposite him. He was immaculate, as always, in a three-piece suit, off white with a blue shirt and tie. Whereas Charlie was tall and broad-shouldered like a boxer, Okoro was short, burly and with arms the size of Georgie's thighs; more like a wrestler.

Georgie tended to feel very safe around her two mentors.

'Morning,' she said brightly, producing a file of papers from her bag and setting them down. The table was covered with files and bundles, some of them bound together with blue ribbon.

'Morning, Georgie,' said Okoro. 'We haven't started yet.'

The meeting had been set for eight thirty. It wasn't that yet but they had both probably come in early.

'How was the search order?' Georgie directed the question at Charlie, who grimaced before replying.

'Rather odd. I'm now the custodian of non-canonised Hebrew scripture that contains a secret so devastating that its former proprietor was willing to die to keep it.'

Georgie nodded keenly. 'That's exciting! What is it called?'

'The Book of Janus.'

Georgie thought for a moment. 'The Book of Janus? I think I read about that recently. Wasn't it found at the same site as the Dead Sea Scrolls?'

'Apparently. Now there's a legal dispute over who owns it.'

'Cool. Can I see it?'

'You can do, but it's contained in a microclimate storage box. You can peep through and see a bit of it but thumbing through to see what you can find is off limits.'

'Do you know what the secret is?' asked Okoro, interested.

'No, Professor Owen wouldn't tell me, and my Hebrew is somewhat rusty, even if I could look at it properly.'

'There's a conspiracy theory about it,' Georgie said, her eyes lighting up. 'The Pope wanted to suppress it. There was something in it that undermined the church, supposedly. How terribly exciting! It's like *Indiana Jones*.'

'No, it's like a search order gone horribly wrong,' Charlie corrected. 'We're going back to court, and I think I've upset the claimant.'

'That's not like you, Priest,' Okoro razzed.

Georgie had looked up Elisha Capindale the first chance she had after she found out about the case. One article from four years ago had stuck in her mind. The headline was: 'Hermit antiquity dealer claims to have sold vial of Virgin Mary's breast milk.' That rather set the tone. Capindale was once a respected art dealer whose reputation had been tarnished in recent years by her obsession with weird and wonderful Christian relics. By all accounts, she was a bit of a joke.

Charlie had apparently decided to ignore Okoro. 'Anyway, on with the business of the day.'

Georgie enjoyed The Sift. Once a quarter, the Priest & Co. team sat round the table and talked about all of the cases they had been asked to take on, scoping out each one carefully. Most were rejected, sometimes all of them. Occasionally, Charlie would bite down hard on something. A year previous, he had taken on a libel action in the High Court. A small online magazine was being sued by a transnational charity CEO. When Priest & Co.'s star witness had turned up dead on the morning of the trial, they had been entangled in a network of murderous obsession. Charlie had almost been killed, twice.

Georgie was hoping for something a little bit more orthodox this year.

'This looks interesting,' said Okoro, picking up a bundle of papers. 'It's a misrepresentation claim started in the Croydon County Court concerning the authenticity of a seventeenth-century taxidermied raccoon.'

'Oh, look,' said Georgie. 'He's wearing a little hat.'

There was silence for a while.

'Who's the junior on the case?'

Okoro leafed through the papers. 'A guy called Jonathan Price.'

'Never heard of him.'

They moved on, spending the next hour reviewing the evidence of another possible case before, distracted, Charlie stood up. Walked to the window and stared down at the passing traffic.

'No, no, *no*. It's all crap.'

'Are you sure, Priest?' said Okoro, raising an eyebrow. 'This one's got "appeal" written all over it.'

Charlie turned back to the table and Georgie noticed how tired he really seemed, as if the sunlight filtering through the window had rubbed off the mask he had been wearing all morning.

'Maybe we could do this some other time,' she suggested.

When Charlie nodded, Okoro took the hint and gathered up all the papers. 'I'll be in my office if you need anything,' he said before leaving Georgie and Charlie alone.

Charlie rubbed his face. 'Sorry, didn't sleep well.'

Georgie shrugged, unaffected. 'It's OK. I'd still like to take a look at the Book of Janus, if I can?'

'Mm. I'm hoping that Elisha Capindale hurries up and amends her court order; the thing is creeping me out. Owen said it was written by the Devil.'

'Do you believe that?' Georgie asked, cautious.

'I don't believe in God, so no. But that doesn't stop it from being a bad omen.'

Georgie understood. She wasn't religious either. Her mother used to go to church, before her father had died. Then she stopped. Georgie had never really thought about it much. That didn't mean that God didn't exist, she just wasn't sure it mattered much. Perhaps He existed, but wasn't interested anymore; like He was a caretaker on sabbatical.

'I get that. Must be weird having it around.'

Charlie nodded. 'It's a bit creepy, like having the Necronomicon hanging around in your basement.'

'The Necro-what?'

'It doesn't matter. Look, let's finish up here and you come over after work to have a peep. OK?'

Georgie grinned. That having been agreed, they filed away the papers spread out across the table and she spent the rest of the afternoon at her desk. It might have been a pleasant afternoon, but something was bothering her. The fragments of information she had picked up about the Book of Janus buzzed around in her head. Whatever she did, she couldn't shake off the unsettling feeling that something was about to happen. Something bad. Something that would change everything, irreversibly.

# Chapter 17

It was past six in the evening and the heat had finally started to dissipate; a patchwork of mottled cloud had partially covered the low sun and Georgie was able to walk through Covent Garden without leaping from one shaded area to the next like a desert lizard.

Charlie didn't seem affected by the weather, although he had taken to slinging his jacket over his shoulder wherever he went, as if he knew a heavy brown wool was completely the wrong type of garment but couldn't quite leave it behind. She had to half run to keep up with him, weaving in and out of the crowds.

Georgie loved the market, with its mixture of tiny shop fronts and ever-changing stalls. Three acrobats had pitched up outside St Paul's church and were throwing themselves in front of a small band of tourists. The music was loud: an incessant thud that would have sounded horrible anywhere else but here, where the streets were alive, it didn't seem out of place.

Charlie detoured them through the market, the smell of spices grabbing at Georgie as she went. They were headed for his penthouse; he'd promised her a glimpse of the Book of Janus, not that there was much to see. Sarah and Tilly were there, he'd explained. Muttered something about it being a holiday but she had played along, not pressed him, and not letting on that

Maureen had already told her the truth. Maybe he knew she knew; it didn't matter.

'We can do it another time,' she had said.

'No, no. Tonight's fine, just ignore Sarah and Tilly. They're staying for a little while.'

'You sure?'

'Quite sure.'

When they got to the flat, Sarah and Tilly looked more like permanent fixtures than short-term lodgers. Sarah was busying herself over a wok; the smell of curry filled the kitchen. Tilly was in the living room looking like a tiny doll with messy hair sitting on a vast leather sofa, *Peppa Pig* playing out in front of her on a screen big enough for a cinema. She sat upright in the middle, a stuffed rabbit next to her. When Georgie waved from the kitchen, she flashed a mischievous grin and turned back to the TV. If she was aware of what was going on, she didn't seem upset by it.

'I'm sorry for intruding,' Georgie said. She didn't get any further. Sarah didn't have any of her older brother's social clumsiness – she was the sort of woman who could put you at ease immediately.

'No, we're the intruders. Don't mention it, Georgie. And I made enough for at least eight people so you're welcome to stay.'

Priest made to say something but Sarah shot him a look and his expression changed instantly into one of obedience. *That's a neat trick, Sarah.*

'Welcome to the family,' he mumbled. 'Come on. Peep show's this way.'

Charlie led her down a corridor to a room at the back. Georgie had lost track of the number of rooms there were. She had spent long enough in Charlie's kitchen to know what that looked like but, other than venturing into one of the spare rooms once to find it had been trashed by a psychopathic journalist Charlie had previously handcuffed to his bed, she hadn't been given a guided tour. And you'd need a tour. The penthouse was titanic, complete with stairs leading to a rooftop garden overlooking the Royal Opera House. The sort of place you could get lost in without a map and a compass.

When they got to the final door, Charlie seemed surprised to find it unlocked.

'Pretty sure I should be taking better care of the most dangerous book in human history, rather than just dumping it on my desk.'

'I'm sure it's fine,' said Georgie.

The study was a mess. Four giant bookcases built around a flat screen TV dominated one wall opposite a window that took up much the same area on the other side. The blinds were drawn, so Charlie hit the lights. The walls were white-washed, as was the ceiling, peppered with LED spotlights. The furniture was black: an L-shaped desk facing the door covered in papers and books, a Mac desktop on one side.

Georgie ventured forward, curious at the slow hum of the microclimate container that sat on the desk. There was something ethereal about it. She could see it was plugged in, but the faint glow from within heightened the throbbing in her chest.

*For the good of mankind*, Owen had said.

'Like I said, you can't see much,' Charlie admitted, letting the door close behind him.

She inspected the container, felt its cold metallic edges. She could feel a slight vibration near the set of dials, the tiniest current flowing within.

She could see the pages of the scripture, just. Charlie was right. The opaque glass, the gloom and the discoloured parchment meant all she could make out was the faintest of symbols. It was both a disappointment and a thrill at the same time.

She stood up.

'What about the translations?'

'Owen says he has them safe. I'm guessing they're not at his home. Hell, they could be anywhere.'

'He seems genuinely scared.'

'He is. I just haven't worked out what of yet.'

'What do you think will happen in the end?'

'In the end?' Charlie smiled, and ushered her out, locking the door behind him. 'Same thing that always happens in court. Everyone will lose.'

Back in the kitchen, Georgie was delighted to find that Sarah was just dishing up.

# Chapter 18

*Thursday*

By the time Rowlinson arrived, the rush hour traffic around Russell Square gardens was easing. He parked his car behind a white SOCO van and got out. As he pushed past the gathered crowd and made his way through the gardens, currents of warm air rustled through the old oak trees; their branches bowed pensively around the dry circular fountain, as if out of respect. He could hear the murmur of people gathered at one end – journalists baying at the uniformed officers, craning around them and taking photos through gaps in the greenery. It was all white noise, like the hum of the traffic. Rowlinson shut it out.

He flashed his identification at a PC who nodded and held the tape up as Rowlinson ducked underneath. A few feet from the perimeter, he was met by the crime scene manager, handed white coveralls, mask, gloves and booties. He put them on, listening but not listening, trying to process it but knowing all the while that he was losing.

*Another body. Same MO. Eight-inch nail driven through the head, probably with a hammer. Symbol on the ground underneath the victim. Dead two or three hours, max. Something else too, as well as the symbol. Dog walker found him.*

*Him.*

*Same MO. Different type of victim.*

There was a tape gangway leading to the centre of the gardens. Everybody went in and out using the same channel. A small viewing area close to the fountain; they'd put a tent up there later. Don't step onto the fountain, change your booties regularly. Wear two pairs of gloves, so you can peel one pair off easily. First Officer Attending: Fay Westbrook. She'd called straight away from the scene, woken him up.

'Boss?'

'Shit, what time is it?'

'We've got another one.'

Westbrook was standing in the viewing perimeter, hands behind her back, watching two CSOs tiptoe around the fountain. She didn't turn when he joined her, just kept on staring.

'We just ran out of time,' she said.

Rowlinson glanced back. The gaggle of press was growing, some journalists he recognised from Sky News, BBC. They'd seen it all. A ritualistic killing in the middle of a public park. Westbrook was right. *We just ran out of time.*

'What now, boss?'

Rowlinson slipped a piece of gum into his mouth, offered one to Westbrook, which she took. Even from here, the smell of decay was noticeable. Gum helped, a bit.

'We don't have any choice but to go public,' he said.

'About all three?'

Rowlinson didn't answer at first. Tried to think but he was still groggy from lack of sleep. His thoughts were jarred, slow.

'Who is he?' he asked at last.

'Driving licence says Alan Burberry. Twenty-two. Address in Islington. I've radioed it all through; should know more shortly.'

Rowlinson felt a tightness in his chest; the stench was squeezing his windpipe, restricting the airway. It was difficult to make Alan Burberry out. His face, pale and horror-stricken, was saturated in dried blood, as were his clothes; looked like he was a jogger. White Nike trainers, seemingly brand new, untouched by the blood. The nail sticking out of his forehead was unmistakable. He couldn't make out much more than that, but it would be the same eight-inch rosehead nail as last time. Sort of thing you could get from any DIY shop for a few pounds.

'The symbol?' Rowlinson asked.

'Underneath, on the far side. In blood, like the rest. He's getting bolder, boss.'

'First he targets two women, one in a hotel, one in her own home. Now a man in a public space.'

'This park is riddled with cameras. Sloppy. It's only a matter of time.'

Rowlinson looked up. Streetlights were dotted around, most of them had cameras pointing downwards. Westbrook was right. But why take such a risk? This Unsub was meticulous. The last two murders were well planned, not a crazed, random bloodlust; carefully planned executions.

*What the fuck are you up to, Unsub?*

'Does the DSI know?'

'He's on his way down,' said Westbrook. 'He's going to want some answers.'

Rowlinson grimaced. 'We'll tell them.'

Westbrook looked at him for the first time. She had deep, penetrating eyes, thick lashes. He couldn't see much else behind the mask, but clearly the early start hadn't affected her. She was wide awake, like a predator.

'Tell who what?'

'The press. About the other two.'

Westbrook turned back to the scene. A breeze shook the tree above them. 'They'll panic. It's what the Unsub wants.'

'It'll be out soon anyway. Plenty of people connected to Jane Vardy and Emma Mendez will sell the story. At least if we control the flow of information, we don't look completely incompetent.'

'Is that important, boss? That we look competent?'

'Yes.' It irritated Rowlinson that she was questioning him. The way her voice – ordinarily monotone, like a recording – rose up at the end. Not disrespectful, but lofty. A little patronising. 'It matters, Westbrook, because public perception matters.'

Westbrook shrugged. 'Thought it matters if we catch killers, not look good doing it.'

'Try telling Eaton that. Let me know how that conversation goes.'

She sniffed the air, didn't reply. Rowlinson calmed down, vindicated by her silence. The sunlight had broken the horizon, igniting the sky with a deep purple glare. Not a cloud in sight. It was going to be another scorcher. The CSOs looked up, chagrined. Rowlinson understood it: hot weather fucks up decomposition. Kills off the bacteria and insects, slows things down but dries things up as well. Makes guessing the time of death difficult, hinders the collection of evidence.

'There's something else,' Westbrook said after a while. It had been playing on her mind, Rowlinson saw it suddenly. He shuffled his feet. The CSM had said the same thing, but he hadn't processed it. Too busy pulling on the coveralls.

'What?' Rowlinson could feel a knot tighten in his stomach. 'This way.'

Westbrook led him carefully around the area where Alan Burberry's corpse was spread-eagled. The symbol was visible from this side, drawn crudely in blood underneath the body.

'There.'

Rowlinson followed her gesture, to a part of the stone pathway that hadn't been in his line of sight from their previous position. The central feature of the park was a circular nucleus from which four paths radiated: the fountain. Rowlinson scanned the area, didn't see at first.

'What am I . . .'

He stopped. The dawn light was reflecting off the stone, making it harder to see but there were words inscribed into the stone, in blood, like the symbol.

'*Kill the Giants*,' Rowlinson read. 'What in God's name does that mean?'

Westbrook shook her head. 'Don't know. But it's meant for us. He's talking to us.'

Rowlinson looked on. *Kill the Giants*. Westbrook was right. The killer was telling them something.

'You said you only knew one person who ever caught a real serial killer,' Westbrook murmured.

'That's right.'

'Well, now's maybe the time to hook up with him again. We need all the help we can get.'

# Chapter 19

*One year ago*

*The vestry to the church of St Swithin's is a small space with oak panels and a thick velvet curtain drawn across to create a windowless enclosure that feels rather like a large photo booth. Behind me, there is a set of stairs that leads to the belfry and a desk to my right, near where Sue is sitting, on top of which various robes and books are piled. Finally, there is a tiny cupboard containing old board games for the Sunday school that finished years ago, and of course my collection of gin and whisky. It is a strange place, a sort of black hole in the church. It's easy to lose all concept of time in there, especially when you've had a few and, after a while, you get used to the musty smell.*

*Sue is waiting for me to hit her with the punchline to this story, but she will be disappointed. For reasons which I hope are obvious, there are certain aspects of the story that cannot be divulged. I sincerely doubt Sue would ever tell anyone about our little encounter today, even if she remembers it tomorrow. There is even less chance of anyone believing her, because she is a drunk. But, nonetheless, I'm not going to tell her about the Binding.*

*God chose me to destroy the blasphemous hybrid race that contaminated our DNA all those millennia ago and I cannot allow anyone to stop me.*

*You see, what the jackdaw told me was one thing, but what I later discovered was something else entirely. I had spent a few nights in a care home after my parents died, wondering what to make of everything. I had never been close to my parents, but equally I had never been detached from them. They served a purpose for me, and I guess I served one for them. That was the sum of our relationship. But I was sad that they had died, especially my father. Because whilst I did not profess to understand his obsession with God at the time, I now recognise that God sacrificed him, despite his faith, to prepare me for what was to come.*

*Throughout his life, my father had served God diligently and, as part of that diligence, he made it his business to collect various artefacts and relics that he thought had significance. With hindsight, most of them did not. He was particularly fond of a piece of wood that he claimed was part of the Ark, washed up on Mount Ararat and salvaged by a Jewish sect in the middle of the fourth century. I had the thing tested. It was about five hundred years old. Nowhere near old enough, and it saddened me greatly to know that his passion was based on a fallacy.*

*Nonetheless, there was one thing he possessed which I did find interest in. It was a sample of translations of an ancient scripture, supposedly one of the Dead Sea Scrolls. Strangely, it was not one of the treasures that had brought him so much joy; I found it stuffed in the back of the tool shed one day when the care home took me round the ruins of the house. Of course, it survived the fire, as was God's plan.*

*I kept the translations for many years, not really understanding them. I read them, of course, and they went straight over the head of an immature ten-year-old boy. But when I returned to them one day, in my late teens, I started to realise that they were perhaps more significant than I first imagined.*

*To my shame, I don't know where my father got them from. I know he visited Turkey a few times in search of artefacts to acquire. Perhaps it was in one of those auctions where he, on a whim, decided to put some money down on something, or perhaps they were part of another deal, thrown in as a sweetener along with something else. I don't know, and it doesn't matter.*

*It took me five years of travelling from library to library, church to church, theologian to theologian, before I established what the pages were. They were incomplete, and I understand the translations aren't of great quality. But finally I pieced it together.*

*'I can't tell you everything,' I say slowly, watching Sue sway back and forth. 'There are some things that must remain between a man and his God.'*

*'Are you a prophet?' she asked.*

*To be honest, I had never thought about it like this, but in a way she was right on the nail and that only made me realise that Sue was, as I had suspected, a partisan sent by God to reward me for my work. So I went with it.*

*'Yes, Sue. A prophet, of sorts.'*

*'My God.'*

*'But that's not why you came here.' She looked confused for a moment, no doubt the last hour of discussion was becoming a bit of a blur. 'The twelve steps?'*

*I raised an eyebrow. She took a moment to gather herself, then stammered, 'Yes. The twelve steps. I'm stuck on two.'*

*'Moving to three is easier than you might think.'*

*'Tell me how.'*

*I sat back and smiled, spread my legs and put my hand over the back of the chair. Waited. Then, when she said nothing, I gave the smallest, almost imperceptible nod of my head towards my crotch,* which I could already feel was starting to react. A warm glow was spreading through me as my body prepared for the possibility, now probability, of stimulation.

There is nothing holy about these visits to the vestry, and I feel no shame. I wash afterwards, as the scripture says, and the girls are given special protection because they have been part of God's plan. Most of them understand this. I am sure that Sue will. She is already catching on, but I can see that, although the alcohol is driving her, there is a part of her that is still anchored to the real world, a part telling her that this sudden change of direction is out of order.

'I . . . I'm not sure . . . I didn't think . . .'

I confess that a part of me is frustrated. 'Sue, relax. Like I said, you have to fail. Did you think that having a few glasses of gin was going to be enough?'

'I just thought that . . . you were trying to help me.'

'I am. But, like I also said you have to help yourself too. Help yourself, Sue, to me.'

It's really too late now for whatever Sue has planned. My body has already prepared for her. I nod again, a little more forcefully. She looks to the curtain, a move I don't like. I don't want to have to chase her.

'Think of it like this, Sue. If I am a prophet, then what would this make you?'

'I'm not sure. A whore?'

I laugh, try and make her feel foolish about the comment, although inside I'm starting to get angry. This should have gone better. I have invested a lot of time in Sue, not just today, but previously and I'm not happy that she is showing signs of more spunk than I had assessed her as having.

'But I'm not paying you. And besides, have more respect for yourself. God is not watching here, but He will know you have served me.'

'Serve you?'

I probably lost a bit of my sense of humour here. 'Yes. Serve me.'

It was enough. I'm not sure whether it was the slight threat in my voice, or the alcohol taking over, or, as I suspect, her coming to terms with the idea and how it could benefit her, but she slips from the chair and glides, a little inelegantly, between my legs.

She starts to undo my belt. I can see down her top, at her almost non-existent breasts. Then she stops, looks up.

'Just this?' she asks, and I know what she means.

'Yes,' I lie. 'Just this.'

# Chapter 20

Priest awoke in the early morning to the sound of screaming.

Alert, light flooding his eyes, his head pounding, he half fell, half catapulted himself out of bed. Wearing nothing but a pair of boxer shorts, he flung the bedroom door open.

The screaming was coming from inside his flat. *Shit! Tilly!*

A hundred different scenes played out in his mind at lightning speed: was she hurt? Was someone else in the flat? Where was Sarah?

He thought of Ryan.

'Tilly!' he yelled.

He hurtled down the corridor and threw open the door to the lounge, his body coiled with energy and aggression.

The screaming stopped. Sarah and Tilly stared at him, bewildered. He stood in the door frame, chest heaving. Surveyed the room. Everything was in order. His sister and niece were in pyjamas. The television was on. Sarah lay across the sofa, the remote having fallen from her grip. Tilly was in the corner, near the lionfish tank.

'What?' said Sarah. 'Why are you stood there in your pants?'

'I heard—'

'I told you not to be so loud,' Sarah scolded, turning to Tilly.

'This fish has been very naughty,' Tilly announced, pointing to the lionfish closest to her. 'He ate *all* the food.'

'So you screamed at him?' said Priest. He wasn't angry – just curious. Why the hell would anyone scream at a fish? Why so bloodcurdling?

Tilly opened her mouth and, from the look of chagrin on her face, she was ready to justify herself, but Sarah stepped in. 'Sorry, she's six. They do stuff like that. Breakfast?'

As the adrenaline receded, Priest's headache took over. He rubbed the back of his skull, suddenly also conscious he was practically naked.

'Breakfast would be swell. I'll have eggs or something.'

As he loped back to the bedroom, he heard Tilly ask Sarah, 'Mummy, will Daddy be home yet?'

He slowed down. 'Oh, I think Daddy will be away a little longer, sweetheart. Shall we make breakfast for Uncle Charlie together?'

'Yes! Do you think he will want cake?'

'I'm sure he will.'

'Mummy, why was Uncle Charlie only wearing silly pants?'

She'll keep doing this, he knows. Assuring her, reassuring her. And as long as Mummy keeps reassuring, there will never be a problem. Ryan never bonded with Tilly. Wanted a boy to play rough with, take out for his first pint, teach how to swear and bet. It's a miracle it lasted this long. A complete mismatch. Sarah, the attractive, smart professional, and Ryan, the . . . whatever the fuck he was.

Priest needed to talk to Sarah, alone. Tilly would be getting ready for school soon; Sarah was taking time off. He wasn't sure what she was doing – planning a divorce? Working out how to break it to Tilly?

He wished he knew what to say to her, but he didn't. He was biased. He hated seeing Sarah unhappy, hated seeing Tilly unhappy even more. The idea swelled inside his head. It felt ready to explode. If he was truthful, he had wanted their marriage to fail, wanted vindication for the years of animosity he'd shown his brother-in-law, the years he'd chided his sister.

He thought it might mean he would stop feeling so guilty about it but he was wrong: now the time had possibly come, he felt even *more* guilty.

'Hey,' she said, smiling.

He was half dressed, hadn't even noticed her standing in the doorway, long blue and white striped pyjamas, just like a pair she had when she was a kid. Back when Mum and Dad had been alive.

'You're going to have to tell her, Sarah,' he said, pulling on a white shirt, cuffed.

'I know.' She was trying to seem content, relaxed, but her eyes betrayed her. He knew that look. He'd seen it at William's trial; when she spoke to her friends, when she had read a statement to the media. A façade that looked impenetrable to anyone else, but he knew it was as fragile as glass.

'What the hell happened?'

'It was exactly like I said the other night. This girl rang me. Told me that she'd been seeing my husband, but she was wracked with guilt. Had to tell me. Also, she doubts she's the first.'

'Who is she?'

'Her name is Gemma, and she's nice. We've met. She was as devastated as I was.' Sarah looked at the floor. Priest buttoned the shirt, tucked it in. Dark blue trousers – they went with a jumper he had somewhere . . .

'Have you confronted him?' he said, starting to peel through his wardrobe. On the bedside table, his phone buzzed but he ignored it.

Sarah paused, the façade flickered slightly, then reaffirmed itself. 'I waited until he got back from work.'

'He has a job?'

Sarah sighed. 'He started at a tattoo parlour last year. I didn't tell you because . . .'

Priest was so taken aback he actually stopped messing around with his cuffs to look up. 'A tattoo parlour?'

'He designs. It's what he's always wanted to do.'

He was about to say more but realised now wasn't the time. So he returned to the shirt, the signal for her to continue.

'He came home and I just said, "*Gemma's been on the phone.*" That was it. Easy. Seven years of marriage destroyed in one sentence.' She was reflective, staring past him, out of the window. Maybe what she had done was registering for the first time. Priest shifted his weight uncomfortably. His phone was ringing, and he couldn't find his jumper.

'How'd he take it?'

'Dismissive, at first. Tried to tell me she was an ex, obsessive and looking to punish him. Then angry, defensive. It's my fault for working so hard. Then sorry, begging. All puppy dog eyes and promises. All that, in less than a few minutes. Like he'd fucking rehearsed it.'

She said the last part with venom, her true anger seeping through. A glimpse of the vast depth of the betrayal she felt.

It was a yawning well, black as night, wherein she had buried everything. For now.

She composed herself, looked up. He realised he was supposed to say something, but his mind was blank.

'I'm sorry,' he said, in the end.

She seemed to snap back out of the daydream. 'You're sorry?'

'Yes.' He felt helpless, drowning in his emotional uselessness. 'Isn't that what people say in . . . these sort of situations.'

'Yeah, people you just met on the bus. Siblings might have something a little more constructive to say.'

Priest motioned with his hands, as if trying to conjure up some form of words from somewhere, perform a miracle. Eventually, he settled for, 'He was a bit of a dick, Sarah.'

For a moment, he thought she might lash out. She always did, always defended Ryan. Always on the offensive, Sarah.

Instead, she hung her head. Laughed. Hollow.

'Yeah. You're right. Total dick.'

He stepped across, took her arm. He meant nothing more than to offer her a pat on the shoulder but she pulled him into an embrace and he realised how unhelpful he had been to her all these years. How absolutely unhelpful. Christ, she'd probably stayed with Ryan just to prove a point.

She cried, juddering in his arms for a moment. 'You're a fucking moron,' she said softly.

He put his hands across her shoulders, wiped her eyes. He remembered doing that only twice in his life. Once when she had fallen from a tree at the age of ten, a tree he had told her to climb. And once after his own divorce. How strange that the situation had reversed itself, but the emotional response from each of them was the same.

'Do you want me to beat him up for you?'

She laughed through the tears, genuinely this time. 'It's about all you're good for, you big dope.'

'We all have our uses, Sarah. Just sometimes they're not immediately obvious.'

She nodded, managed to smile. He let her go. Started fishing around again for his jumper. He didn't need it, but he needed something to do. His chest was fluttering – the sadness he felt for her, and the anger he felt at Ryan, was making him anxious. There had been long stretches of time in Priest's life when he had felt almost nothing at all, and he had sat for hours on his own, sometimes for days at a time, thinking about the emotional cavity that swelled inside of him and how this made him feel. This was the echo of that emotionless vacuum, where all strong feelings seemed to converge into one insipid reaction: a hollow sense of disquiet. *It's not that I don't feel*, he had concluded. *It's that everything feels the fucking same.*

'Jessica seems nice, by the way.'

He faltered, Sarah's observation was so unexpected that he literally staggered backwards a little, light-headed.

'What?'

'Jessica. The woman you've been keeping secret from me.' When he didn't respond, she smiled. 'It's OK. I'm kidding. You don't have to tell me about your life all the time. I'm just pleased you've found someone.'

He wasn't sure what to say. He didn't think he had the capability of explaining how tortured he was by Jessica, how conflicted he felt. And the feeling that haunted him: the possibility that this might be it. He had reached his maximum capacity for love, or whatever twisted version of love he was capable of experiencing. This was the sum of him, the best he could do.

And even that amounted to the same thing. A hollow sense of disquiet.

'Yes,' he heard himself say. 'She's great.'

She nodded, unconvinced. 'You better go.' She pointed to his phone on the table. 'Tiff's rung you five times while I've been in here. He must really want to speak to you.'

# Chapter 21

Priest sat with his arm across the bench, one leg resting over the other, watching the sunlight dance off the water through a pair of aviator sunglasses. St James's Park was quiet, still. People meandered over the Blue Bridge taking photographs of the lake, the London Eye visible on the horizon, the giant metal iris around Shell Tower. It was cooler today; a soufflé of wispy clouds had gathered overhead, veiling the sun and promising a more bearable temperature.

Nevertheless, he had discarded the jumper in a crumpled heap next to him. *What was he thinking?*

Tiff Rowlinson sat down and handed him a plastic bottle.

'What's this?' asked Priest, inspecting the bottle.

'Water.'

'Where's my tea?'

Rowlinson broke open the cap on his own bottle and drank. Then motioned to the sky. 'No good on a day like this. You'll dehydrate.'

Priest stared down, disappointed. 'Tea's good for you on hot days. Keeps your own body temperature down.'

Rowlinson shook his head. 'That's just propaganda that tea companies spread in the nineties. Drink water, live longer.'

Priest watched as Rowlinson brushed a crop of sandy hair out of his eye. He was pristine, as always, in a light grey suit, no tie and expensive-looking leather shoes. He was a little younger than Priest, with sharp features forming a handsome, boyish face. They went back a long way, but the last time Priest had seen Rowlinson was shortly after he'd pulled him out of a burning church just before the building collapsed. The two noticeable additions since then were some crows' feet and a wedding ring.

'Been a while,' Priest remarked, taking the lid off and swilling the water around, purposely letting some of it spill.

'You're so fucking busy, Priest. Did you get my last message?'

Priest thought about it; couldn't recall it. 'No. What did it look like?'

'Looked like a wedding invitation.'

Priest turned and looked, a feeling of embarrassment creeping up on him. *Did I miss that?*

'Ah, shit, Tiff . . . I . . .'

'Shut up,' Rowlinson laughed. Took another long swig of the water. 'I'm kidding. It was a quiet affair, abroad. Family only. You'd have hated it.'

'Who's the lucky guy?'

Rowlinson smiled and Priest saw it right there, in that little hunch of the shoulder, the way his eyes flickered. Tiny subconscious gestures that told Priest all he wanted to know. Rowlinson was happy. 'He works for the government, secret stuff. Gary. You . . . don't know him.'

Priest smiled, Rowlinson's contentment was catching. They had worked together at the Met for a long time, back in the day when Priest had caught criminals for a living. Priest knew him to be a shrewd and resourceful detective, one of the few men he trusted. After he had left the service and become a lawyer they had kept in contact, sharing something that was about as close to a friendship as Priest felt capable of achieving. So when he said, 'Congratulations, Tiff,' he genuinely meant it.

Rowlinson rubbed his chin self-consciously, as if he was a little embarrassed. 'Thanks. Anyway, to business. Seen the news this morning?'

No. Priest hadn't seen the news. He usually checked the headlines online, occasionally watched CNN. American news was far more entertaining. But with trying to coexist with his new flatmates, after having lived alone for so long, he'd no idea what was going on in the world.

'Could be at war with Mexico for all I know.'

Rowlinson handed him his phone. The video took a moment to buffer, then clicked on. A news reporter was standing outside – *was that Russell Square?* Rowlinson turned up the volume.

'Police have launched an urgent inquiry into the discovery of the body of a twenty-two-year-old man who was found in the centre of Russell Square gardens in the early hours of this morning, with what appears to be a heavy-duty nail driven into his head. The man, whose identity hasn't yet been revealed by detectives, was discovered already dead by an early morning jogger. Police are appealing for anyone with any information to come forward. Detective Chief Inspector Tiff Rowlinson said that there are currently no leads and no clear motive for this brutal murder but if anyone was in or around the area between ten p.m. yesterday and five a.m. this morning, particularly if they were driving with a dashcam, please can they come forward. The park will remain closed as forensic investigators establish a—'

Rowlinson stopped the footage. Turned the phone off.

'Nasty,' said Priest. 'I take it you're the SIO?'

Rowlinson nodded. Priest took a sip of water. It wasn't clear what the issue was. Just another murder investigation – another nameless victim in the city. He was damn glad that was all behind him. Priest had spent enough time as a detective to have grown to loathe crime and its detection.

'Who was he?'

'Alan Burberry. City trader.'

'OK.' Priest hesitated. *Surely there was a point to all this?* 'Why did you want to see me, Tiff?'

Rowlinson handed him a picture, folded. Priest opened it out. A black symbol. A cross with a squiggly line running up it. He looked at it, turned the paper over. Didn't mean anything to him.

'What's this?'

'It's a symbol the killer left at the scene. Drawn in blood on the ground near the victim.'

Priest glanced down again with fresh eyes. Something twigged inside of him. A little spring in his chest. Now he got it. *Shit.*

He looked at Rowlinson. Those crows' feet had nothing to do with the wedding stress. 'How many others are there?'

'Two. Jane Vardy, a twenty-nine-year-old married woman with three kids. And Emma Mendez, a thirty-three-year-old unmarried photographer.'

'Two women and one man. Where were the other murders?'

'One in her home, the other in a hotel. Both on our patch. Emma lived in London and Jane, although she was born here, lived in Stroud. She was back visiting family. Apparently she liked to stay in hotels rather than at her parents' house. Mum has early dementia, Dad told me it's just easier that way.'

Priest frowned. 'Same symbol?'

'Same symbol. Same MO – nail in the head. He's starting to get aggressive, too. First one was a clean kill, then it gets messier.'

'He's enjoying it then.'

Rowlinson nodded. 'Media haven't cottoned on yet. Jane Vardy's husband is playing ball for now, but we can't trace Emma Mendez's boyfriend. This could spill out any day.'

'A serial killer. In London.'

'First since . . .'

Priest felt his stomach knot. He closed his eyes. Dr William Priest had been the most notorious London serial killer since Jack the Ripper. He had no pattern, no favourite way to kill people. He had been completely unpredictable, quite unlike any murderer the Met had encountered before. They'd shipped in FBI trained profilers, a ten-man-strong task force. And in the end, they hadn't even caught him. William had decided he had had enough. He turned up at Scotland Yard, sat patiently in the foyer waiting for someone to see him, and confessed.

'First since William,' Priest finished the sentence, breathless.

'I need your help.'

The question caught Priest off-guard. He could feel the world around him slowly turning, the weight of guilt rushing back, oppressive and hot. 'Come again?'

'I need your help, Priest. There's no one with any experience of a serial killer, not like this. Not with this level of organisation. You know serial killers. You've caught one.'

'I didn't catch William. William caught William. I wasn't even on the task force.'

Rowlinson turned and fixed Priest with a penetrative stare. 'I don't know what happened back then,' he said slowly, lowering his voice as a couple walked past arm in arm. 'No one does, 'cept you and William. If you want it to stay that way then fine, I get that. But we all know the myth.'

'Tiff—'

Rowlinson held up his hand, making no room for argument. 'This man will kill again, Priest. Very soon. I'm surrounded by people who are either inexperienced or downright stupid. I *need* help.'

'He's escalating?' Priest asked, referring to the kill pattern. Serial killers often start off slow, then begin to reduce the cooling period between kills. Usually as the thirst for death intensifies, and the reality never quite matches the fantasy.

But Rowlinson shook his head, sighed. 'No. He's not escalating, he's *escalated*. Three or four days between each kill, straight off.'

Priest clicked his tongue. 'What have you found out about the symbol?'

'He paints it in the victim's blood at the scene.'

'Serial killers don't use symbols. That's Hollywood bullshit.'

'This one does.'

Priest thought about it. No known serial killer of any notoriety had ever left a symbol at the scene of the crime. The Zodiac Killer taunted the police with hidden messages and a crude drawing of a target through letters he wrote to the media, if that was even him writing the damn things. Serial killers often took things from their victims – mementoes, souvenirs. Something they treasured, something that allowed them to repeat the kill over and over again in their heads. Underwear, rings. Eyes. William never took anything, though. Just their souls.

'There's more,' said Rowlinson, handing Priest a crime scene photograph.

'*Kill the Giants*,' Priest murmured. Written in blood, the victim's legs and feet were in the foreground but the focus was the words scrawled in blood behind him. 'What does that mean?'

'It means he has a plan.'

'What's the connection between the victims?'

'Nothing.' Rowlinson took another swig of water, checked his watch. 'Absolutely nothing. Different ages, different backgrounds, different genders, different incomes. Different social groups. We can't find any common denominator between them.'

'Were they on a jury together? Same employer? Same school? Clubs, online chats, friends of friends, that sort of thing?'

Rowlinson shook his head. 'No. Checked. Nothing.'

Priest passed the photograph back, stretched out his legs. Stared at the lake. *Kill the Giants.* He thought about the Ghosts, William's victims. They still swam around in his head. He knew all of them, their names, backgrounds, ages, families. Faces. *Shit.* The sun broke the cloud cover, bathing them in light, and in the moment it took him to shield his eyes, there they were again: on the cliff edge. A young boy, barely fourteen but with the beginnings of a muscular frame. Messy hair that covered his eyes, constantly got in the way. A girl, younger than him, lithe and petite, sandy hair and freckles, smiling as she lay on the rocks, head buried in a book like always. And William, older, taller, bigger, wiser William.

'*Hey, Charlie!*' *he shouted. He was dangerously close to the cliff edge, where the lake spilled out below them like the tail of a blue dress, the water shimmering in the sunlight.* '*Charlie, come here!*'

Priest shook the memory off, shivered despite the heat. It still hurt, thinking about it.

'I'm not sure I can . . . do this again,' Priest whispered. One of the victim's mothers had written to him after the trial, angry and desperate. He still had the letter. '*You must have known.*'

Rowlinson stood up, handed Priest the picture of the symbol back. 'Rethink, then call me. But if all you do is use your resources to find out what the bloody hell this is then I'll call it quits.'

Priest nodded, took the photo. As Rowlinson walked off, he could still hear William's teenage call on the wind. '*Hey, Charlie! Come here!*'

# Chapter 22

*Friday*

Georgie stared at the text. Came out of the messaging app, then went back in again. Turned the phone sideways. It was still there, staring back at her.

She was in the living room of the flat she shared with Li, curled up on the sofa, wondering what to do with her day off. Li was bustling around in the kitchen making coffee, humming some Beyoncé song. The television was on in the background: an American daytime programme about a woman who was obsessed with eating dining-room furniture.

'You OK?' Li called through from the kitchen.

'Sorry, what?'

'I keep asking if you want coffee?'

'Oh, right. Sorry. Yeah, I guess.'

Georgie looked back at the phone, then sensed that Li was standing at the doorway, watching her, puzzled.

'What are you doing? You never look at your phone that long. You don't even have Instagram.'

Flustered, Georgie tried to hit the 'home' button but ended up dropping the phone on the floor, which Li neatly scooped up.

'Hey!'

Li held out her hand as Georgie scrambled to her feet, feeling the heat flush around her cheeks.

'What's this? Oh my God, you have a text from—'

'Yes.' Georgie snatched the phone away. Then, realising it was pointless hiding it, sat back down again. 'Yes, I have a text from Andy.'

'Our martial arts instructor, grossly abusing his position of power to let you know how great you're doing, by text. Randomly.'

Georgie looked up – it annoyed her that Li was smiling, that knowing smile she put on sometimes. 'He probably texts everyone now and again. He's conscientious.'

Li waved her own phone at her. '*I'm* in your class, dummy. He hasn't texted me.'

'Maybe it's not come through yet, or he hasn't got around to it yet. I don't know.'

Li sighed, went back to fixing coffee. Georgie heard the machine click and fizz, then the sound of pouring. 'We need to have a talk, you and me.'

'Do we?'

Li came through and handed her the mug. 'You can't hide all your life, Georgie.'

'I've been held captive by neo-Nazis who wanted to torture me for fun and last year a mad woman tried to kill me with a lionfish. I'm not hiding.'

Li was about to respond when the doorbell rang.

'Here.' She handed Georgie the TV remote. 'Find something more stimulating to watch while I see who's at the door and we'll have a girly morning. Then I'm taking you shopping. Those dungarees look fucking awful.'

'They're fashionable,' Georgie protested as Li walked out into the hallway. She could hear her call back as she unbolted the door.

'They are if you're Super Mario. Oh, hello!'

Georgie looked up, detecting the slight change in Li's voice as she had opened the door. *Oh, God, don't let it be one of her regulars.*

Li reappeared at the door, beaming. 'Someone here to see you, Georgie.'

\*

Priest stood in the doorway to Georgie's house, taking in the lime green sofa, wide screen TV and Georgie with her legs tucked under her staring wide-eyed at him, like he was the last person she ever thought would turn up on her doorstep.

'Sorry,' he mumbled. 'I know it's your day off.'

'Oh, you're a bad employer,' said the English-Japanese girl – *what the hell was her name?* – smiling and ushering him through.

She sat him down next to Georgie, who uncoiled herself inelegantly, spilling a cup of coffee over the table in front of her.

'Damn.'

'Nice place,' Priest noted, as she ran around mopping up the mess.

'It came more or less furnished,' said Georgie. 'Landlord lives in France.'

'Can I get you a drink or anything?' asked Georgie's flatmate. Priest wasn't sure, but he thought he saw something pass between them – some unspoken subliminal girl-talk.

'I'm fine, thanks,' he said. 'I'm not stopping. Just came to give you this.'

He handed Georgie the picture Rowlinson had given him of the symbol found at Alan Burberry's crime scene.

She took it carefully and looked closely. 'What is it?'

'I thought maybe you could tell me.'

Georgie readjusted her glasses. 'Looks like a cross with a squiggly line through it.'

'It's exactly a cross with a squiggly line through it,' Priest agreed. 'I'm looking for something a bit more specific.'

'Is it a new case?'

Priest leant back, casual – he didn't want to alarm her, but he had discovered there was very little point in hiding facts from Georgie Someday. 'Murder inquiry.'

Georgie leant forward, closer to the picture. Her movements were always coltish. Priest noticed that her flatmate had stopped whistling in the kitchen and was no longer making any effort to hide her eavesdropping.

'Then, is that . . . ?'

'Blood. Yes.'

Georgie's eyes widened. 'Gosh! Is it Satanic?'

'The cross would be upside down then,' Georgie's flatmate put in.

'Possibly,' said Georgie. 'Could be something else entirely. An anchor, a corporate logo, football club emblem. Anything.'

'Can you find out?' asked Priest, wiping his forehead. His vision was blurred, voices were muffled. All of a sudden, he was drifting.

Georgie took out her phone, took a picture of the symbol, then returned the original to Priest. 'I don't know any symbolists but I can do some research. Sure I can find something.'

'That's great,' said Priest, getting up. He was about to go when he remembered the writing smeared in blood near Alan

Burberry's feet. 'Oh, and one more thing: can you see if you can work out what *Kill the Giants* means.'

'OK,' said Georgie slowly. 'Kill the Giants?'

'Yeah.'

'I'll . . . do my best.'

'That's great,' said Priest, motioning to leave. He was unsteady, but avoided knocking the coffee mug over for a second time. 'By the way, I'm going to be a little busy over the next few days. When you're back in, can you cover some cases I've got?'

Georgie nodded, unsure. 'You're going to be busy because you're investigating a murder? I thought you gave up police work.'

Priest smiled, met her gaze. It was never enough, whatever he said to her. He was always trying to find the right words of praise, but it all seemed so inadequate. The truth was that Georgie reminded Priest of himself, before William had fucked everything up and killed all those people. They shared the same thirst for answers, the same sense of justice. It was just that Georgie's outlook seemed so much purer to him, unadulterated. His was spoilt, his needs were tainted; hardened and dark.

How he envied her.

He needed to get out, since he sat down three black spots had appeared in front of his right eye. Patches of dust, floating in front of his vision. He looked at his hands. They seemed OK, but he had to dig his nails into his palms to feel the pain of their existence, to feel he was alive. *That's what DPD does to you: tricks you into questioning the very core of existence.*

'Seems I'm back in the game,' he said, turning. 'I'll see you in the office on Monday.'

'Charlie, are you OK?'

He paused. *Was he? Was he ever OK?* In the distance, a church bell chimed and Priest felt a foreboding in the pit of his stomach that gripped him so violently he was, for a moment, lost and adrift.

*'Hey, Charlie! Come here!'*

He shook it off. Georgie was staring at him, concerned. He looked down at his hands, white from tensing, but a part of him, evidence of *him.*

'I'm fine.' He was about to offer some form of explanation, but he was interrupted. Georgie's flatmate was standing on the opposite side of the room hopping from one foot to the other excitedly.

'Sorry, I didn't want to interrupt. But I might be able to help.'

'Go on.'

'I have er . . . a friend. He's a lecturer at UCL.' Priest noticed Georgie wince at the term 'friend'. 'He does stuff to do with symbols.'

Priest nodded, encouragingly. 'OK. Can we meet this friend of yours?'

'I'm not sure—' Georgie began but her flatmate – *Li, that was it!* – cut in, eager.

'Sure! I can text him and we can go this afternoon.'

'That's good,' said Priest. He looked at Georgie. She nodded, although with less enthusiasm. Li was busy thumbing through her phone. He waited, leant against the wall. The house was tidy, with a light vinyl floor, Ikea furniture. The lime green sofa was a bit off-putting but just the right side of garish. The room smelt nice, in an artificial way, but even with the windows open the heat was overbearing.

Finally, Li looked up. 'We can go now.'

Georgie got up, stretched. To Li she said, 'Sure you don't mind?'

'Nah. It's fine. Think he owes me one.'

Priest allowed Li to lead the way out. As he turned, he caught Georgie's eye.

'Kill the Giants,' she said so that Li didn't hear her.

'All I want you to do, Someday, is take a quick look at the symbol and then do some lawyering for me while I sort this mess out. No more. Clear?'

She nodded. 'Crystal, Charlie.'

# Chapter 23

University College London's main campus was bathed in glorious sunlight and as Priest, Georgie and Li made their way towards the Wilkins Building, with its Grecian temple frontage supported by ten Cyclopean pillars, Priest couldn't help but feel a twinge of envy at the small groups of students lying on the grass, books and bags spread around them, any cares and worries they may have had seemingly drifting away in the haze of cigarette smoke and soft, undulant music.

Inside, the building was surprisingly cool, despite there being no obvious source of air-conditioning. They passed groups of more students hurrying to lectures down spacious white corridors, clutching cups of coffee and chattering excitedly. Li stopped occasionally, checked her phone. Isaac O'Brien, Li's 'friend', had given them directions to his office, which they eventually came to at the back of the building where the wooden floors and terracotta-coloured chambers of the Flaxman Gallery gave way to a maze of tighter corridors, where great oil paintings became health and safety notice boards and department hierarchy charts.

'This is it,' Li announced, checking the room number.

'Do we knock?' asked Georgie.

'Best to. He can be a little jumpy.'

Priest arched an eyebrow. 'Why?'

Li replied, but skipped over to the door and pushed it open, knocking as she did, before her explanation managed to lodge itself in Priest's head.

'He's married.'

Isaac O'Brien stood at a water dispenser. Whether it was Li's unannounced entrance, or the sudden gulp of air that blossomed up through the clear liquid, something alarmed him enough to spill the water all over the floor.

'Good grief,' he exclaimed, turning with wide eyes.

'Sorry,' said Li. 'It's just us.'

Brushing the excess water off his tweed suit, O'Brien fitted the picture that Li had painted of the awkward academic perfectly. With round glasses, emaciated features and jet black hair, much of it coming out of his ears, he seemed much older than the thirty-five years Li had speculated earlier and stood, wiry and uncomfortable, over a foot shorter than Priest.

'How do you do?' O'Brien hopped forward and proffered his hand, which Priest took.

'Thanks for meeting us, Professor O'Brien.'

'Doctor, if you don't mind.'

'Right. Doctor.'

'Li.' He turned to Georgie's flatmate and there was a long pause as he tried to work out how best to greet her. In the end, another handshake, but Priest noticed that he avoided her eyes. Then, turning to Georgie, his thin lips curved upwards, although it was more of a grimace than a smile.

'And this must be . . .'

'Georgie,' she replied, taking his hand, which O'Brien held for longer than was necessary.

'Charmed, I'm sure.'

He spoke like a minor character in the *Mary Poppins* film, forced and stuffy.

'So.' He turned to Li. 'You want my help.'

Priest stepped forward, and whilst O'Brien's body language suggested he might rather deal with one of the girls, he hadn't got time for social politics. He handed O'Brien the picture of the killer's symbol. The lecturer's eyes widened.

'I need to know what this is.'

'Well . . . I . . .' O'Brien stammered. 'I mean . . . to be clear, I'm an amateur symbolist at best. I lecture in natural philosophy in the main, but . . . I'm sure . . .' He turned the picture round, observed it at different angles. 'Good grief, is that blood?'

'Probably best that we don't go into it too much,' Priest replied. 'And you'll need to keep this to yourself.'

O'Brien looked up from the picture, defensive. 'Look, exactly in what capacity are you asking me this?'

'Does it matter?'

'You've presented me with a symbol I don't recognise scrawled on a wall in what looks like blood without explanation. You're not the police as far as I'm aware. Li said you were a lawyer, or something.'

Priest sighed inwardly – *I could do without the dick-measuring competition* – but thankfully Li took over before he could interject.

'Don't be difficult, Isaac. This is important.'

'I think it's a fair question, don't you? I mean, do you know this man?'

Priest was reluctant to have come all this way for nothing, and O'Brien's air-conditioned office was as cool as he had been in the last twenty-four hours, but time was short. He gently dispossessed O'Brien of the photograph and turned to go.

'What are you doing?' O'Brien asked, indignant.

'You don't recognise the symbol. You said so yourself.'

'Wait. I said I didn't recognise it, not that I can't help you.'

'Well, make up your mind, doctor.'

'There's no need to be rude. Perhaps I can help. Of course, my fees for private work are—'

'Isaac!'

Li's outburst jolted the academic, he stiffened involuntarily at her raised voice. Again, Priest wondered what power Li held over him. *'He's married.'*

'I'm sorry.' O'Brien looked down, child-like.

'If you want to be helpful, look at the fucking picture and give us something. If you don't want to be helpful, fine – but I have a horrible tendency to spout off about people I meet to their wives if they piss me off.'

*Ah. There it is.*

Priest handed the picture back to O'Brien, who took it sheepishly. Looked again. Beside him, Priest sensed Georgie exhale with relief.

'Well,' he said after a moment. 'It's the Latin Cross, of course, but I've not seen this variant before. Is it supposed to represent the letter "S"? I'm not sure. Perhaps two "S"s coupled up. That wouldn't make much sense. It's very unusual to have such a free-flowing line. Most Christian symbols are straight. There are exceptions, such as the Celtic Cross and the Coptic ankh, the Egyptian symbol of life, but these feature circles, not swirls.'

'Could it be Satanic?' asked Priest. 'Something representing evil.'

'The Leviathan Cross is the most recognised form of Satanic Cross. It does feature the symbol for infinity at its base, but it doesn't look like this.'

'I thought Satanic crosses were upside down?' said Li.

'Not really.' O'Brien pinched the bridge of his nose, pushed his glasses back up. 'Catholic tradition holds that the apostle Simon Peter was crucified upside down, at his own request. He considered himself unworthy to die in the same manner as Jesus Christ. The upside-down cross, or the Cross of Saint Peter, represents this. Although Hollywood has hijacked the imagery and turned it into a symbol of the Devil.'

'What about the letter "S", if that's what it is?' asked Georgie.

O'Brien made a noise, flapped his arms, as if trying to grasp at any idea floating around in front of him. 'I don't know of much significance there. The Marian Cross has the letter "M" next to it, to represent Mary, usually sitting penitently at the foot of the cross, of course. I'm afraid I don't know what significance the letter "S" has in Christianity, if anything. You need a theologist, I think.'

'OK,' said Priest, taking the photograph, his temper cooling with the room. 'That's helpful, thanks.'

O'Brien saw them out, flashing Georgie a gawky smile and turning to Li as he ushered them into the corridor. Priest guessed that he thought he couldn't be overheard amongst the din of the chamber on the other side of the wall, but subtlety wasn't O'Brien's strong point.

'Of course, I've helped, so—'

'Yeah, don't worry about it, Isaac.'

'Great. Thanks. Perhaps later—'

'No.'

The conversation might have progressed and Priest couldn't help but be a little intrigued. No doubt about it: the inelegant Isaac O'Brien didn't seem like an obvious fit with the very attractive Japanese-English girl. But there were more pressing matters. A killer was on the loose.

'Just one more thing, Doctor O'Brien.' He caught O'Brien off-guard; he looked startled yet again. 'Does the phrase *Kill the Giants* mean anything to you?'

Whether it was the change in temperature of the corridor, or being knocked back by Li, or the question itself, Priest would never know; but O'Brien shrank back into his room, eyes to the floor in a graceless, surreptitious motion.

'No. Sorry. It means nothing.'

# Chapter 24

By the time Priest had navigated the lobby to his penthouse and opened the door, Isaac O'Brien's odd reaction to the phrase *Kill the Giants* was still swirling around in his head, along with the image of Alan Burberry's mutilated body and other random memories. Like the sweet smell of Georgie's house, the dew on the mountainside that day with William and Sarah. The day it had all changed.

*'Hey, Charlie! Come here!'*

He had thanked Li and Georgie, telling the latter she was to concentrate on keeping the practice running with Okoro for a few days while he sorted this mess out. She had agreed to stay out of trouble but they were both lying, honestly. She because staying out of trouble wasn't in her nature and he because . . . *because this isn't going to be over in a few days.*

Priest unlocked the door, swung it open and looked into the kitchen. A draught of cool air hit him, along with the sound of the television blaring in the lounge and the smell of baking. He made his way in, closed the door behind him. It was chaos. Papers, crayons and paints strewn across the breakfast bar, an open suitcase in the middle of the floor – looked like someone had ransacked it, throwing clothes everywhere. A chalk board had been set up in the corner, on which Tilly had scrawled in red chalk – 'Welcome home, Uncle Charlie.' Every single door was open. Every single light was on, despite the late afternoon sun glaring through the open balcony bi-folds.

'Jesus Christ,' Priest mumbled.

Sarah appeared from the lounge carrying a tray of cakes. She stopped, smiled, but clearly hadn't been expecting him.

'You're home early.'

'I don't work normal office hours.'

'It's great you do flexitime. Want a cupcake?'

Priest surveyed the tray. Eight pink cakes lathered in untidy icing.

'Thanks – feeling in a savoury mood, though.'

'Tilly made them for *you*.'

Priest looked up as Tilly danced into the room dressed in a pink leotard and waving a dangerous-looking fairy wand. She had green wings that looked like they were from a different costume and bare feet with stubby little toes. *Mum's toes.*

'Have a cake, Uncle Charlie,' she sang, spinning round him. Priest picked the smallest-looking cake and ate, waving a hand of approval between mouthfuls.

'It's delicious, thank you.'

'It's made from fairy poo.'

Tilly cackled heartily and danced off, slamming the door through to the lounge behind her. The television was still on loud enough that he could hear every word the Powerpuff Girls were saying.

'Is it really fairy poo?' he asked Sarah.

'No. It's mainly baking mix. You're safe, for now.' She put the tray down and turned to him. 'I'm sorry. I'm doing all the pick-ups from school. Gerry's covering for me at work but

Ryan normally does at least three days a week. I meant to tidy up before you got back.'

'Sarah, it's fine, honest.'

This was true. The mess didn't bother him and the house was usually so quiet. Priest had lost track of how long he had lived alone. Right now, he was glad of the company, even if his electricity bill was about to skyrocket. Sarah and Tilly couldn't fill the cavity in his life completely, but they came close. They were the most important thing to him in the world. They and Jessica, he realised. Maybe that's all he needed: his sister, his niece and a woman he saw rarely and understood less.

'Has he asked about her?' Priest said. He meant had Ryan asked about his daughter. Sarah pulled a face, catching his meaning straight away.

'I'm not speaking to him at the moment.'

'Has he been in touch?'

'A few times. Texts. Stupid stuff. Apologies, that sort of thing.'

'Is it over – for you, I mean?'

She brushed a strand of golden hair out of her eye, went to put the kettle on. 'Yes. It's irreversible.'

'He knows that?'

'I've told him.'

Priest was hardly surprised. Sarah might have taken Ryan's surname, but there was nothing anybody could do to strip her of her father's stubborn nature, a disposition that had latched itself on to her through her genes to an even greater extent than it had with her two brothers.

It was both a blessing and a curse. Maybe if she'd listened to him all those years ago, lying with her back on the moss making pictures with the clouds, then things might have been different. The sound of his juvenile self shrieked at the back his mind:

'*Sarah! Help!*'

'*Go away, Boy who cried Wolf. I'm not falling for that.*'

But that wasn't fair. There was nothing she could have changed. The damage was already done.

They spent the evening playing Pictionary on the chalk board with Tilly declaring at the end that Mummy was the best drawer, followed by her, with Uncle Charlie being the least good, but he was the best guesser. That was generous, given that he had only guessed two correctly the entire game.

Priest had managed to push the puzzle of the symbol to the back of his mind for a few short hours. Then, after a dinner of sausage and mash he had rustled up, despite his sister's offer to cook, Sarah announced that it was bathtime and they disappeared, leaving Priest resting in the armchair, the troubles of the symbol tumbling back into his head.

He was about to call Rowlinson when Sarah appeared; the steam from the bathroom had flushed her face and she had water down her front.

'She wants *you* to read.'

Priest nodded. 'What does that entail?'

Sarah rolled her eyes and handed him a book. *Princess Lollipop*. 'Christ, you're dumb. Read this, in a calm voice. Tuck her in and leave the hall light on.'

Uncertain, Priest took the book and padded through to the spare bedroom, where Tilly was already in bed, the covers pulled right up to her chin.

'It's s-s-so c-c-cold in here,' she chattered.

'It's the air-conditioning,' he laughed, grabbing a remote on the side and adjusting the temperature. 'Better than sweating your brains out.'

'You can sweat brains out?'

Priest hesitated. 'Yeah. I think so.'

Tilly giggled. After he had read the story, he kissed her forehead and she promised to go to sleep straight away, closing her eyes tightly and stiffening, as if tensing herself would help.

'Relax,' he told her. 'Goodnight.'

As he was about to leave, she called back to him, yawning. 'Uncle Charlie, do you think we'll see Daddy soon?'

Priest wasn't sure what to say – he could handle the cruellest, most callous judge in the world, but this bright-eyed six-year-old child had just vexed him.

'I'm sure you will, Til,' he settled on. Mercifully, she seemed satisfied with the answer, turned over.

'Can you send Mummy through?' she requested with a regal wave of one starfish hand.

'Will do.'

Priest loped back through to the lounge to where Sarah lay on the sofa frowning at her phone. 'Emails,' she said, although it wasn't convincing.

'She wants you to go through.'

Sarah hummed, pocketed her phone and left. Priest replaced her on the sofa and checked his own phone for messages. Satisfied everything could wait, he threw the phone on the coffee table and watched the lionfish circle in their tank while he waited for Sarah to return. She wasn't telling him everything. Everything was so quick, so final. He wasn't seeing enough anger, enough resentment. Just acceptance.

Then again, he only had his own bloody divorce to judge against, which was hardly a fair comparison. His walking out had damaged Dee's pride more than breaking her heart. She had seen the end coming just as clearly as he had, but had clung on to the fallacy that they could have continued to live like that – *what?* – indefinitely? Breaking that final barrier down, eventually forcing her to concede that what they had wasn't real, that it was just the semblance of a marriage, hadn't broken her, but the admission that she had been wrong about him, or wrong about the notion that she could have changed him, was the thing that had really terrified her. What had terrified him was not facing *that* truth, but the possibility that her final conclusion brutally explained the whole sorry affair: that he was incapable of real love.

Priest picked up a pile of papers on the side, idly started to leaf through them. They were mostly drawings that Tilly had done. Some, he noticed, were drawn on confidential documents she had obviously found lying around the house. He sighed wearily. To be fair, she had made a good job of defacing some disclosure for a fraud trial listed for next year; the document was much improved, with a picture of what looked like a unicorn sitting outside a house on top of which she'd drawn . . .

Priest stopped. Looked again. Turned the paper over and checked his hands, clasped them together, squeezed tightly. He felt everything. It wasn't a turn, the drawing was there. An icy chill rippled up his arms and neck. Felt like his blood freezing. *My God.*

There it was.

It was without doubt the same symbol that had been scrawled in blood near three murders: Jane Vardy, Emma Mendez and Alan Burberry. A Latin cross, intersected by the wavy line.

Priest flipped through the pages. There it was again. Hovering above a picture of some stick men. And again, in the sky next to the moon and stars. And again, on a space rocket.

And then a whole fucking page of them.

Priest threw the pages down, as if they were burning him. Adrenaline was now coursing through his body, flooding his brain with confusing questions. He jumped up, too quickly, the sudden movement knocking him off-balance temporarily. He managed to regain himself, grabbed one of the pictures and hurtled towards Tilly's room.

When he opened the door, Sarah was leant over her daughter, kissing her goodnight. She looked up sharply.

'What are you doing?'

'Sorry, I just . . .'

He gently eased her out of the way and knelt down next to Tilly, who looked at him, wide eyed but unalarmed.

Sarah protested, but he ignored her. 'Hey, Uncle Charlie!'

'Tilly,' he said softly, showing her the picture, pointing to the symbol. 'Why did you draw this?'

'I liked it.'

'OK. Have you seen it somewhere?'

'Yes.'

'Charlie,' Sarah tried to interrupt but he put his hand up. She stopped, must have sensed his anxiety.

'Where, Til? Where did you see this?' Tilly leant over the bed, pursed her lips. Touched his head. Her eyes were crystal blue, like her mother's, like his. 'You won't be in any trouble. I just need to know where.'

'Can you keep a secret, Uncle Charlie?'

'Yes.' Priest's heart was pounding in his chest. There was a resonance gushing through his head, a droning surge of white noise, increasing in its intensity.

She whispered into his ear, 'There's a funny book in your study behind a glass case. It's in there.'

Priest nodded, forced a smile. The noise was now deafening.

The hot, dry night air clung to Priest like a second skin as he pounded on Owen's front door. He had lost track of time in the early evening but he didn't care if he was disturbing the professor: he had surged into his office and found that when you stared up through the glass case at a certain angle (which would have been more apparent from Tilly's height) the symbol was plainly visible at the top of the page, eerily scribed in ancient carbon-black ink. Whoever had murdered Jane Vardy, Emma Mendez and Alan Burberry had had sight of the Book of Janus.

'Owen!' Priest yelled through the letter box. 'It's important. Open up.'

As he had torn across the city, the sound of the Aston Martin's V12 engine ripping through the air like a chainsaw, he had tried to call Rowlinson, but the inspector's phone went straight to voicemail. Priest had left a hasty message. It might be a blessing: Owen would be rattled as it was. He was secretive about the Book anyway and not likely to open up if he knew the police were involved.

Priest wondered if Owen had an alibi for the murders.

'Owen!'

He was about to give up when, finally, a light flickered on in the hallway, preceded by the door opening. Owen was partially garbed in an ill-fitting dressing gown that looked as though it had seen better days. His bare chest looked blotchy. His eyes were bloodshot. The smell of weed that followed him out was unmistakable.

'Bad time?' asked Priest.

'W-what do you want?'

'I want to speak to you. About the Book of Janus.'

'*Now?*'

'Now.'

Owen stood there, swaying slightly. He seemed to be mesmerised by something behind Priest in the street, but more likely he was stoned.

'I'm not . . . feeling well,' he mumbled.

'There's a symbol in the Book, professor. A Latin cross with an intertwining line. What is it?'

Owen inhaled deeply, but the air caught in his throat and he ended up choking it out. 'Can't we do this in the morning, Priest?'

Priest was surprised Owen recognised him. His eyes were almost sealed shut. Even as they stood in the doorway, the rash across Owen's chest had expanded and his face had grown paler, etiolated. He looked like he might throw up. Priest realised that any chance of getting a coherent answer from him tonight was next to nil.

*Fuck.*

'Be at the Savoy for nine,' Priest told him. 'Bring the translations, and be sober.'

Owen's mouth contorted upwards. He giggled stupidly.

'Right.'

He closed the door, and Priest turned to go, frustrated. To compound his annoyance, the smell of marijuana seemed to follow him all the way home.

# Chapter 25

*Saturday*

To give him his due, Owen was in the Savoy's lobby – the complete antithesis of the wretched soul who had stood wavering in his front doorway last night like something out of a Hammer Horror film. He was wearing a brown suit and a yellow shirt and although his eyes were heavy he looked surprisingly alert for a man who had spent the night getting high.

He looked up as Priest and Rowlinson made their way across the marble flooring, slowing momentarily to let a porter guide a trolley full of luggage in front of them.

Rowlinson took the opportunity to say, aside: 'Did you tell him I would be coming too?'

'He didn't know what fucking day of the week it was last night. He wouldn't have remembered, even if I had.'

'Fine.' The porter moved on, Rowlinson picked up the pace as Owen rose to his feet, concern etched across his cobwebbed face. 'And why the hell did you pick the Savoy?'

'Thought it might encourage him to turn up looking half human.'

No sooner had they arrived and shook hands, a waiter appeared and took orders for tea, as if it was mandatory. Owen just asked for water. When the waiter was gone, they sat down and Priest did the introductions, watching as Owen avoided eye contact.

'Norman, this is Detective Chief Inspector Tiff Rowlinson – Met Police, Serious Crime Command.' He deliberately omitted the word 'Homicide' at this stage. Owen was already anxious, and there was a visible shake in his hands.

'You, er . . . caught me at a bad time last night, Priest.'

Priest waved him away, like it wasn't a problem. 'It was late. Don't worry about it.'

'Can I ask what—'

Rowlinson didn't give the professor a chance to finish. Slapped down a black and white copy of the symbol found at the murder scenes in front of Owen, whose lips parted. There was that sharp intake of breath again.

'What's this?' Rowlinson demanded. Priest shuffled next to him. Rowlinson was keen, but Owen needed boiling slowly, not set alight straight away.

'This is the symbol that appears in the Book of Janus,' Owen said, cautiously.

Rowlinson shuffled in his chair. 'What does it mean?'

'We don't know. It's a variation of the Latin cross that isn't seen in any other texts, even in the rest of the Dead Sea Scrolls.'

'Guess.'

'I don't know. An ancient symbol of the Essenes, maybe.'

'The Essenes were a Jewish sect,' Priest told Tiff, remembering his first discussion with Owen. *Mr Priest, if I have to, I'll die to keep this Book secret.* 'That would be something more like the Star of David, no?'

'Yes. No. Perhaps. Look, nobody knows. But it's not unusual for a small sect to adopt a symbol of their own – there probably isn't much significance in it.'

Owen was defensive, but trying to inject a little joviality into his voice, which seemed to spur Rowlinson on. If Priest could have stopped him without compromising their unity, he would have done. But as it was, Rowlinson went right ahead and threw another picture down. This time a photograph: of Alan Burberry's body in the foreground, the symbol scrawled in his blood behind him.

'That significant enough for you?'

Rowlinson leant back, fingers to his lips, legs crossed. Waited. Owen was silent. The waiter came over. No one spoke as he poured tea; the buzz of the dining room around them, the chink of metal on pot interspersed with an occasional laugh, offered a small mundane relief from an otherwise uncomfortable silence.

The waiter placed the bill next to Priest, and left.

Owen moved the photograph to get a better look, treating it with the lightest of touches.

'My God.'

Priest watched, taking in Owen's expression, as the professor moved his hands sequentially across his chest in the sign of the cross. A tremoring, perfunctory gesture.

'Somebody's read your book, professor,' said Rowlinson evenly.

Owen took a gulp of water. 'This man was . . . ?'

'Murdered. Yes.'

'How many people would know about this symbol?' asked Priest.

Owen hesitated. 'I don't know. Some, but few know the content of the Book. The text has been in circulation for two thousand years or more but for the most part it has been lost.'

Rowlinson leant forward again. 'But not just you?'

'I . . . wait. No. Certainly not just me.' Owen coughed, the seriousness of Rowlinson's intonation dawning on him. 'A number of scholars have seen the Book, there are probably even some pictures on the internet.'

'We'll check,' Rowlinson warned.

'Do so.'

Priest intervened, sensing the rising heat in Rowlinson's tone. 'When we last spoke, Norman, you told me that the Book of Janus contained a secret that was so important you were prepared to die to keep it. You said it was written by the Devil.'

Owen shuffled uncomfortably. He looked embarrassed. 'That's only partially true, I'm afraid. The Book of Janus was most probably written by the Essenes, an ancient Jewish sect, much the same as the rest of the Dead Sea Scrolls. I may have used a little poetic licence. I was trying to make you realise its importance in simple terms. But the secret is real. And I remain willing to die to keep it.'

'Maybe it's time you shared that secret with us, professor,' said Rowlinson, making no effort to disguise his growing impatience.

'If there was some other way?'

'There isn't.'

Owen drank the rest of the water without pausing for breath. Priest picked up his cup of tea. He didn't want it – he craved something stronger, sweeter – but made a show of it. A message. *We're here to stay.* Owen was shuffling around. Itching. Delaying. The internal conflict was painfully evident: his brow was so furrowed it looked like a great weight was pressing down on him.

In the end, no doubt encouraged by the methodical tap of Rowlinson's fingers on the arm of the chair, he came to a decision.

'Fine. I can see that the cat's out of the bag anyway. No point in hiding. Somebody already knows.'

'You mean the murderer?' said Priest, motioning to the photograph.

Owen looked away – didn't affirm or deny it. Instead, he picked the photograph up and turned it over. Slid it back towards Rowlinson. The DCI didn't pick it up.

'Are you a man of religion?' Owen asked Rowlinson.

Rowlinson shook his head. 'Went to Sunday school. That's about it. Never thought about it since. Maybe that makes me agnostic, I don't know.'

'You're familiar, though, with the story of Noah's Ark?'

Rowlinson chewed his lip. Priest sat back, waiting to see how this played out, see if his friend's irritation would boil over before Owen could finish.

'God decides one day that he hates his creation, so He sends a deluge to destroy everybody expect Noah and his family, because of how evil everyone had become.'

'Sort of,' Owen admitted. 'But you have made a common mistake. You said that God sent the flood to wipe out man because of his wicked ways. No doubt that is the version you remember from Sunday school, inspector.'

Rowlinson flinched. 'He did though, didn't He?'

Priest sipped the tea slowly. He wasn't completely ignorant about what the Bible said. In his early teens, he had declared himself an atheist. Looking back on it, that decision was more about wanting to copy William rather than having been based on any particular theological insight. But whatever doubt about the existence of God he harboured as a youth had been extinguished altogether on the death of his parents: a senseless and arbitrary tragedy. He had spent time reading the Bible without really understanding why other than the feeling he had that perhaps somewhere hidden in the pages was some form of justification for him, a reason to believe despite what had happened. He hadn't found one. Decades had passed, and things had only got worse.

'Does this have something to do with the Nephilim?' Priest asked.

Owen nodded slowly. Rowlinson raised his hands, palms up.

'Will somebody please tell me what the fuck the Nephilim is?'

'Not *what*, but *who*,' Owen said softly, looking at the photograph of Alan Burberry. 'They're also known as Giants.' This particular picture didn't show the blood written warning *Kill the Giants*, but the phrase resonated around Priest's head and something clicked into place. He remembered the story of the Watchers, the angels fallen to Earth who, contrary to God's law, had made children with human women. Most people didn't realise that the tale of how a race of hybrid demon-people came to inhabit the Earth was woven into the pages of Genesis. They were the Giants. *Of course.*

'Giants?' said Rowlinson, also realising the significance.

'The word Nephilim translates as "giants" in Hebrew,' said Owen, picking at the photograph with the ends of his fingers. He was pale, and the artificial light of the hotel lobby splashed across his face glared back at them. He looked lost, defeated.

Priest spoke carefully. 'Do you think it's possible that someone is going around killing people because they are – what? – descendants of demons?'

'That's ridiculous,' Rowlinson muttered.

Owen swallowed.

'Norman?'

'Genesis tells us that the Giants were not destroyed by the Flood,' said Owen, avoiding Rowlinson's glare. 'For a long time, no one knew how. One story said that Noah's third son, Ham, was wicked and that Ham's wife was a Pagan who carried the demon seed. Genesis tells the peculiar account of how, after Noah had planted a vineyard, he fell into a drunken stupor, during which he was sodomised by Ham. Rather than curse Ham, Noah, curiously, cursed Ham's son, Canaan. Indeed, Ham's grandson was Nimrod, a Babylonian king rebellious against God through his conception of the Tower of Babel.

'Less convincingly, other stories have said that the Giants *were* wiped out, but able to reintroduce their bloodline through an incubus, an evil spirit in male form capable of copulating, with consent or otherwise, with human women. These stories have festered and brewed for two thousand years; yet the answer was here all along. In the Book of Janus.'

'Who is Janus?' asked Priest.

'A stowaway aboard the Ark. A simple farmer who carried the demon bloodline put there by Satan.'

'So when the Flood ended, he escaped and eventually reintroduced the Giants' DNA into the human race?'

'According to the Book, yes.'

Rowlinson exploded. 'Am I the only one here who thinks this is bullshit?'

'It doesn't matter what you or I believe, Tiff,' Priest replied. 'Most civilisations have their flood story: the Babylonians, the Mesopotamians, the Sumerians. Even the ancient Greeks had a version, although they preferred the destruction of their world to be by fire. Point is: our killer believes it. He believes that demon DNA exists.'

Owen corrected, 'With respect, Mr Priest, that is conjecture. The Book of Janus does not explain how one can tell a pureblood – a descendant of Ham, Shem or Japheth – from the bloodline of Giants, a descendant of Janus.'

'And yet they think they may have found such a way,' Priest countered.

'I don't understand.'

Priest turned to Rowlinson. 'Show him, Tiff.'

Rowlinson, who was beginning to catch on, placed another photograph in front of Owen. This time, mercifully, Alan Burberry's punctured head wasn't visible. But the words written in blood near him were. *Kill the Giants.*

Owen raised a hand to his mouth. '*My God.*'

'You see our concern, professor,' said Priest. 'Rather seems like someone's read your book after all.'

# Chapter 26

The meeting room on the top floor of Holborn Police Station was an eighteen-foot square box with harsh artificial lights and magnolia walls. Three tables had been thrown together to make one large one, around which three people sat sweltering in the irrepressible heat. Above them, an air-conditioning unit teased them with the promise of a short reprieve from the hot weather, but when Priest pointed upwards inquisitively, Rowlinson shook his head.

'Broken. Maintenance guy is on leave.'

The third person shook her head, muttered under her breath, and removed her jacket, revealing a soft white sleeveless blouse and a pair of toned arms. She pulled her dark hair off her shoulder, tied it back; the motion was expertly performed, but with little self-awareness.

'Fay, this is Charlie Priest, as discussed. Priest, this is detective sergeant Fay Westbrook.'

Westbrook offered her hand. Priest took it, expecting a light grip but receiving instead a firm clasp of authority and control. Perhaps that shouldn't have surprised him. Rowlinson had already given him a short breakdown of her CV. She was on the Fast Track programme, what used to be called the Accelerated Promotion

Course. Degree in psychology, masters in Crime Intelligence and Data Analytics, top of every class, that sort of thing. This case would make her career. Being part of the task force that caught London's most prolific serial killer since William Priest? She would make DI in less than a year. Not a bad achievement for someone in their mid-thirties, but incredible considering she came to the force late; just six years ago.

'Welcome to the team, Priest.'

She had a casual smile that didn't quite reach her eyes, but it didn't matter; her heart-shaped face was perfectly aligned for it. Some people just suited smiling, Priest concluded.

'Thanks,' he said. 'Did Tiff brief you about what we know so far?'

She nodded. Tapped a notepad in front of her. 'We're looking for a demon-hunter.'

Rowlinson was about to speak when the door opened and two men in suits appeared. An older man with clout chiselled into an angular face – he held the room's attention immediately and even without introductions Priest knew this must be DSI John Eaton. He fitted Rowlinson's description perfectly. The second man was shorter, younger and, were it not for the enormous sneeze he produced shortly after shuffling in, might have been missed altogether. He hovered behind Eaton, hands clutching a file of papers, nose streaming. Probably the only man in London to have a cold during a heatwave.

'Sorry we're late,' Eaton said, approaching Priest, who rose to greet him. 'DSI Eaton. Call me John, though, for God's sake. You're William's brother?'

Priest was taken aback. No one mentioned William. No one dared even utter his name. Sure as hell, no one ever dared refer to Priest's relationship to William directly. Not in the first sentence. Not ever.

'That's me, the sane one.'

Eaton laughed and took a seat. Priest felt himself instantly liking Rowlinson's boss.

When no one introduced the second man, and he hadn't worked out how to introduce himself, Rowlinson motioned towards him.

'Priest, this is Ethan Grey, a consultant we've brought in. He's an expert on serial killers, like you.'

Priest sensed Grey's hostility immediately. He either hid it poorly, or was making zero effort. But Priest didn't hold that against him. The Met was notoriously territorial, so it was hardly surprising that Grey felt threatened. Someone was pissing on his tree.

'Great,' said Priest, like this was just what they needed: another fucking so-called expert. 'Good to meet you, Ethan.'

Grey didn't shake hands, but took a seat as far away from Priest as possible.

'Of course,' he mumbled.

'OK,' said Rowlinson, sensing the tension and moving on. 'Everyone knows about our meeting with Professor Owen.'

'And we now know that the symbol used by the killer does indeed represent a snake, as I surmised,' said Grey, coughing out the line like he had rehearsed it a hundred times before the meeting. The point scoring had started early.

'So what I understand,' said Eaton, ignoring Grey's triumphant look, 'is that this bastard thinks he's on a fucking mission from God to take out an ancient race of hybrid demons, whose bloodline has survived for two thousand years or more.'

'That's about the size of it,' said Rowlinson.

'Fucking hell.'

Westbrook looked over at Priest, leant across her notebook. 'And Owen was adamant that he didn't understand how the killer had identified his victims? He doesn't know who supposedly carries this demon DNA?'

Priest shook his head. 'So he said.'

'You didn't believe him?' pressed Eaton.

Rowlinson answered for him. 'Owen has agreed to hand over the translations of the Book of Janus to us. It doesn't matter if we believe him or not. We can see for ourselves.'

'We can trust him?' said Eaton. It was more of a challenge than a question. 'We'll never know whether the translations are accurate.'

'We can get an expert,' said Westbrook.

Eaton laughed, but it was forced. 'Bloody joking, Westbrook. It'll take weeks and cost more than your house is worth. This killer is working on three or four days between kills, max. We're due another one any moment.'

'A very unusual pattern for a serial killer,' said Grey. 'Usually serial killers build up; the time between kills shortens on each occasion. This is known as escalation. The down times are known as the cooling-off periods.'

'No, he's not—' Priest was about to explain when Grey cut him off, smugly.

'No. It *is* the case. It has been the case from the Ripper to, well, your brother, I think.'

'I mean, he's not a serial killer.'

Grey shook his head. 'A series of three or more murders, committed as separate events, usually, but not always, by one offender acting alone. Surely that's what we have.'

'Our guy has a plan. He knows exactly what he's doing.'

'He's organised,' argued Grey. 'Like Ted Bundy and John Wayne Gacy. That's all.'

Grey was referring to the FBI's Crime Classification Manual, which categorised serial killers into those who were *organised*, who planned each kill methodically, often abducting their victims to kill later; those who were *disorganised*, killing randomly and impulsively; and *mixed*, those that exhibit the characteristics of both organised and disorganised killers.

William was mixed. In everything he did, he was completely without pattern. Or so it seemed, anyway.

'What's the significance in this, Priest?' asked Eaton. 'Does it matter, or is this a cock fight between you two nerds?'

Priest smiled while Grey winced. 'It matters in how we approach this. Point is: I don't think the time between kills is a cooling-off period. He's not planning between these kills. He's already planned, a long time ago. Maybe years. He knows who the victims are, and he already knows everything about them.'

Grey snorted. 'Impossible. Serial killers tend to have low to average IQ, and few real expertise. There's no way a mad killer could orchestrate a plan that meticulously.'

'You should meet my brother,' Priest retorted. 'Anyway, our guy knew how to get into Jane Vardy's hotel room, into Emma Mendez's house, all without a trace, or without breaking anything. He knew that Alan Burberry would be jogging through Russell Square gardens at that time. He knew where the cameras were. And he's managed to pull off three murders without leaving one tiny strand of DNA. Not one molecule, not one partial fingerprint. Nothing. The guy is a ghost.'

'What *have* we got from forensics, Rowlinson?' asked Eaton before Grey could respond.

'Like the man says. Nada. The nails could have come from anywhere. There's nothing unusual about them.'

'What about the salt?'

Westbook read from a notepad. '*Judeo-Christians believe that salt is a purifier, so it's often used in folklore to ward off evil spirits and demons. It's one of the few substances that can be found almost everywhere on the Earth.* We found traces of salt at all three crime scenes.' She turned to Rowlinson. 'I checked with SOCO. There *was* salt found in Jane Vardy's hotel room; under the bed.'

Rowlinson frowned. 'I don't remember seeing anything at Alan Burberry's scene?'

'They found it *in* him.' There was a short moment's eerie silence as they all took this in. Priest shivered, despite the heat.

'What do you mean?'

'It had been poured into the wound.'

'He's mixing up different traditions,' Grey said presently. 'Not such careful planning after all.'

'He's telling us what he's doing,' Priest corrected. 'He wants us to know his plan. *Kill the Giants.* The symbol. The salt. He knew we'd work it out pretty quickly.'

'He's telling us something,' Westbrook murmured. She looked troubled. Priest kept catching her eye, but the sub-text wasn't clear.

'He wants us to know what his plan is,' said Priest, to Westbrook more than to anyone else. 'So we're a part of it. He wants notoriety, but he doesn't want to be caught. He's intelligent, and he understands how to kill people without leaving a trace.'

'He'll have killed before,' Rowlinson added. 'Three more or less perfect murders isn't a chance occurrence.'

'What do we look for?' asked Eaton, and Priest guessed he was referring to a search for similar crimes through the criminal intelligence system 'CrimInt'. 'Nails, salt, religious motivation?'

'All of the above,' replied Rowlinson. 'Past five years, at least.' Westbrook nodded, made a note.

Eaton looked at Grey. 'When can we have a full profile?'

'Well, that's not straightforward. I have delivered a preliminary analysis but I will need time to complete something more comprehensive. It's complicated – the killer is sophisticated.' Grey shuffled around some papers, stalling. 'Perhaps by the end of the week?'

'That's great but someone else will have died by then,' said Eaton. 'The end of tomorrow will be fine, though.'

Priest suppressed a smile as Grey's face reddened. 'DSI Eaton, the process of accurately profiling an individual as prolific and complex as the Serpent Killer cannot be rushed through—'

'He's Unsub,' Rowlinson interjected.

Eaton raised his hand. Grey was about to protest but clearly thought better of it. 'Enough. Tomorrow, please, Mr Grey. Charlie – what's our next move?'

'Owen is collating the translations for us. He asked for a few hours – he's going to meet us later and hand them over.'

'From which you'll learn nothing,' Grey chided.

'From which we hope to learn how the killer is choosing his victims.'

'I can't make that rendezvous,' said Rowlinson. 'I've got a meeting with the MCM.' Scotland Yard's Media and Communication Officer. Priest nodded. The Press hadn't tied the three murders together yet, but it was only a matter of time before they would – then there would be pandemonium. A serial killer loose in London. No one is safe. Police baffled. Who's next? It would be worse if the killer's motivation were to be made public.

*Kill the Giants.*

'I'll go with Charlie,' said Westbrook.

'Fine,' said Eaton. 'And put a tail on Owen from now on. If he so much as takes a shit, I want to know about it.'

# Chapter 27

By the time Priest pulled the Aston up outside Owen's house, the temperature had dropped a few degrees and wafts of warm air rustled through the trees lining the pavement, shielding them from the perishing sun. Owen's road was quiet – a little pocket of old suburbia where people still had milk deliveries and took Neighbourhood Watch seriously. A woman putting her bin out across the street stopped and stared as Priest killed the engine. It would have been an unusual sight. A heavily built man who hadn't shaved in a week wearing a faded T-shirt and linen jacket getting out of a hundred and fifty-thousand-pound car, followed by a slim mixed-race woman who looked half his age. *Yeah, unusual.* The stare he got was one of the reasons why he tended not to use the Aston for work, preferring instead his brother's dark blue Volvo 940 estate, but the 1992 engine had conked out a few days before and the old car was in for repairs.

'This is it?' asked Westbrook, checking out the house.

'This is it.'

'We should have brought him to the station.'

'On what grounds?'

Westbrook waved her hand dismissively. 'We could have come up with something.'

Priest ducked under a low hanging willow, the only feature of Owen's front garden, and rang the bell, knocked and called through the letter box.

'Norman?'

Westbrook stood behind, arms folded.

'Does he have a car?' She nodded at the empty driveway.

'I don't know. Could be in the garage.'

Priest knocked again.

'Norman? It's Priest!'

'Nobody keeps a car in the garage anymore,' Westbrook muttered. 'He's gone. Long gone.'

Priest straightened up. If she was right, he'd misjudged Owen. He didn't seem the type. But he had been scared. And scared people tend to . . .

His phone vibrated. He pulled it out and found a text.

'What is it?' asked Westbrook sharply.

'It's Owen. He wants to meet elsewhere. I've got an address.'

'Where?'

Priest started heading back to the Aston. 'A lock-up, few miles away. Get in.'

The Aston's six-litre engine roared into life as Priest accelerated out of Owen's road. In the mirror, the woman putting her bin out was still staring, mouth open.

It took them around twenty minutes to navigate the labyrinth of side streets out of the estate to the address Owen had sent to Priest; so by the time they got there the cloudless sky was a deep purple, disturbed only by the undulating flock of starlings retreating as one into the distance.

They were at the start of a corridor of garages, one side of which had been built, relatively recently, underneath a railway line, the new bricks nestled underneath the arches of the old fly-over. Each garage was numbered. Signs warned of closed-circuit television cameras. Gang tags and graffiti adorned the walls.

'Which number?' asked Westbrook, looking up at the nearest garage door.

'Fourteen.'

They crawled through the corridor, then stopped at the right number. Priest left the car idling as they both climbed out. Garage number fourteen was like the others, although the paint-work looked less tired – maybe done recently. Priest hammered on the door. Waited. He was about to turn, ready to admit to Westbrook what she had intimated – they had fucked up. Owen was long gone. But as he opened his mouth to tell her, there was a grinding noise behind him. The hinges and springs squealed as the garage door was lifted from the inside.

'I'm sorry,' said Owen. He seemed to struggle with the door, so Priest took it the final third and made sure it locked open. 'I thought we might meet at my home but, what with everything going on, I can't guarantee that no one is watching me.'

'Why would someone be watching you, Professor Owen?' asked Westbrook.

'Norman, meet Detective Sergeant Fay Westbrook,' said Priest. Owen looked nervous, hung back in the garage. There was a lamp on in the corner casting a weak light over a workbench cluttered with tools and dust. A grey sheet had been thrown over a car that took up most of the space. Priest couldn't see what it was: small and low – sports car probably, maybe a classic. More tools hung on the wall, couple of jerry cans in the corner. Nothing out of the ordinary.

'Good,' said Owen, looking at Westbrook, not with authority but with pained concern. 'If you could keep watch, DS Westbrook. That would be appreciated.'

Priest glanced over his shoulder, expecting Westbrook to protest but, to his surprise, she grunted in reply and stepped back out to where the Aston was.

Priest turned back. 'The translations, professor.'

Owen fumbled for a file of papers on the worktop. 'Of course. I can trust you, Mr Priest, can't I?'

'More to the point, *I* can trust *you*, right?'

'I have done everything to keep these from falling into the wrong hands. It's just—'

'Looks like you either failed, or he got them elsewhere.'

'The latter, I am sure.' Owen handed Priest the file. 'It wouldn't be impossible. Although I am sure that nothing exists as accurate as these, there have been other scholars who have seen the Book.'

'Such as who?'

'Well . . .'

Owen was shivering, despite the warmth. Priest watched as he placed his hands on the car for support, leaning over it, clearing his throat, swallowing back bile. Owen was in turmoil, but why? Was he protecting someone? Priest felt his patience begin to slip away.

'Norman, if you know something, now's the time to say it.'

'A minute, please.' Owen wheezed, coughed again. Priest's phone rang. He snatched it out of his pocket, didn't recognise the number. Owen coughed again, looked like he might retch.

*This is ridiculous.* Priest concluded that the best thing to do would be to let Owen catch his breath – this was getting them nowhere.

He pressed 'answer', placed the phone to his ear. Took five paces out of the garage. Saw Westbrook leaning against the car. She straightened up, seemed surprised to see him.

'Hello?'

There was a short pause – the phone was definitely connected.

'Get out of the garage.'

Priest didn't recognise the voice, but his instinct took him another five paces away from the garage.

The phone went dead.

Even in the short distance from where the explosive discharged, Priest felt it before he heard it – the sensation of weightlessness, of his body being magically lifted into the air. He was flying, hurtling, blind – nothing but light piercing his eyes, the air thundering past him.

Then, a split second later, the noise of the explosion hit him as the garage ripped open and his world collapsed into darkness.

# Chapter 28

*One year ago*

*I become disorientated quickly. The rush of toxins in my blood-stream has gone to my head. I can feel the warmth of Sue's mouth around my cock, but it isn't enough. She looks up at me occasionally, and I see defiance in her expression, and disgust. It angers me. She should be subservient. She should serve.*

*I push her head down. She moans and chokes angrily.*

*She isn't attractive, Sue, but it doesn't matter. I'm not thinking about her anyway. I'm thinking about the woman who stumbled into the church all those years ago. She was like nothing I had ever seen. Tall and lean, with flawless dark skin and perfectly formed lips. Battered, and worn down by her habit much like the rest of them, but she had an aura of strength, despite her problems. It was so noticeable that I might have even called it powerful.*

*I asked her to share her name and she told me, and when it came to the part where I invite members of the meeting to talk about their lives, she didn't squirm and shrink back like most of the newbies, she just started talking: a meandering, captivating mono-logue. Some of it I had heard before. Her father had been abusive, although he had only hit her a few times. Her mother took the brunt of it. She had left home at fifteen to come to London, determined to make something of her life. It hadn't gone well at first. She knew a few people here, but not many. She never slept on the streets but spent a year crashing on the sofas of various people she met and, although she never mentioned it specifically, I suspect she crashed in their beds where it was the only way to get a roof over her head.*

*Then she started drinking and a large chunk of her life, many years in fact, was practically lost in the fog of dependency. She drifted, a lost spirit: a strong, intelligent woman trapped in the body of an alcoholic monster. Eventually, she drifted to Hackney and, somehow, managed to secure a job cleaning for the Council. This represented a small turning point, and although she kept drinking, she rented a room from an elderly couple not far from this church who in turn encouraged her to come here, to seek help.*

*And what was I supposed to do, faced with this confused, susceptible creature?*

*She lives with me now, mostly. The elderly couple ask after her once in a while. Fine, I say. Just fine. They want to see her, but she does not want to see them. I am insistent on that. They know it is suspicious, but they do not have the conviction to object.*

*She gives me almost everything I need. Almost. The rest is supplied by God through people like Sue. She is not legally my wife, and never will be, but she is the only woman who I have seen as more than just an entitlement. She has an inner strength that is, at times, overwhelming, and although I remain in control, I have to watch her carefully. Recently I have noticed a lot of . . . rebelliousness. I seethe, just thinking about it. I am excited by it, terrified and mad, all at the same time. She must be retamed. That look in her eyes nowadays . . .*

*I close my fists into balls, anger raging in me as Sue coughs and splutters her way through her half-hearted performance and my dissatisfaction swells into a blinding headache.*

*This isn't enough.*

*I take Sue by the head and wrench her away. She is stunned, tries to protest but realises quickly that I had lied to her when I take her by the hair and pull her over the vestry table. She tries once to turn around, cry out. I hit her, slap her across the face and she stiffens.*

*'What are you doing?' she whimpers.*

*I take her by the hair again and push her back across the table.*

*'What is my right,' I tell her.*

*As I fumble around for her jeans button, she neither submits nor fights me, but tells me she hates me. I don't mind. What she thinks makes little difference.*

*By the time I have finished, I hate her as well.*

# Chapter 29

At first, there was nothing but silence. And white light.

Then a cool breeze across his face and, gradually, a rushing noise. He thought it might be the wind, but the noise soon cleared – water. The stream, lapping off the rocks in its descent through the valley where eventually it trickled into the lake below. And birds too, overhead, ceaselessly bickering.

The kind of day when anything could happen. The kind of day when you know what it is to be free.

Charlie looked up. It was clear now, the white light gone, replaced with a blue wall of sky, splashed with mottled clouds. Perfect, were it not for soft white contrails in the wake of an aircraft. And the birds, of course.

Charlie sat up. Sarah was pretending to be asleep, snoring in the most unconvincing way, her chest rising and falling with forced gusto. Her way of saying *bugger off and leave me alone*.

William was down by the rocks, studying the water. He had changed dramatically in the last year, bulking out like an evil henchman from TV, and his skin breaking free from the acne that had plagued his early teen years. Like a snake shedding its skin, Charlie had thought. What had emerged was a confident, strong and striking young man.

Seeing Sarah's eyes well and truly shut, he glanced at his own arms. Biceps that were nicely shaped but lacked the power and build of his older brother's.

'Face it, Charlie, you're a scrawny wimp,' his sister chided.

Charlie jumped. Turned, but her eyes were still shut.

'How do you . . . ? You were asleep!'

'Magic,' she smiled mysteriously.

He was about to reply with a new profanity he had been working on when William called from the other side of the stream.

'Hey, Charlie! Charlie, come here!'

Annoyed at his sister's apparent mysticism, he got up. Stretched, walked across to where William was standing.

'What?'

'You think I can make it?'

Charlie glanced over the edge to the lake below. It wasn't that far down, maybe forty feet, fifty at the most. But the scree thrust out – an assembly of jagged rocks and sharp edges through which the stream ran.

'No,' replied Charlie, blinking – his eyes hadn't adjusted from being closed for the best part of an hour.

'I think I can,' said William, trekking back. 'If I run from here.'

Charlie looked again, but his dismay hadn't dislodged. 'What if you fall?'

'It's just a few rocks.'

'Are you crazy?'

'Come on. I can make it.'

William took another few paces back, stripped off his shirt and threw it aside. Charlie was conflicted. He was old enough to know now that William wasn't invincible, but it would be pretty damn cool if he made it. He'd heard some of the other kids at school talk about jumping into the lake from the Crag, the rocky edge near the Priests' house. They'd all shut the fuck up if William had actually done it.

'I . . . I don't know, Wills . . .'

William kicked off his shoes. 'Are there any sharp rocks on the edge? I don't want to cut my feet.'

Charlie looked around, saw a few stones that might hinder William's run up and cast them aside. Realised that this had made him complicit. He felt a change in the wind, a chill in the air. Something felt wrong.

'Wait. Wills, no, forget it.'

'Stand back, Charlie.'

Charlie stepped into the path, put out his arm. 'Come on, Wills. Let's go and swim, but down there. There's too many rocks here.'

'Stand back, Charlie.' This time he was being serious. That was a command, the voice that William used when he wanted something done. If he'd used that voice to tell Charlie to jump in after him, Charlie would have jumped.

So he stood aside.

William hurtled along the path, barefoot, the sun at his back and for a second Charlie mistook him for their father, the powerfully built martinet who would have told William not to be so bloody stupid; told him there was no way he would have made it over the rocks, to the . . .

William was in the air, and for a brief moment, time stood still.

Charlie scrambled to the edge, his heart pounding, tears streaming down his face. He scratched his arm on a thistle, didn't even notice the pain.

'Wills? William!'

He screamed at the lake, desperately searching. Nothing. A glimmer of hope. *He must have made it!*

'William!'

He started to climb down, half skidding, half falling, the rocks giving way beneath his feet and tumbling into the stream before he hit an incline made of dirt and moss. The wet ground provided no traction and he fell the rest of the way, collapsing in a heap at the foot of the slope, the pain in his arm registering for the first time.

*Shit!*

He called out again. The water was disturbed, sloshing up near the bank. He called his brother's name again, this time louder, a pernicious sense of alarm began to envelop him. Checked back up the escarpment. Could Sarah hear him from down here?

He thought about jumping into the freezing water. It was deep, not the gradual slope of a beach but a fucking great big hole filled with solid-looking black water.

He took a deep breath, ready to jump.

The water erupted, and William emerged with a tremendous breath, laughing and shouting his name, then gliding through the water with the ease of a dolphin to the bank. Charlie took his brother's arm but he wasn't much help: the release of adrenaline had stripped him of his strength. Not wanting William to see his quivering hands he pretended to be uninterested, folding his arms and watching insouciantly.

'Miss me?' laughed William, hauling himself out of the lake.

'No. And you're a bloody fool.'

William flung his arm round him and dragged him playfully back up the slope and over the rocks.

'Admit it, Charlie, you were shitting yourself.'

Charlie was annoyed but didn't make any effort to resist his brother's affection. After all, he *had* just made the jump that no one else dared to make.

It could have ended there. Priest knew that. That day, back then. It could have ended there, with William teasing him and his anger subsiding, replaced with relief and admiration, with them all trooping home to Mum and Dad, making a joke of Wills having fallen in the lake. But it didn't end there. Something else happened that day that changed them all for ever, although the change was never as stark and irredeemable as it was in William Priest. A change that saw him shed his skin again, and emerge as something entirely different.

# Chapter 30

There was a buzzing sound, gnawing at Priest's ear like a pneumatic drill. Darkness too, with yellow edges he could only see peripherally, no matter where he looked. And searing pain in his arms.

He smelt something familiar, distinct – sweet but not particularly pleasant. The smell of iodoform, of disinfectant. The smell of a hospital.

When he opened his eyes, the darkness receded, replaced instantly with a blinding white light. He remembered the explosion and, for a moment, a disquieting thought nestled within him. *Am I blind?*

Slowly, a room came into focus. White walls and a high ceiling. He became aware of the mattress, and the stiff sheets, the IV in his arm.

'Welcome back, princess.'

The voice was one he heard every day but it took him a moment to realise that the dark mass sitting on the chair next to him was Okoro.

'Ah, shit.'

'Don't move,' Okoro warned. 'You lost a leg.'

Priest sat bolt upright, spat mucus on the bed sheet, the acidy taste of sick was at the top of his throat.

'What?'

'Relax,' Okoro soothed, placing an arm on him. 'You're fine. Somehow, you managed to stay together.'

Priest reached down, felt both his legs – delight flooded through him.

'Oh, you bastard.'

'Well, that's what you get for taking these crazy assignments without consulting me.'

'OK, last time I checked I thought I was in charge, but point taken. What about Owen?'

Okoro shook his head gravely.

Priest fell back against the bedhead. 'Fuck.' His mind wouldn't focus, too many drugs coursing through him. He didn't want to believe it, but he knew if the explosion had come from inside the garage then Owen wouldn't have stood a chance. 'Fuck! Fuck! Fuck!'

'He wouldn't have felt a thing.'

'No consolation but good try. What about Fay?'

'The policewoman? Fine. Out of range. Called triple nine, looked after you from what I can gather until they got to the scene.'

'And the bomb?'

'Early signs say small explosive device already inside the garage and detonated remotely.'

'Shit.'

'Yeah. Miracle you weren't in the garage, otherwise I'd be taking you home in a bucket.'

Priest hunched his knees up, noticed his clothes in a pile in the corner. Briefly thought that he had escaped death by a few metres, ended up in hospital and his next of kin was down as Okoro, not Sarah. He would have some explaining to do later.

'It wasn't a miracle,' he said quietly.

'What do you mean?'

Priest hadn't recognised the voice on the other end of the line – the accentless, androgynous voice that had saved his life. Solly might be able to trace the call, though. That was something.

'Come on,' he said, ripping the IV out of his arm and swinging out of bed. 'We've got to go.'

'Wait!' Okoro jumped up, blocked his path. 'What the hell are you doing?'

'You said I was fine.'

'Yeah, in the sense that all of your vital organs appear to be in the correct place but you're in here for a while longer. For a start, you're in shock.'

Priest pushed past him and started to pull on his clothes. 'We can assume one of two things: either the person that set the bomb didn't want me dead and I spoke to the assassin, or they did want me dead but someone else knew the plan and warned me.'

'What the fuck are you garbling on about?'

He had finished getting dressed. His arm was bleeding, but not badly. Otherwise, Okoro was right – bruises and cuts, but nothing substantial.

'Are you coming?'

Priest opened the door and peered out, made sure there was no one watching.

'Priest!'

He looked back, assured. 'I said, are you coming?'

Okoro's shoulders slumped, and Priest saw his resistance evaporate. 'One of these days, Priest, you're going to get yourself killed for real.'

He didn't look back – the corridor was clear. He slipped out and Okoro followed.

'Then you can say I told you so.'

Priest sat in the passenger seat of Okoro's Porsche Cayenne on the phone to Rowlinson as the barrister drove. His arm hurt like hell and he was still struggling to assimilate it all – the black spots floating in front of his eyes didn't help either.

'The translations are destroyed,' Rowlinson was saying. 'I don't know whether there are any other copies. We're searching Owen's house now with the help of his ex-wife.'

'Did he have any other family?'

'A brother in Glasgow – we're trying to contact him. And a daughter – nineteen, lives with Mum.'

'Damn. The daughter OK?'

'They weren't especially close, but it's tough losing a parent, even a part-time one.'

Priest closed his eyes and realised what was stopping him from thinking properly: he needed to sleep. The urge to fall unconscious was overwhelming – it was eating him whole. And the disassociation was dragging him under. When he closed his eyes, all he could see was the flash that preceded his flight through the air, and the sound of the explosion in his ears, cut off suddenly when he blacked out. Everything hurt. Every fucking muscle complained, begging for rest. He could hardly keep the phone to his ear.

'Priest? Priest, you there?'

'Yeah, I'm here.'

'You better still be at the hospital.'

'Yeah, still here.'

'Sounds like you're inside a car.'

'How's Fay?'

Rowlinson paused, then carried on. 'Shaken up, but no injuries. She's got your car, by the way. Think she likes it.'

Priest forced his eyes open, stared out of the window. The clock in Okoro's car said 21:08. They'd lost over six hours – most of those he'd spent unconscious, but the drug-induced coma hadn't been any kind of rest. He sloshed back the last of the bottle of water Okoro had given him, conscious that he needed to piss badly.

'Listen, Tiff, I'll be at the office – I need to give my phone to Solly to see if he can trace a call for me.'

'What fo—'

Priest hung up. His head lolled to one side. For a minute, he blacked out, but came to when he felt the Cayenne pull up and the engine die out.

When he opened his eyes, he saw they were parked outside his apartment block.

'What are we doing here? I said the office.'

'I heard what you said,' said Okoro, getting out.

The passenger door opened and Priest half fell out, like a drunk. As he hit the ground, he felt a powerful arm lift him back up.

'Come on, Priest. This way.'

There was another voice too, and another body helping him to the door.

'We should get him back to hospital.'

'I know. But he'll just abscond again. Better here, with you.'

Priest was about to protest but he felt his body go limp, a sense of dread and acid clinging to his chest. More voices, definitely two people carrying him. Then the lights went out again and Priest surrendered to the darkness.

# Chapter 31

*Sunday*

When he awoke, Priest found himself in his own bed. The curtains were drawn but not the blind. Sunlight burst through the gaps, splashing the bedroom floor with a glorious yellowy hue. The clock on the bedside table read 6:45.

He lay still, not even sure if he could move. Above him, the fan rotated, bathing him in welcome cool air; but the sheets were damp. He seemed to have sweated off the worst of the nausea, although his head was still throbbing.

Beside him, a body stirred.

'Are you awake?'

He rolled over, fell into the warmth of her torso, knew it instantly and connected it to the voice last night.

'Barely. What are you doing here?'

'Sarah called me,' said Jessica. 'Okoro brought you from the hospital, called her on the way. She called me at the office, somehow got through. Said you'd been blown up.'

Her head was next to his. Her breath on his face, her scent was everywhere. He breathed in, long and deep; the woman who occupied the space at the back of his mind that niggled and gnawed away at him. The itch he couldn't scratch.

'You came,' he pointed out.

'For Sarah.'

'You don't know Sarah.'

She shuffled further towards him, her hand on his. He felt his body react, as bruised and battered as it was, as a warm sensation flooded through him.

'You were talking in your sleep,' she whispered.

'I do that, so I'm told.'

'Who's Joseph?'

He reacted inwardly at the name, heat spreading out across his chest as if it had opened up and there was now a yawning cavity she could see through. All his secrets laid bare. The day that had changed everything.

Outwardly, he didn't move a muscle.

She shuffled down further in the bed, drawing another gasp of yearning from his groin but her intentions were made clear in her eyes, through her unwavering stare.

'Who's Joseph?' she repeated.

'I mentioned him?'

She nodded, taking a moment to pick something out of his hair. He hadn't washed properly since the explosion – just what they'd done at the hospital. The faint smell of burning lingered in the air – or was it just him who could smell it? The sound of the bomb was still ringing in his ears.

'You said his name, a lot. Is he important?'

'No,' he said, without much thought. 'And yes.'

'Tell me.'

He frowned. It was out of character, and he was disorientated. 'We don't usually . . .'

'Talk? Today's different.'

'What's different about today?'

She leant in and kissed him, tenderly. Not the hard, lust-fuelled annexation he was used to – something softer, something that filled him with warmth, and hope.

In his semi-delirious state, he saw lights flashing in the corners of his eyes, and felt pain across his back and legs. It seemed like every nerve was on fire. He was tired, but he didn't want to sleep. He wanted this moment to last, despite the pain in his body and the pangs of anger in his head – the loss of Owen weighed heavily on his soul.

There didn't seem any harm in it. She might as well know.

'It's not Joseph,' he sighed. 'It's *Jozef*, a Polish immigrant. He worked at the sugar factory near my family home, but he was one of those people Dad used to tell us to stay away from. The Sugar Man, we called him. I didn't really know at the time why Dad was so concerned about him but of course now I realise it was because he knew about Jozef's past through his police contacts. He kept coming onto our land – we had a small wood at the back of the house we all used to play in. It backed out on to a lake, although that wasn't ours and we weren't supposed to go there. I don't know what Jozef wanted but it was kind of a game for us – see if you could spot him in the woods and hide from him. Stupid really, but kids are invincible, aren't they?'

Priest told Jessica the story of that fateful day, when the summer's breeze licked at their bare skin and the days seemed to last for ever – how it had almost turned sour when William had recklessly jumped across the rocks into the lake, how he had been angry with him but tried not to show it, and how they had stumbled back to where they had left Sarah laying on the mossy grass, face to the sun, eyes closed . . .

. . . they had heard the scream when they were about half way up the incline.

Forgetting his brave face, Charlie took hold of his older brother's arm as an icy wave of dread washed over him.

'That sounded like . . .'

'Sarah.'

William bolted up the incline, his back and shoulders were as powerful as any athlete as he tore towards the scream. Charlie wasted no time, but when they were on level ground he proved something else: William was bigger and stronger, but Charlie was quicker.

Overtaking his brother, Charlie charged down to the clearing where they had left Sarah but, on the higher ground, he could already see she wasn't there. William was behind, calling her name, the toxic mix of fear and anger distorted his voice into a shrill cry.

Scanning the woods, Charlie saw movement to the left.

'Over there!'

He didn't think what might have happened. The consequences of charging into the woods at full pelt didn't occur to him – none of it mattered. They had to look after Sarah. They were responsible. That was all that counted.

By the time Charlie broke through the edge of the woods, William was five or six seconds behind, yelling at him to wait. The trees were thick, untouched for hundreds of years and smelt of the earth. It was different in here. Cooler and darker – the woods were their own ethereal world, a secret world of spirits and ghosts.

There he was – Jozef, the Sugar Man. He had Sarah by the arm but he seemed hesitant, disturbed by the shouts of her brothers. When he saw Charlie bursting through the undergrowth, he let go and turned, pushing her to the ground.

Sarah shouted but he barely registered it. 'He wants my bag!'

Charlie flung himself as the Pole started his getaway, but Jozef was five or six stone heavier. He was squat, with broad shoulders and eyes spread wide across his face like a lizard. He was surprised, and Charlie sensed he had the upper hand, but then Jozef took him under the shoulder, using Charlie's own momentum against him and threw him to the ground with ease.

'Stop!' Jozef hissed, his accent making his words difficult to decipher. 'Not what it look like. I mean no harm.'

There was a fleeting moment when Charlie realised that maybe Sarah was right, and all the Sugar Man was doing was stealing Sarah's bag. But it was too late.

In a fury of muscle and testosterone William was on him. They both clattered to the ground. Charlie scrambled to his feet, spitting dirt from his mouth, the pain in his arm was intense. He watched in horror as William and Jozef struggled, each trying to gain the upper hand, a contest of strength and determination.

Charlie spied Sarah – ran to her. She was crying, sat on the damp ground watching the fray, terrified. He put his arm around her, shocked at how violently she was shaking. Her bag lay beside her, the contents scattered everywhere.

'Sarah, wait here. I have to help Wills.'

'No—'

He didn't hear her, the fight arrested his attention completely. William had managed to pin Jozef, had him by the throat. His other hand was raised, fist clenched. His right hand. His strongest. Panic seized Charlie. What if Wills got hurt? What if Jozef beat him? What if Wills won? Would he get in trouble? It was self-defence, surely?

Endless possibilities, doubt and terror passed through him but in a matter of seconds it was over . . .

'What happened next?' Jessica asked, enthralled.

Priest rubbed his face: the memory was painful. It ate away at him. Everything did from that day. The sound of Sarah's scream, the taste of the dead earth, the heat of the sun.

'Wills had him, but Jozef wasn't done. I thought, *Fuck me, Wills is going to kill him*. But it didn't work out. One minute Wills was on top – the next he was on his back; then he was up, but so was the Sugar Man and they were facing each other. It was a simple matter of who got their blow in first. That's what real fights are like. Not like in the movies – it's usually all over pretty quickly. And it was.'

Priest paused for breath; he needed a drink, his stomach was churning. He could hear Tilly running around in the lounge laughing, and Sarah trying to hush her up. Jessica was still looking at him, expectant, tiny signs of anxiety in her eyes, around the corners of her mouth.

'Go on,' she said.

'Jozef hit him hard. Later I found out that he broke more bones in his hand than he did in Wills's face, but it didn't seem like that at the time. Wills fell back, hit his head. Passed out. I screamed, Sarah cried. Then Jozef turned on us both.'

'You must have been terrified.'

'I'd like to say that I was scared for Sarah, or worried about Wills, but yeah I was scared out of my wits, for me.'

'What happened?'

Priest cleared his throat . . .

. . . Jozef advanced on Charlie and Sarah. There was a gash across his eye – must have been where he had fallen – and dirt all over his jacket. Charlie couldn't read his face, though. That was the most terrifying thing. He didn't look angry, or mad. He just looked like Jozef, the Sugar Man: the ugly, slow weirdo his father had said to stay away from. He was saying something, but Charlie couldn't make it out, or even the tone.

His fifteen-year-old self stood up, stepped in front of Sarah. He'd never been in a fight, not a real one. Only once had someone threatened him at school. Wills had sorted that. The guy never bothered Charlie again. But now his brother was out cold and he had to stand up for himself, but he could hardly stand, his legs were shaking so much.

'Back off,' Charlie tried to say, but it didn't sound right – just a pathetic splutter.

Another moan from Jozef, and the larger man waded forward, off-balance and uncoordinated, one tree-branch-sized arm held out.

It all seemed to happen in slow motion. Charlie had been barely aware of the rock in his hand, until it swung out as he launched forward, catching Jozef across the head and sending him spiralling backwards before tipping over and lying in a heap, just like Wills.

Charlie dropped the bloodstained rock. Sarah had stopped crying. For a moment that seemed to last an eternity, nothing happened. Even the breeze stopped, like the trees had held their breath.

Then there was a sound of a man running. A figure appeared through the trees, brandishing a large wooden staff.

'What in the blazes is happening here?' yelled Fagin.

His father's groundsman, who had been part of the family for decades, strode into view, his trademark cane crunching through the dead leaves and branches on the ground.

Charlie couldn't move. He just stared at William's limp body.

Fagin looked from Sarah crouched under a tree, to Jozef lying at Charlie's feet, to the bloodstained rock, and then in horror to William, a little pool of crimson liquid forming under his head.

'My God.'

'Fagin?' asked Jessica, repositioning herself so she was closer to him.

'Our groundsman. Still is.'

'Right. I guess William was OK in the end then?'

'He lived, if that's what you mean. But he was never the same. You know the rest. It's well known.'

She frowned, incensed. 'What? He became a serial killer because of what happened?'

Priest tapped his head. 'The injury. It dislodged something. I'd like to think that, had it not been for that hit to his head, things would have worked out differently, but that's wishful thinking. It was always there, I think. The injury just brought it to the surface somehow.'

'It turned him into a killer?'

Priest swallowed, for a horrible moment he felt a tear form under his eye. 'Paedophiles, fraudsters, rapists. That's what he went after. It was his way of channelling the overwhelming desire to kill into something close to justification. It's why the media dubbed him the Dark Redeemer. Not that he was some kind of hero. Some of them didn't exactly have a trial.'

'What happened to Jozef?'

'Mm.' Priest heaved himself up, threw back the covers. It was so damn hot he thought he was going to pass out. When he looked down, he paused, mesmerised by the network of scratches and bruises on his arms and legs. 'They found him the following year, hanging from a tree a few miles away from our house.'

Jessica said cautiously, 'So, it wasn't . . .'

'No, it was Wills. He never confessed to that one. I don't know why. Perhaps because Jozef was his first. Perhaps because if he did it somehow made Sarah and I complicit, I don't know. But it was Wills.'

'You said, *hanging*.' She didn't understand, her eyes searched for answers, but it was incomprehensible, even to Priest now. He put it the best way he could.

'I know it's hard to understand, but Dr William Priest *did* kill a lot of people. But they were the lucky ones. The *un*lucky ones killed themselves.'

# Chapter 32

Jessica showered then left, telling him that she would be back later to check on him. He'd better not leave. When his headache had receded enough to enable him to get up without passing out, Priest stumbled through to the kitchen where Tilly sat at the table drawing and Sarah was cooking breakfast.

He sat opposite her. She looked up and grinned, then back down to the page.

'You were poorly again, Uncle Charlie.'

'I'm better now, thanks, Til.'

She looked up again, studied him. 'You don't *look* better.'

Sarah placed a bacon sandwich in front him and a cup of tea. He had never tasted anything so good.

'You're dressed in jeans and an absurd jacket,' she observed.

He looked down, puzzled. 'Yes?'

'Those are your work clothes.'

'It's a work day, isn't it?'

'It's Sunday. And yesterday you became a human firework. You need rest.'

She was about to protest further but then the intercom buzzed. Instinctively, Priest got up, then bent and winced in pain. *Shit!*

Sarah sighed, threw a tea-towel down and marched across to the intercom to answer it. A few minutes later, Rowlinson stood leaning against the wall and Sarah was ushering Tilly out of the door. Apparently, she was going to spend the day playing at a friend's house.

'He's not to go anywhere,' she told Rowlinson on her way out. 'Understand?'

Rowlinson sighed. 'I'll do my best.'

Tilly waved. 'Bye, Uncle Charlie!'

Priest waved back, finished the tea, and waited for the door to shut.

'We need to go and see Elisha Capindale,' said Priest, getting up.

'No way. I just made a promise to your sister—'

'To do your best, a duty which no doubt you will discharge admirably. Now let's go before she comes back.'

Elisha Capindale lived in a manor house nestled in the Cambridgeshire countryside just outside of Ely surrounded by evergreens and black wrought-iron railings. The house was typical Georgian – not grand per se but imposing in its regularity, with white-painted sash windows and grey ashlar stonework. The grounds were modest for the size of the house, hemmed in by clumps of ungovernable trees, the boundary marked with a rotting wooden fence through which Priest could see flashes of an expanse of fields and groves beyond. There were two cars in the driveway: a relatively new-looking Jaguar and a Land Rover Defender, the chassis sprayed in mud.

'Pretty idyllic,' Rowlinson remarked, shutting the door of his BMW behind him.

'If you go in for that sort of thing.'

Priest took a moment to scan the outside. On closer inspection, the windows that had looked so perfectly aligned when they had driven up the gravel driveway looked tired and peeling. The summerhouse hidden under the trees in the far corner looked abandoned, with a smashed window and sparrows nesting in the roof. It was all unloved. The house was dying.

'Do we have a plan here?' asked Rowlinson, joining him.

'Capindale commissioned Owen to get hold of the Book of Janus and provide her with it and his translations. When he refused to hand it over she hired some pretty expensive lawyers to wrestle it back. Now people are turning up dead, and everything leads back to the same book. Let's just keep it simple and find out what she knows.'

He walked the short distance from the car to the front door. Knocked. A few minutes later, the door opened and a face Priest recognised peered out.

'Yes?'

Rowlinson held up his identification. 'DCI Rowlinson, Major Crime Unit. We'd like to speak to Elisha Capindale, please.'

The face at the door winced. 'I'm afraid Ms Capindale doesn't just see people like that without any appointment. Not even police officers.'

Rowlinson was about to protest but Priest cut him off, his recall having matched face with name.

'Mr Vose, isn't it?'

Henrik Vose turned, looked Priest up and down, his brow furrowed. Then bemusement turned into recognition, then into annoyance. 'Mr Priest. The supervising solicitor. What are you doing here?'

'He's helping us with our enquiries,' said Rowlinson. 'I rather hope Ms Capindale can do the same.'

'It's not that simple,' said Vose, rounding on Rowlinson. 'Ms Capindale does not take unsolicited visitors, as I explained. What's this in connection with?'

'It would be simpler if you cooperated, Henrik,' said Priest, trying to placate him.

'I'm not even sure it's appropriate for you to be here, Priest,' Vose returned. 'I will need to inform Ms Capindale's solicitor.'

'You can do that while we're talking to her,' said Rowlinson. He stepped forward, but Vose stood his ground.

'That's not happening.'

'Look, it's either this way or we do it down at the station, Mr – Vose, was it? – up to you.'

'He's serious, Henrik,' Priest added. 'This is important.'

Vose stalled for another minute, hovering uncertainly in the door, mulling it over. Then, begrudgingly, he stood aside and ushered them in.

'Fine. But I will be talking to your superiors about you, DCI Rowlinson, and the court about you, Priest,' he muttered, slamming the door behind him. 'I'll show you through to the study but you will have to wait while I explain to Ms Capindale what's happening.'

Vose opened another door and they were hurried through to a large reception room overlooking the forlorn summer-house. In fact it was less of a study and more like an antique shop; not so much because of the quality of the furnishings but the way they were cluttered around the room. A partially filled bookshelf aching with age, two dining-room tables with chairs stacked irregularly behind them, a Welsh dresser, a hideous blue and white settee. None of it worked together. Everything smelt of damp and old wood.

There was no obvious place to sit, so they stood in the middle of the room watching curiously as Vose hurried round, hauling the floor-to-ceiling curtains across and plunging them into gloom. Then he adjusted a switch on the wall and two chandeliers flickered in to life, but whereas Priest had expected them to offer some useful illumination, the light was nothing more than a dim orange glow.

'Ms Capindale objects to light,' Vose said simply before leaving.

After he had gone, Rowlinson turned to Priest. 'Who the hell objects to light? And why?'

'I don't know.'

Priest began to examine the paintings across the back wall. Much like the furniture, they had been hung with no attempt at pattern although, unlike the furniture, there was at least some connection between them.

'Look at these.' Rowlinson joined him. They were forced to inspect the paintings within reaching distance, such was the poor quality of the light.

'They all show—'

'The deluge,' Priest finished for him. 'The story of Noah's Ark.'

'This one's strange.'

Priest followed Rowlinson's gaze to a small canvas hung lower than the rest. The frame was cracked, made from a wood that was either very fragile or very old, or both, Priest couldn't be sure. On inspection, there was the Ark, he supposed; almost imperceptible against the grey background, nothing more than a shadow streaked across a spectral landscape. And the animals, assembled at the foot of the mountain, crudely depicted as a cluster of dark shapes, their individual features barely discernible, and their bodies and appendages seemingly merging into one. Then, unmistakably out of proportion, three impossibly tall, spindly humanoid figures emerging from the trees, each with a weak blue halo capping a small oval head.

'It is called *The Last Gathering of the Fallen Ones*,' said a voice behind them. They both spun round, startled. The speaker was a figure standing at the door, accompanied by a flustered-looking Henrik Vose. 'Alas, nobody knows who the artist was.'

'Elisha, this is Charles Priest and Detective Chief Inspector Rowlinson,' said Vose. 'As I said, I specifically told them that you would—'

'Thank you, Henrik.' Capindale raised a single hand, and Vose fell silent obediently. 'You've said who they are.'

Elisha Capindale shuffled forward but did not offer her hand. Instead, she appraised her visitors' faces with clinical scrutiny, lingering on each of them for a few seconds as if to commit their features to memory. She was a small woman in her sixties, perhaps early seventies, with pallid skin and straggled hair marbled with grey and white streaks. Her movements were slow and delicate. She picked her way across the room to take harbour in a high-backed armchair. There she sat, with one knee across the other and her hands perfectly aligned on her lap.

'That'll be all, Henrik.' She nodded at Vose, who seemed to take on the role of her butler as well as her representative. When he didn't move, Rowlinson looked across at him.

'That'll be all, *Henrik*,' he said quietly, not bothering to disguise the warning.

Reluctantly, Vose withdrew from the room, his last words aimed at Rowlinson but intended to be for his superior.

'I will be right outside, if you need me.'

'We're sorry for the imposition,' said Priest, after Vose had shut the door behind him.

'No doubt it is important,' she replied.

'It is. We're here about Professor Owen.'

Capindale looked fleetingly at the floor, then back up. 'Henrik said that you were the supervising solicitor who oversaw the execution of my search order.'

'That's right.'

'And what of Owen?'

'I'm afraid he's dead.'

She nodded, as if the news was of little consequence. 'And do you have the Book, safe?'

Rowlinson shifted his weight from one foot to the other, incensed. 'Didn't you hear him? He said Professor Owen is dead.'

She turned to Rowlinson, scornfully. 'There is nothing wrong with my hearing, inspector.'

'Did you already know he was dead?'

'No, but given that he stole one of the most precious and sought-after items in the history of Christian archaeology from me, you'll excuse me if I don't shed many tears. Now, is the Book safe?'

'The Book is safe,' said Priest, watching her reaction carefully. 'The police have it.'

Capindale's eyebrow arched in a wave of concern. Then, turning to Rowlinson. 'Why? Why can't it be returned to me?'

'Because it's in our evidence room with a little tag on it marked *Exhibit A*.'

'The police are treating Professor Owen's death as suspicious,' Priest added, quickly before Capindale had a chance to reply – he could see she was ready to bite back. 'It may also be linked to the Book of Janus.'

Capindale sank back in her seat. A heavy silence lingered as she turned her head, touched her brow and stared wistfully at the curtains rippling in the breeze blown from a fan humming on the desk.

When she didn't respond, Priest took a few steps towards her and dropped his voice. 'Elisha, we know that the Book of Janus tells the story about how a stowaway on Noah's Ark spread the seed of the Giants after the Deluge was over.'

He watched as she turned her head slowly so their eyes met, surprised. She reached for the silver cross that hung from her neck. 'Did *he* tell you that?'

'Yes.' She looked away in disgust. 'Why is it such a secret?'

'Why do you think?'

'Does the Book explain how to identify the descendants of the Giants?'

'Yes, of course it does.'

Priest winced. *That's not what Owen had said.*

'Do you know how?'

'No. I don't have the Book. You do.'

'But you know the story,' said Rowlinson, arms crossed and impatient. 'What was your interest in the damn thing anyway?'

Capindale flinched, like she had been slapped, then made the sign of the cross over her chest. 'Forgive them, Lord,' she whispered. 'Please – inspector, whatever-your-name-is, I do not expect you to understand these things. But there are people who would stop at nothing to uncover the secrets of the Book.

It must be returned to me, quickly. Only I can keep it safe.' With that, Capindale got to her feet. She was unsteady, having to use the arms of the chair for support. Priest moved to help her but she shrugged the gesture away. 'I'm fine. I don't need help.'

'I'm sorry,' said Priest. 'But we need your help, Elisha. You're the only one who seems to understand anything about the Book.'

'Then bring it to me – that's how I can help. That way, we can avoid any more bloodshed.'

Priest met her eyes. They were cloudy with age, but resolute: he could see that her body was failing but her mind was as sharp as his. 'I fear it might be too late for that.'

There was a moment's pause before she looked away, her face contorted with anger and regret.

'Then God help us all, Mr Priest. God help us all.'

# Chapter 33

After Priest had pressed Elisha Capindale further about her knowledge of the Book, the encounter had descended into something resembling a farce as their mysterious host had refused to answer any further questions, clutching her chest and spluttering something about not being able to breathe. Vose had intervened and, despite Rowlinson's protestations, Priest had led him away; they weren't going to get any further, not without a warrant or some grounds to charge one or the other. On their way out, Vose had asked for Rowlinson's senior officer's details and promised that a robust complaint would be lodged.

In the car, exceeding the speed limit on the country roads out of Ely, Rowlinson was pensive.

'What now?'

'He's going to kill again, soon,' replied Priest. His heart was heavy; they were sinking fast. They were running out of time if the killer's pattern so far continued. There would be another Alan Burberry any day now. 'If we can understand how the Book of Janus identifies the victims, we can maybe anticipate his plan.'

'Maybe it doesn't. Maybe it's all bullshit. A cover, and this guy is just another Gacy or Bundy, killing for the sheer hell of it.'

'Why bother with the symbol, if that's the case?'

'Same reason Zodiac wrote those letters to the police. Because it's a game to him, and he's enjoying watching us flounder around after him.'

Priest tipped his head to one side. Rowlinson had a point. He had been convinced that the killer had a plan, but he was looking for the tiny glimmer of logic – the semblance of reasoning, albeit perverse reasoning – in a sea of bloody chaos.

*Maybe the killer was just another fucked-up psychopath.*

*But that hadn't necessarily been the case with William, had it?*

His thoughts were interrupted by the buzz of his phone.

'Hello?'

'Charlie?'

'Georgie.'

She sounded concerned. 'Are you OK? Vincent said you were in an accident or something?'

*If you call getting blown up by a remotely-detonated bomb an accident . . .* 'Yeah, I'm fine. Nothing to worry about.'

'OK.' She didn't sound convinced but was apparently willing to overlook it. 'Listen, I managed to track down the company that made the microclimate case for the Book of Janus. It was custom-made in Italy, a factory near Florence. The Book sits inside a matrix of inert, conservation-grade materials, which sits inside an aluminium case. The document is bedded in a product called PROSorb, a silica gel that helps stabilise the humidity. The outer shell, the case, is then sealed, made fireproof and a special glass is used for the display that stops all UV light getting through.'

'Why are you telling me this?'

'Just listen. Inside the case are a series of environmental monitor sensors; they're checking the temperature, humidity and light constantly and making tiny adjustments where there are changes, what they call a fade event. But here's the key: the sensors transmit data via an internet link to a host so you can monitor the status of the container remotely.'

Priest waited a beat, realising the potential.

'So we can hack it.'

'And track where it's been.'

Priest exhaled, he felt a flutter of excitement; but it was a long shot. A trail of breadcrumbs that might lead them to the person who sold the Book to Owen. There was no guarantee they could hack the system and no guarantee there would be any trace of the historical metadata. But if anyone could then . . .

'Georgie, meet me at my house in a couple of hours, and bring Solly with you.'

'Sure – it's Sunday so he'll probably be at home painting. I'll go round now.'

Priest frowned. 'Solly paints?'

'Haven't you seen the portraits he's done of you?'

He guessed by the laugh in her voice that she was joking. At least, *hoped* she was joking. 'No, and I'm not sure I ever want to.'

'I'll get him to send you a copy. See you shortly.'

Priest rang off, quickly explained to Rowlinson, who nodded, pressing his foot down on the accelerator and threw the BMW round a narrow corner. Now they had some purpose.

Georgie was out of breath. Charlie's penthouse was on the twenty-first floor and they had taken the stairs; Solly had refused to use the lift. The only slight compensation was that Solly was apparently less fit than she was.

'Are we almost there?' he panted, using the banister to haul himself up to the next landing.

'Fifteen. Another six flights. Remind me why we didn't use the lift?'

'Lift buttons have forty times more germs than public toilet seats. There are three hundred and thirteen colony-forming units of bacteria per square centimetre on a lift button.'

'But *I* would have pressed the button. All you had to do was stand there.'

'You're missing the point, Georgie.'

Exasperated, Georgie decided to abandon the argument and put her energy into not passing out. They rested on the nineteenth for a few moments before slumping up the final flights to the top. Georgie hit the intercom but couldn't manage to say anything. When Charlie opened the door, she half fell in to the apartment, grasping at a side table for support. Behind her, Solly was bent over, wheezing.

'What the hell have you two been doing?' said Charlie, dismayed.

Georgie felt her cheeks flush at the insinuation. 'We weren't allowed to take the lift.'

Charlie looked over her shoulder at Solly, who was taking deep, laboured breaths. 'Was it the colony-forming units again?'

Georgie nodded. Charlie motioned for her to take a seat at the breakfast bar while Solly went about the business of producing a packet of antiseptic wipes and scrubbing his hands in the sink. While she waited, she took in the bruises and scrapes on Charlie's hands, the cuts on his neck and temple.

'What was your accident again?' she asked.

He waved her away, like it was nothing. 'A Zumba related incident.'

After some further discourse about the cleanliness of the floorboards, Charlie eventually managed to coax Solly away from the sink, on the promise that he could sit in a chair that had been specially covered in clingfilm straight from the box. Georgie watched as the accountant shuddered when he looked around and wondered how debilitating it was to live with such restriction, how difficult even the simplest things must be, like walking into someone else's home.

'Fine,' said Solly, at last. 'Let's get on with it then, Priest.'

Georgie followed Charlie and Solly through to the office where Rowlinson was already waiting for them. The latter proffered his hand, which Solly looked at suspiciously but didn't shake.

'I'm afraid—'

Charlie intervened, hastily taking Rowlinson to one side. 'Don't take it personally, Tiff. But he won't shake your hand.'

For a moment, Rowlinson looked as though he might protest but thought better of it. Seemingly unconcerned, Solly perched himself at the end of the clingfilm-covered chair and opened a laptop on his knee. Everyone else stood around the microclimate case, which took up much of Charlie's desk.

'Is this going to work?' Rowlinson asked softly.

Charlie replied, mimicking Rowlinson's whisper. 'If a group of people in Finland can use a Remote Access Tool to hack a fish tank connected to the internet in a North American casino, we've got a pretty good chance of Solly hacking a box in the same room. The question is whether any of the data will actually tell us anything.'

'That actually happened?'

'In 2017,' said Georgie, remembering the case. 'The tank had its own VPN, so it wasn't connected to the casino's usual security tools. The sensors checked things like the temperature of the tank, just like the sensors inside the case here.'

'VPN?'

'Virtual private network. Like an intranet—'

Georgie was cut off when Solly mumbled, 'That's what happens when you connect everything to the internet, I'm afraid. Someone can hack it. Much like this box. Anyway, I'm in.'

There was a few moments' silence, interspersed only by Solly tapping on the keys. Then, with the gusto of a conductor bringing the orchestra to a crescendo, Solly hit the last few keys and looked up, evidently pleased.

'I have three IP addresses where the data was sent, all at different times. One here in London, one just outside of Florence and one in Geneva.'

'In English . . .' said Rowlinson.

Georgie replied before Solly could, anticipating that his explanation would just add further confusion. 'It's a unique label for the individual device that received the data, which might help us work out who has had access to the Book. The address in London is probably Professor Owen's, the Florence address is most likely the company that made the box running some tests, which leaves the address in Geneva.'

'Which was the second recipient of data over a long period of time by the look of it,' Solly added.

Charlie exhaled. 'Norman said that he had got the Book from a Swiss dealer.'

'Can we work out who it is from his IP address?' asked Rowlinson.

'No. An IP address will give you a rough location, but that's it. Even that can be hundreds of miles off.'

'So, we're no further on?'

'Not quite. As I say, *we* can't get a name. But *you* can. You can apply for a warrant to force the ISP to give us the details.'

Rowlinson growled. 'I'll have to get someone from the CPS in front of a magistrate tomorrow morning. This will take time.'

'We don't have time,' said Charlie. 'But it'll have to do. I'll fly out to Geneva in the morning. Hopefully by the time I get there you'll have a name and address for me.'

Rowlinson shook his head. 'No. I'll arrange for one of my team to fly out.' He looked at Priest meaningfully. 'This is a Met investigation, Priest.'

Georgie thought for a moment that Charlie might protest but instead he nodded. To anyone else, it might have seemed like a concession, but she knew better.

'OK.' Charlie smiled. 'You're the boss, Tiff. How can *I* help?'

'You can speak to the symbol guy. What was his name?'

'Isaac O'Brien,' Georgie said, cringing when she thought about the strange way Li's university friend had looked at her the last time they had met.

'Yes, him. See if he can do any better with a prompt, now we know that the symbol is connected to a Dead Sea Scroll text.'

Charlie nodded, but Georgie could see that he was itching to leave. He tossed the apartment keys to a slightly bemused Rowlinson.

'Lock up for me, Tiff,' he said. 'Let's go, Someday.'

They were on their way out when Rowlinson called after them. 'Priest, *the symbol guy*. Right?'

Charlie didn't say anything but saluted in a less than reassuring way. As they left, he could hear Solly explain to Rowlinson that he would have to disinfect the door handle before he could leave.

# Chapter 34

*Monday*

Priest stood in line at the check-in desk scanning his phone for messages. Nothing from Rowlinson about the IP address in Geneva, but several calls from an unknown number he'd missed and two emails from Sasha Merriweather that he decided to ignore. The gist of it was that she had been told about his visit to Elisha Capindale and she wanted to discuss the 'obvious conflict that now arose'. The calls were probably her as well.

Ahead of him, he could see Fay Westbrook sliding her passport across the check-in desk and fumbling around for her ticket. She looked different dressed in a pair of skinny jeans and Converse trainers, her ankles showing and the intriguing tail end of a tattoo disappearing up her leg. He wasn't sure what it was but it might have been an elaborately designed cross.

He could have announced himself when he first got to the airport but he needed to get through security first. There was less chance of her calling Rowlinson and using her authority to prevent him from boarding the plane that way.

She was eventually passed back her documents and they all shuffled forward. By the time he had checked in and made it through security he had lost track of her. Not that it mattered. He could do what he needed to do in Geneva with or without her.

He bought a takeaway cup of tea and took a seat in the departure lounge near the window. The early start had been disagreeable and the reminiscence of sleep was still crusted around his eyes. Yet, he was alert. It was exhausting, constantly calculating every possibility. Going over the same questions again and again. DPD was a series of irreconcilable paradoxes. During the times when he felt nothing, the lack of feeling in itself made him immeasurably sad. At the times when he couldn't sleep, and tumbled out of bed bleary-eyed and dopey, he was hyper-alert. His heart pounded in his chest. He could feel every organ in his body expand and contract. He felt the blood pumping in his temples, and behind his eyes. He self-ruminated obsessively, but he didn't care about himself.

It was all . . .

'I take it you're not about to go on holiday.'

Priest shook himself out of the daydream and turned. She was standing behind him, a small bag over her shoulder and a cup of hot liquid matching his in her hand.

'Hi, Fay.'

'I let the DCI know I spotted you coming through security.'

'I really fancied a break, and Switzerland has always been—'

She cut him off irritably. 'He's been ringing you.'

She nodded to his jacket where she must have realised his phone was buried. Priest dutifully retrieved it and feigned surprise.

'Gosh. Four missed calls.'

She rolled her eyes. 'Seriously?'

He put one arm out across the seats, yawned. 'I can help you.'

'I don't need your help.'

'Then you can help *me* instead.'

She looked around, sighed. As if she was checking whether anyone was watching them. 'I don't have to let you tag along, you know. I'm a police officer.'

Priest held up his hands. 'Fay, look, why don't we—'

She didn't let him finish but, to his relief, walked off, calling back over her shoulder, 'Just don't get in my way, Priest. This is *our* investigation that you're helping out on. Remember who's in charge here.'

He bit his tongue and watched her leave. Half an hour later, they called his flight.

They touched down in Geneva airport just after nine local time and fought their way through the crowds to the exit. Outside, he waited patiently while Fay took a call. He respected her space and found an interest in examining the various film posters plastered to the side of the shelter until she eventually came over and handed him the phone without saying a word. He knew who it was.

Priest cleared his throat. 'Good morning, Tiff.'

'Don't even start. I had a whole speech worked out; something about responsibility and police procedure but – know what? – it'd be wasted on you.'

He felt more than a twang of guilt. He'd have preferred to hear the speech and take his punishment than that. He considered apologising but it would just come out insincere, and he was keen to ensure that Fay didn't get into trouble.

'I just want you to know that your detective sergeant was *very* insistent that I don't come here, but—'

'Will you please shut up and listen? I'm going to tell you what I told Fay, in the vague hope that you can break the habit of a lifetime and work as part of a team. You're going to try to find one Luca Caspari.' He read out the address. 'He's an art dealer – not big time but we've got some information. I'll send it through to Fay shortly. Had some notoriety for the wrong reasons in the nineties when he was sued by some viscount or other in Romania for undervaluing his collection. Looks like his specialism is Christian artwork – a Dead Sea Scroll text doesn't totally fit with what he does but it's not completely out of line either.'

'OK, thanks. We'll take a look and let you know.'

He looked up. Fay was climbing into the back of a taxi. He hurried over.

'We'll check in with you when we can.'

'You better—'

Priest cut him off as Fay, eyes squinting into the sun, shouted over at him. 'You coming or what?'

After Fay gave the driver the address, they didn't speak, except when she uttered one quiet sentence after about ten minutes.

'I meant what I said, Priest. Don't get in my way.'

He didn't need to respond. The brief eye contact they made was enough.

Half an hour later, the taxi driver pulled up opposite a narrow street and announced that they had arrived.

Luca Caspari lived in Carouge, a place built as a town in its own right. It was later swallowed up by the capital, but in jurisdiction only. With its busy markets and Mediterranean architecture it could easily have been an Italian town, rich in colour and noise with artisanal shops and chic bars, the collision of old and new.

A little higher than the old town, Caspari's house was a white-washed mid-terrace with venetian windows on a pedestrianised street underneath bunting strung from building to building. The din of the old town market drifted on the breeze as Priest tipped the taxi driver and they walked down to Caspari's house.

'Does he work from home?' said Fay. 'It's a weekday.'

Priest rapped on the door. 'Let's find out.'

They waited. Nothing. Priest knocked again, louder this time. It was disappointing but not the end of the road for them. He'd camp outside all day until Caspari came home if he had to. *Hope he's still in Geneva.*

When he knocked for a third time and shouted Caspari's name, he felt Fay touch his arm. 'Priest.' When he turned, she was pointing to a woman in her sixties, round-faced and homely, leaning out of a window of the property next door. She was shouting something in German, not a language he was pro-ficient in, so he tried his luck and replied in French. The woman stopped, surprised, but spoke back, also in French.

'Are you police?'

He frowned, it seemed a strange question. Neither of them were dressed formally. 'We're looking for Luca. Have you seen him recently?'

'Are you police?'

'No. Old friends, from England. We've got some business with Luca. About a collection in London.' It seemed a plausible cover but the old woman wasn't impressed. With a huff, she told them to wait there. In a second, she was gone and the window was slammed shut.

'Good work,' said Fay, dryly. 'Building bridges.'

'She'll be back.'

It turned out to be an accurate prediction as the neighbour's door was flung open and the woman stomped out, wiping her hands on her apron.

'I take it you're not *close* friends,' the woman muttered, this time in English.

Priest hesitated. 'We've not spoken in a while, but we were in Geneva and wanted to look him up.' *How does she know we're not close friends?* He tried to work out what he'd said wrong but in the end the answer presented itself when the woman folded her arms and looked down sadly.

'Well, I'm sorry to be the one to tell you, but Luca Caspari has been missing for days. And after last night you certainly won't be doing any business with him.'

Priest felt something give in his chest, a sinking feeling as another lead started to dissipate in front of his eyes. 'What happened last night?'

'It was low tide. They pulled his body out of the river just before sunset. He'd been shot in the head.'

# Chapter 35

Georgie hesitated before knocking. The main halls of UCL had been easy enough to navigate, with the chatter and laughter of the crowds of students to keep her safe. But the corridor outside Isaac O'Brien's office was deserted and the halls had nothing but a distant hum bleeding through the walls. Even the lighting was dimmer here.

She had considered asking Li to accompany her; O'Brien was after all *her* contact, but a part of her couldn't summon up the courage to ask. And another part wanted to test herself. See how far she had come. It had been two and a half years since her ordeal with Martin – the man who had raped her – and Georgie had climbed a long, steep ladder to leave it behind. She had taken control of her life, re-established her confidence and found a new outlet through her work that helped her to move on. Not that the incident had been forgotten, it never would. But it didn't define her, it didn't weaken her, it made her stronger. Like everything that had happened to her since – she had been kidnapped and held captive by a neo-Nazi cult and threatened with torture. That was an evil that overreached Martin a hundred times over. And last year a woman mistaking her for a love rival had tried to kill her with one of Charlie's lionfish, knowing she was allergic to its venomous sting. All the more reason why she was infuriated at her shaking hand hovering over the door. Sure, her trust in men was fragile but what was knocking on a door compared to all of that?

*It's ridiculous.*

She jumped back, off-guard. O'Brien had chosen that moment to leave his office and now he was staring at her, irritated and confused.

'How long have you been there?' he demanded.

'Sorry – I was just about to knock.'

'Well, if . . . wait, you're the girl from the other day. You were with Li and that rude man.'

That was as good a description of Charlie as any, and O'Brien's attitude cooled on recognising her – although she rather preferred him irritable.

'That's right. I just wanted to ask you a few more questions about the symbol we found. We can link it to one of the Dead Sea Scrolls. Knowing that might help.'

O'Brien glanced up and down the corridor, although for what reason Georgie couldn't be sure, then nodded, smiling.

'A Dead Sea Scroll, you say?'

Georgie explained briefly what they knew – the symbol had been found on a Judeo-Christian text which originally formed part of the Dead Sea Scroll hoard but which had been lost for centuries until recently. The text told the story of how a stowaway on Noah's Ark – a man named Janus – had ensured that the seed of the Watchers had survived the deluge.

'And now there are people who want to destroy the Carriers,' O'Brien completed.

Georgie stopped, surprised. 'Yes. That's right. If by Carriers you mean . . .'

'That is what the Book of Janus calls them. The people who carry demon DNA are Carriers.'

'You've read it?'

'No. But I am aware of the story – I had no idea that this was the symbol of the Book of Janus, though. I can see it makes sense.'

Georgie felt a surge of excitement. 'Do you know how the Carriers can be identified?'

O'Brien screwed up his face. 'You mean, if they were real?'

'Yes, if they were real, how could they be identified?'

O'Brien studied Georgie for a moment. She stood uneasily in the soft light of the corridor, conscious of his scrutiny of her. She didn't like it. There was something cold about the way he looked at her through a pair of eyes that were so dark it was as if they had no corneas at all. It was dehumanised, like the way a dog looks at meat.

'Come with me,' he said, breezing past her and marching away. Realising she had little alternative, Georgie followed. Just before they reached the hall, he ducked through a small door and into the warm glow of a Baronial chamber full of oil paintings and sculptures.

'This is where we keep the things that aren't on display,' he explained. 'The Waiting Room, we call it.'

O'Brien was moving at a determined pace and Georgie was half running to keep up. 'You said that the symbol made sense. Why?'

He called back over his shoulder. 'The snake is a much-confused symbol in Christianity but it would be wrong to associate it with evil, despite the snake in the Garden of Eden. People were worshipping snakes some seventy thousand years before

Christ died on the cross. They were seen as a symbol of fertility and healing.'

'Because the snake can shed its skin?'

'That's right. It can cleanse itself like no other animal. The Mesopotamians thought snakes were immortal, although snake cults were particularly prevalent in the Bronze Age. But in the Hebrew Bible snakes have contradictory symbolism.'

'The snake of the Garden of Eden being evil—'

'Or possibly the Devil himself, but the other story is interesting.' O'Brien pushed open a set of double doors and they descended a flight of stairs. At the end of another winding corridor they pushed through a door and walked into a wall of light and air.

'The library,' said Georgie, looking around.

'A short-cut. Now, follow me.'

O'Brien took the stairs and they headed to the first floor and into a row of books which he started scanning.

'You were saying about another snake story in the Bible,' she prompted.

'Yes. When the Israelites fled Egypt, the Book of Numbers tells us that God sent a plague of fiery serpents to torment them in response to their whining and complaining. Moses was instructed to erect a bronze serpent on a staff which was used to heal those who looked upon it, thus reinforcing the cleansing symbolism of the snake.'

Something Georgie had read a long time ago flickered into life at the back of her mind. 'The Brazen Serpent.'

'That's right. Although there are numerous older examples of snakes symbolising healing. The Rod of Asclepius, for example, is a snake entwined around a staff that represented the Greek

God of healing and medicinal arts. Not to be confused with the caduceus, which is a staff adorned with two snakes and has been the symbol of the US Army Medical Corps since the turn of the twentieth century.'

'Are there any examples of serpents wrapped around Latin crosses, rather than staffs?'

O'Brien seemed to have found what he was looking for: a tatty composition of paper that could hardly be called a book – it was more like a very old pamphlet, with dog-eared corners and faded print. Georgie didn't catch the title.

'There is one,' O'Brien replied, taking the book to a desk and leafing through the fragile pages. 'The World Federation of the Catholic Medical Associations have adopted a logo that features a snake and a cross but that is, I think, a red herring. Ah, here.'

O'Brien pointed triumphantly to a small passage at the bottom of a page showing a picture of a creature Georgie assumed to be an ancient depiction of a demon; a crude drawing, maybe even an etching, of a bearded fawn-like beast with hoofed legs, wings, horns and an erect penis.

'This is Samyaza,' O'Brien murmured. 'Leader of the Watchers.'

Georgie knew the myth. 'The Angels that defied God and fornicated with human women.'

He simpered, and Georgie was suddenly conscious of how close together they were standing. 'Who can blame them, eh?' She moved to the side as subtly as she could. O'Brien's intensity and the swift march through the university had quickened her heartrate and brought a flush of blood to her cheeks. She checked behind them – nothing but rows of books. She breathed in heavily, wondered why he had led her to the library. Hoped that it hadn't got anything to do with the fact that it was so early and the building was alarmingly empty.

'Look here.' O'Brien drew her attention to the short text underneath the picture. He smelt of stale cigarettes and body odour. 'This references the existence of the Carriers, the offspring of Samyaza and his kin; and a prophecy, here.'

She read aloud where he pointed. '*One day a man of worth will come to destroy the Carriers and purge the world of evil. Thence, the man shall stand on the left hand of God to herald a new age and welcome the Christ to Earth once more, and this event shall be called* the Binding.'

Georgie looked up. 'The Binding?'

'I remember reading an article a long time ago about the possibility of the existence of the Book of Janus and its connection to the Binding. It was ridiculous – an alternative ending to the Bible.'

'The Second Coming,' she said, taking another step away. 'Isn't that what Revelations prophesied?'

'In a sense, but the Book of Revelation is concerned with the day of Judgement, when the Beast and the False Prophet are cast into the Lake of Fire and the Dragon, or Satan, is imprisoned for a thousand years, only to rise again and wage war in the holy city against the people of God. The dragon is defeated and what follows is the end of days, and the beginning of a new, glorious heaven in which there is no more suffering and death.'

As he spoke, O'Brien seemed to drift off for periods of time, but whether that was how he recalled things or for some other mysterious reason, she couldn't tell. But it did nothing to rescind her disquiet.

'And the alternative version?'

He turned the page. 'This is the only reference I am aware of in existence, except the Book of Janus itself.'

Georgie scanned down. There was a line of text at the top.

She read: '*And the man shall slay the Carriers and the rivers and streams shall run silver with their blood, and the old Earth shall dwindle and be replaced, not by heaven, but by the Age of Man.*'

She looked further down. *That's it?* Thereafter, the book changed topic capriciously to the legend of Spring-Heeled Jack. She quickly took photographs of the two key pages on her phone, and handed the book back. He took it, and she managed to avoid his clumsy attempt to make contact with her hand. Georgie took another step away, he was looking at her again with those lifeless eyes.

'In the Binding, the defeat of evil does not mean the judgement of the wicked and an eternal reign of man in a new kingdom free from death and with the forgiveness of sin. It means the destruction of the Carriers will avoid Judgement Day altogether, or at least postpone it, indefinitely.'

'The Age of Man?' she asked, timidly.

'We can avoid Judgement if the Carriers are destroyed.'

Georgie checked over her shoulder – her stomach lurched. They were alone. O'Brien was holding the book, grinning at her.

'It's all nonsense, of course,' he said casually. 'Just another fairy tale.' When she didn't reply, he looked surprised. 'You don't believe, do you? You're not religious?'

She was agnostic but not intent on sharing her intimate views right now, or ever, with Isaac O'Brien, so she settled for ambiguity. 'Maybe.'

'I hope I haven't offended you.'

'Not at all. And thanks, that's been really helpful.' She was processing what she had just read – *the rivers and streams shall run silver with their blood* – and urgently calculating her extraction. 'I must go. Thanks again.' She turned with a mixture of anxiety – *must get out* – and excitement: *silver with their blood, the Carriers have silver blood.*

'Georgie, wait.' She froze, turned back. 'That is your name, isn't it? Georgie.' She nodded. He took a few paces forward, licked his lips. 'Look, we can talk about this more, perhaps over a drink. What do you say?'

'That's kind, but I have to get back, let Charlie know all this. It's been really useful.'

'Useful for what, I wonder?'

'Oh,' she stammered. 'You know . . .'

Whether he stumbled or lunged forward, Georgie wasn't sure, but all of a sudden he had hold of her arm and the sense of alarm rang thunderously in her ears and roared through her chest. 'Just a drink, Georgie. After all, I've helped you out here.'

She didn't struggle: O'Brien wasn't big or well-built but he had a vice-like grip and she knew he could easily overpower her if he wanted to. She started rapidly filtering through the judo moves she had learnt but her mind was a blur and she couldn't focus. 'Please let me go, Isaac.'

'I think it's only fair, don't you? *Quid pro quo?*'

Her heart beating fast, Georgie remembered what her judo instructor Andy had taught her. She swung her arm in a loop and pushed forward. O'Brien released his grip instantly and, with a small yelp, fell forward against the bookshelves.

Georgie relaxed. It had been so easy, and O'Brien's shock was almost comical as he wheeled around off-balance, groping for the bookshelf for support.

'Sorry,' she said. 'I don't like people touching me.'

She waited a beat to see if O'Brien might retaliate, but he raised his hands in surrender.

'No,' he stammered. 'I'm sorry.'

As he staggered away, Georgie smiled inwardly.

# Chapter 36

Priest had to give John Eaton his due. When Fay had phoned in to update Rowlinson, who had in turn alerted his senior officer of the situation, the DSI had arranged for them to meet with the Swiss Police SIO, Detective Kim Rising, in less than an hour at Priest's hotel. When she arrived, Rising turned out to be a small, wiry woman of indeterminate age – somewhere between forty and sixty, a quandary not assisted by the contradiction of her smooth skin and old-fashioned cropped hair and shoulder-padded suit.

'DS Westbrook, I assume,' she said, extending her hand and smiling with non-committal ambiguity. 'And you must be Mr Priest, the consultant detective.'

It was as grand a description as Priest had ever heard and one that Eaton had presumably used to avoid any questions over his jurisdiction. He noticed Fay flinch at the label; fortunately, Rising hadn't.

'Thank you for meeting with us, Detective Rising,' said Fay, taking her hand.

'It's appreciated,' said Priest.

Rising motioned for them to sit. Ordered three coffees from the nearest waiter without asking for their preference. 'You two have come a long way to talk to a dead man.' Her English was so perfect it was almost accentless, and Priest felt relieved he didn't have to struggle through another conversation in rusty French.

'We wanted to speak to Mr Caspari in connection with a murder investigation in London,' Fay explained. Priest sat back, happy for her to take the lead. It gave him a better chance to size Rising up, gauge how cooperative or otherwise she might be.

Rising looked down her nose at Fay through a pair of round Harry Potter glasses. 'Is he a suspect?'

'A person of interest.'

'Uh-huh. Well, your commanding officer was very keen for us to be transparent so here is what we know so far. Luca Caspari was divorced, he lived alone in a house in Carouge. He was an art dealer, or at least he thought of himself as an art dealer. His income looks like he was mainly relying on a pension. We can't see that he made any real money from dealing in the last few years, save for one transaction three months ago to an unknown collector in London. I don't know whether you can help us with that?'

'I'm sure we can,' said Priest, avoiding Fay's glare.

'Good. So, three nights ago Luca went missing. We know that because he had a doctor's appointment the following morning he failed to attend, which is highly unusual. His family are in Zurich but he doesn't have much to do with them. Two estranged sons and a sister he visits occasionally. His ex-wife didn't really say anything when we told her. He doesn't have much by way of inheritance to offer. The house was rented. We're having the contents valued, of course, although nothing has surfaced as interesting. A lot of it is fake. Despite the apparent embitterment, the two sons are the beneficiaries.

Both were in Zurich the whole time – they have photographs and friends to prove it.'

'No obvious motive then,' Priest offered.

'None. Luca was neither liked nor disliked by the people he networked with. Just a speck of dust on a large canvas, was how one colleague described him.'

'What about some trouble he had with a viscount in Romania?' asked Fay.

Rising waved it away. Waited while the waiter placed coffees in front of them. No milk. Priest didn't intend to touch it. 'Water under the bridge, by all accounts. The litigation was settled, the viscount had his pound of flesh.'

'You said Luca was shot,' said Fay.

'In the head, twice, with a Smith and Wesson revolver.'

'What model?' asked Priest.

'Ballistics say a six-four-two.'

He noticed Fay watching him out of the corner of her eye, but he didn't react. The six-four-two was a lightweight pocket revolver with a five-round chamber and no good over distance. It was cheap – you could probably pick one up for a few hundred pounds – and easy to use, if you were more or less right next to the target. Easy to carry and conceal but not exactly a professional assassin's first choice.

'When was he last seen and by whom?' asked Fay.

'The neighbour, on Wednesday afternoon, says he was in his backyard smoking, probably pot.'

'How did you know to check the river?'

Rising smiled sadly. 'He didn't sink. There's a jetty, near Hans Wilsdorf Bridge. Looks like the killer managed the murder quite successfully but tried to dump the body in the Arve at night and didn't realise Luca's jacket was snagged on a tree root. He probably just watched the body sink but didn't realise it was only just below the surface.'

Priest realised that that was what Luca's neighbour had meant by the body being found at low tide. Most bodies sink initially because the water runs into the lungs and displaces the air, only to re-emerge later when, during decomposition, the bacteria inside the body starts to eat up the protein and fat to create gas, lifting the body to the surface. Here, there was no need. Luca never made it to the bottom.

'So when the river tide receded, the body was just left hanging there,' he finished.

'Some children found it,' said Rising, shaking her head. 'It's every child's dream to find a dead body, until they actually do.'

# Chapter 37

Detective Rising had promised to let them know if the post-mortem of Luca Caspari threw up anything of interest. She had taken both of their mobile numbers and left them to pay for the coffees that neither of them had wanted. Priest had already resigned himself to at least one night in Geneva and there seemed little else to do but pass the time with a bottle of cheap Swiss lager and a cache of emails to examine on his phone. He deleted the one from Sasha Merriweather without even reading it.

While he sat back in the hotel foyer, Fay Westbrook was restlessly pacing the floor, checking her phone every few minutes and looking out wistfully through the window to the river beyond. She seemed indecisive: she must realise they could be waiting the rest of the day and it was barely mid-afternoon. On the one hand, Priest suspected she would have preferred to amble back to her own hotel and open up a bottle of Prosecco all to herself, but she was anchored to him and this hotel. After all, what if Rising called *him* and not her. Priest might have worried about exactly the opposite scenario but something told him, by the way Rising had written the numbers down, that his was first on her list. Maybe it was that she sensed Priest was more in control, perhaps it was as simple as she had taken a disliking to Fay – easy to see how – but either way he was confident that the DS needed him more than he needed her.

'Why don't you sit down?' he asked when the pacing was just starting to get on the wrong side of annoying.

'We can't just sit here. There must be something we can do.'

Priest slugged back the beer and put the bottle on the table, empty. He nodded at the waiter, who scuttled off to get him another one.

'What would you suggest? Charge in and see if we can conduct the PM ourselves?'

She snorted, turned away and stood at the window. The waiter placed another beer in his hand. He examined it, didn't recognise the brand, but it was sweet-flavoured, and the alcohol was already starting to make him feel more relaxed. Charlie Priest's relationship with intoxicants was complicated: months of sobriety without even a thought for the bottle, then bingeing, even sneaking wine in a hip flask to the office, then back to cold-light-of-day abstinence again. A love-hate circle that rotated endlessly.

'I spoke to Tiff,' she said, turning back around.

'What did he say?'

'Stay put. Wait for Rising to ring us. They've not made much progress back in London. This is the best lead we have.'

'Best not waste our chance by overcooking it then.'

She waited a beat, then kicked a chair in frustration. The waiter looked over at him, one eyebrow arched. Priest held up his hands apologetically, and he went back to cleaning the bar top.

'Sit down, Fay,' he said, and there was just enough warning in his voice to force a reaction. She slumped in the chair opposite him. 'Drink?'

'Beer. Like yours.'

Priest looked over and the barman nodded, already reaching for the fridge.

'They never tell you about this part of the job, do they?' he said.

'Which part?'

'The endless waiting.' She looked down, and he knew she could see they had no choice. 'There's no champagne-popping moments in a criminal investigation, like there is in films. Just a myriad false hopes, dashed expectations, dead-ends and mountains of paperwork.'

She looked at him strangely, her features softened, some of the animosity had ebbed away. 'Is that why you left? Not enough champagne?'

'There's a little of that but being a lawyer is much the same but without the car chases and shoot-outs.' *Jesus, she actually managed a smile.* 'I left because I'd come to the end of that part of my life. Occasionally, I like to reinvent myself as someone else.'

When the waiter brought the beer over, she drank the bottle as good as any university student in one go before slamming it empty back down on the table. Priest raised an eyebrow.

'Thirsty?'

She wiped her mouth, crossed her legs. 'Another would be good.'

He waved at the waiter. He wanted to ask her something personal but he wasn't sure what. It just seemed like the right moment. The silence that followed was interrupted by the buzz of his phone. Glancing down, he saw that it was Georgie.

'Good afternoon.'

'Hi, Charlie, is that you?'

'Yes. Were you expecting someone else?'

'I spoke to Professor O'Brien, like you said, about the symbol.'

'Good. What happened?'

Fay leant forward, craning to hear but he knew she couldn't. He mouthed at her that it wasn't Rising. He could have left it until the end of the conversation. Pleasingly, the gesture was taken as a sign of peace, and she sat back, cradling the second bottle of beer. He sensed a truce had been reached, for now.

'I think I've definitely got a sexual harassment claim against him but the parts of it where he wasn't hitting on me were very useful.'

'I'm sorry to hear that. Remind me to pay him a visit when I get back.'

'Don't worry, it's sorted. Now, he took me to a crappy book in the library which contains a brief reference to the Book of Janus. I'm sending images to your phone.'

He lowered the phone to check the incoming pictures, put her on loudspeaker for Fay's benefit. Another sign of peace. She put the bottle down and moved round to sit next to him, leaning in to hear.

'The book talks about something called *the Binding*, an alternative ending to the Bible in which man defeats evil by destroying the offspring of Samyaza and the other fallen angels – the Carriers – whereupon Judgement Day is avoided. One man is chosen by God to hunt and eliminate the Carriers. This man will, in the end, sit on the left hand of God.'

'That's what our killer thinks he's doing? Steering us away from the Apocalypse?'

'I think so, yes.'

'Bloody considerate of him.'

'There's more. There's a reference in the book to the Carriers having *silver blood*.'

'Sounds like a shitty Biblical thing.'

'That's what I thought at first but all words are subject to interpretation. The blood type Lutheran b negative, which is very unusual anyway, can be combined with O negative to create an exceptionally rare blood type. I checked online. This is all freely available information. The kernel of it is that this blood type has a slight silver tinge to it, meaning that it is often referred to in medical circles as "silver blood".'

Priest let it sink in. 'Shit.'

'That can't be how he's picking the victims,' Fay whispered.

'Thanks, Georgie,' said Priest. 'That's good work. We need to find out what blood types the victims were.' It seemed an outside shot, but it was possible.

'Surely that would have turned up on the PM report?'

'Blood type isn't part of the standard report, and there wouldn't be any reason to check it specifically unless someone asked. That still the case?' He turned to Fay, and she nodded.

'I'll check.'

She left with her phone in her hand, headed to her spot by the window with her back to them.

'We're chasing a lead here in Geneva,' Priest explained. 'Luca Caspari is dead.'

'Dead?'

'Murdered, dumped in the river. Swiss Police are on top of it though, doesn't look like a professional hit.'

'Everyone involved with this Book ends up dead.'

'That's right. Like the damn thing's cursed.'

'What are you going to do next?'

Priest mulled over Georgie's theory . It had legs. *Silver blood*. People had been killed for more elaborate reasons. 'Wait for the Swiss Police to contact us about the progress of their investigation, let Fay establish the blood types of the victims, and, in the immediate future, have another beer.'

He rang off. Right on cue, the waiter appeared.

# Chapter 38

After Fay got off the phone she took the seat next to Priest, leaving the seat opposite vacant; a sign that hostilities were over, for now at least.

'He's checking,' she said. 'But you're right. Blood group doesn't turn up on a PM report unless its requested. It'll take time to sort, though.'

'More waiting then.'

'Guess so.'

He could smell the alcohol on her breath, and something else too. A perfume he didn't recognise. Not like the one Jessica wore, something earthy, organic.

She reached across him to pick up the bottle of beer.

'You think it's possible?' she said. 'Someone thinks there's a better ending to the Bible by killing the last demons on Earth.'

Priest considered his reply. 'What I've learnt is that human beings have an endless capacity to justify their actions on the flimsiest of grounds. But in the end, it doesn't matter *why*. It matters *how* and *when*.'

'What about God? You believe in Him?'

They were silent for a moment, watching people file into the bar, preparing for nights out, nights in, conferences, shows, affairs. A microcosm of networks, intermingling and dispersing randomly. A kaleidoscope of human behaviour. It reminded Priest of something his father used to talk about: two colonies of ants, both living on the opposite sides of the same leaf. They were blissfully unaware of each other's existence because ants can only think in two dimensions. Three is beyond their tiny brains. We only know what we know, nothing more. Like the ants, we have limits to what we can see; there could be something else waiting for us, on the other side of the leaf.

'Not the God of the Old Testament,' he replied. 'Not the omniscient being they call Yahweh.'

'But you believe in *something*?'

'I believe this world is infinitely more complicated than they would have us believe.'

'Who's *they*?'

Priest's phone rang. A number in Geneva. He exchanged glances with Fay and hit 'answer', then 'loudspeaker'.

'Priest.'

The voice that came back was loud and energised. 'Mr Priest, this is Detective Kim Rising. There has been a development.'

'Go on.'

'Our pathologist noticed a small mark on Luca's right hand. We thought it was a rash at first but under a UV light it turned out to be a red stamp, a little faded from the water. We've managed to take a picture and enhance it. It turns out to be an entry stamp for a gay club in Geneva near Luca's house. We thought he must have been there recently so we made enquiries. Looks like he was a regular.'

'Good. When was he last there?'

'The night he disappeared. And the club was good enough to give us the CCTV showing Luca coming in and coming out.'

'Don't tell me he left with someone.'

'Yes. He's known to us. His name is Tobias Haas. He's got pre-vious, including one attempted murder.'

He sat up, alert. They were on to something, he could feel the adrenaline kick in, mixing with the alcohol. 'Can we track him?'

'We're raiding his house shortly. I'm sending a car for you.'

As she spoke, they looked up. A marked Swiss Police cruiser had just pulled up outside.

'Jesus. It's already arrived.'

'It's not just the Germans who are efficient, Mr Priest. We'll rendezvous at Haas's property in two hours.'

The Swiss Police Officer hit the blues and pulled out into the Geneva traffic with expertise well beyond his estimated twenty-one years of age. He didn't speak much English but could utter a little French, enough so Priest could communicate with him, but he didn't know much by all accounts. Priest formed the impression that his sole duty in the operation was to transport the two English observers to the raid before the Swiss Police broke the door down. John Eaton had certainly got them VIP backstage passes when he had arranged their introduction to Kim Rising.

After half an hour of negotiating the Geneva traffic, the city-scape dipped and flattened before disappearing behind them. Very soon, cattle outnumbered houses ten-to-one and the mountains loomed ahead, their snow-covered tips offering the perfect contrast to the lush green vista below and reflecting off the waters of the shimmering lake to their left.

'How far into the mountains are we going?' asked Priest.

'Er, looks like fifteen kilometres or more,' was the uncertain reply. The driver was following the sat nav, and clearly had no more of an idea than they did. Occasionally, he received instructions by radio in German. Priest caught the gist. The house was hidden behind the brow of a hill. The operation had assembled in a quiet rest point further down the mountainside.

Fay was quiet, spending much of the journey staring across the lake and checking her phone. She was apprehensive, but he guessed it was the same thought he had: this was their only lead. He reached across, touched her arm. She didn't flinch.

'You OK?'

She turned, rested her head back. 'Just tired. Wish I hadn't had that last beer.'

'That's what you get for drinking on duty.'

'Hm. Wouldn't be the first time.'

He could have asked what she meant but the driver had slowed, looking for the rendezvous point.

'It's just up here, I think.'

There was a turning to the right at the foot of a steep slope covered in trees. They followed a moss-covered track that wound through the woods with a sheer cliff face to the left and a sheer drop to the right leading to a valley speckled with cabins and tents. The sunlight kept puncturing the green canopy, flashes of stunning light flickered across the face of Priest's Aviator sunglasses and in the end he had to look away. In the distance, the skyline was dominated by a craggy giant of a mountain.

'That's Mont Collon,' the driver offered. 'A favourite amongst climbers.'

He muttered something into his radio and received an instant reply. A few moments later, the track widened out into a grassy terrace above a campsite where two police vans and several other vehicles were parked.

They got out, no one shut their doors. That was a sound that would travel right across the mountainside. Rising met them next to her car. She was already wearing a tactical vest. Several other men and women were stationed by the van, checking assault rifles and receiving a briefing from the commander.

Rising handed them two vests, which Priest and Fay started to pull on.

'Is he home?' Priest asked.

'He's home. We got one of our special friends to make a false call to his landline about a home survey. He picked up. Told us to fuck off, would you believe!'

Priest smiled. You wouldn't catch British police pulling a stunt like that. Too much red tape.

'What's the plan?' asked Fay.

'We've set up a perimeter around the house. The plan is to go in hard and fast, make a lot of noise, and see what tumbles out.'

Priest checked the firepower Rising had at her disposal. At least ten units he could see and clearly a load more he couldn't. These boys meant business too. Most of them were carrying SIG SG 550 assault rifles, manufactured here in Switzerland, as well as a handgun each. They'd probably all been shooting from the age of twelve. It was a national sport for the Swiss, but in a country where there are more gun ranges than golf courses, the crime rate is one of the lowest in the world. The notorious Task Force TIGRIS, part of the elite military police, have been deployed in hundreds of operations all over Switzerland. They've never fired a shot on active duty.

By the time Priest and Fay had squeezed into the tactical vests, Rising had her team in place and the commander had taken over giving orders. They waited by Rising's car, but with no direct view of the house on the other side of the embankment. A hush descended over the mountain: it was a dark wilderness up here hidden in the trees, but now the silence was more noticeable; as if the valley was holding its breath.

The crack of Haas's door caving in reverberated round the mountainside, followed by the whoosh of the trees as a flock of startled birds took flight. Then all hell broke loose. More crashes, presumably other doors being battered down, and shouting. Noise was the greatest weapon a tactical unit had in this situation, and now there was plenty of it. They cycled through different languages to make sure their instructions could be understood, but they needn't have bothered. The tone was universal.

'Armed Police! Get down!'

As the seconds passed, information started filtering back to Rising, who paced the area near Priest and Fay impatiently as each section of the house was checked and cleared. A false hope was raised when someone thought they saw movement in the basement, but it turned out to be Haas's cat. Within a few minutes, it was becoming clear that the element of surprise had been lost.

Rising swore in German. Turned to Priest.

'Think he knew we were coming?'

Priest nodded, and turned away to stare out at the valley below. He didn't want Rising to see his disappointment. It might only be a matter of time before Rising and her team caught up with Haas but time was no longer on their side. The killer was still at large back in London, planning his next victim. The ones with silver blood, maybe . . .

He walked to the edge of the rest area to where the pine-covered escarpment fell away. He could see the campsite below, with a sprinkling of tents and a line of cedar cabins. The valley would be teeming with skiers in high season when the whole area would be covered in a thick blanket of snow but today it was quiet. The hikers who had set up camp were probably half way up Mont Collon now.

He was about to call Rowlinson when something caught his eye. Movement further down the slope, past a clump of trees. At first he thought it was an animal, a hare maybe. But it was too big. He repositioned himself, and caught a better glimpse of a man, snagging his foot on a tree root, fighting to regain balance.

*Oh shit.*

Priest shouted back to Rising – 'He's here!' – before skidding down the mountainside in pursuit. He had no idea whether Rising had heard him so he called again, but aimed at Haas – for that was surely who it was – to stop. *How the hell had he got there?*

The answer came soon enough. As Priest reached the spot where he'd seen Haas fall, he got a look at an opening partially concealed by the trees. *It's a bloody secret passageway through the mountains!*

He hadn't made much ground and now Haas had the advantage. He was in danger of losing him if he disappeared over the next crest. His body ached from the explosion, there was a burning sensation around his hips; his legs felt twice as heavy as they ought to. Then there was another problem. The gunshot rippled through the air as Haas fired blindly over his shoulder.

The bullet was way off-mark but Priest realised that all he had to do was turn round and take aim. Fortunately, for now, Haas didn't seem inclined, perhaps because he didn't know exactly how many people were chasing him. Priest stole a glance over his shoulder. If Haas did the same, he'd realise it was one-on-one and he was the one with the gun.

As they neared the cabins, the gap had closed. Ignoring the pain, Priest thought back to that day in the woods again, at home, when he had raced past William to get to Sarah. He was broad-shouldered, lean and tall. He didn't look like a runner, and maybe he had slowed up a bit in his fourth decade, but he knew that running was about power not weight, and Tobias Haas didn't look like he had either on his side.

But he did have a gun, and another couple of shots kicked up waves of grass and earth in front of Priest. *Getting closer.*

The ground rose up before dipping back down again and he saw Haas scramble over a mound of rocks before momentarily disappearing on the other side. He guessed that he would soon be at the campsite and another troubling thought hit him: was it as abandoned as it had seemed from the top of the slope?

Fifteen seconds later he was skidding down the last section of embankment and scanning the area where the slope levelled out. The red cedar cabins were dotted around the edge of the woods without any apparent order, but he couldn't see anybody around. At first, he thought that Haas had continued towards a cluster of trees further away from the cabins but, if he had done, he couldn't see him.

He checked behind him but there wasn't any sign of Rising or her team. They either hadn't heard him or were slow to react. He couldn't see back up to the rest area anyway. He was on his own, and he just may well have lost one of the only viable leads they had left.

He kicked up a small pile of earth in anger. *How could he just vanish?*

He focused on his descent down the mountain, and on the moment when Haas had dipped out of sight. Judging the distances, where could he have got to in that time to be able to disappear? The trees seemed unlikely. But there was a cabin set off from the others, a single-storey wooden structure to the left with steps leading up to a veranda and a pitched moss-covered roof. *Could he be in there, hiding?*

As he approached, Priest realised that the cabin was bigger than he first thought with a glass frontage and an open gate. Quietly, he took the steps to the front door. As soon as it opened, he realised that Haas probably wasn't hiding. He was most likely gambling on Priest finding where he was and intended to kill him. He was walking straight into a trap.

He stood in the entranceway for a short while, listening.

The wooden floor stretched out to encompass a table and chairs but went off at an angle leaving plenty of places to hide. There were several other rooms containing sparse furnishings. Probably a skiing outlet for hire, although it didn't look like it was currently in use.

He peered down. The boards looked like they would creak, but he didn't have a choice. Keeping to the edge, he inched round the room. Stopped suddenly. He'd definitely heard something. From the room opposite. The sound of something dropping on the floor. He stood still for a moment, conscious that Haas could leap out from anywhere. Or maybe he already had the gun trained on him.

He took a few paces back to the entrance.

But it was the wrong decision.

From behind him, a different door flew open, followed by the sensation of rapid movement. Haas was leading with the gun. That was his mistake. He was too close to his intended target. He would have been better off waiting for Priest to move to the other side of the room.

Priest took Haas by the wrist and manoeuvred his shooting arm away from them both. Two deafening shots blasted harmlessly wide, splintering holes in the side of the cabin.

He drove his left elbow into Haas's neck, drawing from him a strange muffled cry of alarm and pain. Haas kicked out, but Priest was ready, deflecting the blow and taking most of it on the fleshy part of his thigh. He had control of Haas's gun hand. With sheer brute force, he levered his arm down but there was still the problem of wrestling the gun away from his fingers. Haas was stronger than he looked, and although Priest held the superior position, his opponent was fighting back.

Priest tried to slam Haas's hand into the wall, hoping the shock might force him to drop the weapon. He managed to get two clean connections, the second one drawing another bullet from the chamber in a roar of power, the recoil shuddering down his arm.

Sensing an opportunity, Haas used the moment to twist his body round, bringing Priest with him, and using the new-found leverage to manipulate his hold of the gun to turn it on him. With the barrel dangerously close to his head, Priest realised his only hope was to reposition his hands on the gun itself. They were now backed against the wall, with the gun pointing towards the rear of the cabin. Priest took a moment to check the gun. It was a short-range pistol, he couldn't see anymore. Eleven shots, maybe nine. He'd counted three. With a momentous effort, he forced his fingers around Haas's and fired off round after round, cutting holes in the cabin, shattering the glass windows. After six shots, the gun clicked but didn't fire.

Without the need to worry about getting shot, Priest was able to use his superior size and strength to shove Haas away. Sensing victory, he grabbed Haas by the top of the arm and was about to roll him over when he kicked out and caught Priest square in the stomach. Winded, he fell back and Haas seized his chance, bolting for the door and putting his shoulder against it. The door gave way with an agonising sound and Haas stumbled outside into the snow.

'No!'

Priest scrambled up, adrenaline surging him on. Headed to the door. He was about to give chase, but he stopped. Through the broken door he could see Haas wasn't moving. He was standing in the sunlight, looking around him in bewilderment. In front of him, a regiment of armed police had their assault rifles trained on him.

'That's quite enough, Mr Haas,' he heard Rising shout. 'Stay where you are.'

# Chapter 39

After another 'no comment' slurred in German, Kim Rising placed her papers down and left her sergeant in the interview room to watch Tobias Haas and his lawyer fester. Priest waited for a moment before she appeared at the door on the other side of the one-way mirror, exasperation written all over her face.

'We'll link him forensically to Luca eventually,' she said with conviction.

'What about motive?' asked Fay.

'We're already acquainted with Mr Haas. He's got loose ties with a gang that operates out of Liechtenstein. They call themselves mercenaries; it's not been unknown for them to take hit jobs.'

'You think he was hired by someone?'

Rising pulled a face. 'Maybe. He runs for the gang; drugs mainly, but he's got previous, as I said. Knows how to shoot, how to wield a knife.'

'Nice place he's got in the mountains,' Priest remarked. 'With an escape tunnel.'

'It's his late father's, who was also one of our regulars. The tunnels date back to the end of the war.'

She left it there, but Priest knew the rest. A number of cells had sprung up after Hitler's suicide to offer safe passage to senior

Nazis and their families. They used a lot of European countries as safe houses while they arranged transport to South America. It wasn't spoken about much here, but a lot of Geneva's money – their famous banks – had helped fund the Third Reich and, although they were by no means alone, Geneva's secrecy and remote countryside was an ideal hiding place for former Nazis. And no doubt the odd tunnel was built here and there.

'Now you have a suspect,' said Priest, 'do you still believe that the murder was bungled, or Haas wanted us to find the body, or was instructed to leave it that way?'

'All of those theories are possible. Certainly, Mr Haas isn't the most competent criminal, as his track record of imprisonment shows. Did he see a quick buck and bungle the hit? Quite possibly. Was he told to leave the body on show for us to find? Also quite possible.'

'If the latter, he must have known he'd be implicated sooner or later,' offered Fay.

'As I say. Not the brightest criminal.'

Priest checked his watch. It was late evening and he only saw tired faces around him. He guessed Rising was planning to see if a night in the cells would make a difference, although it seemed unlikely. The next flight home wasn't until the morning, so after exchanging some final words with Rising – and securing her promise to call him the minute they knew anything more – he suggested to Fay that they head back to the hotel to call Rowlinson. She didn't object.

Half an hour later, they were back in the foyer, and the familiar waiter had placed two more bottles of the finest Swiss beer in front of them. Fay was on to the second before Priest had even picked his up.

They called Rowlinson and agreed they should return to London on the next flight. Six thirty in the morning. Priest groaned inwardly. He wasn't a morning person. Frustratingly, they still had nothing on the victims' blood types.

'I can't get a pathologist until tomorrow,' Rowlinson explained, fatigue creeping into his voice. 'Two kids were stabbed outside a night club in Soho and they took priority. Mixture of illness and holidays and more fucking budget cuts means we're going to have to wait.'

'Can't the DSI do something?' Fay complained.

'He's not impressed with the silver blood theory. Doesn't believe the killer is a fallen angel or some shit, but I'm checking with UCL library anyway to see if anyone checked out the book your girl found, Priest. I want to get it to the lab.'

'Doubt you'll find anything.'

'Probably right, but we'll look anyway. What about this Liechtenstein connection?'

'It's a tax haven for criminals,' said Priest. 'The centre of most of the significant international banking scandals in the last twenty years. There's a very low crime rate but a lot of gangs use it as a base and operate elsewhere in Europe.'

'Is it possible Tobias Haas was a hired assassin? And if he was, where the hell does that lead us?'

'It means that potentially our killer in London has a longer reach than we thought. Somebody doesn't want us to understand the Book of Janus.' *It also means there's a breadcrumb trail somewhere if Haas was paid. First rule of all criminal investigation: follow the money.*

'All right. Let's regroup in Holborn tomorrow morning.'

He rang off. Priest pocketed the phone. The barman dimmed the lights as the grandfather clock in the corner struck eleven.

The hotel was too highbrow to have a cuckoo clock for the tourists, much to his disappointment. He wondered if there was one at Fay's hotel.

They sat in silence for a few moments, lost in their own thoughts, until she said without ceremony, 'You said that killers don't leave symbols because that was Hollywood shit. But the Night Stalker did.'

Priest nodded, impressed. Between June 1984 and August 1985 Richard Ramirez – dubbed by the media as the Night Stalker – brutally murdered nineteen people in their own homes in Los Angeles. He was mentally disturbed and obsessed with occultism, forcing one victim to recite 'I love Satan' while he raped her. He also left occult symbols at the scenes of his crimes.

'Ramirez killed for pleasure. Our guy's on a mission. They're different types of killers.'

'Ethan Grey doesn't think so.'

Priest clicked his tongue. 'There's a lot you can't learn about serial killers from textbooks.'

She leant back in her chair, finished her second beer and ordered another. He stole a glance at her profile as she stared straight ahead. She had an unusually straight jawline, defined cheekbones, perfect skin, but there was something distant about her gaze that he couldn't quite grasp, as if the real Fay Westbrook was always just out of reach.

'That's how you categorise them?' she said, making eye contact. 'By what they want.'

'Serial killers do what they do for one of four reasons: because a mental illness tells them to; because they're on a mission, usually from God; because they want something, could be money but could easily just be the thrill of killing; and finally because killing is all they know, death is the only release, and murder is the ultimate expression of power and control.'

'Are you married?'

The question caught him off-guard. He blinked. She hadn't taken her eyes off him. The waiter brought over two more beers. When he had gone, she was still looking at him. He realised she was serious.

'I was once.'

'What happened?'

He took a sip of beer. She had a way of asking very short questions that couldn't be answered concisely without a degree in psychology and a whole lot of spare time.

'I used to be married to your boss.'

'Rowlinson?' She didn't break a smile, deadpan. He wasn't sure if it was meant to be a joke or not.

'The AC.'

That *did* surprise her. She actually spilt her beer. 'Assistant Commissioner Dee Auckland?'

'The very same.'

She looked at him, as if in a different light, no doubt a hundred questions filtering through her head. In the end, she went with an observation. 'She's a lot older than you.'

'A few years, admittedly. But don't let her hear you say that, for God's sake.'

'Was it nasty? The divorce, I mean?'

'You have no idea.'

She laughed, and her face changed again. Some people just had laughs that transformed them, like Jessica. Fay Westbrook was just the same. And much like Jessica, he couldn't work out which was the real Fay: the one who laughed as gorgeously as any woman he'd seen, or the reserved, cold woman pissed off to have to get on a plane with him.

'What about you?' he asked. She wore no ring, but that didn't necessarily mean anything.

'Me?' She took another swig from the bottle, nearly half of it was gone in one gulp. 'No. Work gets in the way of things like that. You want something stronger?'

He didn't answer, but she took his silence as an affirmative and slipped off to the bar. She returned a few moments later and placed two glasses of clear liquid in front of them.

'Vodka. Neat,' she said. 'Just like the Russians.'

Priest took the glass and inspected it. He didn't have a taste for vodka but one wouldn't do any harm. Might help him sleep better. She raised her glass to him.

'What are we toasting?'

She thought for a moment. 'You falling down a mountain after a guy with a gun. Funniest fucking thing I've seen in ages.'

They broke into laughter, chinked glasses and threw the drinks back at the same time. The liquid burnt his throat but he was too tired to care. He thought about Jessica, what she would think if she was a fly on the wall, but they weren't in a relationship, as she took the time to repeatedly tell him. They just occasionally slept together; and it was torture, the rushed moments of passion they shared. She rarely stayed the night, and they rarely talked properly. It was business. Nothing more. He wondered if either of them were capable of anything more. Vexed, he put his glass down. She picked up on the signal immediately.

'What's wrong?'

'Nothing. Just tired.'

She smiled, unconvinced. 'Can't do anything on half a night's sleep, as my grandmother would say.'

'A wise woman,' he agreed.

'She also used to tell me that if I ever met a turtle I had to wish it happy birthday.' She laughed, a little giddily.

'What?'

'For years when I was a kid I went round zoos making sure that, if there was a turtle, I wished it happy birthday. Sometimes I even sang to them.'

'That is literally one of the weirdest stories I've ever heard.'

They laughed again, and she got up. Put her jacket on.

'You want me to walk you back?'

She let the suggestion linger for a second. 'You know damn well I don't need walking back.' He wondered if he had offended her again, but, to his relief, she smiled. 'But I can make an exception. Come on.'

Watching her trip on the bottom step of the hotel gave Priest the impression that Fay was more drunk than he had previously thought, or the amount of drink she had had allowed, but then maybe the whole thing was an act. She was self-contained. He got the impression she didn't need anyone. But nonetheless by the time they reached her hotel, a modest three star set back from the street and painted an insipid blue colour, she had slipped her arm around his.

They hadn't talked much, just gazed out at the boats moored along the Arne, and wondered at the beauty of it. Mostly, they had just walked, aware of the closeness they shared but not saying anything. Priest wondered where it would lead, but it still felt like an infidelity and he concentrated not on her, but on the case, the killer back in London, the Carriers and all the ceaseless unanswered questions. How was he choosing the victims? Who had orchestrated Luca's murder, and why? Was the killer responsible for Owen's murder? Was there more than one person involved? How did Elisha Capindale fit into the picture?

It was an endless cycle of dead ends.

Fay unhooked her arm and turned to face him. She had a stare that seemed to look right through him. Or *into* him, he wasn't sure which.

'Want one more drink for the road?'

They both knew what it meant, what it represented. She did nothing to seduce him, there was nothing flirtatious or suggestive about the way she was standing, looking at him. There was a coldness to her proposition, as if it were nothing more than transactional, and inevitable.

He wasn't sure if he was in the moment or if it was just all playing out like a film. It happened quickly, first as nothing more than a flutter in his chest, then spreading across his back to the tips of his fingers. The world slipped away and he was falling. Drifting. He was inside his head, looking out into the eyes of a beautiful woman, a siren. The unreal. The hyperreal. It was all the same when disassociation overcame him. When it came from nowhere.

He checked his feet to see if he was moving, checked his outstretched arm to see if she was taking him by the hand and leading him to the hotel, to her room. That's what he surely wanted? To undress her, feel her skin, her body. Tease her. Taste her. Leave her.

*Not now.*

It didn't matter that he was being unfaithful, if indeed he was. That was someone else's problem, someone else's life.

She said something. His name. Not his surname, like every-one called him. His first name. Charlie.

He didn't move as she leant in and kissed him. He tasted the alcohol on her lips and felt the soft touch of her hand in his hair. Closed his eyes. But he couldn't connect. Something was wrong. He was melting away.

She pulled back, unsure. He should say something.

'Sorry,' she whispered.

'No . . . I . . .'

She walked up the steps to her hotel. He was powerless to stop her. She looked back, once. Over her shoulder. He backed away. Her eyes were gone, replaced with two spotlights, as bright as any that he had ever seen, shining at him. Alarmed, he turned to walk away but stopped. Further down the street, a turtle was ambling towards him. When he looked back, worried, Fay was gone.

As he walked back to his hotel, he noticed the turtle follow-ing him, matching his stride. When he got back to his room, he locked the door and stuck a chair up against the handle. He realised his mistake. He should have wished it happy birthday.

# Chapter 40

*One year ago*

*I can't explain to you exactly how I knew that those few tatty pieces of faded paper my father had left me were significant, but I certainly had a predisposition towards the idea that the Book of Revelation was only one of a number of alternatives for mankind's fate. Even as a ten-year-old boy sat listening to the teachers at school talk about the Bible, I thought it was obvious that God would not prophesise about our assumption into paradise in such inevitable terms. It seemed ridiculous that we, a species tainted by endless sin, had already earned the right to the key of Heaven, and we would just soak into God's world like some sort of spiritual osmosis.*

*No. I no more believe in predestination than the blasphemous atheists do. Destiny is not pre-set. God has a plan for me, for mankind, but it is up to us to execute it, not Him.*

*So I suppose in a way the idea that the scripture I had inherited represented an opportunity for someone to seize the moment, to avoid the End of Days, was already simmering deep down in my core. You can't imagine what it felt like when I discovered the truth, and in the most unlikeliest of places.*

*As I watch Sue ease herself up, stagger away from me and wipe the inside of her legs with her hand, I realise she reminds me so much of a younger version of the woman I met not so long ago at her dilapidated mansion in Ely. Like Sue, Elisha Capindale was reclusive and small, as if she had once been a good person; but something rotten had taken a hold of her, eaten her from within. I recall the meeting well. She sat in an armchair, listening, watching me. Her wraith-like fingers resting on her lap, her watery eyes half glazed over. It had taken me an age to convince her to see me without the German butler strapped to her side. and how she shrank away from the light, like some sort of vampire!*

*'You're not a prophet,' Sue says suddenly. I'm taken aback. I thought she would leave, like the others. Too shamed to even look at me. But whether I had applied too much drink to her or her constitution was stronger than I had originally judged, she sat back down and stared at me, defiant.*

*'You're right,' I admit. 'I'm something else.'*

*'You've done this bef—'*

*I don't let her finish. 'You remind me of someone, Sue.'*

*She blinks, startled. Sways around, her mouth open. She enjoyed it. I can tell. She wants more. It reminds her of how pathetic she is, and this in turn feeds her addiction. Not to alcohol, but to something else. The same thing that I am addicted to. The darkness.*

*'Who?'*

*'Her name is unimportant but she, like my father, spent her life collecting things from the past that she thought might help her understand the future. She had an affliction.' I look down, with genuine sadness because I understand that Elisha is cursed. 'A fear of the light.'*

*She looks at me, and I can tell she is disgusted by what we did but she cannot pull herself away. I understand. God's will is hard to ignore.*

'At least I thought it was a fear of the light, at first,' I continue. 'In fact, it is a fear of the sun.' I get up, she flinches, but I am harmless right now and put up my hands to make it clear that I am doing nothing other than taking down a copy of the Bible. I open it and read aloud the passage from John:3:

'And this is the judgement: the light has come into the world, and people loved the darkness rather than the light because their works were evil. For everyone who does wicked things hates the light and does not come to the light, lest his works should be exposed. But whoever does what is true comes to the light, so that it may be clearly seen that his works have been carried out in God.'

*Sue frowns, her frazzled brain trying to process it. Then she realises. 'She thought that she was evil, because she feared the sun. Or the light.'*

'Perhaps she was right,' I suggest, teasingly.

*Sue becomes angry, her etiolated skin crumples under her grimace. 'You told her that. You made her believe it.'*

'I read a passage from the Bible to her, Sue,' I sigh, a little irritated by the intonation. 'I am not responsible for her interpretation of it.'

*That is not the truth, but for some unknown reason I was content for Sue to believe it. Elisha told me about the passage. Her pitiless mother had read it to her, burnt into her soul when she was a child. It was perfect. I needed her help to source the Book of Janus (my father was an amateur relic hunter: Elisha Capindale was making a living out of it!) and she needed spiritually cleansing. She needed to prove to God that she was not evil. And she needed money, both of which I was able to offer her.*

'She wouldn't have thought she was evil.' Sue says something else but I don't catch it.

'Anyway,' I say, hoping to turn her around. I'm not comfortable with the way she is acting. She doesn't seem scared enough. I don't think she would tell anyone about what just happened, and they probably wouldn't take much notice if she did, but I feel I need to keep talking to her to make sure she understands what she is a part of. 'The woman was not evil. Quite the contrary. She was very useful.'

'Like I was?'

'No. In a very different way. You see, Sue, when my parents died I was left with an incomplete translation of a scripture that would shape my life in a way that I had not thought possible. This woman had considerable understanding of such scriptures and she was able to tell me that what I had was most likely a few pages from an obscure text known as the Book of Janus.'

'I've never heard of it.'

'Of course not. Hardly anyone has. The Book was lost for centuries. But there is a reason for that.'

She screws up her face again and I am angered to see how sceptical she is. 'God's plan again?'

'Have you ever met a fucking demon, Sue?' I kick myself inwardly for losing control of my temper. It is a sign of weakness. I calm myself. Count to ten in my head. Sue has shrunk back even more. 'I'm sorry. But this is . . . difficult.'

She gets up and I feel a strange sense of dread as she looks back at me. 'Like I said, you're not a prophet. You're not even a man.'

*I let her leave. Watch her stumble through the door and into the church and listen as her footsteps on the flagstones grow fainter until finally the oak door is rammed home behind her.*

*And then a disturbing thought crosses my mind:* was she one of them?

# Chapter 41

*Tuesday*

The journey home was characterised by the kind of disorientation and grogginess that only DPD sufferers understand. It makes hangovers look like a walk in the park.

'You OK?' Fay asked him when they got off the plane.

'Sorry. Bad head.'

'Last night. You seemed a bit off. At the end.'

He swallowed but despite two bottles of Evian on the plane his throat was Gobi-dry. He cursed the weather as they walked across the tarmac to the terminal building. The heatwave had subsided. It was warm, but overcast, and the clouds sported a typical English grey tinge. It was all fine, but he couldn't justify wearing the sunglasses that were hiding his bloodshot eyes without looking like a washed-up rocker from the eighties.

*It'll have to do for now.*

'Yeah, sorry. I get migraines. They come on pretty quickly.'

They entered the terminal but he kept the sunglasses on. He bumped into the door but somehow managed to cover it up.

'I misread the signals, clearly,' she said softly, and he felt a crushing wave of disenchantment, guilt and embarrassment. It was awkward – he doubted that Fay was the kind of woman who was regularly turned down.

'It's not that,' he said, lamely. 'It's complicated.'

'OK. I get it.'

Keen to regroup, Rowlinson picked them up from the airport, slung their bags in the boot and pushed the BMW hard up the motorway. Apparently Grey and Eaton were already waiting for them.

'Georgie didn't tell you?' Rowlinson asked, surprised.

Wearily, Priest checked his phone. Five missed calls, all from Georgie.

'No. What's up?'

'She's been looking at this event referred to in the book as the Binding and there's some obscure cult blogs that mention it, but not much. Anyway, long story short, there are some references to the Book of Janus, which is supposed to explain how to bring about the Binding. There's a lot of speculation, most of it is crap, but there's a common thread.'

'The Carriers,' Priest guessed.

'Yeah. The consensus is that whoever destroys the Carriers, brings about the Binding.'

'And takes his reward by sitting on the left hand of God.'

'That's right, but there's more. Georgie found an anecdote from someone who claimed to have seen a few pages of the Book of Janus and there's mention of another story in the Bible about a woman called Yael.'

Priest shrugged, it meant nothing to him. 'And?'

'Yael appears in the Book of Judges as the woman who killed Sisera, the leader of King Jabin's army who was waging war with the Israelites.'

'Forgive me if I'm not familiar with this particular Biblical fable.'

'The story doesn't matter. What matters is that Yael murders Sisera while he's sleeping, by driving a nail into his head with a hammer.'

'Oh shit. Are you tracing these blogs?'

'Yeah, but they're probably just a bunch of middle-aged divorced men with nothing better to do than fantasise with each other about angels and fairies.'

'You just described *me*.'

From the back, Fay leant forward. 'Is the DSI more interested now?'

'He is, but Grey's still insistent we're wasting our time. We'll know more if the pathologist confirms the victims have this rare blood type. But there's more news.'

'Go on,' said Priest. 'I could use a pick-me-up.'

'The International Rare Donor Panel database shows that there are fewer than six hundred registered people with Lutheran b negative combined with O negative, but because blood types are genetic, they're clustered.'

'Let me guess. Most of them are in London.'

'You got it.'

'Are our victims on the database?'

'We're looking at it now. We're also checking family members of the victims, although they're saying inheritance is complicated. You're not necessarily born with the blood type of either of your parents. This was all kicking off before I decided to become your personal taxi service.'

Priest sat back, rested his head to one side. The verge rushed past as Rowlinson urged the car on. It made him feel sick as hell. When they reached the station, he half fell out.

'What the fuck happened to you?' Rowlinson hissed, helping him up.

'Nothing. Lack of sleep.'

The DCI glanced over at Fay, who looked away and went about retrieving her bag from the boot.

Rowlinson whispered in his ear. 'Did you sleep with my sergeant, Priest?'

'No. Why would you think that?'

He walked off leaving Priest to fumble around for his own bag. 'Just an inkling.'

Priest had, at one stage or another, tried most forms of recreational intoxicants, but the cup of machine tea that DSI Eaton handed him when he stumbled in to the meeting room was about the most welcoming cup of liquid and chemicals he had ever been given.

'Welcome back,' Eaton barked. 'Not a completely wasted trip, I understand.'

'The Swiss Police were very cooperative,' said Fay, mechanically. 'If they have further news on Luca Caspari's murder then I'm confident we'll hear it first.'

Priest collapsed in a chair next to Grey, who moved away, much like anyone would if a man in his dishevelled state sat next to them.

'This is great tea,' he said, draining the cup. 'Where's Georgie, by the way? She should be here.'

'I think there's quite enough people involved in this already,' said Grey, folding his arms. 'And I've heard talk about attributing the killer with some bizarre religious fantasy motivation. I would urge caution about such conjecture. It doesn't help us. Serial killers don't choose their victims based on blood type.'

'We'll know soon enough,' said Priest.

'I'm expecting a call later this morning,' Rowlinson added.

'What about the International Rare Donor Panel's database?'

'We've requested the details, which are being assessed by the Treasury Solicitors.'

'Why can't we just have the damn thing?' asked Eaton. He was irritated but Priest suspected it wouldn't be easy.

'The EU's General Data Protection Regulation means it can't just be handed over. The database can only be accessed by medical professionals who are sourcing rare blood for clinical use. In the end, the Department of Health's lawyers will work out if they can allow this exception for crime detection and prevention, but they'll make sure their own arses are covered first.'

'Well, Grey's right,' said Eaton, although he didn't appear to like it. 'It's conjecture, for now. Let's work with what we *do* know.'

Priest considered his options but there didn't seem much point in arguing. Whatever he might have said would have been lost anyway as they were interrupted by a knock at the door preceded by a fresh-faced PC clutching an envelope which she handed to Eaton.

'I'm sorry to interrupt, sir, but this came marked for Mr Priest.'

'What, you're getting post here now?' he heard Fay jest as he took the envelope from Eaton and opened it. 'You'll be wanting a fucking lanyard next and a parking space.'

'While Mr Priest reads his school report card, what else do we know?' Eaton demanded.

'The killer isn't escalating,' Grey replied. 'We were due another victim yesterday by my count and we didn't get one.'

'Not one that we've found,' Fay added.

'He'll want us to find the victims quickly. He's an exhibitionist.'

'Well, I'm not going to get upset that another innocent member of the public hasn't been murdered,' said Eaton dryly.

'It's unusual though,' said Grey. 'I had anticipated that the killer—'

'Copperhead,' said Priest. Grey trailed off as they all turned to look at him. 'His name is Copperhead.'

'How . . . ?'

Priest placed the paper gently on the table, careful to touch as little of it as possible. He was already at war with himself. In his semi-delirious state, he'd torn the envelope open and forced the paper out, not even thinking that it might have been written by the killer.

They all leant across and examined the note.

*Dear Mr Priest*
*Enoch VIII 3-6*
*Your friend*
*Copperhead*

'What does it mean?' asked Eaton.

'It's a quote from the Book of Enoch,' said Priest. 'Chapter eight, verses three to six.'

He looked up. Fay was already typing into her phone. After a moment, she read the passage.

*'And when men could no longer sustain them, the Giants turned against them and devoured mankind and they began to sin against*

*birds, and beasts, and reptiles, and fish, and to devour one anoth-
er's flesh, and drink the blood. Then the earth laid accusation
against the lawless ones.'*

'I'm still none-the-fucking wiser,' Eaton growled.

Priest's headache was pounding but he realised there was no
time to lose. Grey was wrong. The killer *was* escalating, boldly
taunting them. Singling him out. How did the killer even know
that he was involved?

*The killer. Copperhead.*

'The Book of Enoch is a scripture that Owen mentioned, part
of the Dead Sea Scrolls,' he said. 'Same as the Book of Janus. It
talks about the Giants, or the Watchers, the fallen angels that
begot sons and daughters with human women. The Carriers.
The ones with silver blood. The last demons. It all fits. *Kill the
Giants*, the silver blood. The Binding. The killer thinks he's on a
mission from God to avoid Judgement Day.

'And now he's given us his stage name. Copperhead.'

# Chapter 42

Darren Green parked his bike outside the old warehouse and looked around. His dad had told him about this place. It was where gangs came to do drugs and other bad things. But Darren knew about that already. He'd seen them from the other side of the canal when they drove home, always three cars parked up in a line. Always the same cars, with big wings on the back and shiny paint. Nothing like the cars his dad drove. They all had beige leather seats and were constantly breaking down.

He knew they were loud too. The gangs and their cars. Once Dad had let him wind the window down as they passed and he heard the rhythmic thud of the music and their shouts, even from the other side of the canal. Darren wondered what it would be like, to be so free that you could just drive to wherever you wanted, do whatever you wanted. Be part of a gang. But they'd never allow him to join, even though they were his age. He was different, always had been. His dad said he was bad with numbers, but he knew it was more than that. He was bad with everything.

He looked around. The warehouse was massive. Stretched right across to the back field it ran almost the whole length of the canal. His dad once said they called it the *Titanic* building, because it was the same length as the ship. Darren loved that film, except the end.

Dad had gone out for a few hours, so Darren was supposed to stay in, like he always did. Dad trusted him, and he felt bad for breaking that trust. But this was different. The thrill of it was too irresistible, and he knew the gangs wouldn't be here. Not at this time. They only came out at night. This was first thing in the morning. They'd all be at home, passed out. Or in hospital. Or prison.

And Dad would forgive him if he knew.

Lucy Warren was the prettiest girl he had ever seen, and although she went to regular school, she always smiled at him. Didn't avoid him like the other norms.

He couldn't remember the correct word for her. There was a group of boys at school – they called themselves *incels*, or something. He knew that stood for involuntary celibacy, but he didn't know what it meant. He wasn't part of the group; they talked in a different language and one of them knew Lucy. He didn't like the way they talked about her. They just seemed to hate girls. They had a name for girls like Lucy, pretty girls.

They'd be reeling if they knew that he was here to meet her.

Darren started walking towards the warehouse. There seemed to be different entrances but they'd probably all lead to the same place. Part of the roof had collapsed at the front of the building but Lucy had said to head towards the back, she'd be waiting for him there. She was going to let him have sex with her. Because she felt sorry for him, thought he might be in the group, the *incels*. He wasn't, but he didn't want to spoil anything so he just agreed.

She had asked him if he knew what a blow job was. He did. Dad thought that the internet had locks on it. It didn't. Or they didn't work, or whatever.

Once inside, Darren saw how vast the warehouse actually was. The view from the canal didn't cut it. It was unbelievably big. There was graffiti everywhere and he decided to take a few moments just to look at it. Some of it was amazing. Some of it was weird shit, but mostly it was great. After a moment, he realised that he hadn't progressed much further and, fearing that he was now late, hurried past a pile of gas bottles and deep into the back of the building.

After a few minutes of wandering around, Darren stopped. He felt annoyed. Lucy wasn't here. He felt more than annoyed, he felt something else. Stupid. Why would she give him a blow job, or do anything, just like that? It didn't make sense.

He saw a room he hadn't noticed the first time around. It was off to the right and, although by now he thought he had probably explored every part of the warehouse, he thought he might have missed that bit. He decided to take a peek, but something stopped him. He wasn't sure what. He hadn't noticed it before, but inside the warehouse, it was so quiet, so still. It was like those tubes at the hospital he hated so much. He hated them because when he was inside he felt alone, like no one outside of the tube existed.

He had a sudden urge to leave. Get on his bike and ride home. This was a bad idea. He felt like there was something in that room. Why hadn't he seen it before? Was it ever there in the first place? This had been a bad idea. Lucy Warren could stuff her blow job.

Darren spun around and was about to leg it out of there when everything changed; he was suddenly paralysed because standing at the other end of the warehouse, silhouetted against the light gleaming through the doorway, stood a man carrying a hammer.

'Hello, Darren,' the man called. 'Looking for little Lucy?'

Darren shrank further back. He didn't understand who this man was, or where he had come from but one overarching realisation had hit him.

If he didn't get away, this man was going to kill him.

# Chapter 43

Georgie had got the message, but she had found Charlie's office empty.

She studied the email again, but it was quite clear. 'Need a word. Office.' Looking up, she saw that Okoro's door was ajar.

'Vince?'

When she pushed the door fully open the barrister turned and took off a heavy pair of headphones, from which the muffled sound of some off-beat hip-hop emanated.

'What's up, young lady?'

'Have you seen Charlie?'

'He's back from the station. Have you tried the roof?'

'I didn't know we have a roof.'

'Every building's got to have a roof, Georgie.'

'I mean, I didn't know we have an accessible roof.'

Okoro nodded, understanding. 'The window next to Solly's room.'

'OK, thanks.'

She left as Okoro replaced his headphones. Bemused, she went up the stairs. Solly's door was shut, as always, but the window was wide open. She'd never noticed it before but outside was an iron terrace that led to a fire escape and, when she looked out further, she saw a ladder.

Without looking down, she climbed out and up the ladder. Charlie was standing in the middle of the roof, a cigarette hanging out of his mouth, swinging a putter.

'This is new,' she remarked.

'Not at all. I often come up here.' He lifted the putter back and tapped the ball across the green. It hit the side of a windmill and bounced off-course behind a plastic rock. 'Shit.'

She watched, perplexed. 'We have a Priest & Co. crazy golf course. On the roof.'

Charlie pointed with the club. 'Not a course. Just one hole. The windmill.'

'Why do we have this?'

'It was something my doctor told me a long time ago, when I first started experiencing DPD. To anchor yourself back down, you have to find something mundane and repeat it over and over again. Help deflate the balloon in my head.'

'So you play crazy golf. On the roof of the office.'

He put the club down and walked over to her. 'I can hardly play it in the boardroom, can I? What would clients think?'

She blinked, twice. Decided not to pursue the line of questioning any further. 'You wanted to see me?'

'The killer's name is Copperhead.'

She froze, aware all of a sudden that, when the sun was hidden behind the clouds, it wasn't that warm at all, and something about hearing that the killer had a name made her shiver.

'Copperhead,' she repeated. 'That's a type of snake.'

'I think the imagery's clear.'

'Like the snake on the cross, the symbol in the Book of Janus.'

'You found some blogs referencing the Binding?'

'Yeah. I tried to call you but you didn't answer.'

'Don't worry. Is there any way you can interact with any of these bloggers, or whatever they're called? I mean live. In a chat room or something?'

She thought about it. There's a chat room for everything. Biscuits, tasteless jokes, fish tanks, sudoku. Surely there was a chat room for believers in the Binding?

'I'll see if I can find one.'

He nodded. 'I spent some time going through the case files for the three victims. I know that Rowlinson will have already done it, but I wanted to check everything myself. I was trying to do some network analysis, see if I can get any common ground between them.'

'Did you get anything?'

'Yes. I think your theory has been proven.'

He handed her a piece of paper, which she took and read before peering up, her eyes wide.

'So all three victims had Lutheran b negative blood and the killer knew that.'

Charlie nodded. Lined the putter up and swung. The ball bobbed along then hit the side of the windmill, spilling back towards him and finally coming to rest in almost exactly the same spot from where it had been dispatched.

'Shit.'

Georgie checked the page again. It was an email from the Thames Blood Donor Centre telling Jane Vardy that there was a shortage of Lutheran b negative blood – there was an urgent appeal for donors.

'Do the other two victims have the same email?'

Charlie nodded. The cigarette smoke swirled around his head, hardly disturbed by the stillness of the air.

'You want me to check out the clinic?'

'The address is on the email.'

She was about to say something but Charlie turned away to take a phone call. She stood around while he talked. There wasn't much of a view from up here. The building behind Priest & Co.'s office that backed on to the Strand was taller and overshadowed them. She wondered how many times Charlie had slunk up here to pitch a golf ball into a windmill in order to regain traction with his life.

When he turned back after ending the call, he looked grave. This was the worst she had seen him, with dark marks under his eyes, even his hair had lost some of its shine. In truth, he looked beat.

'Got to go,' he said, leading her to the ladder. 'They've found another body.'

The postcode Rowlinson had sent him brought Priest to the shell of a decommissioned factory warehouse in Hackney near a canal. He pulled the Aston up alongside Rowlinson's BMW, two squad cars and a forensics van where he was met by a female uniformed officer, the same one who had delivered him the letter from Copperhead earlier that morning.

'Mr Priest,' she said, removing her cap and brushing the hair out of her eyes. 'It's through here. You'll need to suit up first.'

She motioned to where a tent had been erected behind the van. He thanked her. She made to say something but stopped herself. He noticed a push-bike leant against the wall, cordoned off with tape, before he entered the tent and found the crime scene manager waiting for him – a bearded man in his late fifties with a good-natured smile and a distressing comb over, who introduced himself as Frederick-but-everyone-calls-me-Freddy.

After Priest had hauled on the white coveralls, Freddy caught him by the arm.

'The governor gave me the low-down on you,' he said without a trace of hostility. 'But just to warn you, this isn't for the faint-hearted. No shame in sitting it out. You don't have to see it first-hand.'

'I appreciate the advice, but I've seen a lot in my time.'

'Not like this you haven't.'

Freddy watched Priest for a reaction with an unwavering look, before leading him out.

'Through here.'

As they exited the tent, the PC was waiting for them, a little anxious and much paler than she had been yesterday.

She addressed him uncertainly. 'Sir?'

'Yes?'

'The envelope I gave you this morning.'

'Yes,' he said, reading her thoughts. 'It was *him*.'

She nodded, thankful that he hadn't patronised her with a lie, or fobbed her off, and withdrew back to her position next to the road where her colleague was waiting.

Freddy led Priest into the roofless part of the building. The walls were covered with graffiti. Most of it was just teenage stuff: tags, words and numbers that had meaning to themselves and no one else, scrawled in black and red paint; but some of it displayed real talent. Elaborately coloured images of revolutionary idealism and anti-establishment notions: a picture of a man in army uniform holding a gun to a baby's head while a mother wept helplessly in the background; a laughing clown face with a swastika printed on his nose holding the strings of puppets dressed in suits waving generously at a crowd; children wearing gas masks riding on the backs of Dali-style elephants with absurdly long spindly legs.

The warehouse was a labyrinth of small rooms littered with discarded spray-paint cans, cigarette butts and pigeon shit. They passed a tower of wooden pallets and a room with four inexplicable square holes in the centre, perhaps where once a machine had been cemented in, filled with rubbish and used gas canisters. In the distance, Priest could hear muffled voices, Rowlinson's amongst them. And in the air, the stench of death.

The final room was gigantic and the roof was still intact. Three thick shafts of brilliant light burst through the lead-lined windows splitting the area into sections, in the last of which, four people in the same white coveralls, gloves and masks stood solemnly looking down. One of them approached Priest and from his gait he could tell it was Rowlinson.

'The fatal wound is the same – a nail to the head, driven in so deep there's only a few mill protruding out – but there's more you need to see.' Clearly, there was no time for small talk.

When Rowlinson showed him the body, lying crookedly over a pallet, naked and bloody, Priest could see what he meant. His instinct was to look away, repulsed. The smell was overwhelming, it gripped the inside of his throat and stung his eyes, made his stomach churn. But he looked. Long and hard, knowing that sometimes when he closed his eyes at night, he saw bodies from his past life circle around his mind like vultures. This was another one he'd never forget.

The victim was male, young – Christ, a teenager. Fourteen, fifteen maybe. Rowlinson was right. This time the nail was barely visible. But Copperhead hadn't stopped there. There were deep purple wounds oozing with blood across his chest, shoulders and arms, cuts down his midriff. His right thigh was split open, the muscle and bone partially removed as if it had been savaged by a wild beast. The boy – for that's all he was – hadn't been murdered, he'd been mutilated almost beyond recognition. Most sickening of all, Priest began to realise what had happened.

'Are those bite marks?'

'Afraid so.'

The answer came from one of the other people standing opposite him. He had been so wrapped up with the sick parody of human flesh in front of him he hadn't noticed Fay. His eyes met hers for a brief moment. Something passed between them, but he wasn't sure what.

'Do we know who he is?'

'We know nothing,' said Rowlinson. There was something in his throat that distorted his words. 'No sign of his clothes. We're in touch with missing persons, of course, but as of now we don't know who he is.'

'Cross reference the donors' register with missing persons and we'll find out soon enough, assuming he's registered. Who found him?'

'Anonymous triple nine call from a phone box a few miles away. My guess is some kids came here to shoot up or whatever, saw the body, decided that it would be a whole load of questions if they were found with it, and called it in later. They'll have already found a new crack-den by now, and a cache of pictures on their phones to show their mates.'

Priest clicked his tongue. 'Is there anything . . . missing?'

It seemed an odd question but Freddy took it in his stride. 'If you're asking whether any of the flesh was consumed then the pathologist will tell you more, but best guess is yes, there's a lot of tissue missing from the thigh wound.'

*Fuck me. Copperhead is a cannibal.*

A thought entered his head. *The mutilation was so horrific, so very different, was it even the same killer?*

'Where's the symbol?'

There was a pause before Fay answered. 'It's everywhere.'

He looked up sharply. 'What do you mean?' Then he looked around. He hadn't seen it first time around. The graffiti pervaded every section of wall throughout the building and he saw his mistake. He'd become blind to it. The large room was no different, graffiti everywhere, but when he saw the first symbol woven into the urban artwork the rest suddenly appeared like a 'magic eye' picture coming into focus. Fay was right. It was everywhere. And if there was any doubt about the identity of the killer remaining, it was vanquished by the message on the wall. Not *Kill the Giants*. Something different. Something for him.

'Have you looked up this one?' Priest asked, staring at the words scrawled in the unknown victim's blood on the wall bathed in glorious sunlight:

*'Priest: take heed. Isaiah 13:9.'*

By way of an answer, Fay read aloud from her phone. *'See, the day of the Lord is coming – a cruel day, with wrath and fierce anger – to make the land desolate; and destroy the sinners within it.'*

'A warning?' Rowlinson suggested.

'A prediction,' Priest corrected. 'He's getting bolder by the hour.'

Rowlinson, letting the pressure get the better of him, cupped his hands behind his head, walked away, kicking a pile of rubble. 'Shit! Shit! Fucking shit!'

Priest turned away. He was no less frustrated, but in all fairness he wasn't going to have to tell some mother and father that their son had been butchered and partially eaten by a lunatic who thought he was a demon-hunter. And given that the blood type was genetic, was one of them also in danger?

He was about to address Rowlinson but stopped when he saw the DCI had finished venting and was on his phone. After a minute of listening, he rang off, mumbling a thank you.

'That was our CPS contact. We've got the donors' database. All three victims are listed.'

Priest watched as the implications of this started to settle in. He had already had time to think about it. It raised a grave question. What if you knew a serial killer was narrowing his victims to a few hundred named individuals, but you didn't know in what order he would approach it?

'So we've got a hit list,' said Fay, thoughtfully.

'With over three hundred names on it, many of them family members.'

'Is there any apparent pattern to Copperhead's selections?'

'They're working on it, but nothing's jumping out.'

'He'll be picking them at random,' said Priest. 'He'll have anticipated this.'

'What do we do?' asked Rowlinson. 'We can't possibly protect them all. Do we tell them? Can you imagine the consequences? The panic?'

'Can you imagine what happens if you *don't* tell them.'

Another thought crossed Priest's mind. *Did he know anyone with such a rare blood type?* Not in the family – not Sarah or Tilly, thankfully. He didn't know their blood types but he would know if it was rare. Wouldn't he? And Jessica? What was her blood type? He had no idea. He didn't even know if she had a middle name.

He looked round at Rowlinson, at Fay, Freddy and the two SOCO technicians setting up a camera. No doubt they were all thinking the same thing. Did they know anyone on the database? *Fay looked particularly troubled*, he thought.

It should feel like progress: they knew how Copperhead was choosing his victims. But it wasn't. It was worse than not knowing. They were hopelessly under-resourced, with no way of guessing which potential victim was next. It was probably completely random. And with regard to telling people, they were damned either way. Inform everyone – induce mass panic, alert Copperhead to the only advantage they had, tie up their dwindling resources on managing the outrage and fear that would spill out across the city. And the people on the database weren't the only people with this rare blood type; only the ones who had bothered to register. Or don't say anything, and when the truth finally comes out – as surely it ultimately will – stand accused of abandoning those victims, of withholding vital information, stripping them of the opportunity to flee if that's what they wanted to do.

Priest pinched the bridge of his nose. *To destroy the sinners within it.* He could be imagining it, but it felt like the temperature had just soared again.

# Chapter 44

By the time Priest got back to his apartment he wanted nothing more than to shower off the smell of Copperhead's latest victim but, with all the distraction, he had forgotten about his two temporary lodgers.

After he walked in, he faltered for a moment before it all flooded back; when he saw Sarah and Tilly sitting side-by-side at the breakfast bar, mother on her laptop, child on her iPad. From the subdued '*Hey*' he received, he realised something was wrong beyond the normal shit Sarah was going through.

With a wistful look at the door leading to his bathroom, he pulled up a chair opposite her.

'Bad day?' he asked. She sighed heavily, replied with nothing more than a tired smile, but something was troubling her beyond the fatigue, a feeling that he recalled well. 'Tell me about it.'

She turned to Tilly, placed a hand gently on her shoulder. 'Til, can you play that in the lounge while I talk to Uncle Charlie?' The little girl nodded and got down from the chair, not taking her eyes off the iPad.

'She likes word games,' Sarah explained as she padded out. 'And apps that teach her things.'

'She probably knows more about technology than me. Does she need a job?'

She managed another wan smile before cutting to the chase. 'He wants half of everything, including the rental properties.'

He almost laughed. He knew Ryan was money-orientated but even he couldn't possibly think that that was realistic. 'The properties are in our joint names, from Mum and Dad. There's no way the court would grant him that in a divorce.' She didn't look convinced. 'Does he have an income?'

'From the tattoo parlour, not much. You know what he's like. Always looking for a quick buck.'

'If he had a brain, he'd be dangerous.'

'He does. He's a trained accountant, just fucking lazy.'

'Where did he train? Betfred?'

She laughed weakly, got up to make tea. She was dressed as stylishly as an A-list celebrity with perfectly ruffled hair and to anyone that didn't know her well she looked about as far from a woman dealing with divorce as was conceivable. Only her eyes betrayed her.

'He's got some advice, apparently. He thinks he's got a claim against the portfolio. By the way, you stink. What the hell have you been doing?'

'Me and the gang found a dead body by the mill and we went to poke it with sticks.'

'I thought you didn't do that kind of shit anymore.'

He shrugged. 'Me too.'

She filled the kettle with water and got out two mugs. He stole another glance at the door to the bathroom. The dirt and grime of the warehouse were eating away at him. He also took the opportunity to put his phone on the table to check for messages. The database was due any moment if Tiff had got his act together.

'By the way,' he said. 'What blood type are you and Tilly?'

She looked at him sideways, puzzled. 'Why?'

He tried not to make a big deal out of it. 'Just wondered. Thought I should know. Okoro knows the blood type of all his family members. I don't. It bothers me.'

She considered this, perhaps weighing up whether she wanted to understand the strange request more or move on. 'O negative. So's Til.'

He had been fairly sure but nonetheless a wave of relief took the edge off his anxiety. It was soon replaced with exhaustion.

He picked up his phone, located a contact and sent it to her.

'I've just sent you my divorce lawyer's details. He's still practising and he's still the best in London. Call him. Tell him who you are. He'll look after you.'

She nodded, but still didn't relax. Without thinking, Priest checked her face for bruises. It was an overreaction, he realised. As far as he knew, she hadn't met up with Ryan whilst she had been staying with him but the urge to protect her was instinctual. Anyway, there was nothing.

When she spoke, it sounded more like a confession than anything else and he realised why she had been holding back. A pang of annoyance pricked his side.

'The income goes into a joint account.'

'I told you to keep that money separate.'

She retaliated, ready for a fight – this conversation had probably played out in her head a hundred times before he arrived back. 'And I told you that marriages don't work like that if . . .' She stopped, realising her mistake.

'If you want to make them work,' he finished for her.

She ignored the boiled kettle and slumped down next to him and, for the first time – much to his horror – he thought she might actually cry.

'Fuck. I'm sorry. I fucked up. I just wanted it to work, so badly. For Tilly.'

He softened instantly. There was no chance he could be angry with his sister. She was one of the few people in the world who had stood by him through his divorce, his exit from the Force, the six months working in a bar, the constant rumination, depression-like symptoms, and his failure to detach from William. She had hated all of it. And, yes, they had argued, virulently sometimes. But she was blood, as was Tilly. The only tangible thing he had left in this world and he would give up everything else for them in a second, without hesitation.

'It's OK,' he said, placing a hand on her arm. 'We'll work it out. Ryan's hardly going to win in a legal battle against us, is he?'

'It's his fault,' she sniffed, and he could see she was crying now. 'He started this. He ... did what he did. Won't the court take that into account?'

'Sorry, kid. He could have had a hundred affairs, it wouldn't make much difference. Divorce law is about who gets what, not who deserves what.'

'Your law is an ass.'

'At the best of times. You should see it at its worst.'

'Ah, what a fucking mess.' She buried her head in her arms on the table. The tears had stopped. Perhaps they shouldn't have. Perhaps she should cry, wail, scream, shout – get it all out. Perhaps he should have told her that, but in truth he was worried. Worried for her, but worried about Copperhead too.

'Do you need money?' he said.

'No. I'm fine. The company is doing well. I have savings.'

'The Volvo's in for repair but you can borrow the Aston any time. Or I can rent you a car.'

She laughed. 'It's fine, Charlie. We're OK, and I'm not driving that ridiculous car of yours. I don't need an ego trip.'

He smiled. 'I'll see what I can do on the properties. I can get the tenants to change their direct debit to my account and feed you the money behind the scenes. It'll be a mess if you get involved but I can handle it.'

'He's terrified of you, you know.'

'He damn well should be.'

She lifted her head, leant in to his embrace, and he knew that it was his turn to stand up for her after the years that she had stood by him, tolerated him and made allowances. Finally, a long-established debt could be repaid, at least in part.

'There is something you can do,' she said.

'Name it.'

'I need some things from home for Til. Toys, books, clothes, that sort of thing. If I make a list, can you get them? I don't want to run into Ryan. I don't have the strength right now for another fight.'

Out loud, he said 'of course'. He would do that. Right now if need be. It wasn't a problem. Work could wait. She wasn't causing a problem.

Inwardly, he really wished she had asked for something that could have waited.

# Chapter 45

It was late by the time Priest pulled up outside the black railings fronting Sarah and Ryan's house and killed the engine. He glanced up and down the street but he couldn't see Ryan's motorbike parked anywhere and there were no lights on in the house. Part of him was disappointed.

He slammed the car door behind him and checked the list Sarah had given him. It was quite extensive but there were detailed instructions for locating each item. He checked his phone: nothing from Rowlinson. *What the hell was keeping him?*

He fumbled around with the key and opened the door. Hit the light and the hallway came into view. It looked empty, abandoned. No shoes at the foot of the stairs, or coats hung on the pegs lining the wall, none of Tilly's toys clustered around the little cupboard under the stairs. It even smelt different somehow. Lonely. No wonder Sarah hadn't wanted to come back.

He worked methodically through the house; the list was organised room by room. He was upstairs in the bathroom trying to work out which bubble bath she meant when he heard the front door open and someone enter the hallway.

*This is all I need.*

He grabbed a couple of bottles and stuffed them into a bag, before heading downstairs.

He had seen rabbits in the headlights before. Their wide eyes, mouth agape, fear plastered across their faces. But nothing compared to the look on Ryan's face as Priest descended the stairs carrying a bag and whistling merrily.

'What ... are you doing here?' Ryan stammered, backing against the wall.

'I'm redecorating, what the fuck do you think?'

To his credit, he regained his composure quickly enough and fell into his default combative disposition, hostile and suspicious.

'This is *my* house, Charlie.'

'And my sister's, who gave me a key.'

'Still doesn't explain what you're doing here.'

Priest stopped when he reached the bottom of the stairs. Ryan had retreated further inside the house, allowing him plenty of room to leave. He wasn't stupid. Priest was a foot taller and a good four stone heavier. Ryan swayed warily. Priest didn't move, just watched him.

'OK, so you're picking stuff up,' he said sulkily. 'I get it.'

'Mm. See you around then, Ryan.' He made to leave, surprised at how cool he was acting, but it didn't last. Ryan had always been like that: always needed the last word, even when he knew he was on the losing side. He responded so softly that it was barely audible. Priest could have walked away. He could have ignored it and left. But the last twenty-four hours were catching up with him. The frustration, anger and tiredness all conspired against him.

So when Ryan muttered, 'Good riddance, dickwad,' something snapped inside him.

'Say what?'

Ryan realised his mistake instantly. 'Nothing.'

'No. You said something, *pal*.'

'I said nothing. You were just leaving.'

He backed away, arms out, as Priest rounded on him, dropping the bag on the floor. 'Say that again to me. *Please.*'

'Piss off, Charlie!'

Priest reached out and grabbed Ryan by the lapels, pulled him across the room and slammed him against the wall. He shrieked with pain and for a moment Priest thought he was going to fight back but the pathetic shit just fell limp in his hands, defeated. It was the yield that saved him, and what he said next that avoided Priest putting his fist through his jaw.

'Truth is, Charlie – I don't even know what I did wrong.'

Priest tightened his grip, bringing a yelp of pain in response. 'What are you babbling about?'

'I'm telling you the truth. I don't know why she left.'

'Right.'

'It's the truth!'

Priest paused, unsure. 'Why don't we ask Gemma about that?'

'What? Who the fuck is Gemma?'

Priest realised Ryan could barely breathe. His grip was strangling him, but he knew exactly where the limit was. He relaxed, not enough for Ryan to wriggle free but enough to let him have a gulp of air.

'I swear, Charlie! I don't know what the fuck you're talking about. She just packed her things and said it was over.'

Conflicted, Priest let him go, but not without first shoving him hard towards the kitchen. No harm in letting him know just how easy it would be for Priest to hurt him if he really wanted to. But he had no wish to. There was something in his tone of voice, the pleading look in his eyes. He wasn't sure, but if Ryan was lying, it was a pretty convincing performance.

'She told me that a girl called Gemma contacted her out of the blue and said you were seeing her. You'd met on the internet, and there were other girls too.'

Ryan was shaking, fighting to keep calm. It was a sad sight, watching a man's dignity flake off, even if the man was a dickhead. 'There is no Gemma. I'm a lot of things, Charlie, but not a cheat.'

If there had been time, Priest might have been able to prise out the truth. He could cross-examine as good as any barrister if he wanted to. But he didn't have the privilege of time. He felt his phone vibrate in his pocket. Checked it, and made to leave.

Before he reached the door, he looked back over his shoulder.

'If you're lying to me, Ryan, then there'll be hell to pay.'

This time, his brother-in-law had the sense to stay quiet, but whatever he could have said wouldn't have stopped Priest from leaving at that point. Rowlinson had sent him a copy of the database. And it was bad news.

# Chapter 46

In the car, Priest read Rowlinson's message again and tried to put his encounter with Ryan to the back of his mind. It didn't make sense – why the hell would Sarah lie to him? But there wasn't time to consider it further. It would have to wait.

The database was attached to an email but the attachment was password protected. Priest would need to call the DCI to get the password. He suspected it was more to do with forcing him to speak to Rowlinson first rather than security.

He dialled. Waited. Tossed the message around in his head. There was someone he knew on the list. *But who?*

After five rings, Rowlinson picked up.

'Got your email,' he said, hoping his tone would leave no room for procrastination. 'Who is it?'

Rowlinson hesitated. 'The DSI doesn't want anyone on the list to be contacted. Not yet. Not until we have a full strategy and a plan for dealing with disclosure.'

'Tiff, for fuck's sake, it's late. Just cut to the chase.'

'The DSI was quite clear on this point, Priest. No exceptions. You with me?'

'Fine.'

There was an agonising pause. 'It's Jessica Ellinder.'

Priest let it sink in. At first, he wasn't sure what shocked him more: the fact that Jessica was one of only a few hundred people with an exceptionally rare blood type, or the fact that, by the way he handled telling him, Rowlinson clearly realised that it was significant for him. They hadn't spoken about Jessica since the Mayfly case. *How the hell does he know we're still in touch?*

'OK,' Priest heard himself say. 'OK. Jessica Ellinder.' He felt a tightness in his chest, and a prickling sensation at the back of his neck. *Jessica.*

'Let's not beat around the bush here, Priest. I know that you two are . . . you know.'

'How do you know that?'

'I'm a detective.'

'That's a dragged-through-the-shop-floor answer.' He could have pressed it further but, again, it was another puzzle he didn't have the time or energy to try and fit together.

'Look, we've got a couple of days at least,' Rowlinson breathed. 'Nothing will happen tonight. Not even this killer can mobilise between kills that quickly. We're meeting tomorrow with the DSI.'

Priest realised he was still parked outside Sarah's house. It was a small positive that Ryan was nervously watching him from the upstairs bedroom window, presumably under the misapprehension that he couldn't be seen.

He switched the phone to hands-free and started the Aston.

'Priest, you still there?'

'Yeah, I'm here.'

Except he wasn't. He was elsewhere. In the corner of his vision, something stirred. He blinked several times but it wouldn't go away. A ghostly shape that vanished every time he tried to look directly at it. He shook his head violently. *Not now.*

'That a car engine I hear?'

'Don't worry, I'm not going to see her. Just had to swing by Sarah's to pick up some things.'

'OK. We'll sort this out tomorrow morning. There's nothing more we can do now.'

Priest pulled out on to the main road and accelerated past rows of parked cars and stopped at a temporary traffic light guarding a set of roadworks. He wasn't sure what it was hidden in Rowlinson's tone, but it bothered him.

'Why do I get the feeling there's something else?' At first, there was no reply. 'Tiff?'

'Yeah, you just need to be aware that the AC will be at the meeting tomorrow.'

'*Fuck* me.'

'Yeah.'

'Does she know I'm involved?'

'In a fashion.'

'That means no, doesn't it?'

'The DSI is squaring it with her now.'

'At ten at night?' Priest slammed his hand on the side of the door in frustration, his head spinning. 'Jesus, Tiff! She hates being disturbed at home.'

Rowlinson yawned. 'I know. It's going to be a difficult meeting.'

'Does Dee know about Jessica? Wait. I already know the answer. No.' Rowlinson didn't reply which told him he was correct. 'All right. I'll see you in the morning.'

'Bright and early.'

Priest rang off. The traffic lights turned green. The ghost dissipated.

He didn't move until the car behind sounded the horn. As he drove off, he realised he hadn't even asked for the bloody password.

Priest passed his shopping across the conveyor belt but with his phone in his hand he was only half concentrating. With nothing else to do, and knowing it was unlikely he was going to sleep well despite his tiredness, he had ended up in the twenty-four-hour supermarket trying to work out what food to stock up on for the three of them.

As the checkout boy, whose name was Erik according to his badge, looked doubtfully at his random purchases, Priest reread the text from Jessica, which was both good and bad news.

'*Can't talk. Away on business in Belfast. Back tomorrow. Lunch?*'

Good because she was out of London, *although did that make her safe?* There didn't seem much option – he didn't fancy the 'just to let you know a serial killer might be after you' conversation right now, and he doubted it would achieve much, other than just to scare her. Would she even believe him? It was pretty far-fetched to someone who hadn't lived and breathed the last week or so.

'And this as well?' asked Erik, holding up the PlayStation 4 and VR headset.

'Please.'

'Cool, quite a few games too.'

'Yeah, I don't know what six-year-old girls like, so I just got a selection.' Erik nodded, but Priest could tell he was sceptical, so he explained further. 'It's for my niece. She's staying with me for a few days.' Erik nodded, more relaxed.

Priest went back to his phone. He was just starting to delete another message from Sasha Merriweather when Erik coughed politely.

'I get a few of these,' he said, earnestly. 'For a little kid. But I'm not sure about *Hello Neighbor.*'

'It's rated seven plus.'

'Yeah, maybe, but I've got a copy. Basically you have to break in to your neighbours' houses and spy on them. It don't teach kids right from wrong, you know what I mean?'

Priest nodded, appreciative. 'See what you mean. Stick it back for me, will you? Thanks.'

'OK. That'll be six hundred and fifty-three pounds, thirty pence, please.'

Priest hauled the shopping away and spent the next ten minutes repacking the Aston's boot so that everything fitted properly before heading home.

On the way, a thought occurred to him. Something Erik had said, about breaking in and spying on your neighbours. He had been so obsessed with finding out how Copperhead was *picking* his victims that he'd forgotten to address a more obvious question: how was he *catching* them?

The meeting started at ten, and that gave him enough time in the morning to take some advice from an expert.

# Chapter 47

*Wednesday*

Dr William Priest stared vacantly across the table, his arms hung loosely and his head slightly cocked. Ten years of incarceration inside a high-secure unit at Fen Marsh Hospital had taken their toll on London's most notorious modern-day serial killer, but his younger brother was accustomed to seeing the fire behind his blue eyes – the fire that told him there was nothing diminished about William's brain. If anything, the contrary was true. He had used his time to improve his mental abilities, studying ferociously and devouring literature on every conceivable topic from the mysteries of dark matter and string theory to the wonders of the human mind.

It was outside of visiting times, outside of protocol, but it had happened before and, although Priest detected reluctance, his request was acceded to. Inside Fen Marsh, Dr William Priest was in control. Priest had never dwelt upon it too greatly but he knew that William had spent his time locked away in this unreal, insular world doing more than just studying. They could restrict William's physical movements, but they could never contain him. He was too great a manipulator.

'The secret is simple,' he had once said quietly to Priest, out of earshot of the nurses shuffling their feet nervously behind him. 'Networks are greater than hierarchies.'

Priest had always assumed that what William meant was that the influence he had established inside Fen Marsh was not based on fear, subordination or oppression, but had been created by an insouciant manipulation, much like the British Empire – at its peak, a population of millions controlled by a handful of people. William had got inside the heads of those around him and while there was no outward reason to suspect that Fen Marsh was anything other than a secure hospital with fewer than eighty patients, the reality was that the lunatics were well and truly running the asylum.

The immediate problem was William's current state of mind. Whether it was just his mood or a regression, or he was just pretending for reasons best known to himself, Dr Wheatcroft, who had overall responsibility for William's care, couldn't be sure, but William wasn't showing much interest in engaging.

'I doubt you'll get much out of him today, but by all means you can try,' Wheatcroft had warned. It turned out to be a fairly accurate prediction.

'Wills?' Priest urged. 'Can you hear me?'

William refocussed, and for a moment Priest thought he saw some lucidity in his expression but it was gone in the blink of an eye.

'William?'

Priest waited and eventually the Dark Redeemer slurred out a response:

'I'm sorry, I'm having some problems recalling things this morning, Charles.'

'That's a shame. I'm hunting.'

That caught his attention. 'Hunting?'

Priest glanced up at the male nurse behind them; recognised him as one from his last visit. Sensing Priest's wariness, William said:

'That's Perry, Charles. I wouldn't worry too much. We're all friends in here, Perry, right?'

Perry didn't say anything. Just shifted his weight. Uncomfortable, but under control. Priest dreaded to think how William managed it.

With Perry looking on anxiously, Priest placed pictures of the four victims in front of William one at a time in order. There was a moment's silence while William considered them, the vacancy in his expression having vanished as the fire in his eyes ignited.

'I didn't think you were a hunter anymore, Charles,' he said, so quietly that Perry had to strain to listen.

'Some of us can't escape what's in our nature.' Priest looked at his brother meaningfully. 'Can we?'

'Unfortunately not.' William picked up one of the photographs, pointed to the Janus symbol. 'What's this?'

'His trademark.'

William murmured, almost inaudibly, 'A snake, wrapped around the Cross of Jesus.'

Priest summarised the story: the stowaway on Noah's Ark, the demon lineage, the silver blood, the Binding. And Copperhead.

'Copperhead?'

'The snake. From the Garden of Eden.'

William frowned, strained hard, as if digging right to the darkest depths of his mind. 'Yes, yes. I know. But . . . something else.' Priest waited, but nothing came until William wafted his hand irritably. 'Curse this fog that's clouding everything. You've not caught me at my best, Charles.'

'His name's not important. This rare blood type: the International Rare—'

'Yes,' William interrupted, annoyed. 'The International Rare Donor Panel database. No doubt there are only a few hundred people with Lutheran b negative and most of those are clustered around Greater London. Yes?'

Priest tried not to react, or ask anything that betrayed the fact that he was reluctantly impressed. 'That's right.'

'He can't possibly kill all of them,' William surmised. 'Even the Met will catch him eventually, and of course his chances have dwindled now that you're on the case.'

Priest was finding it difficult to work out what was the most surprising: the speed at which William assimilated the story or the back-door compliment.

'There's no pattern, of course,' said William.

'No. Seemingly random. The only thing the victims have in common is their blood type.'

'Hm.' William studied the photographs again, thoughtful. 'But he knows their movements. The locations suggest so. A hotel room, the victim's house, a park and an abandoned warehouse. Your killer knew where to find them, and how to coordinate this knowledge to spring a trap.'

'He knows how to kill people without leaving a forensic trace, too.'

Priest was about to go on, but William cut him short. 'There's something you're not telling me.'

Priest stopped, alert. *There's plenty I'm not telling you.* 'Your—'

William leant across the table, watched Priest with such clinical intensity it was as if he was trying to split his head open and look inside. 'You know someone on the donors' register.' When Priest didn't react, he carried on, assured. 'Yes. Not just someone. Someone important. A woman. Someone who means something to you.'

Priest felt a wave of heat go through him as William's words sunk in. *How the fuck did he know that?* It didn't matter, and it was obvious anyway. He cursed himself for being so transparent. He had to be more careful; unlike Perry and the rest of them, who would have been such easy pickings for the great manipulator to strip apart piece by piece. It would have taken nothing more than a change in his tone of voice, a twitch, a few blinks out of sequence, a little glance to the right, a sure sign that a right-handed person like Priest was using the creative 'left' part of his brain to mask a truth. And William had no better baseline for detecting the tiny psychological reactions of a person than his brother. He'd been doing it since he was old enough to read and write.

'Have I got your attention now, at least?' said Priest, pissed off but deciding it was best to go with it. No point in pretending.

William sat back, concerned. 'If this woman is important to you then she will only be safe when your killer is dead. You know that, right?'

'Wills, I need to—'

'Listen to me!' William bellowed, making Perry edge forward, alarmed. 'Dead. Not caught. Not imprisoned, especially not in a place like this. Dead. You're not dealing with an amateur here, Charles.'

'I'm helping the police. I'm not a fucking vigilante.'

'You think he'll extend you the same courtesy?'

'This isn't about—'

'If you have someone to protect, then you have a vulnerability. A killer who can plan and execute four near-perfect murders in such an extraordinarily short period of time will have little trouble exploiting an advantage like that.'

Priest gritted his teeth, anger coursing through him. 'He'll not get to her.'

William shook his head, not dismissively, but with disgust. 'How can you be so sure?'

Priest felt under pressure, the realisation that William might be right was starting to weave under his skin. His hands were clammy, his head filled with images of Jessica. 'I can catch him. With your help.'

'And you think a hospital can hold him? You think this place can hold *me*?'

Priest faltered again. He'd considered the penetrability of Fen Marsh many a time. William had never shown any interest in escaping, but this was the first time that his brother had mooted the subject. He felt a rising sense of panic, washing the anger away. Perry had picked up a phone on the wall and was speaking urgently down the line.

'He's just a man, Wills.'

William thrust the photograph of the mangled body they had found in the warehouse across the table. 'No *man* did this, Charles. A monster did this. Remember: there is no greater danger than someone who thinks he's doing God's work.'

Sweat was forming on his brow. He should have insisted on going to see Jessica last night, even if she was in Belfast.

The door opened. Three people appeared, including Dr Wheatcroft.

'I must insist that visiting time is over, Dr Priest,' Wheatcroft announced.

'Wait,' said Priest sharply, then turned to William as two men placed their hands on his shoulders. 'How do I stop him?'

William didn't seem to notice the intervention. He was almost in a trance. 'Stop looking for him.'

'What?'

They started to help William up from the table and guide him across the room. Wheatcroft was frowning at Priest, saying something but he didn't hear it. He was straining to listen to William's last words as he was taken away.

'To catch this snake, brother, you might have to become one.'

They led William away despite Priest's objections, and as the door slammed shut behind them, Priest was left alone with nothing but the sound of blood rushing past his ears.

# Chapter 48

Georgie stood in the entranceway to the Thames Blood Donor Centre and looked around. There was a reception desk at the far end, behind which an orange-faced woman with enormous hoop earrings was staring at her as if something very important had just been disturbed.

'Yes?'

'Hi.' Georgie shuffled to the desk and put her bag down. 'Can I donate?'

From the look she received back, she might as well have asked the woman to lend her ten grand, unsecured and with no interest. The woman waited a beat, before sliding a form across the desk.

'There's a pen on the side.'

Georgie filled out the form and passed it back. The woman indicated that she should sit down and wait.

'You don't ask for blood type?' Georgie asked out of the blue. The woman lowered her phone, gave her an *I can't believe you're talking to me* look. 'On the form. You don't ask for blood type. Surely that's important.'

'Most people don't know their blood type,' she said like Georgie was stupid. 'And those that do are probably wrong. So they just stopped asking for it. The lab works it out then we know it's right.'

'Oh, I see.'

The woman waited to see if there were any more questions, then went back to her phone.

'Well, I can tell you I have a really rare blood type,' Georgie said.

'Right.' She didn't even look up.

'Yeah, it's like a few hundred people, maybe fewer. So I always donate.'

'Good for you.'

'I guess you have shortages once in a while, for things like Lutheran b negative.'

The woman sighed, probably coming to terms with the fact that Georgie wasn't going to shut up. 'That what you have?'

She nodded, did her best to smile but inside she was dying. This was like when they picked her last for the parts in the school play. She couldn't act to save her life.

'That was all last year, wasn't it?'

She felt a jolt of excitement. 'Hm?'

'Last year, when all those emails went out. We never got to the bottom of it.'

'I don't know what happened.'

'Someone sent a load of emails to everyone registered with that blood type you mentioned, but it wasn't us. They all came but they didn't complain. They like rare bloods, like yours.'

She nodded to herself, considered it. Why would the killer want them to give blood? This was an NHS facility, he can't have been able to get hold of the blood after it was donated, and what would be the point?

'How many people came in?'

'Loads, maybe a hundred or something, over three or four months.'

'Right.'

*What did he have to gain from that? Unless there was something about the centre itself that was important. Maybe it wasn't the blood, maybe it was—*

'Say,' she asked brightly, hoping her natural optimism would drag the woman out of her depression. 'Did they book appointments, or just turn up like me?'

She looked at Georgie, puzzled. *Why the hell are you asking that?* For a second, Georgie thought she was going to call her out, but she didn't. Probably concluded that it was easier just to answer the damn question. 'Neither. The email gave set times – that's why we think it was a mistake. We don't do that. Plus the times were all wrong. They all turned up in large groups. It was a nightmare. They had to sit and wait ages.'

*Sit and wait ages.*

She looked around, an idea forming in her head. But it was too brazen. Not even . . .

She stared at the wall. The answer was right there, staring back.

Georgie took out her phone and unlocked the screen.

# Chapter 49

Henrik Vose stood in the corner of the drawing room of Elisha Capindale's home with his phone to his ear and his eyes shut. Shut because Sasha Merriweather – who was on the other end of the line – was going round and round in circles and shut because he couldn't bear to look at his employer's impatient and unflinching glare from across the room where she sat, one thin leg crossed over the other, marinating in anger. Shut because he was tired. Shut because he didn't fully understand why this blasted book was so important. Shut because it was the only way he could concentrate on Merriweather's high-pitched drawl against the shudder he felt in his body every time Elisha's china cup clinked against the saucer.

'Yes . . . yes,' he muttered. 'I understand you've had to go back to the court. We just want the Book. It can't be that hard.'

'It takes time, Henrik.' He detected the edge to Merriweather's tone, the impatience creeping into her voice. 'The court have listed the application to amend the order for Friday afternoon. They wouldn't deal with it on paper. The judge wants a hearing.'

'That's the best you can do?'

'The Book is being preserved by the supervising solicitor. The court won't appreciate the urgency.'

'Bullshit. I explained to you that Priest had crossed a line by coming over here.'

'I'm looking into that but he's not returning my calls. And to be honest, Henrik, you're not helping me out here. What is so important about this book? I understand its archaeological and Biblical significance, but not the urgency that everything has to be handled with.'

'That's none of your concern,' Vose said sharply. 'Just get the damn book. That's what we're paying you for.'

He hung up before she could press him any further. Henrik Vose didn't like being in the dark. At first, his employment by this strange relic dealer, the martinet who was afraid of the sun, had been engaging: flights around the world, attending auctions, acting as the great lady's ambassador, and her eyes and ears on the ground, but at that point her reputation was already on a downward path. He had been naïve to think that he could have rescued it. Her obsession with the weird and wonderful – that fucking vial of the Virgin Mary's milk (probably just sewage water), for example – had blinded her. He increasingly noticed that as he introduced himself to academics and dealers as her representative, there were more and more scoffs, eyes turning away, wry smiles and patronising tones. Slowly, they all turned against her and, by proxy, him.

*Relic.* From the Latin *reliquiae*, meaning *left behind*. The real relic here wasn't the Book of Janus. It was Vose's employer.

'What did she say?' said Elisha, her eyes boring through him from behind the tea cup she had perched at her lips.

'There will be another court hearing on Friday.'

She sipped the tea, the tinkling of the china made him wince. 'I want that book, Henrik.'

'No. *He* wants that book.'

Vose had no idea who *he* was, only that *he* had turned up eighteen months ago clutching a few tatty pages of manuscript, which Elisha had taken copies of and studied for several days before calling him and telling him they were fragments from the Book of Janus. There had been a deal done. He was not privy to the details. Made to wait outside the door like some fucking pet. Then *he* had left and Elisha had told him to track down a scholar by the name of Norman Owen. Oh, and pay this cheque in immediately. It was a down-payment. One of several more to come. Vose had nearly choked. Ten thousand. No questions asked.

'And have a contract drawn up for Owen to sign,' she had said. 'I don't want him getting any silly ideas.'

Fat lot of good that did.

'What does he want with it?' said Vose. It was out of character for him to challenge her, but he was beginning to construct a future for himself without Elisha Capindale. She was becoming too much of a liability. He would go back to Germany, start again if he had to.

'He wants to avoid Judgement Day, of course.'

Vose had heard and seen a lot in the past few years, but that was nuts even for Elisha Capindale.

'He thinks he's Jesus or something?'

'Maybe he is.'

He had heard enough. He swore in German and walked out, slamming the door behind him. Even on the other side of the wall, he could hear that fucking cup and saucer clinking.

# Chapter 50

The desk sergeant, a bald man with oversized ears, barely looked up when Priest announced that he was there for a meeting with DCI Rowlinson. Hassled and agitated after his discussion with William, the last thing he wanted to do was sit down but he did so at the sergeant's behest, and his leg started tapping almost immediately to a soundless beat.

*To catch this snake, brother, you might have to become one.*

He punched through a text to Rowlinson saying he was in reception, wondering if the message would get there quicker. He was anxious to get on. They weren't going to catch Copperhead sitting around a fucking table.

And there was his ex-wife to contend with. Their marriage had been three years of hard work. But they had to have been happy at one point, surely? Funny how he couldn't remember any of it, except that the DPD had been at its worst. It was a corrosive, destructive force. The problem was simple: if the world wasn't real then nothing in it mattered; Priest had found that sooner or later people close to him withered into ash. It had been bad with Dee, but that was hardly her fault. But the shouting, the claustrophobic control, and the manipulation. That had been her fault.

He was thinking about Tilly, about how he had started to get better when she was born. He wasn't sure why. She wasn't his child, but somehow his sister having a baby, even with a dick-shite, represented something for him. Hope, maybe. And also a crushing truth. Charlie Priest had realised when Tilly was born that he would never have children of his own, and not because he didn't want them. He did. But his world was too chaotic, his self-assessment too damning. He wasn't capable of being anything like the father he knew he should be, like his own had been. Attentive, patient, a teacher, a friend.

Tilly was the bolt that had sealed that door shut for Priest. And she was the closest thing he would ever have to his own child. She was still on his mind, her manic laugh ringing through his head and lifting him out of his misery, when the desk sergeant's interaction with someone else caught his attention.

It wasn't that he had taken any notice of the tall, well-built man who had entered the station and was standing at the reception, but it didn't seem important until he started talking. He was around Priest's age and, from his profile, he had strong features, and dark brown hair professionally cut, a smart suit – designer probably – *the warm smile of a good host*, Priest thought.

'Could you give this to her, please? She left it on the side.'

The man handed the desk sergeant a package – lunch maybe? Priest might have looked away, but something held his interest.

'I think Fay is in a meeting this morning but I'll pass it on, Mr . . . ?'

He felt a jolt of guilt, blood rushing to his head.

'Westbrook. Er, David. I'm her husband.'

The desk sergeant thanked him for coming in and David Westbrook turned and left, nodding at Priest politely as he went. Priest nodded back, wide-eyed and slightly shocked. *She didn't wear a ring, and when he had asked directly, she had said she didn't have time for that sort of thing. Now where does* that *leave us?* Maybe the ring is round her neck, dangling from a gold necklace he hadn't seen. She didn't mention him because it didn't suit her to.

He thought about the kiss, the taste of her lips, the smell of her perfume, and of the tall, handsome man who had called himself her husband, worried that she had left her lunch at home, rushing in, taking time out of his day: self-assured, executive, diligent and caring. And none the wiser.

When Rowlinson appeared at the door and invited him through, he was still in shock.

She was there, with a low-cut top and her hair tied back. The top was sleeveless again, her flawless skin glistened in the light. Her jacket was slung over her chair and she greeted him with a smile that didn't quite reach her eyes. He might have contemplated the situation more but he put it to the back of his mind: Fay was sitting next to his ex-wife.

'I can't believe you've allowed this to happen.' Assistant Commissioner Dee Auckland turned to Eaton, who in turn was sat next to Grey. Rowlinson hovered in the background for a moment before taking a seat next to Grey and inviting Priest to sit down, opposite Dee. Neither Grey nor Dee acknowledged him.

'Hello, darling,' he said. 'You're looking well.'

She looked away in disgust. 'John, what the hell?'

To his credit, Eaton didn't show any signs of discomfort. 'So far Mr Priest has been bloody helpful, ma'am. To be fair, we couldn't really have got this far without him.'

Dee was incensed. 'Really? It looks to me like everyone of use in this investigation that you've let him near has ended up dead.'

'You mean Professor Owen? Come on, Dee, that's *one* person,' Priest complained.

Rowlinson sank back in his seat, his body language making it clear he didn't want to be drawn into anything.

Dee turned to him, her lips pursed with anger. 'The trouble with you, Charlie, is that you're incapable of taking anything seriously.'

'Somebody tried to blow me up a few days ago. That serious enough for you?' It had come out sharper than he had intended, but his sense of humour had slipped away. Another thought passed through his jaded mind: *someone had saved his arse that day, too. Called him in the nick of time. But who?*

Dee fell quiet and it turned to Eaton to keep the meeting moving.

'The press have now linked the deaths of Emma Mendez, Jane Vardy and Alan Burberry,' he said, more to Priest than anyone. 'They don't know about the fourth victim yet. A journalist rang – one of the old school. You probably don't know him. Idiot they call Slinky. He knows about the symbol, but he doesn't know what it is.'

Priest winced. He knew Slinky. Every policeman in London knew Slinky, new and old. 'How?'

Eaton made a noise of disgust, took a gulp of black coffee. 'Don't know yet, but if it's a tip-off from within this station I'll string someone up for it.'

'How much time do we have?' asked Dee, arms folded.

'He said he'd wait twenty-four hours but in reality it'll be out by the end of the day. He thinks we've got our own fucking Zodiac. That's too big a story not to cash in on. I've sent a Press Officer round to see him. See if we can buy some more time but the guy's freelance. It'll go to the highest bidder. Fuck the consequences for the investigation.'

'Does he know we have a list of his potential victims?'

'No. Not yet.'

She huffed, loudly to make sure everyone knew how dissatisfied she was. 'How is he doing this? How is he doing these murders so cleanly?'

Rowlinson intervened: 'I have an idea. We've identified the body found in the warehouse as Darren Green. He's seventeen. He has learning difficulties. Lives with his dad and stepmother. Real mother died ten years previous. His dad identified him, and he has the rare blood type. We found messages on his phone from a girl called Lucy Warren the day before the murder asking him to meet up with her for sex at the kill site. But when we talked to Lucy, she denies all knowledge of it.'

'An easy thing to do.'

'Agreed. But her phone's clean. Forensics can't find any trace of the messages.'

'You think Darren's phone was hacked?' asked Priest.

Rowlinson shrugged. 'We're still looking, and Lucy is due back in this morning for another round of questioning.'

'What about the other three?'

This time it was Fay's turn to report back. 'We found out that Emma Mendez's mother has a key to Emma's house but she's now confirmed that it's missing, possibly stolen. Jane Vardy, we're not sure, but if the killer is hacking phones then it probably wasn't difficult to establish that she was in a hotel room on her own one night. Alan Burberry ran the same route every weekday morning.'

Dee shook her head. 'And the nail in the head. What's that all about?'

'It's nothing unusual,' said Rowlinson. 'A rosehead galvanised nail.'

'To symbolise the crown of thorns around Christ's head,' said Grey with certainty. 'Or stigmata.'

They all looked at Priest, even Dee, as if it would be natural for him to either confirm or deny Grey's assertion. 'Georgie found a reference to a Biblical story about a woman named Yael who murders someone by hammering a nail through their head. We think it's connected to the Binding.'

'Is this the alternative ending to the Bible garbage?' asked Dee.

Priest didn't react. Just looked at her, until she looked away. There was silence for a moment, no doubt as they all mulled over the possibilities. Then Rowlinson spoke. 'I think we have to consider telling people on the donors' register. Warning them.'

Dee almost laughed. 'Are you mad? Have you any idea what sort of panic we would create?'

'He's right, Dee,' said Priest quietly. 'They deserve to know.'

'And how do you propose we do that?' She glared at him venomously. 'Send them an email? A tweet, perhaps? We can't possibly get around them all in time. We need to use our resources to catch the killer, not cause mayhem.'

'That's a pretty big decision to make on their behalf.'

Dee raised her eyebrows, then shook her head. 'You don't know the first thing about making big decisions. Ethan, have you completed a full profile? I asked for it by Tuesday.'

'Yes, I will have very shortly,' said Grey, who seemed unfazed by Eaton's tone. 'These things cannot be rushed, but it is worth the wait: I believe that the killer can be caught very soon.'

Priest watched him, surprised. He seemed deadly serious. 'How?'

'I think it would be best if I talk to DSI Eaton. Alone. If that's OK with you, ma'am? There is, after all, a possible leak.' He looked at Dee. She didn't seem pleased. She hated brown-nosing and smugness – two things that Grey reeked of – but any dislike of the situation she had developed was seemingly outweighed by her dislike of her ex-husband, so she relented.

'Fine. Brief me in one hour.'

# Chapter 51

Priest didn't waste any time leaving, not even waiting to speculate with Rowlinson about Grey's conspiratorial approach to speak to Eaton alone, although he clearly wanted to.

'What the hell can he say to John that he can't say to everyone else, including the AC?'

'I have no idea. Look, I've got to go. I'll call you this afternoon.'

'What? Where are you going now?'

He was out the door and in to the warm Holborn air before Rowlinson had a chance to repeat the question. He hadn't been the first one out, though. Fay was making her way across the car park when he caught up with her.

'Nice day for a drive,' he said without any particular tone.

She looked down at the car keys in her hand. 'I'm going to interview Lucy Warren, the girl Darren Green was supposed to be meeting in the warehouse.'

'Maybe we could get some lunch together later?'

Her eye twitched. 'I'm . . . not sure. I—'

'Oh, no, I forgot. You left your lunch at home, but someone dropped it in at reception. Your husband, in fact.'

He watched her lips tighten and her shoulders arch back, almost imperceptibly. In Geneva, he had asked if she was married. Her answer had been clear.

'No. Work gets in the way of things like that. You want something stronger?'

'You don't know me,' she said, looking down.

'Clearly.'

She turned away, shaking her head, like he was being unreasonable. Priest stood his ground. He had to go, but he wanted an explanation.

'It's not what it seems. And you don't get to judge me. My life hasn't always been easy like yours.'

He raised an eyebrow. 'You think my life is easy?'

She started to walk away, but the look on her face was full of regret and anger. 'Stay out of my way, Charlie Priest. I'm bad news. I told you that before.'

He watched her go before doubling back on himself and heading towards Covent Garden, a dark cloud forming in his head. Fay had turned out to be a disappointment, but he had bigger issues to think about. If the press knew about the possible link between the first three victims it was only a matter of time before the whole thing was out in the open, driving the killer further underground. *And what the fuck was Dee thinking by not telling the people on the donors' register, the silver bloods?*

The pub was one of his favourites. With hops strung up on the ceiling, cheap lighting and a pile of glass ashtrays on the side of the bar, ready just in case the smoking ban was inexplicably lifted. The Tuesday night curry was full of sugar and salt but worth the calorie intake. He was wedged in a two-seater booth with a half-wall topped with a plastic panel dividing the centre of the room, separating off a pool table and dartboard surrounded by a few chairs and a table.

He checked his watch. He was early, but so was she.

Jessica was already seated in the corner of the pub scrolling through a tablet, a glass of tonic water in front of her and a pint of dark ale waiting on the opposite side of the table, presumably for him.

She barely looked up when he took a seat, but motioned to the beer.

'I didn't know what to get you, so I got you that.'

Priest inspected the pint. From the chunky sediments clustered around the bottom of the glass, he surmised it was whatever local sludge the landlord had recommended.

'Thanks. This looks like the sort of thing that my grandad might have drunk before the war.'

She shrugged. 'They don't do Earl Grey.'

Priest knocked back a slug of beer; the bitter, metallic taste reminded him of his days at university when shit like this was a pound a pint and you could still buy sixteen cigarettes from a machine in pubs and bars.

'So,' she said. 'I didn't think you could make lunch today. Why the change of heart?'

'Maybe I wanted to see you after all.'

She chuckled, not because she was flattered or embarrassed but because she genuinely found it funny for some reason. 'But here. Not at home.'

He knew exactly what she meant because in that moment she had captured the totality of their relationship. They met and had sex. Good sex, but not close sex. The kind of sex where there's no soft murmurs or intimate kissing, just the sound of the sheets rustling, and her small, distant-sounding moans. Sometimes it felt amazing, euphoric; sometimes it was even a little weird. But mostly it was about raw gratification; something cold and a little primitive. Then she would slink out of bed, walk naked across the room to pick up her clothes, while the mere sight of her supple body, with those extraordinary curves and perfect breasts, would arouse him again almost immediately. Then she would get dressed and leave, occasionally glancing back with an awkward smile and they would exchange a few words – not the words of post-coital lovers, but the words of business people arranging another board meeting.

He wanted more. Maybe she did as well. But they had hit a glass ceiling that neither of them knew how to penetrate, and neither of them were sure they were ready for what was on the other side.

He took another sip of beer.

'We need to talk . . . about us, and this thing we have, whatever it is.'

'Must you insist on labelling it something?'

'It's not a relationship, is it?'

'No. And it can never be such.'

Although he knew that, as clearly as he knew that the grass was green and the sky blue, a cavity had suddenly opened up inside of him. A hole. For that is what loss is: emptiness, and the absence of colour.

He looked at her, his head filled with questions, his eyes filled with sorrow. 'I genuinely don't understand why not.'

The only consolation was that she seemed just as sad about it as he was. Sadder than he had ever seen her. 'It won't work, Charlie. Please. You must understand why.'

'I don't. That's the difference between you and me. I don't understand why.'

She looked around, and for a moment he thought she was sizing up the exits. 'Some things, Charlie . . . some things just can't be built on rot.'

The hole widened. Priest felt it was now large enough to swallow him. 'What do you mean?' He intended it to be a challenge, but deep down he knew what she meant. The Mayfly case had brought them together, but it had tainted them both. They had both been damaged, but more so she – her family had been torn apart by it. Looking at it like that, how could they ever be together? How naïve he had been for even thinking it.

'I can't see you anymore,' she whispered and, for the first time since he had met her, he saw the tiny sparkle of a tear in the corner of her eye.

Priest sat on the edge of the hole that had developed, staring into the nothingness below. The crushing blow was not what she had said; it was what he felt. He knew this had been coming. Sex was never going to be enough. For him maybe, but not for her, and he hadn't ruled out the possibility that he wasn't the only one. Maybe even one of many. Just one of her toys that she picked up and used when she needed a relief.

But all of this was overshadowed by the creeping, insidious dread of what was to come and the toxicity of the blood that flowed through her veins. The blood that put her in mortal danger.

'You need to get away,' he said, softly, avoiding her eyes and running his hands around the sides of the pint glass.

Whatever she was expecting in reply, it wasn't that. 'What?'

'You need to leave London. Maybe England.'

'What are you talking about?'

'Just for a few days.'

Her eyes shifted right, then left. Confused, she reached across and lifted his head up with her hand so their moist eyes met. 'Charlie? I don't understand.'

He brushed her hand away, rougher than he had intended. 'They're back, and they're coming for you.'

'Who?'

'The rot you mentioned.'

He was improvising badly, cursing his lack of plan, cringing at the sound of his own voice, but it was the only thing he could think of that might make her listen to him.

'The . . . ?' The realisation dawned on her. He watched her face change from sudden fear to anger, not the kind of anger he associated with hate but the worst kind – the kind he associated with betrayal. 'So that's it? That's what you've got to say?'

Panicked, he tried to take her hand but she shook him off. 'No, listen to me—'

She stood up. *Shit. She thinks I'm making it up.* 'Jessica, listen to me. Just a few days away. I need you to trust me.'

'Trust you!?' she exclaimed. The pub fell silent. The chatter died, Priest felt eyes on them. A couple in the corner, a couple of groups of co-workers, the landlord. 'You are the least trustworthy man I've ever met!'

'I'm not sure that's fair—'

'I thought we could do this with dignity, Charlie, but you're too thick for that. Jesus. OK, we fucked a few times. It was a mistake. Can't you see that?' She gathered up her bag. He thought about getting up but wasn't sure his legs would support his weight. She was about to leave but turned before she did. Put up a shaking hand, composed herself.

'When I look at you, Charlie Priest, all I see is . . . everything I'm trying to leave behind.'

'I get that, but—'

'No. No, you don't.' She softened as the first tear fell. 'It's not your fault. But you don't get what I'm going through. How I'm rebuilding my life, the company. My entire family are gone. Mum and Dad, dead. Miles, dead. Scarlett's back in the States. I don't even have their memories to keep safe because of what happened, and every night I go to sleep I dream of the House of Mayfly and every morning I wake up I'm bleeding and I don't know why. So, no. You don't get it.'

The chatter had returned slowly, hushed and sporadic. Even the ambience of the pub had been spoilt. The landlord had cast Priest a sympathetic look and brought him over another pint of local bitter, but the last thing he needed now was alcohol to cloud his mind further.

She had left, and the door closing behind her was the sound of his limp body falling into the pit that opened up inside him. But there was hope, a ledge he hadn't seen. Her parting words had given him something to cling on to.

'I have to go back to Belfast tonight anyway. The deal we did with the new investors wasn't as finalised as I thought. So, I'll be out of your way like you wanted.'

It was said with bitterness, and he had not replied. Just watched her leave. But he had felt a spark of relief.

When he sat back with his eyes closed and let the heavy beer slosh down his throat he hadn't noticed the slightly dishevelled-looking man enter the bar, pick his way around the back of Priest's booth and take a seat on the opposite side of the half-wall near the pool table.

When Priest finished the pint and opened his eyes, he sensed the stranger watching him. When he looked round, he didn't think anything of it at first. Just a man a few years younger than him, with a round face, unshaven and unkempt hair, and a slightly weathered look, like he had seen a few too many late nights, knocked back a few too many vodkas. Nothing out of the ordinary for this kind of establishment, except the staring.

But then he froze.

As he was about to say something, the man smiled, and, in that moment, Priest's world collapsed around him. The background noise of the pub stopped and was replaced with a long, drawn-out tone; the sound of static. He felt the veins in the back of his hands prickle and the hairs on the back of his neck rise. Every nerve was on edge, every muscle coiled.

When the stranger smiled, Priest knew straight away. He wasn't sure what it was. Something about the way he sat, his lopsided smile, longer-than-average canine teeth. The way his oily hair was parted in the middle. The glint of madness in his eye.

But if there was any doubt lingering in the back of his mind it was extinguished when the stranger reached over and placed an item delicately on the table in front of him. An eight-inch galvanised nail.

When Copperhead spoke, his voice was unusually high and soft, velvety – almost laughable.

'Hello, Charlie. I think you've been looking for me.'

# Chapter 52

*One year ago*

*I make my way out of the vestry, take a pew at the front of the church and sit cross-legged in silent contemplation, mesmerised by the light sparkling through the stained-glass window above the altar. For the first time, I realise that the gin has affected me and I start to see shapes forming in front of my eyes: blurred patterns like the edges of a flame dancing across my vision.*

*I relax as my head spins. Sue is gone. I had been irrational to think that she was a Carrier. God would not have been so cruel.*

*I check my phone and take delight in reading the message from Elisha, our saviour. She has received my payment and engaged an expert – one Professor Owen – to source the Book. It is possible, it is within reach. Owen knew of its existence, and the rumours that it was in the custody of a Swiss collector. He has an inkling that this collector may be persuaded to part with the Book. Clearly, none of them know how important it is.*

*I ring her. She answers straight away.*

*'This is good news, Elisha,' I say.*

*'Owen is an expert on the Dead Sea Scrolls. If anyone can get it, he can.'*

*'How long?'*

There is a silence, but I am used to Elisha's quirks. 'A month. Maybe longer.'

'Of course.'

I do not betray myself but inwardly I am anxious to get my hands on the full text. There are two reasons for this. First, if I am going to be the one to steer mankind into a new glorious utopia and receive my reward in heaven, I can hardly do so without the complete text in my possession. Second, the translations I have only tell me one thing: that the blood of the Carriers is silver. Hence from this I have ascertained that the Carriers can be identified through their blood group. But the translations do not tell me what happens after the last Carrier dies and although I can put the plan into motion, there are certain details about the endgame which I suspect only the full Book of Janus can provide.

'I will keep you updated. It's good to know there is someone else out there who shares my passion for this subject.'

'Yes. You are not alone, Elisha. Hope and faith ride with you always.'

'And, perhaps redemption?'

'Yes. Certainly, redemption.'

I smile and close my eyes, but I can still see the kaleidoscope of colours moving on the inside of my eyelids.

# Chapter 53

Priest lowered the pint glass slowly and put his hands on the table. The divide that separated them was just above his eye level. He could vault it, but he was wedged in the ridiculously tight booth. Even if he moved deftly, Copperhead, who was closer to the exit, would reach the door in seconds.

He tensed, ready, but didn't jolt up, despite his body instructing him otherwise.

'You're him,' said Priest, watching carefully. 'You're Copperhead.'

The killer ran his tongue across his crooked teeth. He seemed relaxed, pleased with himself. Like he was about to try to sell Priest something. But that was always the disappointment. Killers didn't have horns, or tails, they didn't carry tridents. They just looked like ordinary people. A lot of the time they were insurance salesmen, teachers, statesmen, construction workers, lawyers. Copperhead could have been anybody, or nobody at all.

'I just thought we should meet, Charlie. Have a chat.'

Priest suppressed the urge to launch himself over the wall – surely it would be ill-fated. Copperhead knew he was here. Knew what he looked like. Knew how to find him. But was that so much of a surprise? He had killed four times that they knew of, each time a forensically flawless murder and each time showing that he knew the victim's movements, how, when and where to find them.

'It'll be over soon,' Priest hissed through gritted teeth. 'Give up.'

Copperhead laughed. 'Over? Charlie, we're just getting started. You've seen the list, right?'

'You mean the donors' register?'

'Yeah. That. There's a long way to go yet.'

'You can't possibly think there's any way you can get through all of them.'

He seemed to consider this, but then dismiss it. 'I don't suppose it matters now that everyone knows, does it? If I don't complete the work, there'll be someone else to do it for me.'

'And then what? You think you can bring about an apocalypse?'

He felt a movement building within him, a rage rising to the surface. He saw Darren Green's slashed body, the look of sheer horror on his face. A boy with learning difficulties, who probably hadn't even contemplated this amount of evil could conceivably exist in the world.

'I don't suppose it matters what I think will happen,' said Copperhead with genuine modesty. 'Nor you for that matter. That's the wonder of faith, isn't it?'

'Faith that innocent bloodshed is what God wants?'

'Innocent?' Copperhead stopped smiling, like he had been offended. 'The Giants weren't innocent, Charlie, and neither are the Carriers. They fornicate with animals, mutilate babies, burn down churches. They're beasts, Charlie. That's why God wanted them punished in the deluge. Haven't you done the pre-reading?'

'Then why doesn't He send another flood?'

Copperhead waved his hand, as if his failure to get through to Priest was irritating him. 'For the same reason you didn't get up and walk after the girl, Charlie. There's only so much you can do before you have to let people help themselves.'

Priest flinched at the mention of Jessica, took hold of the side of the table. It was fixed to the floor, and he could pull across to lever himself out of the booth quicker to get over the divide. Copperhead noticed his reaction with glee.

'Oh, of course. The girl. Sorry, *woman*. Jessica, isn't it? Jessica Ellinder. Now, where have I heard that name before?'

Priest felt short of breath, such was the intensity of his anger. 'If you touch her, I swear to God, I'll—'

'Swear to God? You don't believe in God, Charlie. It's what makes you so disgustingly hollow. You're no better than one of them, really. And yet we have so much in common.'

'We have nothing in common, you and I.'

'Sure we do. Both of our parents are dead, for one thing. Yours in a plane crash. Mine were murdered. You'd be surprised how close we are, Charlie. It's why I phoned you outside Owen's garage and saved your life.'

Priest's eyes widened. He thought back to the call. The androgynous tone in his ear. *That was Copperhead.*

'Why?'

'To keep the game going, Charlie. You gotta be alive to play, right?'

*Figures.* There was a moment when he thought he might break for it but Copperhead stayed firm and Priest didn't move again. He decided to change tack. 'I don't think you're doing God's work at all, you know?'

Copperhead arched an eyebrow. 'Really? I'm not sure you're best placed to—'

'No. I think you do it because you enjoy it. You're not an angel. You're a fucking pervert.'

'A pervert?' He was annoyed. *Good.* Priest waited for the reaction, felt a glimmer of hope that he might gain the upper hand. 'Seriously? Then I'd be killing indiscriminately, wouldn't I? Like . . . oh, like your *brother*, Charlie.'

Priest shook his head, forced a smile. 'Nah. I saw the last one. Darren. That wasn't a clean kill, like the others. You ate him. You took your time. You enjoyed it.'

Copperhead's eyes narrowed. 'God chose me because I have a set of special skills, Charlie. Surely you can see that.'

'Do you think *He* chose for you to have a fat erection when you tore out the boy's flesh?'

The killer looked away in disgust. 'If you're going to be like that, Charlie, then I ought to go. I would have thought that you of all people would have appreciated the artistry in my work.'

'You want me to admire you?'

'No!' Copperhead shouted angrily. 'Not *admire*. Fear. I want you to fucking *fear* me! And you should. Because I'm winning. I can beat you. I *have* beaten you.'

'I'm right behind you. It's only a matter of time.'

'Don't make me laugh! You haven't even established a proper motive yet. You're slow, Priest, and I'm disappointed. William would have had me behind bars by now. You're not a patch on him.'

Priest's interest was piqued – Copperhead was raging. Exactly what Priest wanted. Like any other psychopath, he craved respect. 'What do you know about William?'

'I know there was a man who *did* enjoy his work. Who murdered for the sake of murdering. Killed strangers, sometimes in their beds. Sometimes two at a time. Because that's what he wanted to do. How about that for freedom?'

'Don't *you* feel free?'

'Free? Have you any idea how long it took for that clinic to be set up? Free. You have no idea. No, freedom comes when we reach endgame, Charlie. You have to *fight* for freedom. Claw at it. And if that means stampeding over the rest of the herd then so be it. They're just cattle, Charlie. Dumb cattle. Your brother knew that. But you seem intent on being one of the herd, not one of the shepherds.'

Priest made a satisfied noise. He had brought the beast out of Copperhead, roused him. And a man who could be roused, could be caught. That *was* one thing that William had taught him.

'You're right, you know,' said Priest, looking away. 'I don't believe in God.' He looked back, and he felt calmer, seeing the pent-up frustration in Copperhead's eyes; knowing he was right. 'But I believe that there's a special kind of place in the afterlife for people like you. A place that makes your Hell look like a fucking theme park.'

Priest waited, his arms ached from being so tense, the lactic acid burnt his side. But he waited. Copperhead looked uncertain for the first time, and couldn't help a curt glance back to the door, probably measuring the distance. Then he looked back at Priest, expressionless.

'I've seen Hell, Charlie. And you couldn't be more wrong.'

All Priest heard as he launched himself out of the booth and leapt towards the divide was the sound of shattering glass as the pint of half-drunk bitter tumbled to the floor.

# Chapter 54

DSI John Eaton wiped the fatigue from his face with the palm of his hand but found nothing had changed: he still felt dreadful.

An early morning conversation with any journalist was hard enough but one that had his personal mobile number and was known in the trade as Slinky was even more difficult. Eaton had known Slinky – so named because of how bent he was – since he was a wooden top, and although the overweight journalist had held down a few regular jobs with the *Spectator* and the *Evening Standard*, he'd opted to go freelance for most of his career.

Eaton had no idea how Slinky had managed to get hold of a copy of that blasted symbol, or how he'd known it had been drawn in blood at three crime scenes, but he intended to find out. He'd lied to Auckland about sending a press officer over to negotiate an embargo. There was no point. Slinky by name, slinky by nature. He intended to send his best interrogator, Fay Westbrook, to find out where the leak was instead.

As if Slinky wasn't bad enough though, now Ethan Grey was bobbing about in front of him like an impatient child waiting to be taken to the bloody fair. Ominously, he was clutching a bundle of papers. Why this was necessary was anybody's guess. Grey had come highly recommended from Scotland Yard but he could see now that they were just trying to offload him. Frankly, Priest had been more helpful than this nerd who thought he understood police work. The man had a weak handshake and clean fingernails and, in John Eaton's world, that didn't make you any kind of copper.

'Thank you for agreeing to speak to me in private, sir,' Grey bleated.

'Can we cut the bollocks? You call me John, I'll call you Ethan, and we'll all get along better.'

'Yes. Of course. John.' Grey looked crestfallen. *No fair for you today, son.*

'Well, what is it that you can't say in front of everyone else? And by the way, I doubt you made any friends with the AC back there. You made it sound like even she wasn't allowed to know.'

'Perhaps that's the case.'

Eaton might have gone on to tell the profiler not to be so fucking insolent, but something in his tone of voice stopped him. Something he didn't like, beyond the rudeness.

'What do you mean?'

Grey hesitated, then passed Eaton the bundle of papers he was holding. 'I've completed my profile of Copperhead. But I regard the findings as highly confidential. They must remain between you and me, for now.'

'Look, lad, I'll decide . . .'

'John.' Grey closed his eyes and winced, like there was a loud noise somewhere. The performance was so unusual that Eaton stopped what he was about to say again. *What is it with this idiot?* 'Please. Just listen.'

Eaton relented. Held up his hands, motioned for Grey to sit down.

'Thank you.' Grey pulled up a chair in front of Eaton's desk. 'As I say, I've completed my profile. But I am concerned. The killer is showing a number of traits that I would consider to be consistent with one of the standard models of serial killer. You see, critically, serial killing is an addiction, and like any addiction, the subject will do everything he or she can to be able to continue to keep doing the thing that they are addicted to. In this case, murdering people. This, in particular, will usually involve considerable efforts to evade detection and capture.'

'All right,' said Eaton with little interest. 'In forty years of policing, I've found that most criminals have that tendency.'

'Yes, that's true. But most criminals don't go to the same extent as serial killers. For instance, serial killers will become experts on police procedure, and they will often find a way to get close to an investigation so that they can establish the quality of their adversary – usually the SIO on the case – and see how close to detection they are.'

'OK. And?'

'And they use other techniques to try and cause confusion, to throw the investigators off-course. One of those is called staging. Gary Ridgway, for example, known as the Green River Killer, once laid out a sausage, a trout and a bottle of wine on one of his victims to stage a Last Supper scene to try and make it seem as though the killing had a religious motive.'

'So what are you saying?' Eaton was cautious, still not sure where this was going but realising there was a punchline coming. 'That the Book of Janus thing is just a cover?'

'That's exactly what I'm saying.'

Eaton swept his hair back, cleared a ball of phlegm from his throat. He needed some answers on this case, and he wasn't sure this was it. But right now, more than that, he needed some sleep. He'd had two hours last night, if that.

'Look, tell you what,' he said, exhausted. 'Let's run this past Priest. See what he thinks.'

'I don't think we should do that, John.'

Eaton stared at him for a moment. Then he caught on, but he asked anyway, hoping beyond everything that he was wrong, that it was a joke. 'Why not?'

'I don't think we should run it past Priest, John. Because I think our killer *is* Priest.'

# Chapter 55

Priest realised his error almost immediately. The table looked sturdy, and the bolts around the base looked tight enough, but decades of spilt drink, bar brawls and youths climbing all over it had loosened the fastenings so that, when Priest's sixteen-stone muscular frame had tried to use it as leverage, the whole damn thing had come away. Off-balance and now lacking a solid structure to use to haul himself over, Priest was forced to vault the divide further away from the door across a different booth.

He had sensed Copperhead react and felt the rush of air when the door had opened and slammed shut behind the fleeing killer but there was little he could do about it. By the time he reached the door and wrenched it open – his body, still battered and bruised from the explosion, was rebelling against its sudden deployment – he clattered into a group of lost-looking tourists who reacted angrily in some unknown language, although he thought he saw a few of them try to film him on their phones.

He desperately scanned the possibilities. The pub sat on a corner where four streets converged, one of which, the quietest, he could probably rule out straight away. It was a narrow thoroughfare lined with tightly packed shops and cafés, almost deserted despite the time of day. The main roads were more likely, he guessed, where Copperhead could try to lose himself in the crowd.

But there was nothing. No confused people, cries of anguish or alarm, pointing or fuss. Nothing. Just a normal day as Londoners went about their business. *Where the hell did he go?*

Priest was seething. Angry at the audacity of it, angry at being found so easily and being so close, within reaching distance of being able to stop this, to protect Jessica and the others. How many people were now in danger? How many more victims would there be before Copperhead was caught. Dee was right. They couldn't possibly protect them all.

He placed his hand behind his head and, to the dismay and horror of the confused tourists, bellowed a scream of anguish that sent them scattering across the road.

It might have ended there, in the street, alone. With the incessant buzz of the traffic, the distant waft of music from some department store or other, and the unrelenting sun punishing him. But Copperhead's disappearance was simpler than he had imagined and, when he turned around, he realised again the very basic mistake he had made.

Eaton had got up from behind the desk and poured more coffee from the percolator bubbling in the corner. He didn't need it. His head hurt like hell and more caffeine would just add to his problems. But he needed to do something while he processed what Grey was saying.

'You're aware that Priest's brother pleaded not guilty by reason of insanity to a string of murders ten years ago,' said Grey. He was calm – this wasn't the rant of a lunatic, or venomous slander. Grey was reasoned and, Eaton had to admit, making sense.

'Yeah, we all know about Dr William Priest.'

'Did you know that the Priest brothers share the same mental disorder? A condition known as depersonalisation disorder, or DPD?'

'No. I didn't.' Eaton took the coffee back to the desk and sat down heavily. *How the fuck am I going to tell the Assistant Commissioner that her ex-husband is the profiler's number one suspect? No wonder Grey wanted to speak to me privately!*

'A susceptibility to the condition is hereditary, but the symptoms include states of panic, irrationality, lack of control. Sufferers question their very existence as the world slips away from them; nothing appears real. They have no focus, no grounding and, although almost all of the time this is to their detriment only and not society's, I wonder whether the form of DPD the Priest brothers suffer from is so extreme that it conditions them to kill other human beings.'

Eaton shook his head – he wasn't buying that analysis. 'With respect, that's bollocks, Ethan. No better than when after Sandy Hook they all said that Asperger's syndrome was suddenly dangerous.'

'Maybe,' Grey agreed. 'But if not the condition then the commonality of the genes. Think about it. What makes men want to kill, if not a deep-rooted psychological dysfunction, which must, by reason, be genetic in substance.'

'An evil gene? You think there's an evil gene in the family, and the fact that William and Charlie share the same disorder – this DPD thing – means there's an increased likelihood that they share the evil gene?'

'Sort of. What I mean is that, say the DPD was triggered by the evil gene, then the fact of the DPD's existence is evidence of the evil gene's existence.'

Eaton let out a frustrated puff of air, before leaning his head in his hands and massaging his temples. It was the only way he'd now relieve some of the tension headache that was threatening to take over his entire brain.

Eaton exhaled. 'This is sounding like conjecture to me.' It sounded like a conjecture, but he had to admit, there was logic to it.

'Profiling is exactly that, John. But there is considerable method in the madness, so to speak.'

He considered it. It probably made Priest the best liar of all time if it was right. But what about alibis for the murders? Eaton wasn't sure – he'd never even asked. He felt close to defeat and at the back of his aching mind he was trying not to think about the kind of story Slinky would sell if he found out that, not only had the police let a dangerous serial killer be part of an investigation, but they were the ones who'd invited him to join the team!

'What do you propose we do?' he asked.

Grey pulled a face, like he hadn't thought about it much. 'Talk to him, under caution, at least. We can do that without anyone else knowing for now, you and me. What do you say?'

Up-skittled, Priest saw the attack a fraction of a second too late as Copperhead launched himself from behind the pub door towards him. Although he was a foot shorter, the killer's body was a compact mould of hard muscle and, as he went tumbling to the ground, Priest only managed to keep him from gaining complete leverage with a well-aimed kick to Copperhead's stomach.

They were both on the pavement, Priest wishing he had something in reach – anything – to use as a weapon. His assailant was snarling like a rabid dog. He realised that if he made a mistake the killer would tear strips off him in a wild frenzy.

It was for this reason that, rather than try to take advantage of the fact that Copperhead was also down, he rolled backwards, out of reach, intending to right himself first; but the shorter man was too quick for him. Only half way up, Priest took the full force of Copperhead's agile body which sent him crashing back down near the road to the blare of a car horn.

Bearing over him, a nefarious grin spread across his face, the killer thrust his head forward. Panicked, Priest caught it at the last minute and stopped him from burying his teeth into the side of his neck.

He tried kicking with his knees but the squirming, writhing body on top of him, like the snake that bore his name, was too protean to connect with. Instead, he settled for wedging his leg upwards between their bodies and, in a desperate effort, managed to throw his attacker off for a second time.

This time, Priest didn't make the same mistake. He levered himself up, his hand-to-hand combat training flooding back, and shifted his weight forward. Hooked the fleshy side of his hand across Copperhead's face and connected with a satisfying crack of bone and a small explosion of blood as the killer's nose split open.

Surprised, and most likely ill-used to being on the receiving end, Copperhead fell backwards with a shriek of anger and pain. Sensing his advantage, Priest moved in line with the killer's fall and kicked hard into his stomach. His lungs must have erupted with pain as the air was forced out of them. In that moment, Priest stood over him and watched as, dazed and incapacitated, he tried to get to his feet.

When he was half way up, Priest planted the side of his fist across the aggressor's face again, knowing that the killer's nose was already broken and a second strike to the same spot would be painful enough to induce unconsciousness. He was right, although only for a few seconds. He saw Copperhead's eyes glaze over before he fell back down again, his face streaked with blood.

Priest pulled out his phone, hit Rowlinson's number. *Come on, Tiff, pick up.*

Copperhead was choking, coughing up more blood. The phone was ringing. The station was less than a mile away. *We have him. It's over.*

More sounds were spewing from the killer, like he was choking. For a second, Priest thought that he might be hyperventilating, or even having a heart attack.

But then he realised, Copperhead wasn't wheezing. He was laughing.

Priest lowered the phone from his ear.

'What's so funny? You like pain?'

The killer retched up a ball of bloodstained phlegm, laughed again. He was still squirming around, with his hands underneath him, looking like a trapped animal.

'I'm going to fuck you, Priest.'

Priest exhaled, unimpressed. 'You couldn't fuck your way out of a paper bag, you sick bastard.'

'The one who I serve thinks otherwise.'

'You mean God? You don't serve Him. You're a freak. A mutant. And you're going to . . .'

Priest was about to intervene as Copperhead rolled his body off the pavement and into the road, but the flash stopped him. Then something like the sound of a volcano erupting shattered through his ears and, not for the first time recently, Charlie Priest was flying through the air.

# Chapter 56

'OK, it's not all bad. We've got his DNA.'

Rowlinson handed Priest a plastic cup of metallic-tasting water. They were sat in the medical suite at Holborn Police Station – a space that was part doctor's surgery and part oven, with the tiniest crack of open window providing the only source of ventilation. The duty nurse-practitioner – a surly woman in her fifties named Tina – was taking his blood pressure and expressing her dislike of the situation through a series of grunts and huffs.

'He needs to go to A and E,' she growled.

'I don't like the food there,' said Priest. 'Why are my ears ringing?'

'I'm surprised you can even hear anything,' sighed Rowlinson. 'Unsub had a stun grenade in his pocket, looks like a flash bomb or something. Must have pulled the pin, rolled away and waited for you to walk into it.'

'Who the *fuck* gets blown up twice in one week?'

'Apparently, you do.'

'No trace of him, I assume.'

'Long gone. We can do some facial recognition work with you later but there's enough blood on you to fill a tank.'

Rowlinson was about to reply when the door opened. In walked Fay Westbrook. Priest jerked with pain as Tina slapped an antiseptic wipe across his grazed arm with all the care and grace of a grizzly bear.

'Jesus!'

'No pain, no gain,' she muttered through gritted teeth.

'Heard you got blown up again,' said Fay. 'Thought I'd check if you were still in one piece.'

'Apparently I'm indestructible.'

'You need your own personal black box,' Rowlinson mused.

'Eaton wants to see you,' said Fay. There was something about the drop in her tone that caught Priest's attention. She seemed uneasy, as if she knew what she was saying was unusual somehow.

'Anything I should know about?'

She shrugged, touched his arm. A small, delicate gesture, but whether it was out of sympathy for him or something more complicated, he couldn't tell. 'Glad to see you're not dead.'

'Thanks. Tell John I'll be up in five minutes.'

'Better make it ten,' huffed Tina. 'You're going to need stitches on this shoulder.'

Priest had prepared a gracefully articulate explanation for why he had chosen to ignore Eaton's request for an audience, preferring instead to walk straight out of Holborn Police Station, but the truth was twofold: first, there had been some element of reluctance in Fay's tone when she had told him about it that had made him hesitate and, secondly, there was no time for talking.

He had been close enough to the killer to smell his breath, but not catch him. He had failed. Whatever happened now was on his shoulders. It was as simple as that.

Burning with frustration and anger, he had double-backed on the way to Eaton's office, taken the stairs, and headed out, all without Fay or Rowlinson realising. They soon would, of course, when he didn't show, but he didn't care. There would be no more meetings. William had been right. In order to catch a snake, you had to be one. And some snakes don't hunt. They trap. The South American green anaconda, for instance, doesn't wander aimlessly looking for prey, it waits in the murky waters of the Amazon, sometimes for days at a time, for its prey to come to it.

He was trying to figure it out, water the germ of an idea that had taken hold, when his phone rang. It was Georgie.

'Charlie, it's me.'

'Short warning: I'm only in the mood for good news.'

'Something wrong?'

'I just got blown up again.'

She paused. 'You just—'

'It doesn't matter, I'll tell you later. What's up?'

She explained about her trip to the Thames Blood Donor Centre, which he had forgotten all about. She described sitting in the waiting room, trying to work out why, if Copperhead wanted as many people on the list as possible to give blood, he wanted to get them there and why then all at the same time. But the answer was obvious.

'It is?' If it was, he couldn't see it.

'What do you do if you're waiting somewhere nowadays with nothing to do.'

He thought for a while. He tended to write letters in his head, or have weird hallucinations, but Georgie probably meant what normal people did when they were waiting in a public space, not him specifically. Wait. Public space.

'Join the wifi,' he said, amazed.

'That's right. So I did, on my phone, then I got Solly to look at it.'

'And?'

'It's called a man-in-the-middle attack. Hackers use wire-less auditing platforms like Pineapple to take control of wifi landscapes and intercept communications, which is called eavesdropping. Once you take control through the public wifi, hackers can use network protocol analysers like Wire Shark to get user names and passwords. So not only can they see all of your http traffic, they can send you fake messages too.'

Priest recalled what Rowlinson had said in the meeting. 'That's how he's doing it. By manipulating their phones. So he knew that Jane Vardy would be in a hotel on her own, probably either tracked the phone or she told someone about it in a message. She was here visiting her parents so there's bound to be a trail.'

'And Emma Mendez?'

'He knew that her mother kept a spare key at her house, which is now missing. And he could easily have tracked Alan Burberry's running route.'

'You've got to admit, it's clever.'

'Cleverer of you to discover it, Someday. Good work.'

He ended the call before she could reply and was about to call Rowlinson to let him know when the phone rang again. This time when he answered, it was Dr Wheatcroft. William was playing merry hell, demanding to see him, now. Whereas that might have been regarded as an unnecessary distraction in the present circumstances, Priest knew it could only mean one thing: the Dark Redeemer had something to say.

# Chapter 57

It was the same uncomfortable-looking nurse as last time – Perry – who showed Priest through to the meeting room wherein stood a single white table, two chairs, and the hunched-up figure of one of Britain's most prolific serial killers.

William was quiet, unusually so, anxious for Priest to sit down. He was restless, playing with his hands, rubbing them together – a sure sign that something was troubling him.

'Did you—' Priest began but his older brother cut him off, dispensing with any usual pleasantries. There would be no elementary observations this time.

'Charles, I have grave news. The person you're hunting . . . wait.' He studied Priest, looked him up and down. He hadn't changed since the fight with Copperhead. There was still blood on his shirt and mud on his face. 'You're hurt.'

Priest leant forward. 'I need you to focus, William. There is a killer out there that I need to find. Quickly.'

'You've met him, I deduce.'

'We're now acquainted, yes. But I wasn't able to keep hold of him.'

'That's concerning. Very concerning.'

Priest waited a beat, but the punchline didn't come. 'And?'

Despite his dark mood, there was nothing that gave William Priest greater pleasure than being in a position of intellectual advantage over his younger brother, a disposition which was made obvious with the flash of a smile.

'I think I know who he is.'

'Who?'

'His name is Michael. He's one of my pen-pals.'

Priest hovered over the words while William watched. It was completely surreal: hearing William describe evil incarnated in human flesh in such banal terms. A pen-pal. It wasn't even as if Priest could have been excused for not seeing this coming. Media-hype, the popularity of true-crime literature, sensation-alist films, warped crime figures, documentary after documen-tary after documentary. This was the age of the serial killer, an age when memorabilia was traded like football cards, from a Christmas card signed by Ted Bundy to Ed Gein's Ford sedan, and serial killer idolisers regularly corresponded with their incarcerated heroes.

'How do you know?'

'Michael is a troubled man. A very unpleasant man. He talks about a lot of things in his letters to me. I never write back. In fact, most of them I didn't even read. A lot of it was the usual stuff: they're all like it, Charles. They think I'm some sort of god, and by outlining their strange little rape and killing fantasies, that gives them power. The fact that I was never a sex murderer, and indeed loathe the very notion, seems to pass most of them by. Hence why I don't spend too much time on the subject.'

'But you must have read some of it, to know that this Michael is Copperhead?'

'He said when he killed, it was part of God's plan. Nothing unusual in that. People have been doing that since we were evolved enough to hold flint knives. But what did register with me was the nail through the skull, which featured in all of the perverted descriptions I could be bothered to read.'

'Where are the letters?'

'They don't let me keep things like that, as you might imagine. It might be possible to get our hands on them, but I'll need time.'

'I don't have time.'

'Yes, I know. The mysterious woman you mentioned.'

It wasn't a jibe. William was as concerned as Priest was. Therein lay the paradox – the serial killer with such empathy. But the answer was simple: William was not and never had been a psychopath. He was something far more dangerous.

Priest felt the weight of the responsibility on his shoulders, the crushing fatigue that stalked him. It was all too much. His shoulders collapsed, head falling.

'I had him, Wills. I could have stopped him.'

'I told you to kill him.'

'I know.' He realised it now, but although it went against everything he believed in about justice, about humanity, William may have had a point. He closed his eyes. 'It's a mess.'

'There is something.' Priest opened one eye, alert. 'I'll get hold of the letters as quickly as I can but I recall from what I *did* read that Michael did, at least at some point, attend Fellowship meetings in Hackney.'

'Fellowship, as in the AA?'

'I doubt he meant *The Lord of the Rings*.'

Priest got up and broke the protocol by pressing his hand firmly on William's shoulders as an expression of gratitude. Perry winced, but didn't object.

'Let me know when you get hold of the letters.'

'I will, oh and Charles—' William grabbed at Priest's wrist and held it for a moment. 'God's speed.'

John Eaton pinched the bridge of his nose until he felt a swell of pain in his forehead. He couldn't believe what he was hearing. Priest had absconded. Completely ignored his instruction to report back to him, and gone AWOL. And now Ethan Grey was looking as smug as a fucking lottery winner and Tiff Rowlinson looked like someone had slapped him.

Rowlinson said, 'You're not seriously suggesting Charlie Priest is responsible for—'

'We are,' Grey interrupted. 'And the fact that he has now fled rather supports that proposition, does it not?'

Eaton looked at Rowlinson, willing him to say something that would exonerate the man he had decided to bring into the investigation against the AC's express wishes; the man he had effectively staked his reputation on. If it turned out that Grey was correct, it was over for him. And it wouldn't be a fancy early retirement with a gold watch and a fat pension. It would be quick, hushed and involve him having to sign an NDA.

'I've worked with Priest for a long time,' said Rowlinson slowly. 'He's got a few quirks – that doesn't mean he's a suspect.'

'What are his alibis?' Grey snapped.

'I don't know. He just—'

'You mean you never checked, detective.'

Grey let the accusation hang in the air. Rowlinson didn't reply, just pursed his lips. Eaton noticed his fists were balled, his body language defensive. Priest and Rowlinson were friends. His judgement was tainted. Christ, they were all fucking tainted now.

'He's now a person of interest, Tiff,' said Eaton quietly.

Rowlinson turned to him. 'You're not taking this seriously, guv? You think Priest killed all those people and then agreed to join a task force to hunt himself down?'

'We're going to bring him in. For questioning. That's all.'

Rowlinson threw his arms in the air, exasperated. 'You've got to be kidding me!'

'You're very keen not to pursue this line of enquiry, DCI Rowlinson,' said Grey. 'Is there a reason for that?'

Rowlinson turned to Grey, and for a horrible moment Eaton thought he might do something stupid. But the detective waited a beat before saying, 'Fine. We'll go and pick him up. But this is a waste of time.'

# Chapter 58

Despite every ward languishing in the ten per cent of the most deprived in the country, Priest had always been rather fond of the East London Borough of Hackney, with its graffiti covered tower blocks and grey industrial-looking buildings squashed together around a network of roads crammed with the taxis that bore its name. It was real London, a hard man's London. Easily dismissed as run down and dilapidated but actually swimming with colour and diversity.

St Swithin's church, which stood on a mound of earth in the middle of a housing estate, provided such an example of the surprisingly beautiful and delicate architecture you could find hidden amongst the dreary sixties cuboids of bricks and mortar that encapsulated perfectly the history of Britain's ugly class struggle.

He pulled the car up outside and killed the engine. He checked his phone, frowned. Eight missed calls, mainly from Rowlinson. He turned it off. This was more important. Said to Georgie:

'This is it?'

She looked at her phone. 'They've held AA meetings here for ten years, but they stopped suddenly nine months ago. Now I don't think anything goes on here at all.'

They got out of the car, slammed the doors shut and looked up at the eroding spire. 'Who are we meeting again?'

'The church has a sexton, someone who, a long time ago, might have dug the graves and rung the bells but now I guess they just look after it. Her name is Sue Lightfoot.'

Priest nodded. He had called Georgie after leaving Fen Marsh and asked her to try to find out where, historically, someone with a drink problem in Hackney might have wound up. This is what she had come up with.

They passed through a rotting lychgate, walked up the over-grown pathway and past a sad jumble of tombstones, low-hanging trees and rickety benches to the church door. Sat on a bench out-side was a young, desperately thin woman wearing a blue summer dress and white sandals. She got up to greet them in a way that suggested she suffered from joint pain and offered a small, veiny hand, which they each took in turn.

'You must be Sue?' said Georgie.

'That's right. You're Georgie and—'

'It's Priest.'

Sue nodded, but didn't say anything, waiting for them to take the lead.

'When we spoke on the phone, I mentioned we were trying to find someone who might have attended group meetings here, either recently, or maybe a while ago.'

Sue looked uncomfortable. She clearly didn't want to be there. Said nothing, just nodded. Priest wondered if she was just a very nervous person or if there was something else at play.

'It's my brother,' he said, taking over. 'Michael. I lost track of him decades ago and all I want to do is find him again.'

Sue frowned. 'Michael? Well, I didn't really have much to do with the group meetings you mentioned.'

Priest wasn't sure what gave it away but he got the distinct feeling she had just lied. *But why?* 'Please. It's very important to me.'

Sue looked at Georgie, unsure. 'Are you two . . . ?'

Without warning, Priest put his hand around Georgie's waist and pulled her in close. She clattered into him and shuffled around. 'We were married last year. Georgie is the one who has convinced me that to repair the holes in my life, I need to re-establish my relationship with Michael.'

Georgie smiled, but it looked frustratingly unconvincing. *Come on, you can do better than that, Someday.*

'The thing is,' said Sue uncertainly. 'Even if I could help, and there were records or something, I don't think I'm allowed to just hand them over.'

They were getting somewhere. Inadvertently or not, Sue had just confirmed that there were records.

'I completely understand,' he said. 'I'd be the same.'

'What was his surname? Was it Priest?'

'No. That was our family name but Michael . . . chose a different path. I don't even know what name he took, just that he used to attend meetings here, to help with his drinking problem.'

She looked away, and Priest sensed she was making a decision. He waited. Georgie had slipped her arm around his waist, but whether it was that or something else that had prompted Sue to reach a conclusion, he didn't know.

'There were a few Michaels, I think.'

'He's short.' Priest gave an indication with his hand. 'Stocky. Has a very high voice, almost feminine.' She nodded, and he sensed she had someone in mind, so he took a gamble. 'He will have suffered greatly. Very traumatic childhood, probably more so than many of the people who came to these meetings. His parents were murdered when he was young.'

He'd guessed that Michael had been young when his parents had died but it registered with Sue – the little twitch of her lips gave it away.

There was an agonising pause, then she said, sadly: 'Michael was . . . very different from a lot of us.' Then, realising her mistake, she corrected herself. 'I mean, the people who came to the meetings.'

'You don't need to worry, Sue,' said Georgie. 'It's fine.'

'You're talking about Michael Ransom,' she said. *Michael Ransom. Copperhead.* They had a name. Priest felt a spike of adrenaline, remembering the way Michael had rolled on to his side and deftly planted the stun grenade, timing the pull of the pin perfectly so that he practically walked into it. *Michael Ransom.*

'Ransom,' he said softly. 'Yes, that must be right. What do you think, Georgie?'

'It must be.'

Sue looked around, as if checking they weren't being watched. Priest noticed a slight tremor in her hand, and scars on her arms. The scars of a self-harmer. The scars of survival. But what of?

Then she leant forward, conspiratorially. 'Look, I'll just check what we have. But please, don't tell anyone. OK?'

# Chapter 59

Inside the car, waving a hearty goodbye to Sue Lightfoot, Priest felt the swell of anticipation. They had a name, they had an address.

They had the means to protect Jessica.

He pulled off as Georgie started inputting the address into the Aston's GPS. Speed-dialled Rowlinson. He answered after two rings.

'Michael Ransom. His name is Michael Ransom. I've got an address—'

'Whoa, slow down,' said Rowlinson. 'Where are you?'

'Hackney. Did you hear me?' The sat nav finally found a route and Priest accelerated dangerously to the end of the road.

'Yeah, I heard you. You need to return to the station.'

There was something in Rowlinson's tone Priest didn't like.

'No, I've got an address for Ransom. We're on our way now.'

'Priest, Eaton wants you back at base. Now.'

He shook his head, frustrated. *What's wrong with you, Tiff?* 'You're not hearing me. I know who Copperhead is. I've got a name and an address.'

There was a pause on the other end of the line. Some mumbling. *Was Tiff deferring to someone else?* Something was wrong.

'They want you back here, Priest. That or you tell us where you are. We'll come to you.'

He hesitated, but this was Rowlinson he was talking to, and maybe something was up, but he would need back-up. 'You come to me.' He gave Michael Ransom's address. 'It's a tower block, around the corner from here. We're five minutes away.'

'OK – it'll take me half an hour, even with the blues on. Do not, whatever you do, go in. You wait for me. You hear me, Priest?'

'Tiff?' Priest held the phone away to fade out his voice. 'Tiff, it's a bad line. I can't hear you.'

He hit 'end call'. By that time, they had cleared three blocks, Michael Ransom's flat was less than a mile away. Luckily, there wasn't much traffic this time of day but he still spent a lot of time on the wrong side of the road, careering past slow moving vans and buses, narrowly missing a head-on collision with an Outlander.

'I know we're in a hurry,' said Georgie, breathless. 'But could we just slow down a tad in the built-up area?'

Michael Ransom's tower block was a grey concrete cuboid devoid of all character except for the towels and washing hung over the railings of most balconies and the gang tags peppering the walls. It was the kind of Dystopian post-war housing that had sprung up in the sixties, spiritless but functional, without a thought for what progress should really look like.

Michael's flat was 206, second floor. One flight of stairs. Rowlinson had said wait, but he was at least twenty minutes behind, and that was being generous.

'We're not going in, are we?' asked Georgie, looking up at the ominous building and keeping a wary eye on the group of youths huddled around an entranceway, taking a keen interest in the Aston's arrival.

'No. *We're* not. You're staying here.'

He looked over and watched Georgie's eyes dart across to the gang on the corner. Five of them, one looked no older than twelve but a couple were men.

'Nice car,' one of them shouted over. The rest laughed.

'I think I'll go with you,' said Georgie nervously.

They made their way across a small patch of grass, the gang watching them all the way, until the sun disappeared behind the tower and they were left in a world of shadow. One of the gang members climbed down from the wall, shouted something across at them but Priest didn't catch what. He felt Georgie so close to him that he almost tripped over her.

When they reached the entranceway they saw the name of the tower, a misrepresentation if ever Priest had seen one – Paradise Rise. The door was locked, operated by a fob but there were bells for each flat. He hit a few at random until someone answered.

'Amazon delivery, flat above you, pal,' he said gruffly. There was a moment's pause, then the door clicked open.

The first thing that hit him was the drop in temperature. With no glass to let in the sunlight, the dingy concrete tube that ran along the foot of the building towards a lift at the end was like a medieval cell, lit with dull orange lights. They were inside but the floor was covered in pigeon shit, nests lined the ledge above them. There was a man laid underneath a filthy blanket half way down. Everything stank of piss.

'Lift or stairs?' asked Priest.

'Stairs.'

They picked their way across the sleeping man and pushed through a set of double doors to a staircase that took them to the second floor. Here, they found themselves outside again peering down over where the Aston was parked. The gang had moved closer to it and were now taking pictures on their phones. Priest sighed inwardly – at least the damn thing was insured but at times like this he missed William's Volvo.

Flat 206 was a red door next to a window so heavily stained it was impossible to see through. The paint was peeling off the door and a sign read JOVO WITNESSES WILL BE SHOT ON SIGHT.

'You think this is where he is?' asked Georgie. 'Copperhead?'

'No. I think this is an address he wants us to think he lives at, but I doubt he's home.'

'It's like he wants to be caught, without giving up completely.'

The same thought had been troubling Priest ever since his encounter with Michael in the pub. Copperhead had said that it didn't matter if he was stopped because other people would carry on his work. Did he mean others like him, or was there more than one killer at work? Had he reached the burn-out stage already?

Priest tapped across the door and around the handle. It was cheap – hollow, except around the lock. Without warning he aimed a kick at the lock, the wood splintered as easily as card and the door crashed back on its hinges against the wall.

He peered into the dingy hallway. Georgie stayed behind him.

As he stepped over the threshold and onto a brown carpet hardened from decades of use, the smell was overbearing. The last week's weather had baked the small apartment, sealed in a volume of stale air and created a wall of heat that instantly attached itself to Priest like glue. But it was more than that. The air wasn't just stale. It was foetid. The stench of rot and mould permeated everything. There were flies, too – bulky and black, flesh-eaters, darting past him and outside as if even they were repulsed by the rancid interior.

He turned to Georgie, who had her hand over her mouth. 'Keep watch. You need anything, shout.'

This time she didn't object.

Priest ventured further into the apartment, wincing as an invisible line of web caught him across the face. If Michael had ever lived here, he hadn't been recently. No human had been inside this place for months. Maybe years.

Nor had they seemingly decorated since Paradise Rise had been built. The wallpaper was shedding away – an insipid green flowery pattern pasted over a rusty orange-painted wall on both sides. No leaflets or letters littering the floor. No letter box to push them through. They must be downstairs. Just the brown carpet, stained and worn.

To the left was a kitchen which revealed something else about the apartment: there was nothing here. Cupboard doors were open, one hanging off its hinges, but they were bare except for dust and grime. The yellowy work surface looked like a builder's workbench, covered in wood shavings and debris, although from what he couldn't fathom. There were empty spaces where a fridge and, presumably, washing machine might go and a single naked bulb hanging in the centre of the room.

Opposite the kitchen was a living room, stripped to nothing but an old gas fire that had been amateurishly disconnected and some off-white painter's sheets dumped in the corner and, next to that, the explanation for the presence of the flies: a dead rat.

There was only one thing of note in the whole place. In what Priest supposed was the bedroom there was again nothing in terms of furniture. Just a small cavity barely large enough for a double bed with a window smeared with filth. But there was something that confused Priest. More writing on the wall, in red paint, not blood, he was sure. Not a message to him, nor the Janus symbol. Just something that seemed at odds with what he understood Copperhead to be.

From outside he heard Georgie calling his name.

He looked at the words again, confused.

'Charlie! What's in there?'

It didn't make sense. The words stared back at him.

*God is dead.*

# Chapter 60

Priest and Georgie stood outside flat 206 looking out across the street to the row of tatty shops culminating in a boarded-up pub on the corner, all dwarfed by the blocks of high-rises in the background set against a bright, endless sky. It was somehow bleak and somehow hopeful at the same time: the dull grey of the towers and the pastel blue of the sky.

*God is dead.*

'What now?' asked Georgie.

Priest shook his head. 'Why would someone on a religious quest write that on his wall?'

'Maybe it's not his flat. Maybe it's the wrong address.'

He was about to reply, but it would have been nothing other than thinking out loud, when his phone rang. If it was Rowlinson he had a good mind to ignore him. The last conversation had been weird. But it wasn't. It was Sarah.

He answered. 'Hi.'

'Charlie? Are you at work?'

Priest looked down at his bloodied arms, the dirt on his trousers – felt the ache around his shoulder and the pain in his arm where Tina had stitched up his broken skin, badly.

'Yeah, just another day in the office.'

'Great.' She was rushing, not even properly listening to him. 'I would never ordinarily ask this but I'm struggling without . . . you know.'

'How can I help?'

'Look, I'm at Megan's house. You remember Megan?'

'Of course.'

'You're a liar. Well, I came to pick up Tilly, but Megan's mother has been taken ill and she's had to dash off. I need to get home.'

'OK, so just . . .' Then he realised why she was calling. Sarah and Ryan had one car between them, which they used to cart Tilly around; the rest of the time they used the Tube. Tilly didn't like the Tube. And Ryan had the car. He'd offered her use of either the Aston or the Volvo but she'd politely declined. 'Oh, I see.'

'Yeah. I don't think Megan's coming back. She gave me a key and told me to lock up. Sounds bad.'

He could detect the embarrassment in her voice at even having to ask, but the timing was dreadful. Priest closed his eyes. *Not now.*

'What's the address?' he said, reluctantly. He wondered if he could send Okoro, or even Maureen.

'I've texted it to you already. If you could . . . hang on. There's someone at the door.'

Priest rolled his eyes at Georgie and let the phone hang on his shoulder. He could hear Sarah fiddling with the door. Below them, he saw a dark-coloured Audi A8 pull up behind his Aston. The doors opened and he saw Rowlinson, Eaton and Grey get out. It was interesting Grey was with them. He wondered about that for a moment; in the background he could faintly hear Sarah saying something.

There was a strange scratching sound on the other end of the phone. He frowned. Georgie was leaning over the balcony, staring at the Audi. Rowlinson, Eaton and Grey were looking around, probably trying to ascertain which block of flats they were in. He raised the phone to his ear, but he couldn't hear his sister.

'Sarah?'

He froze. There was a bang in his ear, the sound of a muffled cry. Then a thud. Sounded like the phone had dropped on the floor. He listened carefully, trying to work it out, a sense of panic settling at the pit of his stomach.

'Sarah!'

Georgie spun round, watching him, concerned.

Then a voice at the other end of the line. One he recognised. One that made the hairs on his arms and neck rise on end.

'Hello, Charlie.'

For a moment, Priest didn't breathe. His throat contracted. His world closed in around him.

'Michael.'

Copperhead chuckled. 'Ah, so you've found out my real name. How clever of you.'

'What have you done with my sister?'

'She's fine. Just having a little sleep, Charlie.'

Priest felt an anger billowing inside him, he tightened his grip on the phone, his knuckles turning white. Georgie took a step back. He hardly noticed.

'If you harm her I'll tear your—'

'Really, Charlie, there's no need to threaten me. I already know what you'll do. Perhaps you should listen instead. It might just save her life. And the little girl that's here, too.'

His heart stopped for several beats, then thundered into over-drive.

'You *fucking—*'

'Like I said, Charlie,' Michael cut across him sharply. 'You need to *listen* to me.' Inside, he was raging, but he knew he had no choice. Copperhead was in control, for now. 'That's your problem, Charlie. You can't help yourself. Because it's always about *you*, isn't it? Well, not now. Now it's about *me*. So that's where I'm going. Where it all started *for me*.'

'Which is where?'

'You've done so well getting this far, Charlie. You can work it out for yourself.'

He was about to explode, but the phone went dead.

Georgie looked terrified. 'What? What happened?'

He bent over, gripping the phone so hard it felt like it might just break in his hand, then screamed at the ground. *Tilly*. Tilly was there. Surely, he wouldn't . . .

'Charlie?'

He looked up sharply. Fay Westbrook was standing further down from them, having come up from the other side of the building.

He didn't say anything, just rested on the balcony edge, breathing heavily.

'You need to go,' she said.

He grimaced. 'What do you mean?'

'This way, the way I came up.' She motioned behind her. He didn't have time for this, and he didn't know whether he trusted Westbrook after what had happened with her husband.

'What are you talking about?'

'They're coming up the other side: Eaton, Grey and Rowlinson. They only arrived a few moments after I did. I'll say when I got up here, you were already gone.'

'What's going on?' asked Georgie weakly.

He watched her, scrutinised her. Made an assessment. She was trying to help him. But why?

'They think it's you,' she said, and it fitted into place. The weird conversation with Rowlinson. His insistence that he return to base. He looked down. The Audi was there, but there was no one around. 'You don't have any time. They're on the stairwell. Go.'

She stepped aside.

'Why?' He meant why was she helping him.

'Because I want him caught,' she replied. 'Now for Christ's sake, go!'

He wasted no more time and tore down the corridor, Georgie trailing behind.

Luckily, the text Sarah had sent with Megan's address had come through. They had been able to double-back across the grass area below Michael Ransom's block and make a getaway in the Aston before Eaton, Grey and Rowlinson, who were already in the building, had a chance to stop him.

Twenty minutes later, they were skidding to a halt outside Megan's home. It was a detached house on a new estate around the corner from Sarah, with a deep red resin driveway, fake marble pillars fronting the porch and dark Scandinavian cladding across the front gable.

They both half fell out of the car in their desperation to get to the house. Priest had told Georgie in the car about his conversation with Copperhead before Fay had turned up. He didn't think Eaton and company had managed to get back to the Audi quick enough to see which way out of Michael's estate he had gone to enable them to follow, and maybe Fay had delayed them when they got up to the second floor.

Priest burst in through the front door.

Sarah was sitting slumped against the wall, her eyes closed. She could have been sleeping if it weren't for the trickle of blood on her lip and the ghostly alabaster colour of her skin.

'Oh God, no.' He took his sister's head in his hands. Warm. Good. Pulse, and a heartbeat. She was alive, but out cold. He leapt up, hollering back to Georgie. 'See to her. Call an ambulance.'

Georgie shouted back an acknowledgement as he threw the next door open and found himself in a kitchen, with black granite worktops and pastel green fittings.

'Tilly!'

A wave of noxious fear surged over him like a charge, electrifying every nerve as it coursed through his system, spreading outwards from his stomach and storming to his head. For a split second he thought he might pass out but, at the last moment, he managed to regain his senses and wrench the blackness away from his eyes.

'TILLY!'

Frantically, he crashed from room to room, throwing open cupboards, upending furniture, tearing at curtains; like a raging storm he tore through the house screaming her name, the realisation of what had happened – what he had allowed to happen – driving itself further into his chest until he could barely breathe with the agony of it.

'Tilly, where are you?'

He passed through the kitchen, dining room, lounge, toilet, then upstairs – four bedrooms, an en-suite, a family bathroom, the boiler cupboard. Nothing. Fucking nothing. Just despair: cold, cruel and unrelenting despair.

He heard Georgie call up the stairs, terrified: 'Ambulance on its way!'

He shook his head. Her face withered. 'No . . .'

'I should have seen this.'

Georgie's reply was barely audible. 'You couldn't have. She wasn't on the list. Neither of them were.'

'Stay with Sarah.'

He raced past her, back downstairs, intending to leave through the front door and check the street.

He stopped. It wasn't fear this time that pulsed through him; it was something far darker.

On the inside of the front door, in the same scrawled red paint as he had seen inside Michael Ransom's apartment, was a clear message:

*Come alone.*

Consumed with a hatred that almost blinded him, he punched through the window and annihilated the killer's taunt in a shower of broken glass.

# Chapter 61

Five minutes had passed. One of the longest five minutes of Charlie Priest's life, but also one of the most important, because in that time he had reached certain conclusions that may keep his niece alive.

The first was that he had to get a grip. There would be a time for blame, for anger, for self-loathing, but it was not, and could never be, *this* time.

The second was that this was personal – Tilly didn't have silver blood, none of the Priest family did. There was something going on outside of the Binding that he had yet to understand.

He sat in the Aston with the vents blasting cold air at him. Georgie was with Sarah, trying to rouse her but she was out cold. Priest suspected she had been drugged. He had told Georgie that she had to just make sure her airways were clear until the ambulance arrived.

He thought about Rowlinson and Eaton. They were probably on their way. It wouldn't have been difficult to track them.

He had to leave, now. 'They think it's you,' Fay had said. It wouldn't take Eaton long to work it out, he was sure of it, but he couldn't afford even that slight delay.

Besides, Copperhead's instruction had been clear: 'Come alone.' He had Tilly. He couldn't afford for anyone to get in his way. Tilly was his responsibility. She had drawn that symbol everywhere; maybe this was his fault by having that cursed Book in his study.

*But where are you?*

Priest pursed his lips, scrolled through his phone, until he came across a number. After hitting 'call', the sound of a phone ringing rattled through the Aston's hands-free system until it was answered curtly.

'Doctor Wheatcroft, hello?'

Priest waited a fraction of a second. He knew the doctor had his number: they had spoken before. He knew who was calling him but nonetheless he had answered generically, drawing a clear line straight away. Well, today he didn't have time for bullshit.

'I need to speak with him.'

This time Wheatcroft paused, before forcing an unconvincing laugh. 'Charlie, is that you? You know I can't do that. This isn't a hotel and I'm not a receptionist.'

'Dr Wheatcroft, please. It's urgent.'

'Look, Charlie, we did you a favour the other day but, to be honest, your last visit set William back a long way. He—'

'Dr Wheatcroft!' That got his attention. 'Please, shut up. I know he has a phone. I know the level of control he exerts. I know there is a hidden network in your hospital and I know damn well who's the spider sat in the middle of the web. I don't have time for pretence. I need to speak with him now.'

The line went silent. One second, two. Three. Then Wheatcroft replied, defeated. 'I will call back in five minutes.'

'You've got three, tops.'

When the phone rang again and Priest answered, the voice that filled the car was a low rumble, the harrowing tone of the Dark Redeemer.

'Charles? I'm so glad you called, I—'

'He has Tilly.'

William said nothing at first. 'Tilly.'

'This isn't about the Binding, or demon DNA, or God. It's something else. I just can't work out what.'

'I found Michael's letters to me. All of them. I was reading them when you called.'

'Where would he take her? He said it was where it all started, for him.'

'I see.'

'Where?'

William paused again, as if to collect himself. Priest could hear the emotion in his voice, the dryness of his throat. Sarah had cut William off the moment they had caught him; systematically erasing him from her life. Undoing their history. Tilly had no idea she had an Uncle William. There was not one shred of connection there. But Priest knew without question that his brother's love of both members of his family, and his desire to protect them, was as strong today as it had been the day Jozef had attacked Sarah, and that instinct would extend to Tilly. William Priest was a killer, but that did not stop him from being a gentleman, the loyalest of the loyal.

'There is a hospital that was closed in 1987, in the heart of the Lincolnshire Wolds; a hospital for children, I believe, privately funded through a charity of some description in the days when they still thought EST was a good idea. Michael spoke of his fascination with this place on a number of occasions in his letters to me. He connected with it, idolised it. It was his fantasy to be found dead there, strapped to a rusty gurney. Found by me, I should add. He'll take her there. That would be, I believe in his eyes, an ideal setting for the endgame.'

Priest punched the information into his phone. The results sprang back almost immediately. *The Elipmus Hospital for Children, Lincolnshire.*

'I think I've found it.' He entered the postcode and once again the GPS pointed the way. 'Thank you. I know Sarah won't ever know, but—'

'Charles, I don't care about that. Concentrate, and this time, listen to what I tell you. I've read these letters, almost all of them now. I curse myself for not having paid enough attention to them. Wrongly, I wrote Michael off as another serial killer idoliser, a pathetic sheep. He is nothing of the sort. He is dangerous, beyond anything I have ever encountered. He is evil in human form. The devil. He will not hesitate, and neither must you.'

Priest put the Aston in gear and prepared to pull out. 'There's something you're not telling me.'

William took a deep breath. 'Yes. There's something else you need to know.'

Priest sensed the trepidation in his voice. It alarmed him. He had not heard his brother express such open anxiety, not since that day in the woods when he had shouted for Charlie to wait until he got there, but the younger brother had been so much quicker.

'What? What do I need to know?'

'I'll tell you. But you're not going to like it.'

# Chapter 62

Priest tried not to think about Tilly, alone and terrified. He needed to focus, so he imagined she was unconscious, like her mother. Just sleeping. And indeed, why would Michael want her screaming and causing a fuss, drawing attention to him? No, he wanted this too much. He wanted the endgame to play out – his conversation with William had convinced him of it. Tilly would be sleeping.

It wasn't much comfort.

Before he hit the motorway, he had run some calculations. It was over two and a half hours to the Elipmus Hospital according to the GPS, but the Aston had a top speed of two hundred and three miles an hour. He could easily shave an hour off the journey, maybe more. He had thought it might even be possible to get there before Copperhead, but he doubted it; he had at least an hour's head start.

He drove with a single-minded determination; cursing every slow driver, every red light, every touch of the brake. Every mile that passed was agony. Even the rolling clouds kept shaping themselves into hourglasses, slowly revolving again and again as the rumble of the motorway matched the tremor of his beating heart.

William had been right all along. He shouldn't have hesitated. Michael should be dead. Well, not this time. He had taken his beautiful niece, the one thing he was connected to that was pure. He was Tilly's godfather too, and when he had spoken those words six years ago – about loving and protecting her – he had meant every word. He gripped the wheel so tightly his hands turned white. Michael was a dead man walking. He'd see to it this time. He'd show him what happens if you messed with a Priest.

The Elipmus Hospital sat on the edge of a market town in what seemed like the middle of nowhere. A narrow river snaked through a patchwork quilt of green and yellow fields interwoven with red brick farmhouses and gigantic wind turbines that reminded Priest of the Dali-like elephants he had seen graffitied on the walls of the abandoned factory where Darren Green had been killed.

He passed a power station with six cooling towers overshadowing a mountain of coal before the road banked right and an iron bridge saw him over the river. Once he was across the other side, he saw a single-track road with a strip of overgrown greenery running down its centre with corn fields either side. The Aston rumbled along for a mile before the road just seemed to disintegrate and give way to an area of grass and dirt.

He brought the car to a standstill and killed the engine. Got out. Behind him, the sun was setting on a dark landscape of fields and trees and, in the distance, the first sparks of light from the town shimmered like fireflies in the night. Vapour was still billowing from the cooling towers a few miles away against a low plane of clouds ignited in orange and purple from the dying sun.

In front, shielded by a thicket of dense trees, he saw a square of colourless grass fronting one of the loneliest and wretched buildings he had ever seen. A single-storey grey brick building sprawling across the uneven ground with one side clad with decaying wood set around a series of black lead-lined windows. Climbing plants clawed at the walls, reaching the top in places and slithering into the glassless openings, as if nature were reclaiming the house, pulling it back into the earth from where it came.

There was no sign of any other vehicle. That didn't mean much in itself but the intensity of the isolation of the place gave Priest a jolt of apprehension: *what if William was wrong? What if this isn't the place?*

He pushed the thought from his mind and trudged across the lifeless grass to an archway at the gable end. A door had been splintered open and was hanging precariously at an angle from one hinge. He had no plan, but he realised there was no point in being quiet, or sneaking in. The silence of the place was overbearing – only the occasional cawing of a line of crows perched on the roof above him and the slight hint of a breeze nervously brushing through the trees provided the soundtrack to an otherwise forgotten and haunted place.

Priest pushed the door open and, although it creaked at the sudden movement, it held fast in the frame.

He had expected to see a series of corridors and small rooms like a hive but instead he was presented with one large room spanning the width of the gable and ending with a wall and a set of double doors, through which he could just see into what appeared to be a similarly proportioned room, in terms of length at least.

Nothing had been touched in thirty years. The concrete floor was littered with debris, broken glass and dirt. The paint on the walls was peeling everywhere, giving the feel that the building was so fragile a strong wind might be enough to tear it down. The carcasses of four metal beds lined the right-hand side; bare except for one, on which a depressingly thin green mattress lay, torn right up one side and exposing a laceration of rancid, mouldy sponge within. On the other side stood three metal baths fixed to the walls with rusty plates beneath a network of copper pipes stained with blue-green chlorine. A dark patch of moisture ran through the centre of the floor, no doubt contributing to the overwhelming stench of rot and decay.

Priest stood in the entranceway, closed his eyes. And listened. Nothing.

Then he bellowed, deep and loud: 'Michael!'

The sound echoed around the room, repeating itself back to him before it faded, sending the murder of crows on the roof scattering for cover.

But other than that, there was no reply.

'Michael! I'm here. Alone. Like you asked.'

When there was no reply again, Priest started walking towards the end of the room. There was a doorway to the right but he couldn't see through. Evidently, it led to a windowless room – nothing but darkness in there. He ignored it for now, walked through the double doors at the end. The second room was smaller, with a pitched roof and skylights. It was duller, too, the fading light outside was finding it difficult to get in and although the back wall was splashed with amber radiance, the rest of the room was shrouded in darkness.

'Michael.'

'Over here.'

The voice came from behind him. He turned, scanned the first room. Saw nothing. His heart was pounding in his chest, he felt the beginnings of pins and needles in his hands. He had heard Michael, as clear as day, almost in his ear. But there was nothing there.

Angry at how easily he had been spooked, he risked wiping the back of his hand across his face. He was surprised to see how clammy it was. It wasn't particularly warm inside the hospital, but he was sweating openly.

'Where are you?' he barked into the room.

No reply.

There was nowhere to hide in either room. They were open, even the duller room was lit well enough so as not to offer any sanctuary. Which meant that the voice had to have come from the depths of the room that was now to his right. The black doorway, the gateway to a world of darkness.

*Fuck.*

He approached the doorway and flicked on the torch on his phone. The illumination it provided was intense but short-ranged. He could make out that he was in a small room, four or five metres square, with doors off to both sides, stained white walls set around an operating table, over which a series of apparatus hovered, extending from the ceiling on bent mechanical arms. An array of circular lights, like robotic probes from a sci-fi film, threatening an invisible occupant of the table below.

Priest didn't scare easily. He had been the first on scene at the most hideous of crimes, confronted evil that even Dante would have had difficulty conceiving. But the sight of that partially irradiated operating table was something that would stay with him for ever.

The door slammed behind him and he couldn't move.

His first thought was to double back. The door was rotten, he could put his shoulder through it. But something stopped him. He sensed that he was being watched. He scanned the room with the torch, checked every corner but he was alone.

'I know you're here, Michael.'

'I'm sorry it had to be this way, Charlie. But you've caused me problems.'

'Where is she?'

'She's safe, and well. She's sleeping. You've nothing to worry about.'

Priest tried to pinpoint the voice but it was all around him, like it was coming from a PA system.

'It's the acoustics, in case you're wondering,' said Michael, who must have cottoned on to what he was trying to do. 'It's one of the reasons I love this building. It doesn't betray you like other places. It looks after you, keeps you hidden.'

Priest traced the wall with his phone to where he thought Michael's voice was louder. 'I'd like to see you, Michael.'

'All in good time.'

There was a headache forming at the base of his skull, a gnawing pain taking hold. He felt an air vent, or something like an air vent, on the far side of the wall. *Was he talking through the vents?*

'You've no idea how long I've waited for this,' Michael continued. 'To be here with you.'

'You want to get married or something? Come right out. I'll make you one happy psychopath.'

Michael laughed. 'That's funny, but I do hate that word, Charlie. Psychopath. It's so Generation X, you know what I mean?'

Priest thought he saw a flicker of something in the corner of his eye, but when he looked the spot moved to the other side. Then he realised what was happening. *Not now.* His hands were numb, his arms heavy. They no longer felt part of him, but independent – creatures with their own sapient minds.

*Jesus Christ, no.*

He pressed against his temples, desperate to stop the onslaught, and the feeling of detachment.

'They built this place in 1910, you know, when the Catholic boys' orphanage not far from here found it had more sick children than it could care for. It was, like so many good things in this world, started by a priest, although I never got to learn his name. It was a Voluntary Aid Detachment hospital during the First World War, run by the Red Cross before it reverted in 1919 to a children's hospital, specialising in TB. Stop me if I'm boring you, by the way.'

Priest was starting to lose his sense of feeling, the flashing in front of his eyes was starting to worsen. He had an overpowering urge to sink to the floor, but he knew he mustn't give in. He had to see this through. For Tilly.

'Say, are you OK, Charlie? You don't look so good. Maybe you should lie down or something.'

He was crouched down – he had no choice. The pain in his head and the feeling of being on the verge of blacking out was too great. It was that or he would fall. Michael's voice was drifting in and out of his head – his stomach lurched. He was going to be sick.

'Do you know much about TB, Charlie? It's horrible. You can die a horrible death from TB. If it isn't treated the bacilli that causes the disease basically just takes over your immune system and eats you alive. That's why it's sometimes called *consumption*, from the Greek *phthisis*, meaning *to waste away*. Yuck. But the amazing thing – at least the bit I find really amazing – is that it's almost as old as we are. African tribes twenty thousand years ago died from TB. Imagine that. And it's still with us.'

There was nothing else he could do but succumb to the crippling oppression that was taking him over, invading him. He half collapsed on to the cold floor, groaning in pain.

'Charlie? You still with me?'

Before he blacked out, Priest realised all too late that this was nothing to do with DPD. This wasn't an episode, or an hallucination. It was designed. It was a trap that he had walked into, and he had been well and truly snared.

# Chapter 63

*One year ago*

*I am not a killer.*

*That is something that I have had to come to terms with. It has not been easy. While others around me had to come to terms with the limitations of their foresight, or intellect, or sexuality, my cross to bear was far more debilitating.*

*As I walk out of the church, high on the mixture of alcohol and faith, the feeling of pressing inside Sue still throbbing in my groin, I dwell upon this defect in my personality. I am not a killer. I cannot quite see myself being able to watch the life in someone's eyes extinguish, or feel their limbs fall limp in my hands. Perhaps it is a weakness, I don't know.*

*At first I regarded this as a serious setback. I even questioned the philosophy of the whole thing. Why would I have been chosen for this task if I do not have the capacity to push a knife into a demon's heart?*

*But my concern was short-lived when I met Michael.*

*Like so many ghosts who drift in and out of Fellowship meetings he was just another new face staring blankly back at me, as if I held the very answer to his existence in the palm of my hand and all he had to do was sit and wait for it to be delivered to him.*

He was short but there was a breadth to his shoulders and a size to his arms that impressed me. He had small eyes, and the years of substance abuse had hardened his face, drawn lines across his chin and temples that should have been decades off development. But it was his hands that interested me the most. His fingers were padded, stained yellow from holding cigarettes too often for too long. I knew straight away, they were killer's hands.

I walk through the churchyard, marvelling at how the trees bow graciously toward the spire, casting long shadows across the mottled grass and swaying gently in the breeze. Swaying much like Sue had, back and forth. Back and forth. Never once resting, always moving.

In the car, I check my phone again and find that Michael has left me a message. I came up with our method of communication. It is, if I may say so, ingenious. You see, I haven't wasted my life. I could have let my parents' death crush me into the ground, assign me to the dumping ground of obscurity, but God had other ideas. I took a degree in computer science and from there I developed a keen interest in programe language theory. That landed me a job as a coder in my late twenties with a software company and very soon I was taking home a healthy salary. By the time I reached the age of thirty I had acquired enough contacts and knowledge to establish my own business designing, among other things, profiling codes for online retailers.

My first piece of good fortune was a year later when my new business was asked to design the algorithms for a new social media platform called Rylet, owned by a Swedish developer. At the time, I didn't think anything of it. Silicon Valley enjoys an impenetrable monopoly on social networks – Europe lags behind, adopting the American platforms and conforming to its demands, as opposed to

China, which developed its own. So when Rylet said they couldn't afford to pay the fees because they were themselves a start-up, but they would give me personally a five per cent share for the work, I sighed a little and relented.

Five years later, Rylet was bought by Facebook for a billion dollars, and my five per cent paid dividends.

I type a message back to Michael. He wants more money. I have more money, but I resent his continual demands. It was always going to be a risky part of the process, doing a deal with a killer who so enjoyed his work, but money was the only leverage I had. So I didn't have much choice. The only way I could keep his demands down was to feed him the idea that I had less than I actually do.

It will be short-lived. I figured he would get through fifteen Carriers, maybe more if I was lucky, before he was caught and I would have to find someone else. It will be a slow process but Rome was not built in a day, and I had most of their personal data to use when the time came to choose another champion. There would be plenty more ready to take his place. The Watchers saw to the blighting of Earth with enough Godless sinners to create a whole army of potential assassins I could recruit.

The surprise was how easy it has been. I had of course worked on Michael in the same way I had worked on Sue and Elisha and others. Slowly, with patience and understanding, gaining their trust, and blowing holes in their trust of others. Then one day I asked him:

'Would you kill a man for money, Michael?'

He thought about it, before a wide grin spread across his face. 'I've killed a man for less than that before.'

I wait for Michael's reply, anxiously rapping my knuckles on the steering wheel. I could have upped the offer, but my resources are *finite and Michael is going to be the first of many recruits. I can't blow it all just because he has cocaine to buy.*

*Finally, he replies, and I relax.*

*The first Carrier will be eliminated when the final preparations are completed in less than a year's time. Her name is Jane Vardy.*

# Chapter 64

In the darkness, Priest heard his name being called.

At first, he thought it was Jessica calling him; then Sarah, from all those years ago, her scream ripping through the cool summer's air like the crack of thunder.

No, it wasn't Sarah.

Tilly.

He realised that there was a bright light pulsating in front of his closed eyes. The last rays of the sun as it set over the ruins of the derelict hospital, or the blinding flash of a building exploding behind him. He wasn't sure which.

He couldn't remember where he was, but he heard the drop in tone of William's voice as he recited the contents of Michael's letters. *'I'll tell you. But you're not going to like it.'*

Then he remembered the small dark room, the operating theatre with its black, malevolent silhouette of the table and lights poised above. But the table wasn't empty and he could see the outline of a small body writhing in fear and the shriek of her cries, then the agony of looking into her eyes and, even with her child's understanding, the accusation.

*You failed me, Uncle Charlie.*

He gasped for breath as he thundered back into the world of consciousness coughing and spluttering, the pain across his head and chest reawakening him with cruel, raw intensity. He tried to open his eyes but they were sticky, sealed shut. Took him a few moments of furious blinking to shift the glue-like crust that had formed.

It had been gas, he was sure of that. Pumped in through the vents. Something odourless and fast-acting, probably military grade, like BZ, a Swiss-made solvent which the Soviets eerily named Substance 78.

Michael had had this planned for months, years maybe. The whole damn thing, from start to finish. And he had walked straight into the trap with his eyes open.

He tried to move, but little happened, other than a searing pain down both arms. Looking down, he saw he was naked from the waist up and strapped to a bed, his upper half raised at a narrow angle. Straps were wound tightly over his biceps, wrists and ankles. He could hardly feel his hands. There was a bright light above him. Six orbs circling a sun, or so he thought. Then it hit him.

He was in the fucking operating theatre.

Except that it had moved. He was in the far room with the pitched roof. The lights above him seemed like the only form of illumination. It was pitch black outside. *How long have I been out?* He was strapped to a gurney, not an operating table. There must have been another light set-up he hadn't registered first time around. Michael had just wheeled him through.

He checked the restraints, rattled the gurney. It hurt like hell. He did it again, harder. Nothing. Then frantically, desperately: every muscle in his body strained and contorted as he thrashed around with what little movement he had. The gurney moved, clattering across the floor away from the lights, then stopped.

Priest thought he had hit something, but when he twisted his head, he saw Copperhead's dead eyes staring back at him from behind a surgical mask.

'Going somewhere?' Michael removed the mask, grinned. There was something reptilian about it. His nose was badly damaged, bent and with an angry wound that ran from the bridge to his lip. 'Give it another go if you want. See if you can break the restraints, but I doubt you can. Not even someone as strong as you.'

Priest roared in frustration, but even a final effort encouraged by the prospect of getting hold of Copperhead's throat fell flat and he felt his body fall limp, his chest heaving and the pain in his head close to unbearable.

Michael was wearing green scrubs and a white apron. In the pub, he had seemed so small. He was not without athleticism – Priest recalled how agile he had seemed in the scuffle outside – but no match for his nemesis. Only the stun grenade had given him a lucky escape. Now, he looked as mad and threatening as anything Priest had ever seen, with his damaged face, twisted teeth and manic eyes. And the set-up he had engineered – the gurney, the surgical clothes – all designed with a clear intention.

A thought flashed through Priest's head: he might genuinely die here, alone with this fucking lunatic in the middle of nowhere.

Then what would happen to . . .

'Where is she?' he hissed, breathless.

'The little girl? Like I said, she's fine. You don't need to worry about her. It's you I'm interested in.'

'The fuck you want from me?'

Michael reached out, touched his shoulder, made a little circular movement with his finger. It was an odd thought, but Priest registered the softness of his hand, and the warmth in it. Maybe the last warm flesh he would feel.

'You've no idea how much I've waited for this moment.' He said it almost to himself, in a dreamlike trance, his eyes fixed on Priest's torso. He reached across, felt his chest, the contours of his abs, stopped short of his waist and removed his hand.

'You could have bought me a drink like any normal person,' Priest breathed.

Michael laughed softly, then turned away. Priest couldn't see what he was doing but he heard the sound of scraping metal on the concrete floor, like a heavy piece of furniture being dragged toward the gurney. Then there was the sound of more metal, as though he was rifling through a cutlery drawer.

'That's funny,' said Michael. 'I love that even when faced with the prospect of a slow and painful death you keep your sense of humour.'

'I don't have silver blood, so it won't help your tally.'

'What, you think that's really important to me? Really?'

Priest wasn't sure, not after what William had said. *You're not going to like it.* But he had to keep Michael talking.

'It's what you want. The Binding.'

There was more movement and Michael came back into view. He was carrying a stool, or something like a stool, which he placed next to the gurney, almost within reach. Then any tiny shred of hope that Priest might have had died. He saw Michael take a tray and place it on the stool. From the tray, he produced a small metallic object; the unmistakable shape of a scalpel.

'The Binding?' said Michael, arching an eyebrow. He took out a small bottle of fluid with a spray cap – it could have been household detergent. He sprayed the scalpel. Stopped when he saw Priest watching, then explained. 'We can't have germs, now can we?'

He placed the scalpel down on the stool next to Priest and took out another implement – it was much larger, looked like a pair of pliers. He had spent enough time in the morgue as a young detective to know what it was. A rongeur: from the French word meaning rodent. It was used for gouging out bone.

Priest turned away. He didn't want to see any more. His heart was threatening to tear itself out of his rib cage. The only consolation was that he might pass out from hyperventilating before any real damage was done. His body felt like it was already preparing to shut down.

'You didn't answer my question,' he wheezed. 'Your God isn't going to reward you for this.'

'*My* God?' Michael shook his head, tutted. Sprayed the rongeur and placed it next to the scalpel. Reached for the tray and fished out something else. Priest didn't look to see what. 'Not *my* God, Charlie. And certainly not yours either. No. I think we can safely say that, in this room, there is no fucking God. Right?'

He thought back to Michael's apartment, and the scrawl on the wall. *God is dead.* It was the same hand that had written *Kill the Giants* at the murder scenes, and the symbol of Janus crudely drawn in blood.

He turned his head towards Michael, angry and scared. 'Then what? What do you want?'

The question seemed to make him think. He placed the instrument he was holding back on the tray. Maybe it was something in the tone of Priest's voice, the hint that his nerves were finally cracking.

'You really don't know, do you?' He pursed his lips. *You're not going to like it.*

Priest's neck was cramped from straining, the top of his arms felt like they were about to explode out of their joints. Every fucking nerve was ablaze. Every neuron on fire. His brain felt like it was too big for his head; any moment now it would tear his skull in two.

'Fine.'

Michael breathed in deeply, like he was about to tell a favourite story. Priest watched him, now focussed on making sure he gave nothing away if he could. He needed to keep Michael talking, keep him occupied, keep his hands away from the surgical instruments. Anything to prolong his life, give him a chance to save Tilly if he could. He would die, of course. He was resigned to it. But if he could understand what this mad fucker wanted then maybe, just maybe, he could save his niece and if that meant enduring more torture under an amateur knife than a man had ever endured, then so be it.

'What you need to understand, Charlie, is that, in a way, it's nothing personal.'

'Now you're the fucking comedian.'

'No, I mean it. But the problem is, I can't get to your brother. In an ideal world, it would be Dr William Priest on the slab, watching me with a mixture of terror and awe, much like you are now.'

'Not awe, you freak. Pity.'

'Well, have it your way.' Michael smiled, like he'd come to the magic part of the story that some of the older children didn't believe. 'William would understand me. He'd recognise my talent, how hard I'd worked to get to this point. How I use fear as a weapon. It's a skill, you know. The subtle art of inducing shit to splurge from the anus of a grown man. I mean, take this.' He picked up the spray bottle, pulled the trigger and watched in wonder as a splattering of clear liquid fell on Priest's chest. 'It's just water. It's all an act, that bit.'

'You are one fucked-up—'

'Thank you,' Michael interrupted.

Whether it was also on the tray or behind it, Priest couldn't tell, but from somewhere Michael produced a hammer and an eight-inch nail, the same as they had found lodged in the brains of the first four victims.

Priest had thought that the sight of the surgical instruments was the pinnacle of fear. But he was wrong.

'I didn't want to kill people this way,' he said, examining the nail. 'All that stuff about the Israelites and Yael. It didn't really do anything for me. But the truth is that I found it very satisfying. The moment of penetration and the luscious sound of the skull cracking. I practised on watermelons. Oddly, it's a very similar sound.'

There was another moment when his heart rate reached a crescendo and his back cracked under the strain of his body: Michael wasn't smiling anymore. The laughter had extinguished from his eyes, the playful, almost sensual movements of his hands were replaced with rough, primal dexterity as he took one of the nails and, without warning, smashed the hammer downwards and drove it into Priest's hand.

# Chapter 65

Priest's hand erupted with a pain he had never experienced and, for a second, he blacked out.

When he came to, his hand and arm, right up to his shoulder and neck, were on fire. The nail had burst through his hand as easily as a juice carton and latched itself on to the edge of the bed.

He let out a wail of agony; a primitive, defeated cry.

Lights danced in front of his eyes, waves of nausea swept over him. His head swam with oxygen. His body told him it was time to give up.

Michael laughed, and it was only the arrogance of his tormentor that hauled him out of the abyss and back into the real world.

'Does the name Michael Ireland mean anything to you,' asked Copperhead with acrimony.

Priest fought for lucidity. The name *did* mean something. From the depths of his scrambled memory, he recalled William's words. *You're not going to like it.*

'Michael. Ireland,' he managed. 'I thought . . .'

Impatient, Michael picked up another nail. 'You thought my name was Ransom. It is, but only because I changed it from Ireland to give myself a little more anonymity. Maybe this will help. From 1956 until 1987, the date it was decommissioned, my father was the head surgeon of this institute. He was a good man, who gave up thirty years of his career to saving children: kids with nobody, no family, no friends. Destitutes. Do you know what that feels like? To even save one life?'

He didn't move. He was on to his reserve levels of energy and expending them on the task of staying awake. But yes, he knew. William had told him.

Michael was ranting, drooling like he was possessed. 'Well, let me tell you, it's not what you think. You think it makes you feel better, but it doesn't work like that. Never has done. The world is far crueller. No. Every life you save, Priest, it takes a little piece of your soul and crushes it. So one day, you look at all the happy little children you helped bring back from the dead and realise that He took everything from you. God did that. Because you're defying Him, denying them the one-way ticket to paradise, starving Him of souls. So, one day, He sends one of *His* angels to take yours.'

In a moment of heart-stopping clarity, Priest remembered what William had said. He remembered who Michael Ireland was.

'I told you that my parents had been murdered but I never said who by. I was eight years old when I hid in a cupboard and watched your brother, London's most notorious serial killer, come into their room at night and slaughter them with a hammer, a claw hammer just like this one.'

He slammed the hammer down into the middle of Priest's chest. He stiffened. Ribs cracked. Another lightning bolt of pain ripped through him. But that wasn't the worst of it: the worst of it was he couldn't breathe. His lungs simply refused to draw in

oxygen. And after only a couple of seconds, they started screaming for air.

He tried to speak, but the blow had robbed him of his voice.

'Do you have any idea what that does to an eight-year-old
boy, Priest? Watching someone murder your parents? I'll tell
you. It turns them into a killer in his own right. You think you
know pain, right now? You have no idea. The care system. Foster
parents who beat you, kids at school who taunt you every day,
the teacher who rapes you in the school toilets. *That's* pain,
Charlie. And over time, something happens. A shell forms over
you; a hard, cruel shell, and it makes you do things, like drive
nails into people's heads. And it helps, because for every child
that my father saved he lost a piece of his soul, and for every
body that I deliver to Satan I get a piece of mine back.'

Finally, just when he thought he couldn't take any more, his
lungs kick-started, and, through a splutter of blood and bile, he
sucked in as much air as he could and God it felt good.

'So imagine my luck,' Michael was oblivious to the torment of his captive, 'when I'm recruited. Because that's all I
am, Priest. A recruit. The fall guy. A pawn in someone else's
game. You must have guessed by now that I am not Copperhead. I never said I was. I didn't send you that letter. I killed
those people, and I wrote those messages on the wall, sprin-
kled the salt around. And the symbol, of course, because I was
instructed to.'

Priest managed to turn his head to look at Michael, who must
have read some element of puzzlement in his expression because
he explained:

'They say never turn a hobby into a business, don't they?
Well, they're wrong. It can be done. Copperhead believes in the

Binding. He believes that people with a certain blood group carry the DNA of a stowaway on Noah's Ark that descends from the Watchers, the human hybrids spawned from unions between human women and the fallen angels led by Samyaza. Well, here's news for you, Priest . . .' Michael knelt down so that his mouth was close to Priest's ear, and whispered, 'Copperhead is a fucking lunatic. There's no such thing as God, let alone a special place in heaven for the person who kills all the Carriers and brings about a new age of paradise on earth.'

Priest summoned up his last remaining strength to say, 'How did you know . . . I was involved?'

'I didn't. That was the magic of it. That's true fate. I fucking didn't know until Copperhead had me try and blow you sky high and I saw . . . well, I saw you. You made it. I'm pleased for you. You flew in the air like a bullet, but you made it, thanks to my phone call. So, I go and see Copperhead and he knows exactly what's happening in the investigation. Doesn't have a clue why I'm asking and he just says, *yeah, that's Charlie Priest: who gives a shit?*'

Michael laughed, clapped his hands together once.

*Ah, fate. We meet again.*

'You knew about Owen, and Capindale?'

Michael shook his head sadly. 'They were pawns, foot-soldiers in a war that I don't care about. But I know that Owen knew what Copperhead wanted the Book for. You see, nobody wanted the Book out in the open. Owen didn't want it out because he didn't want anyone trying to take on the role of the hero in the Binding. Exactly the role that Copperhead had taken on. And Copperhead didn't want anyone to get their hands on the Book because he didn't want anyone else to rival him in the quest to kill the Carriers, or find out how he was choosing the victims. Not that he ever would have succeeded. I told him that. I said we could do sixteen, max. The same number that your brother was prosecuted for, although I know there are more you two don't talk about. But no, not three hundred. But that was Copperhead for you, him and his blind faith.'

'Who killed Luca Caspari?' Priest wheezed.

'The art dealer? Copperhead arranged it. He paid some idiot he found through the Darknet, but he didn't pay good. Got a dud, by the sound of it; a local thug who thought he was an assassin. Still, he did the job. Just ended up getting caught, I hear.'

'Why? What did Caspari do?'

Michael huffed, impatiently. 'He didn't *do* anything. But he had translations, same as Owen. He knew about the silver bloods. Copperhead knew that if Owen was clinging on to the Book of Janus, you'd eventually link it back to one of the only other people who knew what the fucking thing says.'

By now Michael was leaning on the gurney, gesticulating enthusiastically with his back half turned to Priest, as if he had almost forgotten about his victim. It was agony to talk, but he had to know – this might be his last chance.

'How did . . . Copperhead know what the . . . Book of Janus said? How did he know . . . to go after the . . . silver bloods?'

Michael turned around, intrigued, as if he hadn't thought of the question before. 'I think he said he inherited some scraps of translated pages, or something. From his father. What does it matter?'

'And Capindale?'

'Ah, yes, the collector woman. She was sponsored by Copperhead to use Owen to get the Book, and the translations. But the arrogant bastard decided to keep it for himself, claiming he was the one who translated it. As if. And who would have guessed it? He was also a religious nut. She had the connections, you see. And she needed cash. She has some strange condition that means she can't go outside or something, and her career was down the swanny. It was easy for Copperhead to use her to get the Book.'

'Why did he need it . . . if he had the translations?'

'Well, every now and again Copperhead would have a small dose of reality in terms of the scale of his venture. Three hundred people is a lot to kill. So he realised that if the police got hold of the Book of Janus, they might have someone amongst their ranks with enough brain cells to work out how he was choosing the victims. Blood types don't come up in tox reports; he knew that. Also, the translations he had were incomplete – enough to know how to start but there could have been more in the Book.'

Priest couldn't think straight, but the occasional clear message was floating through the fog: *Copperhead was close to the investigation, and understood police procedure.*

Michael straightened up, stretched. It looked like he had just remembered what he was doing there. Priest looked around frantically, sensing his time was up. He had more questions, but he couldn't put it all together, he was still missing something. And Tilly: he needed time to negotiate, the clarity to think straight.

Michael picked up the hammer and another nail.

'I think that's enough talk now, Charlie. Don't you?'

There was no point in fighting it. The pain in his hand, arm and chest were too great. It was over. Michael measured the nail against a spot between his eyes. He didn't even bother moving his head, just stared straight up, closed his eyes, then he did something he didn't expect.

He prayed to God.

# Chapter 66

In a mysterious world of colourless dreams accompanied by the sound of static, Charlie Priest spoke to God.

He wasn't ignorant of these things. After all, the Bible was a contract, with clause numbers and interpretational issues. The covenants contained therein might be binding; equally, they might not. He lived in a world of perpetual grey, where one man's benefit was another man's burden. The Bible was no different.

He thought about the snake from the Garden of Eden. Some people thought it was the Devil, others the demon Samyaza. Equally, there were those that thought the snake was another demon altogether: Lilith, the whorish Babylonian siren who stole babies in the night, the reason why we sing our children lullabies before bed, to keep them safe from her malevolent clutches.

Or perhaps it was the first Copperhead, the snake's namesake, a creature who later took on the role of saviour, the destroyer of the Carriers, trying to redeem himself in the eyes of God for his breach of contract: what they call original sin.

There is some significance beyond the symbolism in the story of the snake. It is, after all, the only talking anthropomorphised animal in the Bible. True, there is a talking donkey in the Book of Numbers, but that is merely the exception that proves the rule.

So when Priest prayed, he prayed that if he was permitted a second chance, he could come back as a snake, the most sacred of all God's creatures.

He felt the cold hard iron of the nail on his forehead, the flicker of wind on his cheek. He was peaceful, for once. He couldn't feel his hand anymore, or the burning up his arm. He was in a different place. An ethereal sanctuary. Only the buzzing of the lights reminded him of the material world.

He couldn't see, but he knew Michael had the hammer raised, but there was time for one last moment of triumph before death. One last war cry.

'He was a paedophile, Michael.'

There was a pause, and he guessed his words had struck a chord, enough for Michael to delay his moment of triumph.

'What? Who?'

'Your father. He wasn't a good man like you say. Your mother was complicit in it. They abused scores of children in this hospital and sold hundreds more to Russian smugglers. They got what they deserved.'

His words had had their desired effect. Michael was infuriated, seething in his ear. 'You're wrong. They never proved anything.'

'I know. That's what William did. Got the ones that beat the system.'

'*No*. See you in hell, Priest.'

Michael raised the hammer, but there was no moment of cessation as he had expected. Death would have been instantaneous. No blackness. No tunnel offering a pinprick of light at the end. No flashbacks.

Or perhaps there was. Perhaps the whole expansion of his life so far *was* the flashback, and that was how it was experienced, in real time speed.

He felt the gurney crash violently to one side. Something had hit it. Sent it sprawling across the room. Fresh surges of pain shot up his arm. He was suddenly wide awake. There was a commotion, shouting, confusion and anger.

He twisted his head. And God, what a sight.

Michael was off-balance, pinned down in a crouch with a pair of trained hands gripping his hair, holding him in a way that made it impossible for him to do anything other than clasp his own hands over those of his assailant to try to relieve the pressure. He thrashed around helplessly, but he stood no chance. The man who had him trapped knew exactly what he was doing, knew where to hurt, and where to hold. A human vice. Michael could have resisted for hours, it would have made no difference.

Then the man raised Michael up, and the killer could do nothing to stop himself from being lifted from the floor so he was nose-to-nose with his aggressor, whereupon his expression changed from anger and fear to one of total incomprehension. And when the man spoke, it was with total authority.

'Know this, Michael: the only one who gets to torture my brother . . . is me.'

# Chapter 67

Priest had to blink several times to check it wasn't an hallucination: but there he was. Dr William Priest in the flesh, in a hospital, but the wrong one. Standing as tall and powerful as he had that day he sent Jozef sprawling through the forest.

'What . . . how?' Michael stammered, recognising the man he had obsessed over for so long.

'They were part of a paedophile ring, Michael,' William lectured. 'Deep down you know it. It wasn't a teacher who raped you and that didn't take place after you went into care. You've got it all wrong.'

'No . . . I—'

Evidently not intent on listening, William pushed Michael around and let his grip relax for a split second, long enough to bring the flat of his hand down hard across the back of Michael's neck. He went crashing to the floor. Priest knew that the blow wasn't fatal but designed to render Michael unconscious. William knew what he was doing: they still had to find Tilly.

'What the hell are you doing here?' Priest coughed.

'No time for that. Ah, I see you got nailed finally.'

With no warning, William took hold of the nail and yanked it out. Priest screamed in agony as a volcano of blood erupted from the wound.

'Stop being a baby,' William chided, undoing the straps. 'What was *your* plan, by the way? Sit around and let him bleed you to death?'

'Tilly!'

'Yes, I know. Straps first, then we'll get to her. I'm sure our friend can be persuaded to help.'

When the last of the straps was off, Priest eased himself up. William tore off a section of his shirt and wrapped it around the gaping hole in his brother's hand, but every breath was agony.

'Thanks,' Priest rasped.

'Don't mention it. Now, our niece. Oh, *Michael*—'

William turned and stopped. Priest saw his fists ball. Michael was gone.

'I thought you coshed him.'

William turned to him gravely. 'It appears I'm out of practice.'

There was no time for blame, and he would be dead if William hadn't intervened, however the hell he had got there.

'Split up.'

Priest took the door to the right that led back to the main hospital wing, off from which was nestled the operating theatre. He wouldn't make the same mistake twice. William took off the other way, although for the first time, Priest noticed his brother had a limp.

It struck him as unlikely that Tilly was anywhere in the hospital building itself – perhaps a car or van outside but he hadn't seen anything on the way in. He was also concerned that, having let Michael slip through his fingers for a second time, Tilly might represent a very useful hostage. It was this thought that spurred him on despite the pain that threatened to bring his body crashing down.

'Tilly!'

He was about to kick the main door off its hinges and go outside when he heard a muffled shout from the other room.

'Charles! This way!'

*'Charlie, come here!'*

He raced as fast as he could back past the gurney and into a room at the back, lit with another series of operating lights. It was similar to the operating theatre, windowless and airless, but larger, with two other doors leading off to the left and right.

William was standing in the entranceway, stock-still. There was Michael, standing behind a table, on which lay . . .

'Tilly!'

Priest made a move forward, fuelled with rage, but his brother caught his arm, squeezed it hard enough to catch his attention.

'Charles, wait.'

Tilly was laid on the table on her side, looking like a sleeping doll, her mass of tangled hair cascading down her back. But she was peaceful and, more importantly, breathing.

Michael was holding a scalpel, not a particularly big one, but enough to cause permanent damage to a grown man, and probably fatal to a little girl. In the other hand, loose at his side, he held the hammer.

'Stop there,' Michael commanded. 'One more step and I'll fillet her.'

Priest was filled with disgust, and consumed with as much hatred as he had experienced in the sum of his life to date. His body trembled with it.

'Let her go, Michael,' said William. 'It's over.' He was the calmest of the three of them but there was a quiver in his voice.

'You've no idea how long I've waited for this,' said Michael. 'To meet you, in the flesh. The great Doctor William Priest. The Dark Redeemer. How I've longed for it.'

'Do you want to kill me, Michael?'

Michael didn't answer at first, it seemed to Priest that he was incapable. The prospect filled him with such vivid possibility that it seemed too much for him to process. He shuddered, for a moment the scalpel seemed to slip from his hand but he noticed Priest's tiny step forward and corrected himself.

'Back off, Priest. I'll do it. I'll kill her.'

'I asked you a question, Michael,' said William, who had seemingly found his composure.

'I . . . kill you . . . ?'

'You can do so if you wish.' Priest glanced right but his brother was deadly serious, and he caught on straight away to the proposal. 'Why don't you? I'll make it easy for you. All you have to do is let the girl go, Charlie will walk out with her, and you'll be left to do whatever you want with me. You can drive one of those nails through my head if that's what you want, or string it out. As long as you let our niece go.'

'Do you think I'm stupid?' Michael hissed.

'Not at all. I don't think you're a lot of things, Michael. For one, I don't think you'll kill a little girl. That's not your MO, is it?'

'You said they were paedophiles. My parents. But you're not the judge and jury. You don't get to play God. Why did you have to do that, take them away from me?'

'This isn't about me, Michael. It's about you. It's about the choices you make now, and the consequences that they have for us all. My past is not the issue.'

Michael was building up pressure, there were tears in his eyes. He was staggering around, waving the scalpel. Priest glanced at William again. They had to do something soon, or Michael might just crack. William gave a look back, and the tiniest of nods. He understood. Ten years of incarceration seemed to have vanished. William Priest was as arrogant and dangerous as he had ever been.

The moment of understanding that had passed between them was simple enough: they had allocated parts to each other. Who was going for Michael, and who was going for Tilly. It was an invisible bond. The bond of kin.

They moved as one, covering the short distance in the blink of an eye, their respective injuries suddenly forgotten.

Priest had the longer way to go, because his target was Michael. He had to come around the table. William had the shorter distance, but would be directly in harm's way, since he was going to shield Tilly from the inevitable thrust of Michael's uncontrolled hand.

The way it played out could have been better, at least for William. The Dark Redeemer brought his body crashing down over the table protecting Tilly from the swipe of the scalpel. He raised his arm in an effort to parry Michael's attack, but the contact wasn't clean and he was only able to partially protect himself; the scalpel buried itself in the top of William's arm.

To the sound of William's cry of pain, Priest smashed into Michael from the side, pulling him away from the table and sending them both sprawling across the floor.

He had then intended to push himself over Michael, and pin him down, but while William was busy picking out the scalpel from his arm, Priest's cracked ribs and near useless hand were a significant disadvantage. As he grappled for leverage Michael had the upper hand, kicking out into his stomach and causing more shock waves of pain through his broken body.

He realised to his horror that Michael was now standing over him and still had the hammer, which he raised above his head with a primal roar.

This time Priest didn't close his eyes, or pray. He had seen what was coming.

William had pulled the scalpel free, and although he was struggling to move freely, he wasted no time in taking hold of Michael's arm and seizing the pressure point at middle distance between forearm and bicep, neatly dispossessing him of the hammer.

With his other hand, William took Michael by the scruff of the neck and kicked his feet from under him, wheeling him around to the edge of the table where Tilly was out cold. Michael attempted to wriggle free but he was off-balance and confused, unable to do anything except hit out lamely at William's torso. It did nothing to free him, but served to annoy William even more and, before Priest could say or do anything, William pushed Michael's head down onto the table, put the scalpel against the side of his temple, and drove it home with the hammer, cracking through his skull like a watermelon.

# Chapter 68

Priest carried Tilly across the sad patch of grass outside the Elipmus Hospital and placed her gently in the back of the car. William looked pale. They had torn more of the shirt to wrap around William's arm. This had stemmed the bleeding for now but Priest was trying not to think about where Michael might have acquired the scalpel.

When Tilly was safely in the car, William sat down heavily, leant against the passenger door and closed his eyes.

Priest knelt down near him and for a few minutes they did nothing but breathe in the cool night air and listen to the breeze disturb the copse behind them.

In the end, Priest had to ask.

'How did you get out?'

William's reply seemed distant, to such an extent that Priest wondered if he was having a moment of detachment. 'How do you think?'

He considered it, but there was only one viability. 'You took a sharp object, maybe a pen if you were lucky or a toothbrush if not, and stabbed yourself. They came rushing at you but you made sure you were bleeding heavily. You're not known for self-harm so they called Wheatcroft. Fen Marsh isn't a prison, but it's not a full hospital either. They didn't have the right facilities. Maybe Wheatcroft was in on it, I don't know. They take you in one of their own ambulances to A and E, whichever is closest: Guy's Hospital, Newham maybe. There's a four-man transport team: a driver, Wheatcroft and two nurses. How am I doing so far?'

William smiled, impressed. 'Pretty good. You got the tooth-brush, that's very good.'

'There are some quieter roads leading out of Fen Marsh. You're acting docile, so the two either side of you are pretty relaxed. And Wheatcroft keeps reiterating the Deprivation of Liberty Safeguards in the Mental Capacity Act: you're a patient, not a prisoner. Then – what? – you strike the windpipe of the man to your right, with your stronger arm, this instantaneously incapacitates him. Then you put the other in a sleeper hold. The driver stops the ambulance, but by the time he realises what's happening you're on top of him. And Wheatcroft . . . well, you either easily overpower him or you shake hands and walk away. I haven't worked that bit out yet.'

'Bravo.'

It must have caused him considerable pain, but William applauded his recital. He offered nothing on the question of Wheatcroft's complicity, but it was one of the mysteries of life that Priest had decided he didn't really want to know about. Networks are more powerful than hierarchies; that's what Wills would say. Al-Qaeda was a hierarchy, as their defeat demonstrated. ISIS is a network; attacking them is like trying to pin jelly to a wall, as Bush famously said. Wheatcroft was part of a hierarchy. What hope did he have against William's insouciant network?

'How did you get here?' Priest said.

'Taxi.'

He turned and saw where William was pointing to a black cab in the distance. He hadn't seen it, hidden in the copse.

'You steal that?'

'No. I borrowed it. And—' he looked at the Aston, frowning – 'where's my car?'

'The engine control unit's shot to pieces, the mass air flow sensor's failed, there's oil leaking from almost every part of it and there's a bloody great big hole in the fuel tank.'

'At the garage then.'

'Again.' He waited another moment before asking the question he had been dreading. 'What are you going to do now?'

He didn't get an answer. At that moment, there was a sound from the back of the car. Tilly was awake, and crying.

Priest scrambled to get up, flung the door open and reached out. Through a flood of tears, recognition lit up across her reddened face. She tried to speak but just produced a whimper before flinging her arms around him.

He felt the warmth of her body, the clutch of her starfish hand on his neck. The relief was so intense it nearly knocked him out.

'You're OK,' he whispered. 'You're safe.'

'Where's Mummy?' she managed.

Priest had received messages from Georgie. Sarah was awake, in hospital being monitored. Fraught and scared. Georgie had done her best to explain everything. Rowlinson was with her. He must call as soon as he could. Where was he?

'She's waiting for you, sweetheart. We'll ring her now and tell her you're OK.'

She didn't let go at first and he held her for a few more minutes as the twitching of her body subsided and she started to relax.

'Who is that man?'

He let her go and followed her gaze. William was crouched down, watching. Then he smiled.

'I'm your Uncle William.'

'I didn't know I had an Uncle William.'

'Yes, quite.' William looked down at the ground. 'And you should know that I don't hold that against you.'

'Are you a friend of Uncle Charlie's?'

William gave a small gasp; whether he was impressed by her polite articulation, or the fact that she showed no fear of him, Priest wasn't sure, but he could see he was touched, and slightly out of his comfort zone. He wasn't known for his skill with children. Then he nodded.

'Yes. Yes, I am. A friend of Uncle Charlie's.'

That seemed to be more than sufficient for Tilly. She turned to Priest. 'My tummy hurts.'

'You've been a little bit poorly, Tilly,' he said softly. 'Can you remember what happened before you fell asleep?'

She shook her head. *Good.* It might have been more gas, and something mild along the way. She was going to be all right.

He straightened up, took out his phone and dialled Sarah's number. She answered immediately, panicked and alert.

'Charlie.'

'There's someone here who wants to say hello to you, Sarah.'

He handed the phone to Tilly. She took it gleefully and put it to her ear, as practised as any teenager. 'Hi, Mummy! I'm in Uncle Charlie's posh car.'

He couldn't hear what Sarah was saying, just the muffled noises of love and joy that, even without knowing what words were spoken, were enough to bring a tear to his eye.

He watched in wonder as she told her about how she had fallen asleep and woken up in Uncle Charlie's car. Her tummy hurt, but it was OK because Uncle Charlie had promised to take her to McDonald's, even though he hadn't, but of course he would, and was that PlayStation at his house really for her?

Deciding to leave them to it for a few moments before he would call Rowlinson, Priest turned and opened his mouth.

But William was already gone.

# Chapter 69

*Friday*

For once, Georgie hadn't set an alarm, but she still woke at six thirty precisely, sitting bolt upright in bed and cursing the accuracy of her internal clock. It had been the second long, mainly sleepless night, filled with a collage of intel on what had happened a hundred and fifty miles away in a decommissioned TB hospital from Tiff and Charlie.

Two nights ago, she had tried her very best to comfort Sarah but she had never seen the grief of a mother so powerfully and despairingly exposed. It was nothing short of harrowing.

But Tilly was safe. And Sarah's relief and joy had been as overwhelming as her desolation. Plus, the little girl didn't have any recollection of what had happened. She had been subject to some sort of gas, and then an anaesthetic. She had had an overnight stay in Great Ormond Street but early indications were that there would be no lasting damage.

Charlie had spent the night at the hospital with Sarah, apparently spending most of the time on his phone playing a game, but there was a lot of missing information, much to Tiff's infuriation, about what had happened. Charlie had a bad injury to his hand and some cracked ribs – they wanted him to attend

A and E but he had refused, predictably, and the good doctors and nurses at Great Ormond Street had done their best to patch him up.

Copperhead was dead, except he wasn't Copperhead. He was somebody called Michael Ransom – formerlly Michael Ireland – whose father had been one of the surgeons at Elipmus Hospital thirty years ago. He had been the subject of a number of serious allegations of sexual misconduct with children, and trafficking, along with his wife, but nothing was ever proven. Now the hospital was hosting a hefty SOCO team at Rowlinson's behest.

The year after Elipmus Hospital closed, Michael's parents were murdered by William Priest. The coincidence of this or otherwise was now the subject of fervent speculation from those that knew, but only Charlie really understood what had happened two nights ago. And he wasn't talking.

Georgie kicked a pile of clothes out of the way and got out of bed, stumbled to the shower. Forty minutes later she was sitting downstairs, her wet hair covering most of her face, shovelling in mouthfuls of Rice Krispies, when the doorbell rang.

She glanced upstairs, not sure if Li was in or out. *Who calls at this hour?*

Sighing, she got up, unlocked the door and opened it. A tired face stared back at her.

'Too early for a conference?'

She shook her head. 'It's way too early.'

Charlie nodded, then padded in when she held the door open for him. She showed him through to the kitchen and poured the glass of water he requested. He didn't want Rice Krispies. No, she didn't have any sweetcorn.

He sat at the table in the kitchen, one hand over the glass, looking like he'd been to hell and back. There was a fresh bandage wrapped around his hand, bruises up his arms and he seemed to be struggling to stand up for any length of time. His hair looked like a bird's nest, and he stank.

'How's Tilly?' she asked, taking the seat opposite him, conscious her hair was wet and she was wearing a scraggy Nirvana T-shirt.

'She's good.' He rubbed his face. Looked at his hand like he'd never seen it before. He seemed distant, more distant than usual. Perhaps that was hardly surprising. Then, before she could ask anything else, he produced a Samsung smart phone and placed it on the table in front of her.

'What's this?'

'It's Michael Ransom's phone.'

'You took that from him?'

'He didn't need it anymore.'

She couldn't help but smile, though she didn't dare touch it. 'Shouldn't you have given that to Tiff?'

He ignored her. Picked up the phone again and examined it. 'I've spent all day and most of last night looking at this.'

'Does he have a contact called Copperhead?'

'Regrettably not, that would be too easy. There aren't many contacts in here at all, and what there are appear to be sex lines and pizza outlets. Took me ages to work out how they were communicating.'

Georgie shuffled in her seat. She had an urge to ask to see the phone, rifle through it – accept the challenge.

'Show me.'

He smiled knowingly – and this was a man who never smiled knowingly, he wasn't like that – and replaced the phone on the table face up. He lit the screen, and typed in the password. The phone unlocked.

'How did you know that?'

'The date William killed his parents, easy. Watch.'

He scrolled through the two pages, littered with apps. Heart-rate monitors, weather, news, photos, games, iBooks, the usual.

'What don't you see?' he asked. She took a moment, then realised.

'Social media. Facebook, Twitter, WhatsApp. That sort of thing.'

'OK. There's IMs but not very many and I can't see anything interesting.'

'So, how did he communicate with Copperhead?'

'Through this.'

He picked out an app, and pressed it. It looked like a game. It started with a few indie software logos she had never heard of. Then a brightly coloured pixelated title screen presented itself. She read:

'Sword of Zenil. It looks awful.'

'It really is. I guess it's like World of Warcraft – a role-playing game with swords and sandals. Solly probably plays it.'

'Still not seeing this.'

'OK, well basically you make an avatar, give it a name, choose a tribe and an appearance then proceed to roam a mystical world interacting with other avatars, some of which are AI and some of which are real people and, if you join their tribe, you can communicate with them in an online chat.'

She saw instantly what he was referring to when he hit 'play' and a goblin carrying a crossbow appeared on a sandy beach over the message 'Welcome back, Samyaza'.

'Let me guess,' she said, watching Charlie start to wander around randomly shooting bolts into trees. 'There's another avatar named Copperhead.'

'If you can find him, you can instant message him through the game.'

'Is he a snake?'

'No. Oddly, he's a squirrel. But don't get too hung up on that.'

'What if Copperhead isn't online when you find him?'

'Then, if you know where his base is, you can post a message for him and he'll pick it up when he goes online.'

Georgie sat back, impressed at both the ingenuity of the secret messaging system, secure in the confines of a limitless virtual world, and the fact that Charlie had found it.

'So, what do we do? We can't ask Tiff to arrest an avatar. The internet won't allow it.'

He smiled the same smile again. 'We do what someone told me to do a while ago. We become a snake. An anaconda, to be precise.'

She looked at him reproachfully. It had been a pretty torrid week, even by his standards. He had been blown up twice, had his niece kidnapped and narrowly avoided death at the hands of a vicious serial killer bearing a grudge. Maybe it was getting to him.

'What do you mean?'

'I mean, rather than start to charge down the Amazon looking for fish, we wait in the water for them to find us.'

Georgie exhaled. It was obvious. 'He doesn't know that Michael's dead.'

'He probably does now, but he didn't initially.'

She looked at him, again puzzled. 'But shouldn't we be going to the police with this?'

To her surprise, he shook his head. 'No. Michael didn't tell me who Copperhead was, but he did tell me that he was Copperhead's recruit and his principal was close to the police investigation and knew everything we were doing. There may be a leak somewhere. So, *we* have to do this. You and me.'

Georgie shivered, but whether it was out of excitement or fear, she wasn't sure. Probably both.

'But we have to wait for the squirrel to make contact with our goblin, right?'

'No.'

She waited for him to explain, but he wasn't in the mood for making it easier for her.

'OK, why?'

'Because he already did, yesterday. He provided a time and a location to meet.'

He looked at her and she realised he was waiting for her to cotton on to something. Then she realised what. 'We're going now, aren't we?'

He nodded. She jumped off the chair. It dawned on her: she was going to have to go with wet hair.

Her heart beating fast, she pulled on a pair of black and white Converse and grabbed her phone from the kitchen table. Charlie was waiting for her outside. They walked briskly down Georgie's street, past the pharmacy and the chip shop to where the Aston was waiting. She wondered whether after prolonged use he would ever go back to the Volvo but somehow she knew he would. It was William's car and it meant a lot to him. For some strange reason.

They got in and Charlie started the engine, but immediately she knew that something was wrong, and so did he. He just stopped, as if sensing danger. Slowly they turned around in unison.

A man in his early fifties wearing a black shirt and trousers was sat in the back of the car pointing a gun at them. Georgie had to blink several times to make sure he was real. Sure enough, he was there, staring at them with neither hatred nor malice. Just a cold indifference.

'Hello, Charlie,' he said. 'We meet again.'

# Chapter 70

Priest took his hands off the wheel, careful not to react too quickly. He had locked the car, he was sure of it. That made Copperhead's little trick all the more impressive. Very theatrical. Still, he had been right about who Copperhead was.

The gun was small, 9 mm – probably a Glock 26 or something similar, maybe even a Springfield. Either way, good for carrying around concealed. And very real.

He caught Georgie's eye, tried to transmit a vibe to her. *It'll be OK.* By the look on her face, she didn't pick up on it.

'You have Michael's phone,' said Copperhead evenly.

'That's right.'

'Is he dead?'

'Afraid so.'

He didn't show any concern. 'Hm. Very clever of you to find the app, but you forgot to turn the tracker off. And I knew that you weren't Michael.'

'What gave me away?'

'Nothing in the dialogue – that was perfect. You must have studied Michael's mannerisms carefully. But what you didn't know is that I was watching you for a long time stumbling around the virtual world with your stupid crossbow shooting trees. Michael wasn't a very good human being but he was very good at playing Sword of Zenil.'

He nodded, slowly. *Should have thought of that. It was their world after all.* 'Does Fay know about you?'

David Westbrook laughed but it wasn't the kind of laugh that made him endearing. He was handsome, with an angular jawline and sleek brown hair streaked with grey. The kind of man whose aging just made him look better and better. But that laugh, all crooked and lifeless. That was ugly.

'Georgie, get out of the car,' said Priest, hoping he might be able to cajole David into letting her go. This was bad news and he needed Georgie out of harm's way.

She put her hand on the door handle, but David wasn't going to be pushed around easily and quickly trained the gun on her.

'I don't think so,' he said. 'You can stay with us, Miss Someday. You'll make an excellent substitute if I end up having to shoot your employer prematurely.'

Georgie swallowed and took her hand away from the door. David smiled, pleased with her obedience.

'Good. Now, drive. That way.'

He indicated ahead. Priest clicked his tongue but realised there was no choice. David was sat behind him. There was no way he could get to him without the gun going off first.

He pressed the Aston Martin crystal key fob into the start ignition with a satisfying click and the engine roared into life.

'You haven't introduced yourself, David,' said Priest, trying to keep it casual. Georgie looked at him, amazed that he seemed to know who this was.

'You're right, how remiss of me. My name is David West-brook. I am married to DS Fay Westbrook, whom you are already acquainted with, Miss Someday. She was one of the people trying to catch me. It's left here.'

Priest gripped the wheel, indicated, then turned at the junction. Luckily the traffic was already starting to build. He knew where they were going and it was going to be a slow journey.

'Where are we going?' asked Georgie.

'To an airfield,' said David, confirming Priest's supposition.

'She was in on it then?' said Priest.

'She does what I tell her.'

He tightened his grip on the wheel despite the pain from his right hand that ached mercilessly from where Michael had stabbed it with a nail. He wondered what else Fay Westbrook had done in her life because she was told to by her controlling husband. It explained why she seemed so unhinged that night in Geneva, why she denied his existence.

'I guess you recruited Michael at the clinic,' he said to try to keep David interested. He needed him calm and engaged if they were getting out of this one alive.

'That's the amazing thing about the Fellowship. It's one of the only places in the universe where an entire cross section of society sits in one room together. Where you can find lawyers next to vagabonds, all sharing the same story, the same problem.'

'You ran the meetings, right?'

David shuffled in his seat. 'My father was a reverend and the church has always been the centre of my family's life. We like to give things back. Whoever is generous to the poor lends to the Lord.'

'And He will repay him for his deed,' Priest finished.

David looked away. Priest couldn't see his face but he could tell that he was displeased at the intonation.

'It's right here, at the end,' he said coldly. 'Then go over the roundabout and head towards Dartford.'

Priest decided to let it ride for a few moments, until he reached the roundabout. 'And what about Fay? Was she also a recruit?'

'Fay had many demons in her life before she met me,' David said, but there was an edge to his voice, as if he was warning Priest off the subject. 'But, yes, I met her because she was in the Fellowship.'

'How did you persuade Michael to kill for you?'

David winced at the sound of Michael's name. 'Killing his fellow man was in Michael's nature. It was hardly difficult. I had money, and he gained a certain sense of purpose from the transaction that pleased him.'

'But he was just another pawn. You orchestrated everything, which makes you the sacred one, doesn't it? The one who sits on the left side of God after the Binding is complete?'

David said nothing so Priest tried his luck again. Beside him, Georgie shuffled uncomfortably.

'You must have recognised Michael's talents in a private session at the Fellowship.'

'Michael was a complicated character, but I certainly became aware when he started writing to me, sharing his fantasies, and at first I thought he was sick but then I realised that he was part of *His* plan, and I could use him to rid the world of the Carriers. So I encouraged him. He didn't believe in the cause but that wasn't my concern; God had delivered him to me for a purpose, that of the demon-slayer.'

Priest thought back to the letter Michael had written to William in which he had said that if he killed it was part of God's plan, and the scrawled writing he had seen on the wall in Michael's flat: *God is dead.* Michael didn't know what he believed. He didn't care. He had wanted revenge for the murder of his parents; he didn't give a shit about the Binding. David probably didn't even know what his true motivation was.

'Where did you first hear about the Book of Janus?'

'Ah,' David sighed. 'My family came from Cumbria, a little place called Maryport on the west coast. As I said, my father was a holy man, my mother worked in an office. It was all very humble, all very quaint. I had been brought up to love God, as one should, although to my shame I never took the Bible seriously until the fire – the other boys would tease me. Say I was the son of a paedophile, just because my father was a vicar.'

'Fire?'

'My parents died in a house fire when I was ten years old and although I miss them terribly I realise this was my calling. You see, I was there, in the house, but something had woken me. I had the strangest impulse, an overwhelming desire to put on my dressing gown and wander outside. I didn't know what it was at the time, although I now see it was God's guiding hand. He took me to a place where I was safe, so when the gas leak happened and the house erupted in flames I was spared. This was, I now see, part of God's plan for me.'

They pulled up at a set of lights, three cars back from the turning and waited. Priest thought about the possible outcomes, testing each one. None of them looked promising. His best bet was to keep David talking, keep him slightly distracted. He doubted he would have any hesitation in pulling the trigger.

'How do you know it was God? Could have been coincidence?'

'Spoken like a true atheist, Priest. Why bother with faith if you can't see and touch it? Well, the night my parents died I had a vision. God came to me, in a dream, in the form of a jackdaw.'

Priest looked in the rear-view mirror, made sure David was watching him. Time to risk a little inflammation. 'A talking bird told you to recruit someone to go on a religious killing spree.'

David wasn't rattled, he'd probably had years of ridicule. 'I don't expect someone like you to understand, Priest. The power of the Lord is beyond some people's grasp, that's just the way it is.'

'And what about Janus?'

'After my parents died a man came to me. He was a lawyer, like you. With a smart suit and long words. He told me that my mother and father had bequeathed me two things. One was a bunch of bills and the other a few tatty pages of translated scripture, which bore the same symbol as I had seen in my dream. A snake wrapped around a cross. Go straight over here.'

Priest did as instructed. The road was clearer up ahead but he kept to the left lane, as slow and steady as he dared without arousing David's attention.

'How did your father get hold of the translations?'

'Does it matter?' He seemed unimpressed with the question, but offered an answer anyway. 'He collected things like that. Most of it, all of it in fact apart from the crucial pages from the Book of Janus, were either unimportant or unauthentic. Old copies of the Bible that were too common to have value, a piece of what he supposed was the Ark but turned out to be nothing. I was close to throwing the Janus pages away, but after a while I realised how important they were.'

David didn't expand and Priest thought it best to take a break from the questions. David was more likely to give him answers if he didn't feel like he was being constantly cross-examined. They were pulling away from the city now. The high-rise flats were behind them. He could only see low, suburban housing ahead and signs telling him they were only a mile or so from the Dartford Crossing. He exchanged glances with Georgie, tried to reassure her with his look. It didn't work.

After a while, Priest asked: 'Do you really believe in it, David? The Binding?'

When he answered, it wasn't to Priest, but to some invisible speck in the middle distance.

'Oh yes. Yes. I believe that Judgement Day can be avoided.'

'It seems strange to me,' Priest mused. 'That God wrote a get-out clause into the deal that requires breaching the commandments.'

'Thou shalt not kill?' David seemed surprised. 'That applies to men, Priest. Not half-demons.'

'I don't understand,' said Georgie out of the blue. 'You couldn't possibly think that you'd be able to kill them all. And there are people with Lutheran b not on the donors' list, and in other parts of the world. It's an impossible task.'

Priest watched in the mirror for David's reaction. He had put the same thing to Michael, only to be told that others would take over, although he thought he was talking to Copperhead at the time.

'But that's the nature of faith, Miss Someday. It requires you to believe in the impossible. This will be a lifetime's work. Just getting to this point has been a lifetime's work. I don't expect you to understand that.'

'And what happens when you get there, David?' asked Priest. 'How will we know when paradise on Earth has been achieved. When the last Carrier dies?'

David smiled to himself. 'When the new sun rises, Priest. Anyway, we're here. It's this turning.'

# Chapter 71

The airfield was really nothing more than a hangar that had seen better days, a white-box control tower and a single landing strip facing east. David's plane was already out on the runway and although the propeller wasn't spinning Priest realised that they could be in the air in less than a few minutes and he had absolutely no idea where they were going.

David instructed him to drive into the open hangar, which was empty apart from the workbenches at the back, and a cluster of apparatus, stepladders, fuel pumps and tools lining one side.

He got out first, made sure the gun was aimed at Priest, before inviting them to join him.

'This is over, David,' Priest warned. 'Where do you think you can possibly go?'

'There are people sympathetic to the cause,' he replied, motioning for Priest and Georgie to head to the back of the hangar. 'You wondered how it was all going to get done. Whilst I will be credited with the initiative, and take my place at God's left side, opposite Jesus, I have partisans in Europe.'

'So what's the plan? Fly out there and let them take over?'

David produced a pair of speed cuffs from his jacket pocket and tossed them at Priest.

'Cuff her to that.'

David indicated the metal framework of the hangar. The design was such that the primary support struts were welded to the ground and thrust upwards like pillars.

'One guess as to whose these are then,' Priest said, nodding to the cuffs.

'Just do it.'

Gently, he moved Georgie and helped her put her arms round the pillar, then cuffed them in place as lightly as he could. He caught her eye. She was defiant, but her breathing was short and intense, and he could see the rapid rise and fall of her chest.

'Don't fight it,' he said. 'They get tighter if you wriggle. I'll be back for you.'

She nodded, fixed him with a stare that told him she would be OK, before he walked away.

'Touching,' David said, indicating that Priest should move away while he checked the restraints. Satisfied Georgie wasn't going anywhere, he turned back to Priest. 'Are you two more than colleagues?'

'No, but I kissed your wife the other night in Geneva. Funny, she didn't mention you when she was inviting me up to her room.'

'That's amusing,' David said evenly. 'But don't bother trying to goad me. It won't work.'

'I think otherwise.'

They were standing in the middle of the hangar, three metres apart. David was aiming the gun at Priest's chest. He wasn't an amateur – correct distance and correct target. He wouldn't miss, and if the first bullet didn't kill him, the second one would. There was nothing he could do. He glanced across at Georgie. She was pleading with her eyes for him to do something, but he was powerless. David Westbrook held all the cards. He just had to hope that he could get what he wanted first.

'Before you do that, I'm interested in one thing,' Priest said.

David moved his head, which Priest took as a sign that he might be willing to answer one last question before he dispatched him.

'Why didn't you do the killings yourself? Why did you have to use Michael?'

David winced, as if the question was insulting. 'Probably the same reason you have a cleaner, Priest. I don't like getting my hands dirty.'

'But you like violence.'

'I don't know what you're talking about. Anyway, goodbye.'

He was about to squeeze the trigger. Priest had to think fast. 'Sue Lightfoot thinks so.' It was enough to make David pause, let the name register with him. He watched Priest curiously. 'She has some interesting tales to tell about you.'

David shook his head, like it didn't matter. Like it was nothing. 'Sue was my entitlement. It really doesn't matter what she says. No one will believe her.'

Priest nodded. It was enough. From somewhere, he heard Georgie's voice shouting his name. The last thing he saw was David's smiling face as he stared down the barrel of the revolver pointing at his heart, just before he pulled the trigger.

# Chapter 72

Georgie rattled the cuffs, pulled against the steel bar she was attached to. It was futile. Her wrists hurt. Charlie had been right: the cuffs tightened the more she struggled.

David was holding the gun and aiming at Charlie, but what was that he had said about Sue? She was trying to process it, but it didn't make sense, unless . . . David had said that Sue was his *entitlement* but there was a hidden meaning in his tone; a sinister, proprietary intonation that buried itself deep inside of her, leaving no room for doubt. She knew exactly what he meant.

But it was too late.

'Charlie! No!'

She cried out. *Why wasn't he doing anything?* This was it. She was going to watch him die, and then what? Was she next?

Georgie closed her eyes and prepared for the sound of gunshot.

But it never came.

She opened one eye. They were still standing there: Charlie and David, a few metres apart. Nothing had happened. But David had fired the gun, and he was still firing it. At least, he was pulling the trigger and the hammer was snapping shut, but she realised the chamber was empty.

She opened her other eye and her muscles slowly uncoiled; she relaxed her hold of the steel pillar, stood upright. Charlie was looking at David, waiting for him to work it out but stupidly he kept focussing on the gun, like he couldn't remember how to use it.

'What . . . I—'

'Having problems with the gun, David?' asked Charlie brightly. 'Perhaps it would work better with bullets.'

'No.' It had hit him. 'No. This cannot be—'

'Is that the gun that Fay gave you, by the way?'

Georgie did a double take, recalled what Charlie had said a few moments ago. He had kissed her, in Geneva. She had never considered her role until now. There hadn't been time to take it all in. Was she complicit? Or was the whole thing her idea?

Right now it didn't matter. Charlie Priest had never looked so in control. With a pair of busted ribs, and a bandage wrapped around his hand that was weeping blood, his chest heaving, he was ferociously triumphant. Her heart leapt as she realised what had happened: the whole thing had been a ploy. From the moment he had knocked on her door this morning, every question he'd asked, every gesture, every subtle change of tone. He had known all along what he was doing, and if there was any element of doubt left in her then it vanished the moment she heard the glorious sound of sirens in the distance, growing louder by the second.

'What have you done?' David gasped. He paled as he cowered in Charlie's shadow.

'It was pretty simple really,' Charlie said, examining his bleeding hand. 'I spent a long time wandering aimlessly through the land of Zenil in the guise of a little goblin and, occasionally, as you rightly pointed out, I fired crossbow bolts into trees. But then I met a turtle. A turtle that kept following me around. And I remembered: someone had once told me, if you ever see a turtle, wish it happy birthday.'

Georgie had no idea what he was talking about. It was gibberish. But it was having a profound effect on David. *He* understood. The words were stripping him bare, every syllable was undoing him layer by layer.

'You did what?'

'Looks like you and Michael weren't the only ones using the app to communicate.' The sirens were loud enough to suggest that the first car had pulled off the motorway. 'Fay was on there too. Your wife, or at least you say she's your wife. You discovered her all those years ago at a little church in Hackney, the same as Michael.'

'It's not true—'

'No. I think she was ready to tell me in Geneva but I missed the signs. She knew that you were the killer all along but you control her, completely. When you realised that Michael was dead you decided the best thing to do was kill me and make a quick escape to somewhere in Europe. Fay told us that the plan was for her to join you later, when the heat had died down, but I think you sacrificed her.'

'You're bluffing. Fay would never betray me.'

'She did a deal with us. She's a smart girl, more than you give her credit for. This way, by painting you as a man who picked her up when she had hit rock bottom in an AA meeting you were running, then controlled every aspect of her life ever since, right down to pretending that you're married when it suits you, she might even avoid a custodial sentence.'

'No! She believed in the cause, in God!'

'She believed what you told her to believe. She was a child when you met her, but she evolved into a woman that you couldn't control. You were just too parochial to see it.'

'She was *mine!*'

'Yes, once. But over time she realised what *you* were capable of, and of what *she* was capable of. She sorted herself out. Got a degree, a masters in Crime Intelligence and Data Analytics. She outgrew you. By the time you were putting your lunatic plan into place she was already planning her way out.'

Two marked cars, sirens blaring, burst across the tarmac and slammed their brakes on outside the hangar. Doors opened as armed officers scrambled to get out, drawing assault rifles and advancing on David. There were shouts from all directions, commands aimed at him to drop the gun and place his hands behind his head.

He just looked at them, baffled.

'Give it up, David,' Charlie said. 'It's over. We know everything.'

He turned to Charlie. Something had clicked inside of him. He no longer looked confused, but livid, the depth of Fay's betrayal had finally taken hold.

'I never killed anyone, Priest,' he roared. The armed police were within ten feet, still shouting at David to throw the gun down. 'You can't stop God's will. Your precious courts have nothing on me.'

Charlie narrowed his eyes. 'Conspiracy to commit murder is still a crime last time I checked, and there's the rape of Sue Lightfoot for a start. And there are others.'

'You think they'll believe the word of a drunk?'

Georgie felt a hatred of her own burning inside her but, to her absolute delight, Charlie smiled, fiddled behind his ear, and pulled out a wire.

'Maybe, maybe not. But they'll believe a recording.'

The nearest officer took hold of David's arm, twisted it around until he dropped the gun while two others wrestled him to the ground.

# Chapter 73

Priest slumped down next to Georgie and leant back against the steel pillar. She crouched down next to him, put her head against his shoulder. He was breathing hard. The pain in his chest and hand had returned with a vengeance, the mental barrier he had erected had come crashing down the moment they had jumped on David Westbrook.

In the end, David had forced every muscle in his body to stiffen. He didn't resist, but closed his eyes and allowed them to inject his rigid bulk into the back of a prisoner transporter. Rowlinson said later he was muttering something that resembled a prayer the whole time but one of the handling officers, a devout Christian, told him to shut up. God wasn't listening.

Priest closed his own eyes, let his head fall back. He was beat. Every speck of energy was spent. It was over. Jessica was safe. She'd probably never talk to him again. But she was safe.

'Can you let me out?' said Georgie. 'I'm so damn uncomfortable.'

Priest breathed out heavily. 'They're trying to find the keys now.'

'Great. What was all that about a turtle?'

He tried to swallow but found his mouth was sticking together. 'Fay was a prisoner, trapped inside David's controlling world. But she had come a long way from the alcohol-dependent girl he met at his Fellowship meetings. She had turned her life around, fast-tracked through the police force. His control was slipping away. They all used the odd little role-playing game to communicate with each other about the Binding. Fay wasn't difficult to find. She was the only turtle.'

'Did she know?'

'Yes. She knew David was behind it. She knew the plan, but he was steadfast in his belief that she would protect him because she was scared of him and because he thought she believed in what he was doing.'

'What changed?'

Priest scratched his head. *The kiss? No, something far more complicated.* 'When she met us outside Michael's flat, she made a very clear decision to ensure that I wasn't delayed by Grey's stupid idea that I was Copperhead. What changed? I'm not sure. Maybe something just snapped inside of her.'

He thought back to the broken woman he had watched through the CCTV monitor yesterday; she had been slumped back in the interview chair facing Eaton and Rowlinson, her bloodshot eyes staring at the papers in front of her.

'Why didn't you tell us before, Fay?' Eaton had asked gently, or as gently as his Yorkshire manner allowed. 'You could have saved four lives.'

She had looked at them and Priest had seen defiance spread across her face, a flash of the old Fay Westbrook. 'David took me in when I was just a teenager. I . . . I owed him everything. And, yes, he was charming, persuasive, manipulating.'

'Priest said that you allowed him to find you on the app. You gave up. Why?'

'Because of *him*,' she had said. 'Priest.'

'What about Priest?'

'I realised that there was someone out there who might actually stop David. Someone who could beat him. And by capturing him, I would be free.'

'They're not actually married?' said Georgie.

'Apparently not. He just poses as her husband when it suits him. Tells her to use his surname. In his own mind, he was married to all of his girls, the special ones he chose, the vulnerable ones. Like Fay, like Sue. No doubt we'll find there were others. He just chose to keep each one in a different loop. Fay just happened to be the favourite. I think it made him feel powerful, thinking that these girls thought he was some sort of prophet.'

Two officers had climbed in the back of the transporter with David and they had shut the doors. The van rolled out, followed by two of the marked cars. The third car stayed behind. One of the officers waved at Priest to let him know they were there when he was ready. They had been instructed to return him to Rowlinson, where they were continuing to interview Fay, but he couldn't face it yet. He waved back, indicating he wanted five minutes. The officer nodded and started talking into his radio.

'How did you know David had raped Sue Lightfoot?'

'I went to see her yesterday morning. When we spoke to her, she wasn't telling us everything. I knew that Michael wasn't being manipulated – he had his own agenda. But there was somebody out there who *thought* they were manipulating him. That person would, to have any degree of credibility, have been someone able to exert some level of control over Michael, so I figured that Michael might have been recruited through the Fellowship meetings in Hackney. I started asking about the person who regularly led the meetings. Low and behold Sue told me it was David Westbrook. She never told me that he had assaulted her but she was clearly terrified of him, broke down while we were talking about it. I just took a punt on what happened. If she came forward, maybe there'd be enough for a prosecution for her ordeal.'

'How did you know the gun wasn't loaded?'

'I didn't. As part of the deal with Fay, she agreed to unload it. I had to trust her on that one.'

Georgie wiped her head across her sleeve. 'What happened when you confronted her?'

'Michael had already told me that the real Copperhead was close to the investigation. The way that Fay acted in Geneva was really strange. She had a taste for drink and the passive-aggressive act was odd. By yesterday morning I had figured out I was speaking to Copperhead through the Sword of Zenil app. He was trying to arrange a meeting with me. Kept mentioning an airfield, this airfield, I assume. I managed to get Tiff interested in the app. At first, he was pissed off that I'd kept Michael's phone – something about police procedure and evidence. I said he would have bagged it up and we would never have got to the bottom of how Copperhead and his killer were talking. Anyway, when I told him I thought it was David Westbrook and that Fay may well be in on it – the very fact that she was also on the app made that possible – he started to listen.'

'Did he arrest her? His own DS?'

'He thought that she was out speaking to Darren Green's father but we found her at home. She was waiting for us. She—' again, he thought back, to the look on her face when they had found her sat at her kitchen table, a look that conveyed regret, desperation and the feeling of release all in one moment – 'she knew it was over. Took us a few hours to extract the story, but eventually she told us about the airfield, and the fact that David had a pilot's licence. The plane's rented. The airfield is private, apparently.'

He stopped, out of breath. The officer by the marked car was checking his watch unsubtly. Priest acknowledged him. Started to get up but his legs felt like jelly. He wondered what would have happened if Fay hadn't agreed to cooperate. He had had to trust her to remove the bullets from the gun and, although Tiff had watched her do it, so she could later give it to David, there was nothing to stop her from reloading it.

In one way, David had achieved something extraordinary. Fay had a drink problem. It had developed in her late teens after she had fled her abusive father to London. When she first met David, she was vulnerable, at her lowest. An easy picking. But as she weaned herself off the drink, she started to succeed. She was a confident, reliable and competent detective. How had David managed to keep control of her for so long even after she had broken out of the drink-survival cycle?

Maybe it was the same way William had operated. Networks are stronger than hierarchies.

But his control was finite. For every minute of the investigation that had passed, her attachment to him had dwindled. When body after body had been piled up, and she had started to realise the full extent of the Binding plan, she grew more and more uncertain. In the end, it hadn't taken much to make the walls he had built around her collapse. A simple 'happy birthday' had done it.

*By capturing him, I would be free.*

'Hang on,' said Georgie, as Priest managed to get to his feet. She tugged on his sleeve, motioned towards her cuffed hands. 'Aren't you forgetting something?'

Priest nodded and got up. He walked over and had a quiet word with one of the officers before returning, grim-faced.

'Apparently he didn't have the key on him.'

'Say again?'

'He didn't have the key. Why would he? His plan was to kill me and leave you tied here, or kill you – I'm not sure which, while he flew off into the sunset.'

She looked down at the cuffs, troubled. 'Then what do we do?'

'Well,' Priest looked over at the marked car and the open door. 'See that guy over there? He's going to find a bolt cutter.'

'And if he doesn't?'

'I'm going to leave you here as a new piece of modern art.'

'What are you going to call me?'

He smiled, and put a hand on her shoulder. 'How about the Binding?'

# Chapter 74

'I don't understand,' said Priest. '*Kneef* isn't a real word.'

It was eight o'clock at night and the sun was still streaming in through the open bedroom window but Tilly insisted that she liked both the noise from the people milling around Covent Garden below and the light splashing off the den she made for herself in the corner of the room out of blankets and the boxes of PlayStation games, nor could she possibly sleep without both.

'It's a nonsense word,' she explained. 'To help me learn to read, silly.'

'That's ridiculous. Why do you need to learn words that don't exist?'

'The teachers say I do.'

She was deadly serious. Priest flipped through the cards once more and asked her to sound out a few more. They did *glibbing* twice, because it was her favourite.

Her recovery had been remarkable; she didn't seem to recall anything from the point of falling asleep at Megan's house to the point of waking up in his car. She had claimed not to have been scared at all. He was both delighted and envious: his own scars were going to take a long time to heal.

After another ten minutes, he tucked her in, kissed her on the forehead and said goodnight. She squeezed her eyes shut and pretended to snore. By the time he was out of the room, he heard her singing merrily to herself.

Sarah was slumped in an armchair with a glass of red wine dangling out of one hand, staring vacantly at the lionfish swirling around in their tank. She was wearing a sports top and shorts although she hadn't been to the gym, she'd just taken to wearing them around the house. Priest hadn't questioned it. In the circumstances, she was entitled to a bit of oddness now and again.

He took the seat next to her and mirrored her expression. He still hadn't slept properly. It had taken them an hour to rescue Georgie and by the time he had got back, the ordeal of having to recount what had happened at the airfield to Rowlinson and Eaton had forced him wide awake again. Even Dee had shown an interest, not complimenting him exactly but equally not insulting him, which he took as a compliment in its own right.

He had expected to sit in silence with Sarah for a solid hour, wondering what she was thinking but not having the courage to ask but, to his surprise, she spoke almost immediately.

'I don't blame you,' she said. There was a tenderness to her tone that left him in no doubt that she was being honest. 'The one who took her – this Michael – he was the son of one of William's victims. He wanted to lure you to him so he could take his revenge out on you, as if you were William.'

'Actually, I think he fantasised about *me* killing *him* not the other way around, in substitution for William.'

She blew out a long, tired burst of air. Who knows if he was right? He wasn't sure if Michael himself knew what he wanted.

He had copies of the letters he wrote to William and the fantasies worked both ways: in some William killed him, in others he killed William. In one, he, Charlie, killed both of them. Michael was a mental car crash, no doubt about it.

'You saved her,' she said. 'You didn't stop, didn't think. It didn't bother you, did it? It was just . . . you know, you did what you needed to do.'

He turned to her. 'I'd never let anyone harm her. Or you. That clear?'

Sarah nodded. A single tear fell down her cheek. She mouthed *thank you*, and smiled. For a moment, they didn't say anything. There was nothing to say. Maybe the silence itself could heal them.

'There was one thing,' Sarah said after a while. He nodded for her to continue. 'Tilly said that her Uncle William was with you, in the car.'

He let that hang between them for a moment. News of William's escape wasn't widespread. Fen Marsh, like most secure units, had their fair share of disappearances. The standard procedure was to keep such incidents away from the public. Priest had spoken to Wheatcroft. He had been right. William had stabbed himself with a toothbrush and escaped while being transported to a regular hospital. He'd knocked two guards out cold but they'd be back on their feet in a few days. Did Priest have any idea where in God's name his brother was? No, was the truth of it. They were coming round first thing in the morning to interview him again. The manhunt was on, but not even Sarah should know.

'That's strange,' he said. 'He couldn't possibly have been there. Maybe she just heard the name in her sleep, somehow it just slipped into her subconscious mind. She was very drowsy when she woke up. A bit giddy.'

Sarah pursed her lips and he could tell from her expression that she wasn't convinced, but for now she let it slide. Besides, he had a question of his own for her.

'While we're here,' he began. 'When I got Tilly's stuff the other day, I met Ryan.' He could see her stiffen up and that told him she knew what was coming. 'He told me he has no idea who Gemma is.'

'I guess I didn't want to tell you. I don't know whether I was embarrassed or scared you'd do something. But, with everything that's happened, I'm past caring.'

He braced himself. Something in the pit of his stomach had given him an inclination about what had happened. He hoped he was wrong.

'I found pictures on his computer.'

There it was.

'What of?'

'Girls. Young girls.'

'How young?'

She winced, closed her eyes. Welled up. She answered in a muffled tone. '*Too* young.'

*Jesus*. Priest took her hand, squeezed it. But it wasn't going to be OK quickly. Not this time. Maybe not ever.

He was about to say something when the doorbell rang. He hesitated, checked the time again. He might have ignored it but she told him to go, it could be Tiff again.

Troubled, he walked through to the kitchen and opened the door.

Jessica stood with three boxes of steaming pizza, her hair immaculate but a slightly reddened face, like she had taken the stairs and not the lift. He blinked a few times to check it was really her, still reeling from what Sarah had said.

'You're here,' he observed.

'Good spot, genius.'

She pushed past him and placed the pizza boxes on the side. *Please, come in.* He closed the door. She arranged the boxes and opened them up, then took three plates out of the cupboard.

'I didn't know what you all liked. I assume Sarah is here.'

He started to fumble around with his words. 'Last time we spoke, you said—'

She cut him off. 'I know what happened. The silver bloods. I know what you were trying to do.'

He was suddenly conscious that his mouth was wide open. 'Who . . . ?'

'Your friend, DCI Rowlinson, told me. He is your friend, right?'

'Yeah. He's kind of my *only* friend.'

'Well, lucky him.'

She rummaged around in another cupboard and found three glasses. Placed them next to the plates. Then went to the fridge. She was uncorking a bottle of white when Sarah came through, a little red around the cheeks but otherwise there was no way you would have known anything was wrong.

As Priest watched Jessica take her by the hand and sit her down, pour her a glass of wine, he thought about Ryan and his computer, and what was to come. It must have torn Sarah apart to have found those pictures, then to find Tilly was gone, and her family's shameful past dug up and spread out in front of her, the whole thing laid bare.

Yet here she was, laughing and joking with Jessica, sipping wine. Anyone looking in on that moment right now would have thought neither of them had a care in the world.

Priest sat down, looked at the wine glass. Two bottles later, they were still going.

# Chapter 75

*Sunday*

The runners and students were out in force and St James's Park was teeming with clusters of people sitting around in the shadows of the oaks and mulberries with plastic cups of coffee and piles of books, passing around cigarettes and looking as much a part of the green vista as the regiments of mallards that floated across the lake.

Rowlinson joined him, handing him a bottle of water, but he thought better of complaining and slipped the lid off to drink appreciatively. The DCI was still pissed off that he'd gone to the Elipmus Hospital alone, and kept Michael's phone, but his annoyance had subsided since they had apprehended David Westbrook; for now at least, the Met looked partially competent.

'How is she?' Priest asked.

'Fay? Remanded. I'm not letting her anywhere near David. She's asked to see you a few times but the CPS have said no to that. They don't want anything that could jeopardise a prosecution.'

'He's not going quietly then?'

'No. Now he's saying it was all her idea. Anyway, we'll see how long it lasts.'

'The recording will help. It's not a confession but if Sue comes forward it'll be enough.'

For a minute, neither of them said anything. Priest gazed out across the lake, to the thick clumps of lush trees and the Eye glinting above them. The sky was a deep blue, as vast and endless as he had ever seen it.

*It's there,* he thought, remembering what his mother used to say to them. *Where's your blue sky?*

'Where was he going to go in that little plane of his after he killed me?' Priest asked.

Rowlinson sucked his lip. 'We found the outline of a flight plan on board to a private airfield in Jersey but I've no idea what he was going to do from there.'

'He mentioned others – partisans, he called them.'

'Maybe. I don't know. Right now, that sounds like someone else's problem.'

Priest clicked his tongue in agreement. 'Amen to that.'

'Thanks for the Book of Janus, by the way.'

He stretched out, twisted his neck around until it clicked. Every time he woke up he heard the sound of the explosion in Owen's garage, or the stun grenade, sometimes both. That is, if he was lucky enough to drop off to sleep in the first place.

'I assumed you'd regard it as material evidence in your case against David. What about Capindale?'

'She's helping us with our enquiries. I'm waiting for the CPS to make a decision. It boils down to whether or not she knew what the Book was going to be used for. Chances are, she didn't.'

'I'm told that she sensibly discontinued the case against the late Professor Owen. I wonder if Vose stuck around?'

'He's disappeared. I suspect he fled back to Germany. We've let him go – it doesn't look like he had a clue what was really going on.'

Priest nodded. He glanced at the ring on Rowlinson's finger. Nothing outrageous, a gold band with a simple engraved pattern running through the middle. Suited him.

'Did you really think it was me?' he asked.

Rowlinson shuffled awkwardly. 'Me? No. Never. You're not clever enough to pull off four perfect murders.'

He smiled, and Priest managed to laugh, although his body ached with it. They sat in silence for a while watching the sunlight dance off the lake. 'Thanks,' he said presently. 'For looking out for Jessica.'

She had told him that she thought uniform police officers had been following her. He guessed where the instructions had come from.

Rowlinson shrugged. 'She means a lot to you?'

'I've no idea.'

'Probably best that way, Priest. The game's a lot easier when you've got nothing to lose.'

Rowlinson looked at him meaningfully, and he nodded. He appreciated him not making a big fuss out of it. Most others would have fished for better compliments than that.

'I paid a visit to someone I used to know when I was a detective,' Priest said after a while.

'Who?'

'A journalist named Slinky.'

Rowlinson perked up. 'I'm listening.'

'Anyway, it turns out that Slinky remembers me really well from the old days. For some reason, he's terrified of me.'

'I can't think why.'

'Anyway, the leak to the press. It was Grey.'

Rowlinson smiled, breathed out. 'That's helpful.'

'Here's a copy of the cheque Slinky gave him, made out in his name.'

Priest handed him a copy of the cheque and Rowlinson, looking like the cat that got the cream, tucked the paper into his inside pocket.

'By the way,' the DCI said. 'I'm told that Fen Marsh has lost track of one its most notorious inmates.'

'Oh, really?'

'Yeah. Something about one of the largest manhunts in modern history?'

Priest shook his head. 'He'll turn up. He once told me he's too institutionalised to make it now in the outside world. Give him a day or so, he'll be back. He'll miss the hospital too much.'

'You really believe that?'

'Yeah – why not?'

Apparently satisfied, Rowlinson patted down his trousers before getting up. 'I'm off the case anyway. Our alleged friendship rules me out – so you're going to have to get your story straight about what happened at Elipmus. They'll want to speak to you about your statement soon.'

'No doubt.'

'Call me old-fashioned, but I don't think that they're going to buy the idea that you blacked out and you have no idea who killed Michael Ransom.'

Priest shrugged. 'I'm prone to black-outs.'

Rowlinson laughed, but without a trace of humour. 'You're going to have to do better than that. Anyway, I've got to go. Paperwork looming. Good luck.'

'Are you sticking around? Or is the Welsh hillside and low crime rate calling you back?'

Rowlinson paused. The two men stared at each other for a moment. Then the detective looked away wistfully into the distance.

'I'm not sure.'

'You could make a difference here, Tiff.'

'So could you.'

Priest didn't answer, he had the sense that the conversation was at a close. Rowlinson looked as though he was about to leave but something was troubling him. He looked over his shoulder, then back at Priest. There was something on his mind.

'I've got to know,' he said softly. 'Why protect him? William, I mean.'

Priest studied his friend's face and saw genuine curiosity. It wasn't a challenge, or an accusation. It was nothing more than a simple question.

'Because there's more to it. More than you could possibly imagine.'

Maybe it was the finality of Priest's tone, or the feeling that he was stepping on cursed ground. Whatever it was, Rowlinson didn't go any further. Just nodded and doffed an imaginary cap.

'OK. Mind how you go, Priest.'

Rowlinson walked away. Priest might have got up himself but he remembered the phone call he was supposed to make. He lifted out his phone and flipped through the contacts until he found the right one before dialling.

The voice at the other end was disengaged and muffled by the sound of a radio and clanking in the background. 'Yeah?'

'It's Priest. Just wondered about the Volvo.'

'Volvo?'

'My car. You're fixing it. Have been for a couple of weeks now.'

'Just hang on.'

The phone crackled, as if it had been put down. Priest heard some shouts in the background in Polish before the speaker returned to the phone.

'There must be some mistake. You picked it up yesterday.'

He breathed out, licked his lips slowly. 'I did?'

'Got the paperwork right here, pal. Signed by Dr Priest. Can I just ask—'

Priest rang off, cutting the mechanic off mid-sentence. Pocketed the phone and relaxed on the bench with his arms hanging over the back. Looked out into the hazy distance. Somewhere, out there, another killer was on the loose. He got up and pulled his jacket around him. The breeze had picked up. The heatwave was over.

# Acknowledgements

This book is the culmination of a year's work, but it would never have gotten to print without the industry and dedication of a number of people.

To Oliver, Grace and Archie, you are a perpetual source of inspiration, support and wonder. None of you read nearly as much as you should, and you all possess an uncanny ability to drive your mother and I into both despair and hysterics all at once, but you are all uniquely gifted and I am truly blessed to be in your lives.

To my stoic mother, whose attention to detail and genuine devotion to the Priest series is both amazing and slightly frightening, thank you for once again spending hours poring over my poor spelling and grammar.

To Denise, thank you for your beta reading – I always enjoy your updates. It was fitting that a lot of the later stages of the novel were written at your kitchen table late at night!

To the kind people at Lincolnshire County Council who let me in on the secrets of the Magna Carta microclimate container, you are custodians of the most important legal document in British history (which of course was sadly breached almost as soon as it had been signed!), and your help was much appreciated.

To my editors, Katherine Armstrong and Jennie Rothwell, I am indebted to you for your insightful suggestions that have helped steer the story into a coherent novel, and for putting up with my horrendous timeline issues.

To Gordon, your counsel on the darker aspects of this book was invaluable and I treasure the day we spent in the summer of last year, which I hope to repeat soon. You've always been there for me – thank you for your advice and friendship, without which the world would be a poorer place.

Finally, to my tenacious alpha reader, Jo. Thank you for putting up with me for all these years and for your belief in me as a writer. I wouldn't have written a damn word if it hadn't been for you. I still remember you throwing the first draft of *The Mayfly* at me because the original ending made no sense at all (which is true, it didn't). Every word I write has always been for you.

Dear Reader

It has been a privilege bringing the first three Charlie Priest thrillers to life and I hope you enjoyed reading *False Prophet* as much as I enjoyed writing it (don't tell anyone I said this, but it's my favourite so far!).

Most of this book was, like the novels that preceded it, the product of countless late-night toils, months of exasperation, early morning splurges of inspiration followed by lengthy droughts of creativity, about a million cups of tea and prolonged periods of research, some of it even turning out to be mildly helpful.

So thank you for taking the time to read it, because time is so precious. If you have been with me on this journey from the start then you have my utmost respect and gratitude; if you're new to the Priest chronicles, then welcome – I hope you get a chance to check out *The Mayfly* and *The Ash Doll*.

If you have just two minutes left, then we authors always appreciate a fair and honest review – it's positive feedback that keeps us in the job. If you like Priest, spread the word; people value a good book recommendation.

Priest will return, and if you want to hear more, then you could join the James Hazel Readers' Club. You can do so by emailing me at james.hazel@myreadersclub.co.uk. It only takes a moment to register. There'll be important updates about forthcoming titles and some exclusive VIP content.

It's also a really great way to get in touch. I'd love to hear from you and get to know what you liked and what you didn't like.

Your data will never be passed to a third party and I'll only be in touch now and again. You can unsubscribe at any time.

I hope you stay with me though because we've started this adventure together, you and me, and it's going to be a great ride!

Once again, thank you for reading.

With best wishes,

James Hazel